Praise for *Earthway*

"Exciting...The authors smoothly blend personal and professional concerns as the Navajo police sort through a tangle of lies and loyalties while respecting the values of traditionalists and adapting to modern intrusions."
—*Publishers Weekly*

"The informative look at conflict on the Rez between old ways and new that the Thurlos always provide comes packaged this time with an unusually tense mystery."
—*Kirkus Reviews*

"This Navajo police procedural is strongest when it explores a side of Indian life outsiders rarely see—the ongoing battle between traditionalists and modernists. In its way, *Earthway*'s conflict of values reflects the cauldron of suspicion that exists across much of post-9/11 America. Our Native and non-native customs may differ, the writers seem to be saying, but our loves and fears are exactly the same."
—*Mystery Scene Magazine*

"Fast-paced. As always in Clah novels, Navajo traditions and ceremonies are seamlessly woven into Ella's character and her ability to unravel the case. In this instance, she must use every bit of her trademark leadership and ingenuity to stop the terrorists before anyone else is injured—or worse."
—*New Mexico Magazine*

Praise for *Coyote's Wife*

"The landscape of the American Southwest is so gorgeous it leaves some people speechless. It inspires others to write mysteries. Aimée and David Thurlo have a robust regional series going with Ella Clah, a Navajo tribal police officer whose investigations usually involve a standoff between tribal tradition and modern ways. Clah is always good company, on and off the reservation."

—Marilyn Stasio, *The New York Times Book Review*

"Razor-sharp suspense, deep atmosphere, and compelling characters make this another Ella Clah winner." —*Booklist*

"Expertly works Tony Hillerman country."

—*The Times-Picayune* (New Orleans)

"The Thurlos immediately caught me up on Ella's continuing struggle between the old ways of her traditional Navajo family and her duties as a special investigator with the tribal police. Events gradually intertwine and come to a head, concluding with Ella's deepening understanding of her heritage, her family, and herself."

—*Albuquerque Sunday Journal*

Praise for *Never-ending-snake*

"A well-paced story built around the timely and dangerous effect international politics can have on the lives of everyday people." —*The Denver Post*

"This is a terrific and powerful Ella Clah police procedural. Enhancing the story line is a profound, timely look at alternative energy. A great entry." —*The Midwest Book Review*

EARTHWAY

Also by Aimée & David Thurlo

Ella Clah Novels

Blackening Song
Death Walker
Bad Medicine
Enemy Way
Shooting Chant
Red Mesa
Changing Woman
Tracking Bear
Wind Spirit
White Thunder
Mourning Dove
Turquoise Girl
Coyote's Wife
Never-ending-snake

Plant Them Deep

Lee Nez Novels

Second Sunrise
Blood Retribution
Pale Death
Surrogate Evil

Sister Agatha Novels

Bad Faith
Thief in Retreat
Prey for a Miracle
False Witness
Prodigal Nun
The Bad Samaritan

EARTHWAY

— ✗ ✗ ✗ ✗ ✗ —

AN ELLA CLAH NOVEL

AIMÉE & DAVID THURLO

A Tom Doherty Associates Book
New York

EARTHWAY

Copyright © 2009 by Aimée and David Thurlo

A Forge Book
Published by Tom Doherty Associates, LLC
175 Fifth Avenue
New York, NY 10010

www.tor-forge.com

Forge® is a registered trademark of Tom Doherty Associates, LLC.

The Library of Congress has cataloged the hardcover edition as follows:

Thurlo, Aimée.
    Earthway : an Ella Clah novel / Aimée Thurlo and David Thurlo. — 1st ed.
      p. cm.
    "A Tom Doherty Associates book."
    ISBN 978-0-7653-1717-9
    1. Clah, Ella (Fictitious character)—Fiction. 2. Police—New Mexico—
Fiction. 3. Navajo Indians—Fiction. 4. New Mexico—Fiction. I. Thurlo, David.
II. Title.
  PS3570.H82E26 2009
  813'.54—dc22

2009028187

ISBN 978-0-7653-2487-0 (trade paperback)

First Edition: November 2009
First Trade Paperback Edition: March 2011

To Jan E.,
who was with us from the very beginning

ACKNOWLEDGMENTS

With special thanks to Detective Ryan Tafoya of the BCSD Violent Crimes Unit for all his help and patience answering our questions.

The Earthway: Sing that counteracts bad dreams involving the land.

ONE

✖ ✖ ✖

Today was one of those days when "Indian Time" just wasn't good enough. Special Investigator Ella Clah of the Navajo Tribal Police checked her watch for the second time in five minutes. One way or another, she wasn't going to be late. Reverend Bilford Tome, "Ford" to his friends, was giving a special talk at the Navajo Community College this afternoon and Ella had promised to be there.

She glanced at the file folders and forms stacked in five piles on top of her desk. Not much had happened lately that involved her Special Investigations Unit. Perhaps because of it, she had an incredible amount of paperwork to catch up on—a bureaucratic snoozefest that she'd ordinarily brush aside for more important work.

Although she might have normally welcomed some slow moments like these, nothing was normal about her life right now. Her eleven-year-old daughter, Dawn, was spending the last of her summer vacation with her dad, Kevin, in Washington, D.C., and Ella missed her terribly. Her mother, Rose, active with Plant Watchers committees, was almost always gone until evening and Herman Cloud, Rose's husband, was spending more and more time watching TV in the new addition they'd built onto the house they all shared. He still made those beautiful piñon lamps once in a while, in the garage, but lately he'd slowed down a lot.

Their normally active home seemed uncomfortably quiet these days, particularly after suppertime. It was then that Ella felt Dawn's absence the most. During those hours, the only sound disturbing the silence would come from Two, the old family mutt, who'd be on his rug in the kitchen, snoring away.

Spending time with Ford—the Navajo minister at the Good Shepherd Church—had become her way of staying sane. All too often during quiet moments, memories of past cases haunted her. Police work always took its toll. Like most seasoned officers, Ella lived with a darkness in her soul—the cost of dealing with criminals day in and day out—that touched all other aspects of her life.

When Dawn left town, as she did from time to time to be with her father, Ella could visualize dangers that would be unknown to most moms outside the PD. That ever-present dread tempted Ella to fight hard to keep Dawn close to her, but overprotecting her daughter was wrong and Ella knew it. Dawn deserved freedom as well as the right to try out her own wings.

After a quick drive down the streets of downtown Shiprock, Ella arrived at the visitors' lot of the community college—a mixture of hogan-style structures and more conventional modern buildings. There were few trees on campus, most of them small, drought-resistant Navajo willows that granted welcome circles of shade. The campus had been xeriscaped with various tints of gravel, rocks, and native plants selected for the desert climate. Lawns were for water-rich regions, Ella knew, not the Navajo Nation, where farmers and ranchers struggled against nature for every drop of irrigation water.

Following the narrow, reddish orange-tinted sidewalk,

she strode quickly toward Edmond Hall, a boxy, modern building where the lecture would be held. Ella enjoyed reading the faces of the students she passed, each with unique agendas and goals. Unlike high school, nobody came here except by choice, and that positive viewpoint often led to success. These young people, and some of them not-so-young, were the future of the *Diné*. They'd bring hope and skills to the tribe through education and training.

Ella's pace quickened naturally when three young women rushed past her, probably on their way to a class. The dark-haired students were carrying book bags, and two were discussing an upcoming test. The third, lagging behind a few steps, was distracted with her cell phone, chattering away in Navajo, her voice light and happy.

The community college vibrated with life, and that kind of enthusiasm was contagious. For a moment, remembering the freedom of thought and action of her own college days, Ella wished she were back in school.

As she stepped into the foyer of the cinder block-walled building, a stand-alone structure that had once been an office, Ella glanced at the clock on the wall—three-fifty. Ford wasn't scheduled to speak for another ten minutes. The realization that she'd actually arrived early surprised her. Talk about standing "Indian time" on its head.

The lecture hall was filled to capacity—at least a hundred people. Ella spotted Ford at the front, by the podium, getting things ready.

He smiled and motioned for her to join him. "You're either early, or I'm running way behind schedule," he said only half-joking.

"Believe it or not, I'm actually early. Can I help with anything?"

"Thanks, but I'm almost ready." He gestured toward the green chalkboard, which held a brief outline of his presentation, all written in his neat, precise handwriting.

"Professor Begay is supposed to be joining us shortly to make the introduction. Now where did I put my notes?" He looked back toward the instructor's desk, several feet away and closer to the chalkboard.

Ella spotted a nylon book bag on the lectern's shelf. "Maybe they're still in your bag."

"My what?" Following her gaze, he shook his head. "That's not mine. I'm an old school nerd, I carry a leather briefcase. There it is, on the chair," he added, gesturing with his chin.

"So who does the book bag belong to, then?" she asked.

"I have no idea," he answered, getting his notes. "Maybe one of the instructors found it after the last class and put it there for safekeeping."

Ella looked at a clear plastic storage container on the floor against the wall by the door. It was labeled "Lost and Found" and inside was a textbook. "Or maybe not," she muttered.

Glancing back at the black-and-red nylon bag, Ella felt a prickling at the base of her spine. As a detective, she'd never liked the unexplained—things that didn't belong or were out of place. Even if it turned out to be nothing more than books some student or professor had left behind that hadn't been placed in the lost and found bin, she felt compelled to take a look . . . just to make sure.

Ella brought out the bag carefully by one of its shoulder straps. It felt heavy, yet the contents rolled—not what one would expect from books. She was undoubtedly being overly cautious, yet her skin was prickling and the badger fetish she always wore around her neck felt uncomfortably warm—an almost sure sign of trouble.

Careful not to jiggle the bag, she pulled it closer and lifted the flap, held down by self-sticking fabric. A paperback dictionary was at the top, resting on some kind of round contraption.

Ella raised the dictionary slightly, and immediately recognized the device below it. Nails were duct taped to the outside of an eight-inch piece of galvanized steel pipe. One end had a metal cap, and at the other was a taped piece of green circuit board, wires, and what looked like a battery. The rest of the bomb was hidden beneath the tape. Ella remained as still as possible, not even daring to set down the dictionary she'd lifted to see inside. If it touched the wrong thing—

Trying to remain calm, Ella glanced around for Ford, her mouth suddenly very dry and her heart hammering.

Ford looked up, notes in hand, and saw her expression. "What's wrong?" he asked immediately, stepping up beside her.

"Pipe bomb. Get everyone out of this building as quickly as you can," she whispered.

He nodded, then turned to face the room full of students. "Welcome, everyone. This afternoon is so nice that I've decided to speak outdoors. In order to begin on time, I'd like everyone to proceed immediately to the shaded benches in the commons outside the student union building. I'll join you there as soon as I gather up my materials."

Once people began leaving, Ford glanced back at Ella. "I'll set off the fire alarm as soon as the room's empty. After that, what do you need me to do?"

"Go outside with the others, keep everyone clear, and call 911. We need our explosives expert here as soon as possible."

"I've had some training with explosives. Remember my background," he added softly. "I can do more to help."

"No. I need you to let the other instructors know what's going on, then make sure the rest of the buildings are evacuated. This may not be the only bomb," she said.

"All right. I'll pass the word . . . and pray every step of the way."

"Do that," Ella answered in a whisper. She didn't follow the Navajo Way, nor was she a practicing Christian like him, but right now she'd take help from wherever she could get it. Though she wasn't sure that prayers did much of anything except offer comfort, they couldn't hurt.

Soon Ella found herself all alone, the flashing strobe only a slight annoyance compared to the din of the fire alarm. No matter how hard she fought against it, fear pried into her, the gut-clenching kind that made it nearly impossible for her to even think. With a bomb beneath her hand, knowing that each second could be her last, cold sweat poured down her body. Yet somehow, she had to keep her body steady and her hand from shaking.

The ever-growing possibility that she'd never make it out in one piece—that she'd never see her daughter or Rose again—clawed into her. Blinking back tears, she forced herself to take a deep breath. It couldn't be her time to die. She had too much left to do. In the back of her mind, she'd always planned on settling down again someday, maybe even having another child.

Seconds passed with agonizing inertia as she waited for help to arrive. Trying to stay calm, she cleared her thoughts, and concentrated on what was in the bag. She wasn't a bomb expert, but unless the explosive was C-4 or the equivalent, it probably wasn't powerful enough to blow up the entire building. The nails—wicked shrapnel when flying at supersonic speed—told her it was an antipersonnel weapon.

Judging from the location of the bomb, she guessed Ford had been the intended target. As a Christian minister on the Rez, he had his share of enemies. The question was, who hated him enough to want to kill him—along with maybe a half-dozen other innocents who just happened to be seated at the front of the room?

That brought up yet another question. Had the bomber somehow known *she'd* planned to be there, probably in a front-row seat? As a police officer responsible for putting a long list of criminals in jail—and the deaths of several over the years—she had no shortage of enemies.

Before she could give that further thought, Ella heard sirens outside, above the din of the alarm. The police station was close by, and their response time had been quick.

When Officer Ralph Tache failed to immediately appear, Ella reminded herself that it would take him several minutes to suit up. The possibility that he'd arrive seconds too late ate at her, undermining her confidence. She took an unsteady breath, trying to suppress a bad case of the shakes.

The book bag was heavy, and she was relieved to finally see a big shadow appear in the doorway. It was Ralph, suited up in his PPE—personal protective equipment—and carrying a heavy ceramic-plated vest for her.

Looking more like a GI astronaut than a police officer, he shut off the annoying alarm, then waddled over in his heavily armored suit. "How long was Reverend Tome supposed to speak today?" he asked without preamble, as he put down the duffle bag that held his equipment. His words sounded hollow behind the clear, thick faceplate, and unnaturally soft after the din of the alarm.

"Forty minutes—then twenty minutes for discussion," she answered. If there was a timer, and that appeared likely based on the circuit board she'd seen, the bomb was probably set to go off during that time period. Ella looked down at her watch. "The class was scheduled to end at five, but we have no idea when the bomb was left here."

Without touching either her or the book bag, Ralph glanced inside. "I wish our PD had a portable x-ray machine," he said. "There's a lot of duct tape around the mechanism, but I can still make out a battery, and what I think is an electronic timer on the circuit board. Typically, pipe bombs are filled with black powder." His voice was as calm as if he'd just given her a weather update. "Dynamite and other high explosives usually don't require a container. I'm going to use a high-powered water gun to short out the circuits. After that, I'll haul the device out of here and put it in the vault."

"You know what you're doing, Ralph," Ella said in a surprisingly steady voice.

"I appreciate your trust. Just don't move your hand yet. I don't think there's a pressure switch, but we don't want to put that to the test," he said, helping her put on the extra vest. As soon as that was done, he slipped his now-gloved hand over hers, in the same place as hers, and gave her a nod. "Okay, let go and step back."

Ella didn't breathe again until she'd completed his instructions. Every instinct she had told her to run as far away from the building as possible, but she remained where she was, several steps from Ralph. "Tell me how I can help you."

"I've got the protective suit. I can handle this," he said. "Go outside."

"You may still need an extra pair of hands, and I'm already here. I'll duck down behind one of these tables, and you let me know if you need my help."

He considered it, then nodded. "Deal."

Ella moved the chairs away from the farthest table, then tipped it on its side, using the two-inch-thick top as a shield. As she watched, Ralph opened the book bag wider and studied the bomb. Then, moving slowly, he pulled back his hand, and placed the bag gently on the floor. A moment later he stepped away from the bag, and brought out a high-pressure water gun.

Ella knew it was protocol, but she could feel her skin crawling. "Are you sure about using that thing?" She was shivering, but her entire body was covered with sweat. The badger fetish around her neck felt scalding hot, too, but with her own body temperature rising because of the vest, she didn't know whether to make something of it or not.

"Super soaking usually works. Don't worry. Once the circuits are saturated with water, I'll take this outside and place it in the containment vessel. Stay low." He aimed the nozzle at the open bag, pinned the straps down with his foot, then soaked the interior thoroughly. Finally, with a satisfied grin, he turned and gave her a thumbs up. "Let me check things out just to be sure. Then we can go outside."

Ella relaxed and took an easy breath. No one would die today. The bomb was inoperable.

Ralph took out a metal manipulating tool, then extended the telescoping rod. As he grabbed the straps of the soaked bag with a clamp, raising it off the ground a few inches, there was a blinding flash and a roar.

TWO

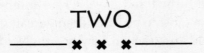

The table slammed into Ella like a wooden fist, hurling her backwards, and her head hit the wall with a crack. Alternating waves of darkness and light swept over her, but she fought to stay conscious.

As her vision came back into focus, she pushed away the table, which was blocked by chairs and pieces of other tables that had been thrown against it by the blast. It took all her strength just to clear enough space to stand in the gray pallor that now encompassed the room.

The air was filled with smoke and the overwhelming smell of gunpowder. With the fluorescent lights shattered, it was difficult to see through the thick haze. Leaning against the wall for support, she edged forward on rubbery legs. "Ralph? Come on, buddy. Talk to me," she said, coughing.

Ella called out his name several more times, but there was no answer.

Slowly, she worked her way through the wreckage of table and chairs, orienting herself with the help of the light coming through the open door. With every step, her boots crunched on broken glass and plastic from the light fixtures. There was something sticky and slippery on the floor, too, and it made walking difficult. Although she couldn't see clearly, the coppery scent told her it was blood.

"Ralph!" she called out again.

Hearing a gurgling sound ahead, she moved forward, finding footing difficult on the shredded metal and chunks of wood that covered the floor.

As the haze began to clear, she was able to make out a dark shape against the wall below the chalkboard. Ralph had been blown backwards away from the bomb, and was sitting with his back to the wall.

When she got up close, Ella saw that a nail had imbedded itself in the clear face plate, but thank goodness it hadn't gone all the way through. Nails were also stuck in the fabric of his protective suit, which was blackened and shredded in places.

"I'm here," she said, reaching his side. "The EMTs are probably on their way, too, so hang on."

"Something caught me in the side. Must have ricocheted off the wall and penetrated between the armor plates. . . ."

He began coughing, and in the dim light, Ella saw blood trickling out of the corner of his mouth.

"Don't talk," she said softly, sitting next to him. "You'll be okay."

An officer appeared in the doorway a second later. "Get the EMTs in here," Ella snapped. "We've got a man down."

As the seconds passed, Ella held Ralph's hand, encouraging him, though he appeared to have lost consciousness.

Finally, rescue personnel came in and Ella moved out of the way to give them room to work. She stood beside the chalk board, which had been cracked by a jagged piece of pipe the size of her fist. At least the portable electric lantern they'd brought in provided much-needed illumination.

As the dust settled, one EMT checked Ralph's vital signs while his partner did a visual inspection and found the source of the bleeding. "The ballistic cloth was punctured by some really nasty stuff," he said, dialing the hospital, and getting instructions directly from the emergency-room doctor on call.

As the rescue team worked to stabilize Ralph, Ella felt someone touch her arm. She looked over and saw it was her partner and second cousin, Justine Goodluck.

"It's bad, real bad," Ella whispered.

"I know, but Ralph's getting the help he needs now. You and I should step outside and let the EMTs work," Justine answered.

Ella knew her partner was right, but she couldn't make herself leave. She still wasn't even sure what had happened. In the blink of an eye, the situation had gone from under control to total chaos.

After removing his heavy armored suit, two EMTs placed Ralph on a gurney and hurried past Ella and Justine. The third member of the team was picking up their gear when Ella went up to him.

"Is my officer going to make it?" she asked quickly.

"It's hard to say. He took a piece of shrapnel through his side, maybe a nail, judging from the wound. The suit protected his front and his spine, but the sides . . . the armor's not so thick there. A bullet or a blunt object wouldn't have penetrated, but something slim and sharp, like a knife or nail, can slip through sometimes."

"How bad is it?" Seeing his reluctance to reply, she added, "Best guess."

"We can't tell what kind of internal damage he's suffered, but from the loss of blood, I'd say it's going to be touch-and-go for a while."

Along with Justine, they picked their way through the debris and walked toward the exit. As soon as they were outside, Ella breathed in her first lungful of clean air. She took a quick survey to assure herself that nobody else had been hurt by the blast. Nobody was down anywhere, so she assumed the building had contained the explosive force of the bomb. Ford was at the forefront of the gathered crowd of students, standing taller than most of them, craning his neck to see. She managed a wave in his direction, and saw him wave back.

"You look like crap, Ella," Justine said, her voice gentler than her words denoted. "You'd better have those cuts and bruises checked out."

"Later. Right now let's cordon off the crime scene and get to work. One of ours is down, and the sleazeball who did this to him is going to pay," Ella said, her anger coming through loud and clear.

While Justine returned to her unit and opened the trunk to get her gear, the ambulance raced away toward the hospital. The EMT who'd remained behind came up to Ella with a medical kit and insisted on examining her. After checking her vitals and disinfecting her many cuts, he released her, asking that she visit her doctor for a more thorough checkup as soon as possible.

The EMT was packing away his gear when Ella spotted FBI Special Agent Dwayne Blalock stepping out of his Bureau vehicle. On the Rez he was known as FB-Eyes because of the unusual color of his eyes—one blue, the other brown. Blalock was in good physical condition for a man in his early fifties. He'd mellowed in temperament slightly over the years, but today his expression was grim.

She watched him study the crowd of students, faculty, and onlookers standing across the commons. A good agent, Blalock was hoping to recognize a face or even an expression that might lead him to the perp. Sometimes they stayed around to survey their work.

Ella heard a door slam, and turned around. Justine, Officer Marianna Talk, and Sergeant Joseph Neskahi were unloading essential gear from the crime-scene van and putting up the perimeter tape. Because of the nature of the incident, evidence would have scattered considerable distances, maybe across the sidewalk and onto the grounds. There were no windows in the lecture hall, but debris had blown out through the foyer and beyond. At least both doors had been open, so the blast hadn't been completely contained. That had saved her, and hopefully, Ralph.

Officers would be flagging every piece of debris—metal, plastic, and paper—to find the remnants of the bomb. Hopefully, they'd be able to reconstruct the device and find additional clues. From the looks of it, this wouldn't be an easy job. They'd be here well into the evening.

Blalock walked up and gave her a slow once-over. "You okay, Ella?"

"Yeah, except my ears are still ringing."

"What's the situation with Officer Tache?"

"Not good," she said. Swallowing to keep her voice from breaking, she added, "He was alive when they took him away, but he's lost a lot of blood, and there's internal damage."

"Ralph's a tough old guy. If anyone can live through that, he will," Blalock said. "You ready to get to work?" He gestured toward the crowd. "I called in all the officers I could find, county deputies included, to keep all the potential witnesses on site until they're interviewed. We also have explosive ordinance teams from other communities checking the campus for bombs. They're going to tag each building after it's cleared."

"Good. Since that's covered, let's you and I start with the students who showed up for the lecture," Ella said. "It wasn't a suicide attack, so the perp probably didn't remain in the lecture hall after leaving the bomb. Maybe someone noticed a student or faculty member who left the building early."

"Did you get a good look at the device, Ella?"

She described the bomb as well as she could remember. "It was in an ordinary-looking student backpack, nylon, probably. Red and black. I didn't notice the brand."

"We'll get that from the debris. Now let's go round up some of our witnesses," Blalock added, walking over to where the crowd had gathered behind the yellow-tape line. Three department officers and two deputies from the county sheriff's office were keeping people from crossing into the crime scene.

"Excuse me, officers?" a voice called out from behind them.

Ella turned and saw a Navajo man, about thirty-five years old, clad in gray overalls and wearing a tool belt. He was waving to get their attention. Recognizing his uniform and the logo of the college on his shirt pocket, Ella walked over to meet him.

"Are you with campus maintenance?" she asked, noting the electrical devices and rubber-handled tools at his waist.

"Yes, officer. I'm Chester Tso, and my supervisor wants me to check out the wiring in Edmond Hall as soon as possible. Circuits were tripped in some of the other buildings, and we need to know if it's safe to turn them back on. Computers are running on backup batteries right now and the staff's worried about losing data, like grades and attendance records."

"I can't let you roam around in Edmond Hall right now. The building is a crime scene," Ella said.

"I understand, Officer. But if you'll let me make a quick inspection, I can also make sure there aren't any electrical hazards for your people. I could cap any potential live wires and maybe restore some of the lighting and power to some outlets. I won't touch anything without permission. You can even send one of your people in with me," Tso said.

Ella wrote a quick note, handed it to Tso, then pointed toward Joe Neskahi. "Give this to the sergeant. You've got ten minutes, but don't touch anything without clearing it with him first. Got it?"

The man nodded. "Thanks, Officer . . ."

"*Clah*." Ella said, already turning toward Ford, who was standing in the distance behind Blalock, a myriad of questions on his face. She went to him.

He reached out as if to hug her, then, instead, touched her lightly on the arm. "I'm glad you're okay, Ella. How can I help?"

"You'll have to make an official statement, but that can wait until later. Right now, could you gather everyone together who was there for the lecture? Each person will have to be interviewed."

With Ford's help, Ella and Blalock quickly recorded the names of all present, then split the large group into two. Ella chose a small empty office to question the witnesses she'd be interviewing, while Blalock took the classroom across the hall.

Leaning back against the desk, Ella waved the first student inside. "Your name?"

"Gladys Joe," the black-haired Navajo girl answered. She was short and stocky, and her face animated. Not waiting for Ella to ask questions, she started speaking immediately. "I've been wracking my brain, trying to figure out who could have done this. I'm taking police-science courses, so I think I know what you're looking for," she added. "The bomb was in that book bag you were holding when we left, right?"

"Yes, it was."

Before Ella could say anything else, Gladys continued. "I don't remember seeing that particular bag before, but then again, practically everyone carries a book bag these days—at least here at the college."

"Did you remember seeing anyone go up to the podium?" Ella asked.

Gladys shook her head. "I came in just before you did, and was just sitting down when you picked up the bag. When Reverend Ford asked us all to go outside after that, I *knew* something was going on."

Gladys was a young wannabe police officer if she'd ever seen one. Ella envied her enthusiasm. Even at the beginning of her career, her past had made that kind of excitement and optimism impossible. She'd been led into law enforcement over twenty years ago by the death of her husband. By then, she'd had few illusions about the human spirit—except that it could survive, and endure almost anything.

"The way I see it," Gladys continued, "the target *had* to be Reverend Tome. There are some Traditionalists who resent Christian preachers trying to spread their religion here on our land. As Navajos, we have our own traditional beliefs."

Ella looked at her, and blinked. Somehow she couldn't see Gladys, who was dressed in tight jeans and a sleeveless sweater vest, as a Traditionalist. The chocolate brown cell phone at her belt suggested that, if anything, she was a New Traditionalist. That group was growing in numbers on the Rez nowadays. New Traditionalists professed their belief in the old ways but, by and large, followed that lifestyle only as far as practical. "Designer hogans with cable," her mother, Rose, often muttered with mild contempt.

"Can you name some of Reverend Tome's enemies?" Ella pressed.

Gladys' eyebrows knitted together as she considered the question. "Not really, but like paying a traffic ticket, evangelism on the Rez can get people ticked off. Of course that's usually not enough to kill somebody over." She paused, then continued. "Have you considered looking for someone who might be jealous of you and the Reverend—you know, personal stuff."

"That's a thought. Thanks for your cooperation," Ella

said, wondering if there was anyone in the town of Shiprock who *didn't* know she and Ford were dating. Curious to know Gladys' future plans, she added, "Are you thinking of joining our department after you finish your education?"

Gladys shook her head. "I want to get away from the Rez for a while," she answered. "I've never been farther west than Flagstaff, and I'd like to see California and the ocean. I thought I'd finish school, then sign up for one of the federal law enforcement agencies."

Memories stirred at the back of Ella's mind, and she nodded. She'd felt that urge to see the world once. And she had. But now she was glad to be home.

The next three hours of interviews yielded nothing of substance. The position of the lectern had hidden the book bag from view, and nobody remembered anyone other than Reverend Ford and her going up to the front.

A half hour later, Blalock came into the room. "I'm finished with my interviews, but I've got nothing solid. Some of the kids had interesting theories, though."

"What kind of theories?" she asked.

"Some thought that Ford got targeted because he's done some work for the tribal police, or because his church is always pushing to get new members. But then, why not bomb the church?"

"A church is just a building. You have to take out the people—or at least their leaders—to shut them down. Or maybe I'm thinking too much about terrorism here," Ella added with a shrug. "As one of the students I spoke to pointed out, evangelism alone isn't a reason to blow someone up, at least not in this country. But I wonder if this may have something to do with Ford's past." Although she'd tried several times to find out what Ford had done prior to his arrival on the Rez, that part of his life remained a mystery to her.

Blalock nodded slowly. "I know where you're going with that. We both know he worked for some federal agency, and that he's a trained cryptographer. I tried to dig up his record a few times myself, mostly out of curiosity, but then orders came down from D.C. to back off."

"We may have more luck checking his background now that it appears he's a target for assassination." She paused, then reached for her cell phone. "Give me a second to make a call and see if there's any news about Ralph."

"I checked a few minutes ago. He's still in surgery."

Ella nodded, silently replaying the scene in her mind and wondering if she could have done something—anything—to prevent what had happened.

With effort, she pushed the thought aside. Those questions would be answered later. At the moment, there was other work that needed to be done.

"I wish this campus had security videos inside the classrooms," Blalock mused.

"There's never been a reason for anything like that. Except for an occasional student protest, nothing much ever happened here—until now."

THREE

— ✖ ✖ ✖ —

After gathering all the statements taken by other officers, Ella joined her team. With one of their own close to death, everyone was determined to find the bomber. No clue would be overlooked.

"We need to talk," Blalock said, coming up to Ella, who was looking for deposits of bomb debris on a scorched wall inside Edmond Hall.

"What's up?"

"If Ford was the target, not the school, the bomber will know soon enough that his attempt failed—meaning, Ford's still a target."

"And if the perp hung around afterwards like some do, he might already have another hit planned," Ella added, looking outside through the opened door. Ford was talking to students from one of the benches on the commons. "I'll follow him home when he leaves. If anyone shows an interest in him, I'll be there."

"I'll keep working here with the team until we wrap up, but you might want to interview Ford now, while everything's still fresh in his mind. I left him for you. I figured you'd want to talk to him yourself," Blalock said.

"I've got a better idea. Let's question him together," Ella said. "I may be too close to this."

A few minutes later, they joined Ford, who'd said good-bye to the last of his students. He was now sitting alone on a bench, sipping coffee from a Styrofoam cup. To Ella, it looked like he'd aged ten years in the past few hours.

"Are you up to some hard questions?" she asked, leading him away from the benches and back in the general direction of the crime scene.

"How can I help?" he asked, falling into step beside her and Blalock.

"Reverend, there's a really good chance that *you* were the target today, not this campus. If Investigator Clah hadn't found that bomb when she did . . ." Blalock purposely let the sentence hang.

Fear flashed in Ford's eyes, but in an instant that was replaced with understanding and acceptance. "If you're right about that, then I'm still a target, and I could endanger whoever I'm around. That means I can't go back to our church or hang around any group of people. I should probably go home right now."

"I need you to think really hard, Ford. Do you have any idea why someone would come after you?" Ella asked.

Almost a minute passed before Ford finally spoke. "At this point in my life I'm no threat to anyone, so the answer's no."

"What were you going to speak about today?" Blalock asked.

"Evangelists on the reservation. That's scarcely a controversial subject—except maybe to a few fringe historians," Ford answered.

"The bomb was placed right in front of where you'd be standing. Someone wants you dead. Why do you think that is?" Blalock pressed.

"It doesn't make any sense to me. It takes a powerful hate to want to kill me at the expense of all the students in the room," Ford said, shaking his head slowly. "My activities on the Rez just don't warrant that."

"What about activities *outside* the Rez?" Blalock said immediately, following up.

"Except for an occasional meeting with other ministries, I spend most of my time here, Agent Blalock," Ford answered.

"That's not what Blalock was asking," Ella said firmly. "Think hard, Ford. Could someone who knew you before you became a preacher have tracked you to the Rez?"

"I don't see how—or why. My past isn't all that interesting."

"Stop avoiding the issue," Ella snapped. "Ralph Tache went into that classroom to protect your life, now his own hangs by a thread." Her words had the desired effect, breaking through Ford's reserve.

"If I knew anything at all that could help you, I wouldn't hold back, Ella. Don't you think I realize that *you* could have been killed today by a bomb that was clearly meant for me? Now one of your men is in the hospital, and here I am, safe and sound. I wish I could trade places with Officer Tache. If I could, I would in an instant."

The quiet desperation that colored his words touched her deeply. "Ford, I know this has been one heckuva day, but we need your help. You're the key to establishing a motive. That's what's going to lead us to a suspect."

"I'm willing to do whatever's necessary to help you. But I can't you give answers I don't have."

"Let's try a different tack," Ella said. "Where would you normally be right now?"

"This late in the day, I'm usually home feeding Abednego," he said, referring to the large mutt he'd adopted.

"Okay. Let's keep to your schedule. I'll follow you from a distance, and if you pick up a tail, I'll move in."

"So be it," he said with a nod. "Should I leave now?"

"Give me a moment to confer with Agent Blalock, then I'll follow you to the parking lot. We'll say good-bye there, and leave separately. I won't be far, but don't look for me."

As soon as Ford was out of earshot, Blalock's gaze locked with Ella's. "Watch your back. Although he kept talking, he still didn't give us any information. That's classic training. Divert and misdirect, don't oppose. While you're with him, I'm going to do a little digging into his background, off-the-record, and see how far I get."

"Good," she said. "I'm hoping that I can get him to open up more when he and I are alone, but I'm not counting on it."

Ella met Ford a few minutes later. "Stay in the left lane on your way home, and stick close to the speed limit."

The highway had four lanes, two eastbound and two westbound, and was separated by a wide median most of the way. Ella suspected that Ford, in his previous career, had been cross-trained in pursuit driving and ambush tactics. He'd automatically make it hard for anyone trying to get in right beside him to take a shot.

"All right, and I'll also make sure not to deviate from any of my regular patterns."

"Good." Ella studied his expression. Despite an afternoon filled with moments of terror and the threat of more evil to come, Ford appeared calm. Half of her wished he'd yell, joke, or do something . . . more human. It was that reserve of his, one she suspected was a part of the training he'd received somewhere along the way, that made her uncomfortable. That quality had always kept her from completely lowering her guard around him.

"I'll also be praying for Ralph," he said quietly.

"He'll appreciate the gesture," she said. Ralph wasn't a Christian, but he also wasn't the type to turn down well-intentioned help, regardless of where it came from. "Keep a sharp eye for anything or anyone that doesn't look right. Call me on your cell phone if you spot anything open to question."

"Count on it."

She gazed at him wordlessly. Ford noticed details most other people overlooked. His powers of observation would be his greatest ally now, something he hadn't lost simply because he was no longer an employee of the CIA, NSA, or whatever he'd been involved with before.

"Once we're both at your place, you and I need to talk. I mean *really* talk. No platitudes or evasions. You get me?" Ella said.

He didn't answer right away. "What you're asking—and what I can give you—are two very different things."

"I'm going to need your cooperation, and you're going to need mine to stay alive *and* avoid risking other innocent lives. Talk to whoever you have to, or reconcile yourself to the inevitable. But we need to be on the same page on this, Ford."

"I understand," he said.

He said the right things, but gave her nothing. It was like trying to nail Jell-O to the wall.

"Your imagination is working overtime and you're seeing way too much in my past," he said after a moment. "I *am* the man you see—a simple minister on the reservation."

She shook her head. "You may want to believe that, Ford, but it's what came before that turned you into the man you are today. And my gut's telling me that we'll find our answers back there—in your pre-minister days."

He didn't argue, and that worried her even more, but she didn't say anything else as he got into his old sedan and drove off.

Ella waited thirty seconds, then set out. The taillights on his car were distinctive, making it easy to find him. Once she had his vehicle in sight again, driving down the only real main street in Shiprock, she varied her distance, trying not to make it look obvious that she was following him. At this point, with so many people heading home from work, it wasn't possible to tell if anyone else was interested, but she watched every car that passed her and then him.

Several miles east of the Rez, traffic was lighter and there were still no complications. Ford turned off the main highway into the inexpensive semi-rural subdivision where he currently lived, and she closed up the distance quickly until she was only a few car lengths back. It was almost completely dark outside when they drove up the gravel driveway to his home, a small three-bedroom wood-frame house.

The house was as dark inside as out, and this set off alarms for Ella. She knew Ford had a lamp that came on at night—for security, and for the dog. Grabbing a flashlight from the glove compartment, she hurried out of the car. Aiming the beam toward the porch, she could see the front door was ajar a few inches.

"Don't go in, not yet!" she yelled, seeing him rushing forward.

"Somebody broke in! I have to check on my dog, Ella," he replied, slowing down only slightly.

Abednego, Ford's enormous dog, stuck his nose out the opening, hearing his master's voice. Then the animal pushed the door open with his muzzle and took a step forward.

"He looks okay," Ella said quickly, directing the light toward the dog. "But there's glass on the porch. Put him at stay."

At Ford's signal, Abednego stopped and sat just past the threshold, watching Ford, his tail wagging furiously.

Ella rushed past Ford and saw a lump of something on the step in front of the dog.

"Keep him there, Ford," she said, aiming her flashlight at it as she stepped closer. Resting on a carpet remnant that the dog used as a bed was what appeared to be a pound of raw hamburger shaped into a ball. Abednego hadn't touched it, thanks to Ford's training.

Glass crunched beneath her boots, and Ella realized it had come from the broken porch light. Directing the flashlight beam, she noted what looked to be a pellet stuck in the siding just beyond the place the bulb had been. Beside that fixture was a new motion detector, but the two floodlights connected to it had also been shattered by pellets.

Ella went into the darkened house, gun drawn. She flicked on the living room light, then, using the walls and furniture as protection, checked out each room. Although nothing appeared to have been taken or even disturbed, the home still held a few surprises for her.

Standing at the doorway of Ford's office, she could see a new computer and a variety of unfamiliar electronic hardware. Ford had gone high tech—very high tech—making her wonder if he was moonlighting for NASA . . . or, more likely, the NSA.

Questions filled her mind as she headed back outside. When she reached the entrance, she realized that the sturdy metal door hadn't been kicked in—the normal method of entry for small time burglars. From what she could tell, the perp had picked the lock, and since it had been equipped with a high-end deadbolt, that had taken some serious skill. The one mistake the otherwise professional burglar had made was not counting on Abednego's loyalty to Ford—or his intelligence. The dog knew how to push the door back with his nose. Whomever had picked the lock must have had to retreat fast and hop the fence to avoid getting nailed.

Ford was poking the lump of meat on the steps with a stick when Ella came back outside. "Good thing I trained him never to accept food from anyone except you and me," he said. "There are capsules in this mixture—maybe poison or tranquilizers. Your lab will be able to tell you for sure."

Ella walked back to her unmarked tribal cruiser, retrieved an evidence bag from the storage compartment, then labeled the outside with a marker and put the tainted meat inside it. "I'm going to put this into your refrigerator for the moment. You and I need to have a talk."

"You're connecting this to the bomb," he said with a nod.

It hadn't been a question so she didn't answer. "You've recently acquired some new, exotic-looking electronic equipment. You've also taken time to install a top-notch deadbolt and that motion detector," she said looking directly at him. "What's going on?"

Putting the dog at stay, Ford started to pick up the shattered glass on the porch and Abednego's carpet. Among the pieces, he found a pellet. "You probably noticed these," he said, handing it to her, then pointing to another pellet in the wall. "This could have been the work of kids looking for something to steal."

Ella gave him an incredulous look. "Kids who can pick a hundred-dollar deadbolt, bring tainted meat for the dog, and just happen to strike on the same afternoon that some lunatic tries to blow you up? You don't believe that any more than I do."

Making sure there was no more glass around, Ford took Abednego by the collar. "Let's go inside. Then we can talk."

Ford closed the door before switching on a desk lamp, then turned off the living room light. "It's clear they never got beyond the door," he said, walking to the hall and taking a look inside his office. "Nothing was touched." He bent down to pet the large mutt. "Good boy!"

"So what were they looking for, Ford?" Ella demanded. "What's put a bull's-eye on you?"

FOUR

———— ✖ ✖ ✖ ————

Ford's gaze remained on the dog. "You *do* have a need to know, so that'll help," he said at last. "But I need to make one call—in private."

"All right. I'll be in the kitchen. Just stay away from the windows, okay? And keep the lights low."

"Understood. Will you take Abednego with you and give him a large slice of cheese from the fridge? He earned it today."

Ella took the dog by the collar and led him away from Ford. It wasn't easy. All ninety pounds of him wanted to stay with Ford.

"If he resists, just say the word c-h-e-e-s-e in an upbeat tone," Ford said. "He'll follow you into Hell itself for that."

Ella glanced down at the dog and said, "Abednego, cheese! Let's go, boy! Let's go get some cheese."

Abednego looked up at her, his tail started wagging, and before she knew it, the dog was barking and pulling *her* into the kitchen.

Ella placed the tainted meat in the refrigerator, then brought out a one-pound brick of cheddar and, using a kitchen knife, cut a generous chunk. The dog swallowed it in two chomps, then barked for more. Ella gave him a second slice, this time about the size of a sugar cube, then started moving toward the hall, hoping to eavesdrop, but Abednego began barking again.

Suspecting that had been part of Ford's plan all along, Ella returned to the kitchen. With Abednego insistent on more cheese, there was no chance of her slipping away anyway. Taking advantage of her experience with dogs, she decided to turn it into a training session. Every small piece of cheese came only after he'd sat, laid down, or spoke.

She was working on rollover when Ford came back into the kitchen. He took one look at the pieces of cheese still in her hand and started laughing. "Hey, who's training who around here? Or is that whom?"

"The big guy and I hardly ever get quality time together like this. I wanted to take advantage of the opportunity."

Ford reached down to scratch the dog behind his ears. "You're spoiled, my friend, but I don't know what I would have done without you today."

"Tell me you weren't counting on him keeping me in the kitchen," Ella added with a smile.

He looked up at her and grinned. "There are very few things a man can count on in this life, but Abednego's love of cheese is one."

"Boy, are you good with non-answers!"

Ford gestured for her to sit down at the kitchen table, then started a pot of coffee brewing. "I spoke to the people I work with—yeah, I said work, not worked—and I've got permission to tell you whatever you need to know. But I think you've already put a few things together."

"I know you haven't always been a pastor and that you have experience in code breaking," she said, remembering a case he'd helped her with in the past. Justine had done an unofficial background check on him back then and had discovered that Ford had more security clearance than both of them put together.

When Justine had tried to dig deeper, her computer screen had flashed an "access denied" warning, followed by a blank blue screen.

A week later, Ford had warned Ella about being too curious and encouraged her to talk to him directly. He'd promised to answer what he could—which had turned out to be darned little.

"It's been a while since I've worked for the government—the FBI actually—but I'm doing classified work for the Bureau again, this time on a contract basis," Ford said. "Before I became a minister, my Bureau cover was that of an analyst working on scams and crimes involving Native American casinos."

"If that was your cover, what was your real job?"

"I was analyzing all forms of communications coming from, and passing to, foreign nationals—suspected terrorists—living inside the US. I was based in various tribal offices—away from Washington and prying eyes and ears, even the innocent kind."

This was the kind of directness that had initially drawn her to Ford, and she was glad to be getting the real story at long last.

"I hadn't done that kind of work in years. Then a few weeks ago, I was contacted again," he continued. "They'd picked up messages in one of their big data-mining operations that suggested terrorists were planning to take some action against our nuclear power plant here on the Rez. They wanted me to identify all the players involved and thought my work as pastor would be the perfect cover. The basic problem is that *Tsétaak'á* Generating Station has received too much attention, being the first of its kind in the US."

"It's the first new commercial reactor of *any* kind in this country in around thirty years." The Navajo tribe had named it *Tsétaak'á*, Hogback, after the prominent rock formation close to the site. *"Specifically*, what did the Bureau want you to do?"

"The FBI asked me to monitor all communications to and from a local Navajo professor at the community college, Dr. Jane Lee."

"What tipped them off to her?" Ella asked, wondering why her department—at least Big Ed Atcitty, her boss—hadn't been alerted. Homeland Security, for one, supposedly encouraged interagency communications and information sharing. Yet Dr. Lee, at the moment, was just a name she'd heard before, nothing more.

"They'd been watching Dr. Lee because of her ties to old anti-nuke activities, in and out of state. She's also got a record of arrests at several of those demonstrations."

"Along with maybe a hundred other activists, I imagine."

"There's more. She subscribed to one of those Internet services that's supposed to create a virtual link between her computer and the company's proxy servers. Theoretically, that makes any e-mails she sends out anonymous. The service is called Kloset. Only the company itself knows who you are and where you've been."

"Kloset—and the Feds?"

"Yeah. They have some people on the inside, naturally, looking for this very thing. And for a very brief time, Dr. Lee corresponded with someone—still unidentified—and they discussed 'taking out' the Hogback reactor, 'one way or the other,'" Ford said, emphasizing the words. "But now the messages have stopped. She's switched to sending, and receiving, coded messages through another, less attention-gathering Internet service. Maybe something tipped her off."

"So the Feds think Dr. Lee and this unknown person plan to attack *Tsétaak'á*, maybe with a bomb? Or are you guys thinking of a takeover, like that raid several years ago on the coal power plant?"

"We don't know," Ford answered.

"Either way, that would be nearly impossible to accomplish with anything other than a Special Forces team. From what I know, and have seen on recent visits, security at the facility is excellent. Their guards have received the best training available," Ella said. "What else does the Bureau have besides these e-mails?"

He gestured for her to follow him back to his office. Sitting in front of his computer, a model and make Ella wasn't familiar with, he soon accessed the file he wanted.

Ford brought up digital images of a middle-aged Navajo woman with grayish-white hair taking photos of the plant with a telescopic lens. From the various backgrounds, it was obvious Dr. Lee had been observing the facility from different locations.

"These were taken by hidden security cameras at the plant. Since then, I've also learned that she's downloaded design schematics that only an engineer would find useful. Thing is, Jane's no engineer."

"And the FBI thinks she's working with one or more other individuals?"

"It's my job to determine who, how many, and what they plan to do—without tipping our hand. The biggest concern is that she may have been recruited by foreign agents eager to use anti-nuke Navajo activists like Jane as assets. If there's a terrorist cell working here, other Navajos, some highly placed, may be involved, too. That's why the Bureau's keeping a real tight lid on this. I doubt that even Police Chief Atcitty knows."

"If he does, he's kept it to himself. Is this why you got involved with the college and agreed to give the lecture series?" Ella asked.

He nodded. "It was a way to get closer to the chief suspect. But I still have nothing. So far, we've spoken on several occasions, but always on a professional or friendly basis."

"Have you talked to her about the *Tsétaak'á* Generating Station at all?"

"I brought up the subject in passing. It's a hot topic right now since the installation of the pebble-bed reactor vessel is imminent. But she refused to discuss it. She actually told me she had no opinion on the subject." He paused and rubbed his neck.

Jane Lee's lack of response surprised her. Ford always made whomever he was speaking to feel as if nothing elsewhere on the Rez could possibly matter as much to him. It was that special charisma that had made him such a popular pastor.

"You got *nothing*?" Ella asked incredulously.

"Jane told me that she wasn't in the least bit interested in that place. Her tone was so dismissive I almost believed her." He smiled slowly. "But I don't give up that easily."

Ella laughed. Now *that* was the Ford she'd come to know. "So what did you do?"

"You've noticed I've recently acquired a lot of very handy hardware. One little gadget looks and functions just like a generic ballpoint pen from the bank she patronizes, but it's also a tracking device. I slipped it into her purse. I figured she'd be easier for me to follow that way, and I wanted to keep track of her comings and goings. I also made it my business to gain access to her laptop, though that was trickier. To do that, I had to wait until she got online, then I hacked into her system."

He paused, and after a beat, continued. "But I suppose it's also possible she 'back hacked' me. Or maybe she found the tracking device in her purse, and figured out who planted it. The signal went dead five days ago, and if she'd just thrown it out, I would have been able to track it. The device was very durable."

Abednego put his paw on Ford's lap, removed it, and repeated the process several times. Ford petted him and smiled. "He wants to go lay on the porch. He's used to doing that for an hour or so every evening. He was on his own for a long time before animal control found him, and the big guy obviously likes the outdoors."

Ford opened the front door, allowing the dog to go lay on his square of old carpet. "If it gets too cold for us with the door open, I'll bring Abednego back inside. After everything that's happened, I want to keep an eye on him."

"I'm fine. In fact, I think you keep your house too warm," she answered, leaning back in her chair and stretching out her legs.

"I grew up east of Gallup, and it was really cold in wintertime. In order to keep from running out of propane when our money got low, Mom kept the house temperature as low as we could stand it," he said. "When I finally left and got a place of my own, I swore I'd never wear my coat indoors again."

Ella listened without interrupting, hoping he'd continue. When he didn't, she wasn't surprised. Ford seldom spoke about his past.

Ella heard Abednego sigh contentedly from his bed on the porch, his gaze on Ford. As she watched master and dog looking out for each other, she wasn't sure who took the most comfort in the constant eye contact between them—Ford or Abednego.

"How big a threat do you think Dr. Lee poses?" Ella asked, bringing their focus back to the investigation at hand. "What do your instincts tell you?"

Ford had an almost uncanny sixth sense about people. He attributed it to his religion and his deep connection to the God he served. She was more inclined to believe it was a result of his training as a pastor and his firsthand knowledge about the weaknesses of human nature.

"Do you think that Dr. Lee could be behind the attempted break-in here at your house?" Ella added.

"Without the tracking device, I can't verify that for you one way or the other."

"If she managed to connect the device to your visit, that could explain her coming here," Ella said slowly. "She'd want to know how much you've uncovered about her—especially if she's involved in criminal activities."

"If you're right, then Dr. Lee will probably try again," he said. "And next time, she'll have another way to deal with my dog."

She was about to reply when they heard two dull pops outside. Abednego scrambled to his feet and ran out into the yard, barking furiously.

Reacting instinctively, Ella flipped off the lamp switch and raced to the door, gun in hand. Crouched low, using the wall as cover, she looked out. She saw a flash from beyond the fence and the whine of a ricochet off the sidewalk.

Dropping to the floor, she rolled to her right, bringing her pistol up, the faint glow of her sights lining up on a dark, moving shape in the yard.

"Abednego! Get out of the way," she yelled.

Gravel flew and an engine roared as a car raced away, its lights out. She didn't have a good target, and in the quarter moon, the only thing Ella could determine was that the vehicle was light—maybe white or yellow.

Ford reached the doorway and crouched down beside her as she was putting away her pistol. "Did someone just take a shot at you?"

"No, at Abednego. But the shot missed. You hear it ricochet?" She stood and pointed toward the highway a quarter mile away. The shooter had turned east and was racing away at high speed, lights now on. "There he goes."

Ford hurried out to check Abednego, who was sitting by the fence. He grabbed the dog's collar and ran his hands along the animal's head and sides, checking for wounds, and finding none. "Did you get a look at the shooter?"

"No, just a muzzle flash, but those pops were too loud for a pellet gun. I'm thinking it was a .22 this time."

"Yeah, I agree. If you've still got your flashlight, let's take a look around."

Ella checked the inside wall of the entryway first, wondering if the rounds had impacted there. The shooter had been aiming at a low-lying backlit shape on the porch, a difficult shot.

Ford moved past Ella and took Abednego inside. When he emerged again, he was alone. "I put him in the back bedroom for now. I wouldn't want him to make a mess out of any evidence that might be here." Ford had also brought out a huge lantern, which put out a great deal of light.

"Here's the thing," Ella said, thinking out loud. "The shooter wasn't after the lights this time. Nothing came through the window in our direction or the open doorway, and that last shot passed right by Abednego."

Crouching down, Ella ran her hand over the wall directly behind Abednego's doggie bed. "Here we are." She reached for her pen knife and pried out the round from the wood siding, being careful not to deface the bullet.

"Thank the Lord I hadn't replaced the bulb yet," Ford said in a heavy, weary voice. "I'm obviously still a target, and anyone—man or beast—who's around me gets to share in that danger." He paused and looked directly at her. "You shouldn't be here."

"This is exactly where I should be, Ford. Trust me, I know my job," she said, her heart going out to him. Ford wanted to protect others. It was part of his nature and the essence of his work. "Tracking criminals down is what I do best, and we now have solid evidence. We'll put this person—or people— away." She looked down at the small, nearly intact .22 round in her hand. Due to the softness of the wood siding, the bullet still had rifling marks that could be compared.

"A twenty-two short?" he asked.

"Yeah. It's quieter than the longs, or long rifle cartridges. Even so, chances are the shooter also made, or purchased, a sound suppressor. Being basically illegal, those aren't very common. I'll use that to start the tracking process."

Ford expelled his breath in a hiss. "Bombs, bullets, silencers . . . this isn't what I'm about. I made a commitment to bring good into the lives of those around me," he said, his voice filled with disappointment . . . or maybe despair. "I wish I hadn't taken on this Bureau work."

"What's happening is *not* your fault. You're trying to save lives." Seeing his pained expression, she continued. "My job is to restore the balance between good and evil so that all can walk in beauty. That's what *I'm* all about. And Ford? I'm *very* good at what I do."

"I know," he answered, nodding slowly. "I believe you were born to be a detective, just as I was born to be a preacher."

"We both give the work our all. That's why we make a difference," Ella said, then she picked up the phone and dialed.

FIVE

✖ ✖ ✖

Since Ford lived off the reservation, he was outside Ella's jurisdiction, but she could still call in favors. Ella reported the shooting and made arrangements for the county sheriff's department to increase patrols in Ford's neighborhood.

Once finished, she went back outside and met Ford, who was busy replacing the porch lights. "County's going to send over a deputy to take a report," she said. "They'll also be increasing patrols in this area, and keeping a special watch on your place for the next few days."

"Good. But I'm worried about Abednego. He has no business being in my church office, but maybe an exception could be made . . . ," Ford said as they went back inside. Leading the way into the kitchen, Ford handed her a storage bag for the evidence, then poured himself and Ella some coffee.

"Your door and frame are steel, which stands up to being kicked in. Abednego was exposed because the intruder managed to pick the lock. You might want to switch to one of those high-tech locking mechanisms that requires a number code, or fingerprint. Other than that, I think Abednego's safe and should continue to come and go through the doggie door leading to the backyard. That ten-foot-tall cinder block wall should protect him from all but direct gunfire, and your neighbor on that side would spot anyone who even got close. Didn't you tell me once that she's retired and usually home?" Ella took a sip of the hot brew.

Ford nodded. "Mrs. Tanner's always watching, which probably explains why the guy tried to come in through the front. But I sure hate having to hunker down for anyone out to do me or my animal harm," Ford added through clenched teeth.

"Once we catch the guy, Abednego will be able to enjoy his evenings on the front porch again," Ella said.

They both looked over as the flash of headlights showed through the front window. "Here's the deputy, I bet," Ella said. "He didn't take long."

They were halfway down the walk when the uniformed officer stepped out of his unit. The deputy, an ex-military-looking Navajo in his mid-forties with tightly cropped hair, nodded to them both. "Investigator Clah? Looks like we're having another of those never-ending days. I was at the college campus earlier, helping question the students and making sure my girlfriend was okay. She works for one of the professors. I hope your officer makes it, by the way. The whole department is pulling for him."

"I'll pass that along. Thanks for the support, Deputy Whitefeather." Although she'd recognized him and remembered seeing Whitefeather at the college today, she'd forgotten his name until she was close enough to see his name tag. They'd been on the same arrest team during joint agency outstanding-warrant sweeps last fall.

"Dispatch said shots were fired at *your* residence?" Whitefeather asked.

"No, the shots were fired here at Reverend Tome's residence. I've recovered a small caliber bullet for your crime lab to process."

Ella handed the deputy the bullet, now in a plastic freezer bag. On the bag's label space, she'd written the date, time, and location, then signed her name. She repeated the process with half the meat sample, having kept the other portion for Justine's lab.

"Reverend, meet Officer Henderson Whitefeather," she said, turning around.

Ford stepped forward, acknowledging the man, but didn't hold out his hand, not knowing if the other Navajo disliked shaking hands or not. The gesture was still not common practice among the *Diné*, the Navajo people. "Good evening, Officer."

Ella sniffed, noting a floral scent in the air.

"That would be me, smelling like lilacs or whatever," Whitefeather said, shaking his head. "Had to use a lot of air freshener in my unit a while ago. A drunk cowboy puked all over the upholstery."

"I can relate to that," Ella responded, leading the way back toward the house. She'd arrested many drunks during her career.

Once inside the yard, Whitefeather raised the small clipboard he had in his left hand. "Shall we get down to it, folks? Reverend, can you give me a rundown on what happened tonight?"

"Okay, I'll start. Jump in whenever you want, Investigator Clah," Ford said as they reached the porch.

Ten minutes later they watched from the sidewalk as the deputy's car headed back toward the main highway.

"You think the deputy was right, that this was just a meth addict trying to set up a burglary? There *have* been some residential burglaries in the area recently," Ford asked.

"Anything is possible but, in my mind, it's just too coincidental, especially after what happened this afternoon. It also doesn't fit the MO of a meth addict. They tend to be the smash-and-grab types. Instincts tells me these incidents are connected."

"So what's next, Ella?"

"There'll be patrol cars around, so if you hear or see anything out of the ordinary, call 911 immediately. One more thing: Stay at home until I've got a better handle on things. A day or two at least, okay?"

"What will you be doing?"

"I'm going to start by seeing how much Dr. Lee could have learned about your background by searching the Internet. To see you through her eyes, I'm going to have to follow the logical investigative footsteps that would be available to her."

"That makes sense." He walked her to the door, Abednego beside him. "Do you honestly think he'll be all right in the house while I'm gone during the day?" he asked, glancing at Ella, then back down at the dog.

"If it'll make you feel better, we can arrange to loan him a Kevlar vest like some of our police dogs wear. We'll get one for you, too."

Ford shook his head. "Not for me. This is all the protection I need," he said, holding out the small silver cross he wore on a chain around his neck. "But I will take a vest for Abednego."

She thought about arguing that he'd need more than the cross to protect him from a bullet, but one look at his face told her his mind was made up.

"All right then. I'll be back later."

Ella stopped by the station and spent the next few hours in her office at the computer. It was close to one-thirty in the morning by the time she looked up, and she was beyond tired, but she still didn't want to go home. Normally, whenever she got off work this late, her first stop would be Dawn's room.

She'd check on her daughter, then turn in for the night. But with Dawn gone, there was no need for her mom skills—what had become the dearest part of her soul.

Ella called the hospital next. Ralph hadn't regained consciousness since his surgery, but although his condition was still listed as critical, he was stable. Grateful he was still alive, she tried to do some more work, but her attention kept wandering. She finally decided she wasn't doing the case any good, picked up her keys, waved good-bye to the dispatcher, and headed home.

Two, their old mutt, greeted her at the door, and she scratched him behind the ears. The dog sighed contentedly, then went back to the kitchen and lay down on his bed. Not knowing which side of the house to sleep on since the new addition, he'd compromised by picking the most commonly shared room.

Ella stopped by her daughter's room and stared at the made-up bed and stuffed toys around the pillow. She missed Dawn so much, it was almost a physical pain. But Ella was determined to encourage her to build her own dreams and follow them wherever they might lead.

She wanted the very best for her daughter, but beneath the love, or maybe because of it, Ella struggled with fear. It continually tempted her to keep Dawn close, where she could be watched over. But her daughter deserved more from her.

Ella lay down on Dawn's bed and picked up the teddy bear that had been her daughter's favorite toy well into her fifth year. It usually sat on the night stand, seldom used except in emergencies. With a sigh, Ella hugged the stuffed toy close, then leaned back against the pillow.

She was so tired. Maybe she'd just rest her eyes for a second or two. . . .

Ella didn't wake up until the alarm on her nightstand down the hall began to buzz loudly. It took her a second to get her bearings, then she hurried down the hall and turned off the racket. Hoping the noise hadn't carried to her mother's side of the house, Ella showered and dressed. A short time later, she headed out the door, a cinnamon roll left over from yesterday in hand.

Ella entered the station a little after seven-thirty and stopped at the break room to pour herself a cup of coffee. The carafe was half full, but the second the strong black liquid touched her tongue, she gagged. The coffee, far from fresh, tasted like acid syrup. Ella promptly poured it down the drain and discarded the foam cup.

Justine came in while she was brewing a fresh pot. "Hey, partner. I see you worked late last night."

"How did you know?" Ella asked.

"My computer's on the fritz, so I went to your office to use yours and noticed your log-off time. I also saw that you'd picked up the crime scene reports I left on your desk," Justine answered.

"Yeah, I did," Ella said, then added, "Anything new on Ralph?"

"I called the nurse's station a while ago. He made it through the night, but there's been no change. I'm still praying for him," Justine replied.

"He's got a lot of support in our community. Now we have to nail the animal who did this. Why don't you follow me to my office and we'll get started," Ella said. "I need to fill you in on a few things."

Fifteen minutes later, Ella had updated Justine, relating what had happened last night at Ford's home. She then explained what she could about the possible terrorist threat to the nuclear facility. "What do *you* know about Dr. Lee?" Ella asked at last.

"She's just a name to me, but I think Marianna Talk arrested Professor Lee several months ago, during a demonstration on campus. The activists wanted to force some tribal council members to talk to the students about the nuclear plant's safety procedures. Dr. Lee and some others were arrested when they refused the order to disperse."

"Is Marianna on duty now?"

"I saw her a little while ago meeting with the watch commander," Justine said, stepping toward the door. "I'll take a look in the briefing room, and if she's still there, I'll send her your way."

Marianna Talk had been with their department for only a few years, but she was already on the radar for a promotion. Ella had heard rumors that Marianna had set her eye on the Special Investigations Unit. Considering that Marianna was only a few inches over five feet—a weak point when encountering drunk drivers—Ella thought it was a good career decision.

Marianna entered Ella's office minutes later and took a seat. "Justine said you needed to talk to me."

Ella nodded. "I wanted to ask you about Dr. Jane Lee, a professor at the community college. I understand you had to place her under arrest several months back."

Marianna nodded slowly. "Professor Lee's a strange one. She never said a word after her arrest. Maybe she thought that was the best thing she could do for herself, and I don't dispute that strategy, it just surprised me. The only time she spoke at all was after I'd booked her. She thanked me for all the work I and the other officers do for the *Diné*. What struck me as odd was that she looked at me directly—and you know Diné hardly ever do that. It's considered disrespectful."

"She's in a leadership position at the college. She's used to dealing with Modernists. Did any of the others arrested on that occasion make any comments about Dr. Lee?"

"Gladys Joe did. She was one of the students I arrested that day. I've known Gladys and most of her clan all my life and we spoke for a while. She told me that Dr. Lee was one of the finest minds on campus. According to Gladys, her professor wasn't a rabble-rouser, but she had some very deep beliefs and wasn't afraid to stand up for what she felt was right."

The news didn't give any comfort. Some of the worst felons throughout history had been ones who'd professed to be acting according to their highest sense of right. But before she could ask Marianna anything more, Big Ed Atcitty, the chief of police, appeared in the doorway.

"My office, Investigator Clah," he said without preamble.

Ella thanked Marianna, then followed Big Ed down the hall. Along the way she met Justine, who'd apparently also been summoned. It was going to be a busy Saturday.

As they stepped into his office, Big Ed glanced at Justine, the last to come in. "Close the door, Officer Goodluck." Their broad-chested superior stepped behind his desk and took a seat, motioning them both toward chairs.

"I received a one-of-a-kind phone call this morning," he said. "At first I thought it was someone playing a joke on me. FBI in Washington doesn't generally communicate directly with the tribal police. If it's important, they contact us through Blalock." Big Ed stared at the swinging pendulum of a cuckoo clock his wife had given him last Christmas. Silence stretched out.

At long last he spoke again. "Assistant Director Hansen said that Reverend Tome is working for the Bureau on a sensitive assignment involving national security. They want us to provide him with protection—immediately. They're concerned about a possible connection between yesterday's events and an article that appeared in the *Diné Times* a few months ago. Apparently, the reporter mentioned that Reverend Tome was skilled in cryptography—codebreaking, specifically."

"I don't remember seeing that," Ella said, thinking back.

"I didn't either, and said so," Big Ed answered. "Then I

was told that it was part of an editorial that appeared after we closed the case involving that murdered serviceman just back from Iraq."

Ella and Justine nodded. Two years ago Ford had helped unravel a coded message sent by a National Guard soldier serving overseas. He'd hidden it within some Navajo creation stories. The disclosure had helped solve a much larger crime.

"I'm surprised that the FBI is monitoring the Navajo newspaper that closely. That was quite a while back," Ella said. "Ford must be even more important to them than I'd realized."

Big Ed nodded slowly. "I asked about the work the reverend's doing for the Bureau now, but the AD told me you'd been briefed, and I should get that information from you."

Ella gave him the highlights from her discussion with Ford the night before. "The way I see it, there's only one way we can protect Reverend Tome and not interfere with his assignment. I'll have to become his bodyguard. People won't think twice about seeing us together."

"Resources are tight. The department needs you to investigate the bombing," Big Ed countered.

She considered for several long moments. "The reverend wants to be at his church, and maybe we should make that possible for him. Good Shepherd's on the Navajo Nation, so maybe the Cloud brothers can keep an eye on him there— one outside, one inside."

Big Ed nodded. "Good idea. When it comes to surveillance, they're among our best. I'll speak to the men," he said, then continued. "Anything new on the bomber?"

"Not yet."

"*Nothing's* more important than finding him, you get me? One of our own is fighting for his life, and I want the SOB who did this. Clear?"

"I'll let you know as soon as I've got something," Ella said.

"Needless to say, we're going to have to keep all this on a need-to-know basis. We have no idea if this conspiracy against the Hogback facility is for real, or just another wild goose chase," Big Ed said, standing to announce the meeting was over.

As soon as they left his office, Ella glanced at Justine. "I need to know what was in the bait that was left for Ford's dog. Then I want to know who in this area supplies it."

"I'll work on that," Justine said with a nod. "By the way, the pellets you recovered won't be much help. They're too common and leave no marks, so we can't link them to a specific gun. I'm still waiting to hear from the county crime lab on that .22 round you turned over to Deputy Whitefeather. Maybe we'll get lucky."

"Unless it matches a bullet they've already recovered from a previous crime scene, we'll either have to find the gun—or wait for the next bullet."

"Not something I'm looking forward to, Ella," Justine said.

"Me neither, cuz. I'll be in my office."

"One more thing," Justine said before Ella could walk away. "You staying close to Ford at night. . . . That's going to be tricky. Nobody's supposed to know that he's a target and needs a bodyguard, so having you there at all hours is going to get people talking. A minister is supposed to serve as a role model for his church. . . ."

Ella nodded, only too aware of that, having grown up with a father who was also a very hard-nosed conservative preacher. "I'll figure something out," she said, then went to her office.

Ella knew that Ford would never willingly upset his congregation. Spending the night at his house would be completely out of the question. Somehow, she'd have to find a way to protect Ford without destroying his reputation. His conservative Christian congregation wouldn't be as understanding as the tribe. To Traditional Navajos, sex wasn't linked to moral standards. It was considered a basic physical need, much like eating, and had its place in the scheme of life. The key to harmony was balance.

There was only one solution to the problem. She'd have to arrange for the Cloud brothers to take turns, keeping watch day *and* night, and give them permission to recruit a third member for the operation, if needed.

She made the call attending to the arrangements. As she hung up, Justine returned.

"I've got the results of the screen I ran on the capsules. It's rat poison, strychnine, essentially. Most feed stores carry it. The empty gelatin capsules can be purchased online or at any health food store. Both might have been shoplifted, too."

"Check area stores and see what you can get. I'm going to talk to Clifford. Dr. Lee's in charge of the guest speaker program, and my brother accepted her invitation to give some talks on the roles of *hataaliis* on the Rez. If I gave him a ride to and from campus, that'll give me the perfect opportunity to make a connection with Dr. Lee."

"What about Ford?" Justine asked. "Who's protecting him now?"

"The county sheriff will help with his deputies, and Ford agreed to stay home until we've worked up a security plan. My guess is he'll call in sick today."

"But what if he gets called on an emergency?" Justine answered.

Ella considered it and knew Justine was right. "He'd go anyway." If a parishioner became seriously ill and specifically asked for Ford, nothing would stop him from going—with or without her okay. "Good thinking, partner."

"What gave me the idea was reading the notice on the bulletin board in the squad room. Did you know that Reverend Tome is expected to lead a special prayer for Ralph tomorrow at our early Sunday service?"

"Couldn't he turn that over to Reverend Campbell?"

Justine shook her head. "Reverend Campbell's got a wedding to perform in Gallup."

Ella's phone rang, so Justine waved and left the room. As Ella picked it up, she heard Dr. Carolyn Roanhorse's familiar voice. Loosely connected to the New Mexico Office of the Medical Investigator, Carolyn was the tribe's only ME, and, as such, had very few friends. No one wanted to be around a person who exposed herself daily to the *chindi*.

Carolyn and Ella had hit it off from the first day they'd met. Knowing firsthand the cost of walking the line between cultures—raised by a Bible thumping minister father and a Traditionalist mother who followed The Way—Ella understood Carolyn better than most people ever could.

"How are you holding up?" Carolyn asked. "I figured this case would tug at you, and thought you could use a friendly voice about now."

"You're right, but I'm snowed under with work. I was just going to call the hospital again and check up on Ralph. Have you heard anything?"

"I try to stay away from the upper floors for obvious reasons, but I checked a few minutes ago by phone. He's stable, but he's still got a long way to go."

Before Ella could respond, her other line began to ring. "I better get that, Carolyn. I'll check in with you later," Ella said, then picked up the second call.

"Ella, this is Lori, Ralph's younger sister. I don't know if you remember me from school."

She didn't, but that didn't matter. "Lori, how can I help you?"

"I went by your brother's hogan twice this morning. The second time, I waited, hoping he'd return, but I never saw him. His wife was out, too, or I would have left a message with her. My family wants to hire him to do a short blessing here at the hospital as soon as possible. We'll have a

full Sing done later when my brother is released, but we
need a *hataalii* now. Could you find him for us?"

"I'll see what I can do," Ella said, wishing Clifford would
agree to carry a cell phone. To date, her brother refused to do
so, claiming that it interfered with the mind-set he needed to
do his work.

After giving Lori some words of encouragement and support, Ella hung up and called Ford. At first she assumed that
she'd be catching him at home, but when she heard voices in
the background, she realized that he'd forwarded his calls to
his cell.

"Tell me I'm wrong and you didn't leave the house . . . ,"
Ella said.

"Don't worry. One of the county deputies followed me
right to the reservation border. Then, before he left, he noti-
fied the tribe, and a tribal officer met me and followed me the
rest of the way to church. That's where I am now. Abednego's
here, too. I decided to take him with me wherever I go."

"You and I had an agreement." Ella clipped her words.

There was a brief pause, and when he answered, it was
in a soft, gentle tone. "It was my duty to be here. I have to
write a special sermon for tomorrow and I needed some references I keep here. There's also a faculty event at the college this evening. I'd assumed they'd cancel, considering
what happened yesterday, but they didn't, so I've got to attend that, too. The patrol officer outside said he'll attend
with me. The college is still on full alert, so there'll be plenty
of security there. I'd never endanger others by not taking
precautions."

When she didn't answer right away, he added, "It's my
responsibility to show everyone that I trust in God's protection. I won't be cowed into hiding." When she didn't respond,
he continued. "I never figured I'd have to spell this out for
you."

Ella took a deep breath, then let it out slowly. She should

have known. Ford could no more be kept from his duties as a spiritual leader than she could hers as a police officer. In that respect, they were two of a kind.

"Who's there with you now?" she asked.

"Officer Charlie's by the side door just down the hall. He said Michael Cloud has reassigned him, with your permission. There are also two ladies from the women's auxiliary taking care of flower arrangements in the chapel."

"I'm going to send Justine Goodluck to relieve Officer Charlie. From now on you'll be guarded by plainclothes officers only."

"Excellent idea," he said. "Justine's perfect. She's a member of our congregation and no one will think twice about it."

"I'll try to take over from Justine before the faculty thing tonight, and go there with you myself," Ella said.

"Great. I'll look forward to that."

"Don't count too heavily on it. It'll all depend on what else is going down at the time," Ella answered.

"I expect you have your hands full," he said.

"My next job is to track down Clifford and take him over to the hospital. The Tache family wants a blessing done. Hospitals—the doctors, the smells, the sounds—can be very frightening. The family needs to cling to something more familiar right now—ways they trust."

"On the drive here I passed your brother in his pickup, heading west out of town. He might be going home."

"Thanks for the tip."

Ella hung up, then hurried to find her partner. She walked into the department's tiny lab, and found Justine behind the computer.

Justine gave her a quick half-smile. "I called the county crime lab to check on the .22 round you recovered from Reverend Tome's porch. They can't find any record of it, but they promised to check with Deputy Whitefeather, just in case there was a screw-up. He filed the report, right?"

Ella nodded. "If they've mislaid evidence, heads will roll. Sheriff Taylor doesn't tolerate sloppy paperwork."

"On the good-news side, I've got the phone numbers of three area merchants who carry those gelatin capsules."

"Save it for later," Ella said, and filled her in on the current situation. "Right now I need you protecting Ford, partner. You're the logical choice."

Justine nodded. "This'll be a first for me. I've never gone inside a church packing." She looked at Ella. "I'm assuming you want me to take my service weapon?"

"You'll be on the job, so don't close your eyes even if they have a prayer or moment of silence. Trust no one."

Justine nodded once. "Nothing will happen to Ford, Ella, not on my watch."

Ella left the station shortly afterwards, driving west out of Shiprock, then turning south. Once clear of traffic, she asked to be patched through to Officer Charlie, whom she'd met several times in the past.

Officer Charlie was a dedicated tribal police officer who came from a long line of Traditionalists. Walking the line between Traditionalist and New Traditionalist, he'd found a way to make peace with his job. After all, Navajo police officers restored the balance between good and evil and that was at the heart of walking in beauty.

Ella reached Officer Charlie on a direct channel a moment or two later and listened to his report. So far he'd encountered nothing unusual. After warning him to stay alert because things could change at a moment's notice, she let him know about Justine. "SI Goodluck will be replacing you soon, but until she gets attuned to things there, she may need your backup. Will you be able to stick around?"

"No problem. I need the overtime."

Fifteen minutes later, Ella turned up the road leading to Clifford's medicine hogan. The house beside it was his family's home. Although she'd never liked Loretta, his wife, Ella was the first to admit that Loretta and Clifford had done a wonderful job raising their son, Julian. Almost thirteen now, Julian went to visit patients with his father as often as possible. He'd made it clear, too, that he wanted to be a *hataalii* like his dad, something that had pleased Clifford to no end. Since it was Saturday, Ella was hoping she'd get a chance to see her nephew.

When she drove up, Ella saw a chestnut horse loosely tied to a hitching post near the front of Clifford's hogan. The animal was grazing on the meager grasses and weeds within reach. Ella parked next to Clifford's truck, fifty feet away, then turned off her engine and prepared to wait until she was invited to approach.

As she settled back in her seat, she could hear her brother's voice chanting a healing song in Navajo. Loretta soon came out of their home, about twenty yards up the road, to hang an old bedspread on the clothesline. Without so much as a glance in Ella's direction, Loretta went back inside.

Ella hadn't expected her sister-in-law to invite her into their home. Loretta would have known that she wasn't here just to visit. Word traveled fast on the Rez, and the news of the bombing and Tache's injuries would be common knowledge by now.

Ella got out of her unit and glanced around for signs of Julian, but didn't see him or his bicycle. Just as she was stretching her legs, her brother's patient came out of the medicine hogan. The wrinkled, silver-haired Navajo man, despite his obvious advanced age, mounted his horse with the ease of a twenty year old, then rode away.

Clifford, wearing his white headband, looked out of the blanket-covered entrance, saw Ella, and waved for her to come in.

Ella stepped inside, and watched as he put away jars filled with various collected herbs and powders, illuminated by the light of a kerosene lantern. The dry painting that had been created on the hogan floor as part of the treatment was no longer there. Only its outline remained. Those sand paintings were often incredible masterpieces, particularly the intricate ones she'd seen Clifford create for special Sings. Yet because they were a way of connecting a patient to higher powers, they had to be destroyed after each ceremony.

Clifford sat on a sheepskin on the dirt floor at the south side of the hogan, as was customary, while Ella took a seat on the blanket placed on the north end.

"You look as if you haven't had a good night's sleep in days," he said gently. "It must be hard for you when your daughter's away with her father. And now with your injured friend . . ."

"Which brings me to the reason I'm here," she said, not wanting to get into personal matters now. After explaining that the Tache family was requesting his services, she added, "Will you come to the hospital with me?"

"Of course."

As he started to gather his ritual items, she stood at the doorway. "Where's Julian?" she asked, curious. It was unusual not to see him hanging around his dad.

Clifford's expression darkened. "My son's visiting a friend who has a big-screen TV." He shook his head slowly as if still trying to understand the unexplainable. "Last week he told me he's longer interested in becoming a *hataalii*. He wants to leave the Navajo Nation as soon as he finishes high school, and go to college somewhere outside New Mexico. At the moment he can't decide between Los Angeles and New York."

He paused, then in a heavy voice, added, "In a lot of ways he's starting to remind me of you at that age. The reservation was your home, but you didn't make it so until after you saw what the rest of the world had to offer."

Ella remembered how badly she'd wanted to leave home. She'd wanted nothing to do with the hardships and poverty that surrounded them here. "To find myself, I had to leave. Have you ever understood that?"

"Eventually I did. I just never thought my son would go through the same thing you did. I'd hoped he would find his path among us. Here, he would have been protected just as we are. Our sacred mountains watch over the *Diné* and our ways continually guide us. We know the power of the spoken word and are careful not to call evil to us. We greet the dawn with an offering of pollen, the gift of life, and walk in beauty," he said, then fell silent. "That's the world that I wanted to share with him."

"He's thirteen, and is starting to realize that he's not just an extension of you. He wants to be himself, but first he has to find out who that is."

"I know. It's all a natural progression, but it still worries me. Right now he's with his friend, and the boy's father is a medical doctor. Their beliefs and ours . . ." Clifford took a deep breath, then shook his head. "Let's not get into this now. We have other business to attend to," he said, gathering his medicine pouch, and adjusting his white headband. "Once we're at the hospital, I'll speak to the family first. Then as soon as the doctors give me permission, I'll do a pollen blessing over the patient."

"You won't have any problems." Doctors who worked on the Rez soon learned that, to walk in beauty, the spirit of a Navajo needed its own medicine.

SIX

✖ ✖ ✖

Soon Ella and Clifford were on their way to the hospital in her vehicle. As they traveled down the highway, a long silence stretched out between them.

"What's bothering you, sister? I sense something is," Clifford said at long last.

"Dr. Jane Lee was the one who invited you to do your talks at the college, right?"

"Yes, and I agreed because I think our young people would benefit from them. They're being taught all about Christianization among the *Diné* and I think there should be more balance. I plan to do my part to provide that. Is there a problem?" he asked.

"No, not at all. How about letting me drive you to your lectures, to and from, at least for a while? I need a reason to be around Dr. Lee. I'd also like you to help me keep an eye on her, and see if she's in regular contact with anyone in particular."

"I'm assuming that you have a very good reason for this request . . . that it has something to do with the bombing that took place on campus yesterday?" he asked.

"Feel free to assume anything you like," she answered

with a quick half-smile. Then in a more serious voice, she added, "I trust you with my life, brother, but the less you know, the safer you'll be."

Clifford considered the matter for a moment, then nodded. "I'll be happy to have you do the driving. I'll be giving morning and evening lectures starting this coming week. I also have to be there later tonight. There's a get-together for everyone participating, and I agreed to go."

"I heard about this evening's function. I'll take you to that, and also pick you up for your lectures, unless something comes up that make it impossible."

"All right. I'll let it be known that I'm having problems with my old truck. That way no one will think twice about you giving me a ride," he said.

When they arrived at the hospital in Shiprock, Ella led the way inside. As soon as they joined Ralph Tache's family, she stepped away quietly, allowing Clifford some privacy with them.

Walking farther down the hall, Ella went to the nurse's station to get an update on the officer. The news wasn't good. Ralph was still listed in critical condition.

As she glanced back, Ella could see pain and worry on the faces of Tache's family. The realization of what they were going through—and what still lay ahead—tugged at her, and she turned away. Searching for something to do, she walked to the soft drink machine.

"Hey, Clah," came a familiar voice from somewhere behind her.

Ella turned around and saw Blalock. "What brings you here?" she asked.

"I came to update you. I stopped by the church to speak to the reverend. He was offering prayers for Tache's family at the request of his sister and a few other close friends who'd come by to talk to him. Officer Goodluck was there as well. Tome's back is well covered, so don't worry."

"Thanks for letting me know," she said.

"The fact that Justine was there to act as his bodyguard wasn't obvious, and Officer Charlie's out of uniform now, too, so that helped keep everything low key," he added. "I also managed to scrounge up a vest for Abednego, that moose of a dog. Seems you promised Reverend Tome one."

Ella smiled. "That dog means the world to him. Thanks. I owe you one."

"You bet you do," Blalock said with a grin. "Those vests cost around seven hundred bucks, and county didn't have any to spare. But I managed to get one up from the DEA."

Ella updated him on the details of the 'round-the-clock coverage she'd put in place to protect Ford.

"Ford's coming up here as soon as he gets word that your brother's finished the blessing," Blalock added. "He wants to pay his respects to Officer Tache and say a prayer at his bedside."

"I'm not sure how that'll play out—half the family's Christian, the other, New Traditional."

"Stand back and let them figure it out," Blalock advised.

"Yeah, you're right," she said. Turning her mind back to the case, she continued. "I'm going to need you to get me everything you can on Dr. Jane Lee. I tried the Internet, but I didn't get far. You've been briefed, right?"

"I got a call right after AD Hansen spoke to your boss, so I'm up to speed on the situation. We can't risk tipping our hand. I'm in the process of getting a sneak-and-peek warrant so we can enter her house without her knowledge. I'll let you know when I've got the paperwork wrapped up."

"I'll be driving my brother to the college campus right after he finishes here. While I'm there, I'll find out what Dr. Lee's teaching schedule and office hours are. That way we'll know when she's not at home."

"From everything I've turned up so far on this woman, I really doubt she's responsible for what happened to Tache.

There's nothing in her background that indicates she'd have the expertise to make a bomb," Blalock said.

"You can get almost anything you want these days via the Internet—including know-how. I don't know how complicated that bomb was, that report's not in yet. But if it was black powder in a pipe . . . how much training could that take?" Ella asked.

"You're making premature judgements and that's a good way to get broadsided when you least expect it."

Before she could answer, Ella saw her brother come out of the critical care unit. "I've got to get going," she told Blalock.

Clifford came up to them, and Blalock nodded, greeting him merely as *hataalii*. The two had been forced to work together several times in the past, and had gained a mutual, if grudging, respect for one another over the years.

"It's time for us to go to the college," Clifford said, looking at Ella.

As they headed down the hall, Justine and Ford came around the corner. Clifford slowed slightly and smiled at Justine, but his face became politely neutral as he glanced at Ford.

Ella signaled to her brother that she needed a moment, but Clifford seemed reluctant to stop.

"I'll meet you downstairs by the SUV," Clifford said, then strode off.

Ford stopped to talk to her, but didn't relax until Clifford was out of view and the hall was empty. "Did he finish his blessing?"

Ella nodded. "I can't say I envy you going up there. The New Traditionalists won't want you there at all, but the Christians need your support."

"When Ralph's sister Trudy asked me to say a prayer by her brother's bedside, I couldn't refuse. That's what my job's all about."

Ella nodded. "I know. The good thing is that you're safe

here at the hospital. Once you leave, stick close to Justine. She'll keep you safe."

"But what about later, at my home? I understand that you don't think Abednego will be enough protection."

Ella looked around. "Where is he, by the way?"

"Out in my car. The temperature's nice and cool in the evenings, and he knows to stay put," Ford said. "But getting back to what I was saying, I got a call from Michael Cloud. He told me that you'd given him and his brother orders to watch over me tonight."

"It's the best way. I'd stay with you, but that would create a whole new world of problems."

"You're right," he answered. "I'm glad you understand."

Glancing down the hall and seeing that Clifford was long gone, she added, "I better get going, but I'm glad that Tache's family has both you and my brother to rely on. You're each needed now."

His parting expression left no doubt that she'd said the wrong thing. When it came to certain matters, Ford's mind was completely closed. Her father, also a minister, had been the same way. His belief in the God he served required that he accept no other powers. It saddened her to think that the two men closest to her, Clifford and Ford, would never get along.

A few minutes later, Ella joined Clifford, who was standing beside her police unit. "I wish you'd try to be a little friendlier to the reverend, brother," she said, not referring to Ford by name out of respect for her brother's beliefs.

"We have fundamental differences, so that's as friendly as it'll ever get between us," he answered. There was no anger in his voice, just acceptance.

They climbed into the vehicle, and Ella drove out of the hospital parking lot. As she thought about what Clifford had said, she realized that some things would never change. Religion, for all its talk about brotherhood, had, over the years, built insurmountable walls between millions of people.

"Once we get to the college, how can I help you?" he asked, breaking the silence after they'd traveled a few miles.

"Keep people focused on you. I'll do my wallflower bit, then sneak away for a walk. If I can, I'm going to take a look inside Dr. Lee's office."

"Be very careful. They're bound to have heightened security on campus, especially after yesterday."

"I know, and if it turns out to be impossible, I'll just talk to the other professors and staff and try to find out more about her that way. I'm in the perfect position as the sister of one of the guest speakers."

When they arrived at the college, Ella followed Clifford's directions and parked in the faculty slots beside the administration office—Narbona Hall—named after a Navajo warrior. Inside, Clifford reluctantly picked up a name tag then, together with Ella, joined the small crowd already gathered in the spacious lobby. Refreshments had been placed buffet-style on a hexagonal table, and Ella suddenly realized she couldn't remember the last time she'd eaten. Almost as if to emphasize it, her stomach growled.

As Clifford mingled, Ella stopped at the table and picked up one of the small club sandwiches comprised of cheese, bacon, and a delicious, tangy sauce. As she ate, she carefully watched the people there. The administrators had all dressed conservatively in business suits, or long Southwestern-style dresses with silver and turquoise jewelry.

The faculty, including guest speakers like Clifford, were almost too casual in comparison. Several of the professors wore western-style jeans, boots, and leather vests or jackets. Most had chosen bolo ties. Her brother, with his white headband, colorful western-style shirt, jeans, and his best deerskin moccasins, fit right in.

Just as Ella turned to track down another sandwich, Dr. Lee, dressed in a black velveteen dress and wearing a multi-strand liquid-silver necklace, entered the room. The middle-aged woman was accompanied by a long-haired Navajo woman in her twenties, wearing a pale-green knit top and multicolored broom skirt that nearly reached the floor.

Dr. Lee quickly worked the room, introducing herself and her young teaching assistant, Mona Tso, to the guest lecturers and full-time staff. As the group of mostly gregarious people continued to mingle, Ella grabbed a cup of punch and retreated to the perimeter, listening and watching from the shadows, but never looking directly at a person long enough to catch anyone's eye.

To Ella's surprise, Dr. Lee seemed to do the same, taking a few snacks on a paper plate, then stepping out of the way to observe. Her gaze darted around the room, studying faces, listening in on conversations, and occasionally checking her watch. When the professor looked in her direction, Ella always made sure to be seen looking at a painting on the wall or studying one of the printed bulletins, which listed all the faculty members and guests.

Time passed, and though the professor still seemed pre-occupied, she began smiling more and engaging others in conversation. Ella made it a point to listen to Dr. Lee, but found nothing particularly memorable or noteworthy about her exchanges.

Ella then turned her attention to the people gathered around her brother, and joined them for a few minutes. When she looked around again a short time later, Ella realized that Dr. Lee was nowhere in sight.

Ella excused herself, stepped out into the hallway, and caught a glimpse of Dr. Lee going into an office farther down the hall. Moving as quietly as she knew how, Ella followed. The door had been left wide open, and she listened for the sound of voices, but there was only silence.

Ella edged closer, wondering why Dr. Lee had left the gathering. Boredom was a possibility, but that seemed unlikely. Before she could give it any more thought, Ella heard Dr. Lee call out.

"Detective, I'm waiting. You have questions, so come on in and we'll talk." Dr. Lee poked her head out of the office and met Ella's surprised gaze. "Do hurry, will you? I haven't got all night."

Ella knew she'd been silent. Even over rough terrain, she could track without making a sound and here, there'd been very little to give her away. She'd greatly underestimated Dr. Lee. When Ella entered the small office she found the professor sitting behind her desk, leaning back on her chair, her hands folded on her lap.

"About time. Both the Feds and the tribe have been showing a great deal of interest in me lately. So let's get to it. What's the problem?"

Ella wondered if she'd made those assumptions after finding Ford's listening device, or if she'd had more to go on. "You have a history of demonstrating against the operation and construction of nuclear power plants," Ella said, not elaborating. Her gaze stayed on Dr. Lee but the woman gave nothing away.

"And you want to know if I'll be a problem once the *Tsétaak'á* Generating Station opens? Is that it?"

"In a nutshell," Ella answered, glad to take the direct approach.

"As I'm sure you already know, I've discontinued my efforts to prevent the opening of the Hogback facility." She met Ella's gaze and, though it was an atypical response for a Navajo, held it. "I've come to realize that other types of influence are more effective—and are more long lasting—than demonstrations."

"Explain," Ella prodded when Dr. Lee didn't elaborate.

"Women are the real source of power on the reservation.

We're the property owners, and always get custody of the kids. Our primary clan, the one we're 'born into,' is our mother's. It's through our women that change—the real kind—will come. That's why I teach women's studies these days. Influencing those who'll impact the future, that's the legacy I want to leave behind. *My* voice won't prevent future nuclear power plants, but the young women who are in my classes today may someday accomplish that goal."

It was a practiced speech. Ella could feel it in her gut. "So you're no longer interested in stopping the opening of our nuclear facility?"

"No. This is a fight for the next generation," Dr. Lee said. "Does that disappoint you?"

Ella blinked, surprised by the aggression in her tone. "I'm neither pleased nor disappointed. I'm only after the truth."

Ella allowed the silence to stretch out between them for several long minutes. Dr. Lee scarcely moved, her breathing regular and slow. Intuition assured Ella that she, too, was being methodically sized up.

"What's frightening you?" Dr. Lee asked at last, her gaze narrowed. "Has there been another threat against the plant? Are you here to determine if *I'm* involved?"

"What makes you think anyone has made any threats?" Ella deflected. Dr. Lee's tactic disturbed her. The activists she'd met in the past had usually been argumentative and highly driven people—warriors of a different kind, anxious to take action. Yet there was a coolness about Dr. Lee that seemed out of character with the radical, outspoken activist her old files claimed her to be. Maybe age *had* mellowed her, or maybe she was just fishing, trying to find out what Ella knew.

Dr. Lee stood. "I'm here most mornings, teaching, but I have office hours in the afternoons. If I can help you with something, Investigator Clah, don't hesitate to ask," she said. "You might consider stopping by and acquainting yourself with what we have to offer in women's studies these days. We give the students plenty to think about, and there's more than enough to satisfy anyone who needs a commitment to a cause."

"I didn't come here tonight only because of you," Ella said, just to gauge her reaction.

"I'm sure you didn't," Dr. Lee answered with a laugh. "Multitasking is the province of a skilled law enforcement officer."

"You say you're no longer involved with the activists who've worked hard to stop the power plant from opening. Does that mean you've lost contact with those people?" Ella glanced at Dr. Lee's desktop computer. "Or do you mean that you only stay in touch via e-mail?" It was a shot in the dark—a way to see how Dr. Lee would react more than anything else.

Dr. Lee calmly pulled back a strand of gray hair that had worked itself loose from the traditional Navajo bun at the nape of her neck. "They've gone their way and I have mine, so we've lost touch. And, no, Detective, you can't browse through my mail. There are some rights I *will* fight to preserve. The right to privacy is one. But if you really suspected I was involved in something dangerous, I'm sure you'd already have found a way to check my computer and private mail. Seems like these days, the government can invade almost every aspect of a person's life without due process."

"Thank you for taking time to talk to me, Professor," Ella said, following her to the door.

"For the record, if I had been communicating with those activists and trying to hide it, I wouldn't be stupid enough to use a computer that's on a college network. My e-mails are subject to examination at any time by the administration— standard policy. If I were hiding something, I'd make darned sure no one would ever find it." Dr. Lee stepped back so Ella could pass, then locked the door behind them.

Whether Jane Lee was involved in a plot against the power plant remained an open question. To Ella, the professor was now even more of an enigma than before. She was clearly a woman of layers, not afraid of a challenge and still defiant.

"By the way, have you seen the new generating station close up?" Ella asked without any particular inflection. There was no denying the photos she'd seen of Dr. Lee photographing the plant. "It's state-of-the-art. Safety's been the primary concern, if you believe such publicity."

Dr. Lee smiled. "So *that's* where this is all coming from! You're right, I *have* looked at it from a distance, and I even took photos," she answered. "Who wouldn't? It's a piece of history in the making. From that standpoint, it interests me, if only as a visual I can share with my classes."

Again, Ella picked up nothing from either Dr. Lee's inflection or her body language. That alone made her suspicions grow. Instinct told her that Dr. Lee had learned from past mistakes, and that would make her a formidable enemy.

SEVEN
✗ ✗ ✗

As they walked down the hall, Ella noticed Ford and Justine just inside the reception area, talking to one of the faculty members. Apparently having seen them, too, Dr. Lee excused herself and walked ahead to greet them.

While Dr. Lee and Ford spoke, Justine stepped away discreetly and joined Ella.

"How did it go at the hospital?" Ella whispered.

"There was an ugly scene. Ralph's sister is a devout Christian, but the rest of the family got their backs up the second they saw Reverend Tome. Rather than make things worse for everyone, Ford spoke briefly to Trudy, then left. Afterwards, we dropped Abednego off at the house—he's now wearing his canine ballistic vest—then drove straight here."

Ella watched Ford and Dr. Lee in conversation. Her gut was telling her that Jane Lee was guilty of something. Jane's failure to even mention the bombing, which had to have been on everyone's mind at the college, assured Ella that she was hiding something.

When Justine went to get herself a cup of punch, Ford came over, greeting Ella with his usual warm smile. Glancing around casually, he lowered his voice, and added, "I was hoping to make myself a little more useful here tonight."

"There's a desktop computer in Dr. Lee's office. . . ."

"Say no more," he answered.

"Her door's locked."

"I'm sure you can get around that," he answered, "so the real question is whether you think the risk is worth it."

Ella took a deep breath. "How fast can you work?"

"Depends on what I'm up against," he answered honestly.

Ella considered it for a moment. If they both disappeared for more than just a minute or two, Dr. Lee would go check on things. Ella was as sure of that as she was of her next breath. And if they left Justine to stall Dr. Lee, she'd catch on immediately.

"The risk is unacceptable," Ella said at last. "You recently hacked into her laptop but found nothing?"

"That's right."

"Did you access all her e-mails?" Ella asked.

"There were some encrypted files I couldn't access without the passwords. It's been a while since I did this kind of work," he admitted grudgingly.

"I have an idea," Ella said, thinking of Teeny, the nickname she'd given her old friend, Bruce Little. He was the best hacker she knew. "But it'll have to wait until tomorrow. I'll swing by your place shortly after seven. That okay with you?"

"That's fine," he answered.

Putting away her cell phone, on which she had been talking, Justine joined them again. "I just spoke to Phillip Cloud. He's on guard duty by your house, Ford. He and his brother will be taking turns tonight, watching with night-vision binoculars. He wanted us to know that your dog began barking like mad a short time ago. Then he stopped."

"Abednego needs a reason to bark. . . ." Ford said slowly.

"Could you take my brother home?" Ella asked Justine. "I want to go check on Abednego."

"Not a problem." Justine answered.

"Thanks," Ella replied, already on the move.

"Let me go with you," Ford said, quickly falling into step beside her. "Abednego's reliable. He *knows* something's not right or he wouldn't have been barking."

"Dogs can also bark at silly things like a cat on the cinder block wall. Let's not see too much in this," she said, reaching the door. "Maybe it's the vest."

"No, if that was bothering him, he'd just try and take it off. When Abednego barks, there's a reason," Ford said firmly but softly, following her out. "Dogs have very highly attuned hearing, and often pick up what a human ear can't."

Ella still wasn't sure how much credibility to give his view of the dog. Ford was very fond of the animal and that tainted his judgement.

When they pulled up to Ford's home twenty minutes later, nothing looked disturbed.

"The lights aren't on, so no one's approached the house. The motion sensors I installed are *very* sensitive," Ford said. "That means Abednego must have heard or smelled something."

Once again there was no hesitancy or doubt in his voice.

They went inside, but it was soon clear nothing was amiss there either. Abednego, wearing the loaned blue ballistic vest, was waiting in the kitchen, and greeted them eagerly. Ford scratched the big animal between the ears, checking him out for wounds or injuries. "His muzzle is wet, and from the water on the floor around his dish, he just drank."

"That vest has got to be hot, or maybe he's just nervous. A lot has been happening lately," Ella suggested.

"If he'd kept on barking I would have been more inclined to agree with you. But he only barks when something's not right. Take a look in that arroyo out back just beyond the block wall. If I'd have wanted to approach this house and not be seen until I got real close, that's the route I would have taken."

"Okay, I'll check it out. Stay here. I'll be back as soon as possible," Ella said. Once outside, she grabbed a big flashlight from the glove compartment of her SUV, then contacted Phillip via her hand-held radio.

Moments later, Ella and Phillip met out back and, together, climbed down into the six-foot-deep, rainfall-carved arroyo. They found a variety of footprints, most small, indicating the presence of children, who tended to play in arroyos. Yet one set, much fresher than those kid-sized impressions, caught Ella's immediate attention. They were barely visible and without patterns, as if the person had worn moccasins and worked hard not to leave a trail. After a careful search, Phillip found a spot where that same person had climbed up on the side facing the rear of the house, and had lain flat on the ground. The size of that impression suggested an adult.

"It looks like he stopped here to case the place. But he'd have needed a night-vision scope like mine to see anything at this time of night," Phillip said.

"He was looking for weaknesses," Ella said after a moment. She thought back to Dr. Lee, but the professor's whereabouts were accounted for tonight. Her teaching assistant had left the gathering early, but Mona Tso wasn't very big, and these impressions seemed more man-sized.

Ella was now sure that there were other players she'd yet to identify lurking about somewhere, maybe watching them right now, hidden by the darkness. That possibility unsettled her, and for the first time, she found herself grateful that Dawn was away with her father.

Ella walked into the kitchen to fix herself some coffee before leaving for work. She'd just turned on the pot when Rose came in.

"I haven't had a chance to see or talk to you lately and

I've been worried," Rose said. "I heard about that blast at the college. I understand it even made the national news on TV."

"I'm working the case. That's why I've been putting in such long hours—even working on Sunday," Ella said. Her mom had stopped watching the news a few years earlier after noting the increasing number of commercials advertising prescription medications. As a Traditionalist, Rose believed that speaking about something could bring it into existence, and had refused to listen to companies talk about diseases so they could sell their pills.

"I've heard that the officer who was injured is a member of your team and that you were there when it happened. Is that why you've been avoiding me?" Rose asked.

"Mom, I haven't been avoiding you. Really. It's this case . . . it's taking up all my time."

"Are you really all right?" Rose asked, her voice a taut whisper. "You have a bruise on your forehead, and scratches on your cheek."

"I'm fine, Mom," Ella said softly.

"So many things are changing here," Rose said with a long sigh. "The Navajo Nation was a place of peace once. Now harmony is something we have to struggle to maintain so we can continue to walk in beauty."

"Progress can be good, but it also usually brings things no one wants."

Rose nodded slowly. "The Plant Watchers have to meet more often now because it's harder to find the herbs we need. Did you know that? The earth is suffering. So many of the Plant People are moving away. Even our *hataaliis* are having trouble finding what they need for our ceremonies."

Ella poured herself a cup of coffee and proceeded to drink it standing up. "*Tsétaak'á* Generating Station is supposed to be much less polluting. It uses less water, and no smoke is produced. Our air should be cleaner in the future."

"Only if they get rid of all the cars and trucks. Every family wants two or three of them these days. Sit down," Rose added in her best mom's tone. "I'm fixing you a proper breakfast."

Ella started to argue, then changed her mind. She *was* hungry, and Rose's special breakfast burritos had no equal anywhere. More importantly, Ella had a feeling her mother had something else she wanted to talk about.

Silence stretched out between them. As she waited, Herman came in, saw them together, poured himself a quick cup of coffee, then wordlessly left the kitchen without even glancing their way. That alone assured her that something important was going on.

Rose finally placed her specialty breakfast in front of Ella and, as Ella began eating, spoke again. "My friends and I have heard a rumor. Some are saying that government people have been sent here to spy on us because they're expecting violence at the power plant. They might even send in the National Guard."

"I haven't heard anything about government agents coming into the area," Ella said, wondering who was spreading these stories.

"Even if you had, I know you probably couldn't say so. I just thought I'd pass these stories on in case it could help."

"You did the right thing, Mom," Ella said, taking another big bite of the burrito.

"Would you like another one?" Rose asked.

"No, I'm fine," Ella said with a happy smile, looking down at her plate.

"You don't eat much when your daughter is with her father. You worry all the time she's gone."

Ella didn't bother to deny it. "A part of me thinks she's still too young to be away from home. We talk every day on the phone, so I know she's homesick, but she wants to act all grown up for her dad."

"And the fact that she tries to impress him bothers you," Rose observed.

It hadn't been a question. "I just wish I could convince her that she doesn't have to impress *anyone*."

"She idolizes her father. He's important to the tribe, working for the Navajo Nation in Washington D.C."

"I know and that's okay, to a point. But she shouldn't feel the need to become someone else just for his benefit. I intend to talk to her about that when she gets back."

"She's not sure who she is, daughter. She's trying to find that out, just like you did at that age. She's growing up so quickly," Rose said sadly.

"I just wish the house didn't feel so empty when she's gone. Believe it or not, I miss the chaos—the radio blasting, the constantly ringing phone, and that cartoon horse announcing she's got e-mail. . . ."

Rose nodded. "Children remain children such a short time. But it's not too late for her to have a sister. . . ."

Ella laughed. "I don't think that'll happen, Mom."

"Are things okay between you and your friend?"

"I have feelings for him," Ella said, always avoiding names out of respect for her mother's traditionalist ways. Names were said to have power and weren't to be used lightly. "But his religion creates some problems between us that I'm not sure we'll ever be able to fix."

Rose nodded. "It was that way between your father and me, too, but I never regretted marrying him." She smiled slowly. "Well, hardly ever."

Ella laughed, then after a moment, grew serious again. "You know, at the beginning, I never thought religion would matter, but the longer we see each other . . ." She exhaled, expelling her breath between her teeth. "I like having the freedom to follow my instincts and my heart, but he lives by so many rules."

Aware that she'd said too much already, Ella stood. This

wasn't something she'd meant to discuss with her mother. It was something Ford and she would have to figure out for themselves.

Or maybe they never would. Some problems had no solutions, and he still carried a considerable amount of baggage from his dangerous past. Those memories seemed to make him cling even more tightly to his beliefs. Perhaps he was afraid of reverting to his old ways if he wasn't strong or pious enough as a minister. Or maybe it was more complex than that. Either way, she'd try to be more understanding.

Ella reached for the top of the cabinet, where she normally kept her weapon. When Dawn had been younger, Ella had stowed it there to make sure it remained out of her daughter's reach. Somewhere along the way, it had become a habit.

"I don't suppose I should count on you for dinner?" Rose asked. "We're having green chile stew and fry bread."

"You really know how to tempt me," Ella said. "Unfortunately, I can't plan on anything until we catch the person who planted that bomb."

Moments later, Ella hurried out the front door. While she was driving north toward Shiprock and the station, Justine called.

"Big Ed has called a meeting this morning, and he wants us there ASAP. Joe Neskahi and Marianna Talk have also been called in. I'm on my way to the station now. Do you have any idea what's going on?"

"No, not a clue," Ella answered.

"There's more. Ford and Blalock are also coming."

"When did you hear that?"

"About three minutes ago. I ran into Blalock at the Morning Star when I stopped by for coffee. He was finishing breakfast and mentioned he was on his way to pick up Ford, who conducted the seven o'clock service this morning without a hitch. An officer was watching the grounds, by the way."

Ella wondered if Big Ed had also heard the rumor going around. Either way, she was about to find out.

"One last thing, Ella. I sure could use some help with the lab work. I've been trying to run down the lead to the rat poison by talking to the feed store owners in the area, but when I have lab work *and* field work I'm stretched to the breaking point."

"I hear you, but our budget problems haven't changed," Ella answered, wishing she didn't have to give Justine the same answer each time she asked for help.

"Could you bring this up again with the chief? I'm burning the candle at both ends each time we work a top-priority case, and that's how mistakes get made. So far nothing's happened, but I don't know how long I can keep this up. I was at the station until two this morning, and it's Sunday. I'm pushing my luck."

"I know. You're carrying too heavy a load, cuz, though you're still doing an incredible job for the department. Let me see what I can do, but no promises."

"It's not like I'm asking for a raise. I just need help to keep doing the job right."

"I wish I *could* give you a raise," Ella answered honestly. "If anyone deserves one, you do."

Ella hung up, the knowledge that her team was stretched to the limit weighing heavily on her. The SI unit had lost two people to higher-paying jobs at other agencies these past few years, and she'd only managed to find one replacement, Sergeant Neskahi. Then he'd been pulled back to patrol duty after three other officers had left the force. Though Ella desperately needed more people, the budget hadn't allowed her to recruit any more officers or techs. Now with Ralph Tache out of commission, it came down to herself, Justine, and whoever happened to be available.

Ella was about a mile from the station, crossing the eastbound bridge over the San Juan river, when her cell phone rang. Without looking at the caller ID she picked it up, hoping it was Dawn. Her daughter usually called early. She was a morning person, and woke up with lots of energy, ready to talk to anyone who would listen.

To her surprise, it wasn't Dawn, but rather her old friend, Teeny, whom she'd been planning to call anyway. Ella greeted him warmly. Despite being one of the best support assets their PD had, Teeny was also a friend she could count on. Friendships like theirs were rare, and all the more precious because of it.

"Hey, Teeny," she said, knowing she was one of only a few who could call Bruce Little by that nickname and live to tell the tale.

"Hey, Ella. After hearing about the bomb and the injuries to Tache, I thought I'd check in and see how I could help out. I worked with Ralph a few times when I was still on the force, and I'd like to help nail the sicko who did this to him."

"Great minds think alike, don't they? I was going to pay you a visit this morning, but Big Ed called a meeting. I'm on my way to the station now. As soon as I can, I'll head over to your place."

"Good enough. I'll be here all morning," he said, then added, "Oh, I also spoke to Eugene Garner this morning. He finally took over the feed store from his dad. I stopped by because I'd picked up a story that someone had tried to poison Reverend Tome's dog, and thought Eugene was the man to talk to. I got a hit. Someone shoplifted a box of rat poison the other day from his shelves."

"The timing's right. Thanks for the lead, Teeny. It's much appreciated."

"See you later."

Ella parked in her usual spot near the station's side entrance. Inside, she saw Blalock and Ford standing in the hallway right outside the break room, cups of coffee in hand. Justine came out a moment later and gave her a nod.

"What's going on?" Ella asked, pointing down the hall. Big Ed's door was shut—a *very* rare occurrence unless an officer was being reamed out.

"We don't know," Justine said. "Joe and Marianna are in there with him now. All I can tell you is that there hasn't been any shouting—yet."

Ella was about to respond when Big Ed stepped out into the hall and waved an invitation to them. Folding chairs were soon brought in, and moments later Big Ed regarded all of them with a satisfied smile. "I'd like to introduce you to the new, permanent members of the SI team—Sergeant Neskahi and Officer Talk."

Ella blinked in surprise but before she could comment, Big Ed continued.

"You've apprised me many times of your team's situation, Ella, and how critical your manpower shortage is. Now you're down an officer again, though for a tragically different reason. Unfortunately, it's precisely at a time when you'll all have to give one hundred ten percent. To wrap this story up, I went directly to the tribal president and he guaranteed funding on the spot. He needs the *Tsétaak'á* Generating Station to succeed. Hundreds of millions of dollars are at stake. You all know that."

After everyone had welcomed Joe and Marianna, Big Ed looked back at Ella. "I've briefed Neskahi and Talk on the terrorist threat to the Hogback reactor, but I leave it to you to deploy the new members of your team. Just keep me updated."

"Done. And thank you," Ella answered.

"Now for the other reason you're here," Big Ed said at last. "The attempt on Reverend Tome's life is apparently connected to the threat on the *Tsétaak'á* facility. From now on we have to stay one step ahead of these individuals. We need to make certain that whatever's being planned *never happens*. Be smart, people, and work fast."

"We'll do our best," Ella answered, "but if we encounter

another bomb threat, we'll have to pull in outside help. With Officer Tache out of action, we don't have anyone on this part of the Rez with the expertise we'll need."

"I'm ahead of you," Big Ed said. "Our department's getting a new bomb tech. Anna Bekis worked for ATF for five years, then decided that the tribe needed her more than the Feds. For the past few months she's been working patrol out of Tuba City, but I heard about her and put in a call. She'll be coming in later today, and I'm going to assign her to work with your team. Bekis has also done field work, so I think you'll find her a good addition."

"We can certainly use her help," Ella said.

"Now tell me what you've managed to put together on Dr. Jane Lee. Is the professor a threat or not?" Big Ed asked Blalock.

"The FBI has had her on the radar for quite some time," Blalock said. "She's the tip of the arrow, but there are others. That's what I've been told anyway."

"I've spoken to her and she's trying very hard to disassociate herself from her past anti-nuke activism, but I don't buy the turnaround," Ella said. "Some of the coded e-mails she's sent, and we've intercepted, directly contradict that. Based on what Ford has learned, it's clear she never really dropped out of the game."

"Lee maintains several blogs on Native American women's issues," Ford said. "Although they appear perfectly legit, there's a near certainty that she's switched tactics and is now sending coded messages via those. I've been monitoring the comments on her Web page, too, and they've really picked up these past few days, for no apparent reason."

"Replies in code?" Big Ed asked.

"I believe so," Ford answered.

"How long will it take you to find out for sure if that's what's happening, and be able to decipher their messages?" Big Ed asked.

"A week, or maybe a few days less, if I'm lucky. I have to analyze previous and current passages and look for patterns, anomalies, and other characteristics. I have some computer programs that'll help me do all that, but the problem is that this will take time."

"Which is exactly what we don't have," Big Ed said. "It looks like you've got your work cut out for you, so get going, people," Big Ed said, standing.

Ella motioned for everyone to join her in her office, and a minute later they gathered there. "Okay, team, we need a game plan."

"We should concentrate on adding names, besides Dr. Lee's, to the list of people opposed to the Hogback plant," Justine said.

Neskahi cleared his throat. "Many clans have members who died from radiation sickness caused by the mining operations that took place here in the '50s and '60s. There are many safeguards today, but most Traditionalists don't trust them. I can think of at least half-a-dozen people in my clan alone who oppose the plant because it involves what they call 'yellow earth.' "

Marianna Talk nodded. "It's the same in my clan. The older ones . . . they've learned not to trust. They think we're being naive. The only thing that has kept them from openly opposing the plant is that they know the tribe needs money for practically everything these days. Let's face it—about half of all Navajo homes still burn wood for heat, but a big percentage don't even have real wood stoves. Those homemade heaters made out of barrels and scrap metal can be death-traps, even if they're properly ventilated. Our tribe's not greedy. We're talking about money to help our people survive. The *Tsétaak'á* Generating Station will generate a lot of that income, especially if they add more units, like they're already talking about."

"Almost all the Christians I've spoken to are for it as

well," Ford said. "God expects us to work together for the common good and this power plant will benefit the Anglos *and* us. It's a godsend. Demands for heat and electricity are growing, and we can provide those resources."

"There's a rumor going around that *bilagáanas* from the federal government are here to make sure we get that facility up and running no matter what," Ella said. "Of course, that story was deliberately planted to stir things up and generate mistrust—to play on traditional fears. Whoever started that knew our past and how our people think. That's why I think it was the work of well-educated Navajos."

"Then Dr. Lee remains the obvious suspect," Justine said. "We'll have to mount a twenty-four/seven surveillance."

"That woman's intelligent and careful," Ford said. "If you're expecting her to lead you to the others who may be working for her, or with her, you're wasting your time. She's even stopped using those anonymous Internet services subject to compromise. In my opinion, we're dealing with professionals, so the key will be electronic surveillance—watching with untraceable eyes and ears."

"Let's do both electronic and physical surveillance," Neskahi said at last. "Maybe I should sign up for one of Dr. Lee's courses."

"In Women's Studies?" Ella countered, fighting a smile. Joe was a bit of a chauvinist.

"I'm already taking one of her courses at night," Marianna said. "My presence in or around the building won't send off any alarms. I have the option of attending other sessions, too, if I miss a class."

"All right. Keep track of whoever she meets, but don't let her catch on. If she does, she's likely to start feeding us false information. In the past, she's been involved in highly organized demonstrations in Arizona and California, and she's well schooled on government agencies and their tactics," Ella said.

"Could Joe help me with the leg work on the rat poison we found and the other leads we need to follow up on?" Justine asked.

"Absolutely," Ella replied, quickly giving them the feed store information update she'd gotten from Teeny. Lastly, Ella glanced at Blalock. "I'm going to need everything the FBI has on Dr. Lee. I mean *everything*."

"Some of that stuff's classified, Ella. *I* don't even have clearance to see it."

"The Bureau brought us into this investigation. If they want us to work this case effectively, they're going to have to cooperate with us. We have need to know."

"I'll see what I can do."

"That's it, then. Get to work everyone."

As the others left the office, Ford looked at Ella. "Is there anything specific you're going to need from me?"

She nodded. "You and I have someplace to be this morning." Ella led Ford outside to her unit, then drove out of the parking lot.

EIGHT

——— ✖ ✖ ✖ ———

They rode in silence for several miles. Ella was still lost in thought when Ford spoke.

"You never mentioned any of the actual evidence we have against Jane, like the downloaded schematics, or even the FBI data mining that triggered the investigation. Neither did Big Ed," he said.

"I know. I thought Big Ed had the right idea about that so I followed suit. Half of the stuff we're dealing with is classified, and I want to respect that by going on a need-to-know basis. For example, the Cloud brothers, who've been told to protect you, have only the information they need to adequately do their job."

"All right," Ford said. "I'll continue what I set out to do—gather intel on Jane and try to determine what codes she's using."

"There's one problem I need to talk to you about. Protecting you during the day is going to pose a variety of challenges," Ella said slowly. "The Cloud brothers and Officer Charlie can rotate their schedules, but there's only three of them, and sooner or later, they'll be spotted. During the day, it's harder to find concealment in such open country—and vehicles tend to stick out."

"And you don't want to give rise to too many questions," he finished for her, nodding.

"Exactly. So how about telling everyone that you've been assigned to me as a 'community ride-along'? We could just say that it's a public relations thing, and avoid specifics. Since everyone knows the bomb was planted at your lecture, they'll assume I've signed up to protect you—just in case you're really the target."

"That's a good idea."

"Could you do your work on a laptop while riding with me?"

"Considering what I'll be doing next, sure," he said, then explained. "I need to research some new, more advanced computer programs now available. Mine are too outdated."

"Your old ones were good enough to get you the data from her computer, so maybe you shouldn't discard them yet."

"I worked around their limitations. What I did was hack into her laptop while she was online. She doesn't stay on very long, so I had to work fast, but while I had access to her hard drive, I discovered her laptop has unaccounted memory—meaning memory that's being used, but isn't stored in any particular file or place. I need more sophisticated software to track down what she's hiding on her system."

"I know someone who can help you figure out your computer questions," Ella said. "We're heading there now."

Ella pulled up to Teeny's place about ten minutes later. Her old friend, who served as an IT and computer consultant, also did PI work on the side. He lived in a square, industrial style metal building surrounded by electrified fencing. As she pulled up to the gate, the camera monitor moved down to focus on her face.

"Hey, Ella," came Teeny's disembodied voice. "Come in. I've been waiting for you."

The gate swung open and Ella drove through, parking

next to the metal structure, which also had a two-car garage at one end.

Ella led the way inside the small warehouse. Long wooden tables were covered with sophisticated computer equipment. There were at least twenty different kinds of laptops, servers, and mainframes placed along the walls and in a center row.

Seeing Teeny, a big bear of a Navajo, video conferencing in front of one of the computers, Ella led Ford to the inner courtyard. Once outside, they sat at the coffee table in the center of a square patch of sunlight.

"Mr. Little's ability with computers is almost legendary," Ford said. "I understand that the Albuquerque office of the FBI offered him a tech job once, but he turned it down."

"Teeny's not much for rules and regulations," Ella said. "But his heart's in the right place."

Ford gave her a long look. "You're close friends?"

She nodded. "We grew up together in Shiprock." She looked at Ford, wondering if his curiosity had gone hand-in-hand with a spark of jealousy.

Almost as if reading her mind, he added. "Everyone needs friends. Your work takes up too much of your time— and heart. I'm glad to see you haven't neglected yourself completely."

Ella smiled. "Reverend, doesn't that sound a lot like your own life as well?"

"You've got me there," he answered with a grin. "Working for God is as full-time as it gets. But I have friends. Reverend Campbell is one, and some of my parishioners. I like to think you and I are close, too."

Ella didn't comment. Had he allowed it, they would have been even closer than they were now. But his ways wouldn't permit a physical relationship. Their special friendship had demanded an entirely new level of intimacy, and maybe that's why she felt closer to him than anyone else she'd ever dated.

"Sometimes I wish that the rules of the One I serve weren't so specific. But marriage comes first. Is that so out of the question between us, Ella?"

She stared at him in surprise. "Is that a proposal?"

He started to answer when Teeny opened the sliding glass door and came out into the courtyard. "Sorry that took me so long. It was a client, and I couldn't afford to put him on hold. I do quite a bit of work for his company."

"Someone here on the Rez?" she asked, mostly out of curiosity.

"Nah, most of my big clients are off the Rez. This man has a company in Albuquerque. Teleconferencing lets me help anyone, anywhere." He took a seat in an empty chair, then looked at Ford and back at Ella. "Okay, fill me in on what's going on."

This time she didn't hold back, and seeing the surprise on Ford's face did nothing to slow her down. Teeny was one hundred percent trustworthy. Even more importantly, Teeny didn't like to play games. If she'd held back and he'd found out, there was a good chance he would have refused to work with the department again. That was Teeny, and to work with him you had to know the way his mind worked.

Teeny then asked Ford a few technical questions about his setup and software. Satisfied with the answers, he continued. "So you need a method of hacking into Dr. Lee's computer, whether or not she's online," he noted. "I'm assuming she doesn't have dial-up?"

"No, she accesses through the phone company, DSL, but doesn't leave it on—at least so far. I'll be monitoring her IMs and e-mails when she's online but I also want the ability to access her other files whether she's online or not. The thing is, I've seen her laptop," he said, explaining what he'd found there. "I could get a government tech to come in and teach me what I need to know, but—"

Teeny nodded. "A new non-Navajo hanging around,

particularly in view of the recent rumors, would make you more of a target than you already are. You don't need more attention, you need less."

"That's it in a nutshell."

"Okay. I think I can help you. I've got this little piece of hardware that's got its own power source, so it's nearly impossible to detect," he said. "The tricky part will be installing it in her computer—particularly if you have to do it quickly."

As Teeny and Ford discussed software, Ella watched the men. Teeny was the kind who didn't make friends easily because he never quite lowered his guard—a trait that put others on theirs. Yet Ford's ability to give the person he was speaking to his entire attention, coupled with his knowledge of computers, had made Teeny relax almost instantly. He was now speaking to Ford as if he'd found a soulmate.

Smiling, Ella called Blalock. "What's the status on that sneak-and-peek warrant?"

"It came through a little while ago. You've got a free hand now."

Ella contacted Marianna next. Officer Talk was still at the station.

"I need you to drop whatever you were planning to do this morning and go check on Dr. Lee's whereabouts," Ella said. "I specifically need to know if she's teaching a class this morning, and how long she'll be on campus."

"I'll get back to you as soon as I find out."

"Also, get me her street address. If there's no street name, then directions to her home," she added, aware that streets on the Rez were often nameless dirt tracks.

"Got it. How fast will you need all this?"

"Yesterday."

"All right. I'll be in touch shortly then," Marianna answered.

Ella rejoined Teeny and Ford as Teeny began explaining where the small device—disguised as a battery—would have to be placed inside the computer. The directions seemed unbelievably complicated. "And that will allow him to monitor her computer whether she's online or not?" she asked.

"Yes, but if a good tech got a look at the motherboard, he or she would probably notice the extra 'battery.' The second that gets pulled off for a closer look, the cat's out of the bag. This device isn't foolproof. Nothing is—not these days. The best advice I can give you is make darned sure she doesn't suspect the cover's been opened."

Marianna called Ella just then, and Ella stepped away from the men. "Dr. Lee's on campus now," Marianna said. "Her classes are popular, and she has three back-to-back sessions this morning. She won't be free till noon at the earliest."

Marianna then gave Ella directions to a newer model home on Shiprock's northwest side, several miles from downtown and just above the bosque of the San Juan river. "She's renting the place from Professor Anita Todea, who's on sabbatical."

Ella knew that area of former farmland, where old-timers had once grown alfalfa, corn, and melons. As the years had gone by, the land had been broken up into smaller lots to accommodate population growth. There were more than double the number of houses around there these days, but unlike modern developments, the expansion had been haphazard and the buildings weren't right on top of each other. The Modernists who lived there only needed enough acreage to raise a few sheep, cattle, or horses, and maybe have a small orchard.

Ella watched as Teeny demonstrated, opening up the cases of two different laptops, then a desktop computer, showing where the device would have to be placed and how it had to be attached. It was a delicate process, and even trickier on the smallest laptop, where there was less available space.

Once Teeny finished, Ford sat back and looked around.

"I really like your office. You have a lot of nice toys," he said in an almost boyish voice.

Teeny laughed. "One of the perks of the job," he answered. Glancing at Ella, he added, "I have some other new equipment you might find useful." He brought out what appeared to be high-tech binoculars. "These are night-vision and have a digital camera built in. Anything you can see you can photograph at the same time."

"I've never used one of those," Ella said, not surprised that Teeny's equipment exceeded what the department was able to get.

"It's off-the-shelf technology, and this baby's reliable. Hang onto it until you're done with the case." He gave Ford a long, speculative look, then added, "If you'd like, you and your dog are welcome to stay here, Ford. You'd have everything you'd need to do your work and the place is secure—day or night."

Ella stared at Teeny in surprise. Teeny didn't issue invitations like that lightly. From a security standpoint, there was no place outside a military base where Ford would be safer. On top of that, he'd have every technological advantage in the world.

When Ford didn't answer right away, Ella added, "That's an invitation you might want to consider very seriously, Ford. Your cover story could be that you needed to get some plumbing work done at your home, or that your cooling system is out."

"I don't know what kind of software or hardware you have, or will need, but I've got state-of-the-art," Teeny said. "I've also got some goodies not yet on the market that I'm using on a trial basis. You could use whatever's here in addition to what you already have."

"I accept your invitation," Ford said with a happy smile. "Thank you."

Ella breathed a sigh of relief. One problem—Ford's

safety—was now resolved. "Now, about this thing that needs to be added to Dr. Lee's computer . . ."

"I'll have to put the device into the computer myself, Ella," Ford said, preempting her. "There'll be less margin for error that way."

"I'd volunteer to go along, but I've got a court appearance today for a client. How about waiting until tomorrow?" Teeny asked.

Ella shook her head. "We need to do this ASAP."

"I can handle this," Ford assured both of them.

"All right. Let's move," Ella urged Ford. "We'll be back later," she added, thanking Teeny for his help.

As Ella hurried out with Ford, she filled him in on the particulars of the warrant and Dr. Lee's schedule.

"If she's in class, that'll give us a set amount of time we can count on," he said, shifting the laptop computer he'd brought along from one hand to the other as they climbed into the car. "That's good, because I'd also like to search her place and get some insight into how her mind works. That's always useful when you're trying to decode encrypted messages. Even if the code isn't one she thought of herself, the way she employs it will be indicative of who she is."

"I hear you. I also find that kind of familiarity an asset when conducting an investigation. I think the Bureau's making a huge mistake denying me access to all the materials they have on her."

"For what it's worth, I agree with you," Ford said. "The problem is that bureaucrats don't always see past the rules and regulations they've been taught to worship."

She smiled. There were times when she would have said the same about preachers.

Silence stretched out between them, then Ford spoke again. "Bruce Little's in love with you."

It had come out of the blue, at least as far as she was concerned. She glanced over at him, but could read nothing in his expression. "Teeny *was* in love with me at one time—in high school, actually—but not anymore. In fact, he's been seriously dating my second cousin, Jayne Goodluck."

"Maybe so, but he's settling for second best. *You're* the one he really wants."

"What on earth makes you say that?" she asked, a little annoyed.

"It's the way he acts when you're around. His voice even softens a fraction when he talks to you."

"We go way back, like I said before. I've helped him, he's helped me. What you're seeing is fondness—that of two people with a long history behind them."

Ford just shook his head, smiling smugly.

As silence stretched out between them again, she remembered the question Ford had asked her back in Teeny's courtyard. She still wasn't sure if that had been his way of proposing or not. But she didn't want to bring that up now. The truth was, she wasn't ready to make that kind of commitment.

"I'm glad you're going to be staying at Teeny's. Whether you realize it or not, you two are a lot alike," she said, mostly to fill the silence. "You both like working with clear goals in mind, and technology fascinates you. The biggest difference I can see between you is that Teeny dislikes structure and you thrive under it."

"I *accept* structure if I'm convinced there's a purpose behind it, but I make up my own mind. I expect others to do the same, too. That's why I'd never ask, or pressure you, to accept Christ and join my church. That would have to be your own decision. You know that, right?"

"You'd wish it deep inside, but you wouldn't ask," she said, with a ghost of a smile.

He laughed. "True enough."

"I don't want to change anything between us, Ford. I like the way things are," she said after a thoughtful pause.

"There's only one change I'd make, if it were up to me," she said, giving him a playful look.

He gave her a knowing smile and nodded. "I'd like that, too—if it were up to me."

"Any room for negotiation?"

"No, I'm afraid not." He reached for her hand, and kissed her palm. "It's my willingness to be faithful to the Lord I serve that makes me the man I am. I'm part of a package deal."

"Then I'll live with it."

"There *are* other options," Ford said, and left it hanging.

"Let's not get into a rush and risk ruining a good thing. Who knows? We may find that nature has its own plans for us."

"Accidents . . ." He shook his head. "I'm human, and our relationship poses certain temptations, but I'd hate to add regret to what we share. The right time . . . that's all part of God's plan, too."

There was nothing more to say. Silence fell between them again until they reached the general area of Dr. Lee's home.

They drove down a paved road that bordered the neighborhood. To the north were houses accessed by long, gravel lanes, and beyond them the narrow bosque, the vegetation-rich flood plain lining the river with cottonwoods, willows, and tall grasses. On the far side of the river were fields of melons and corn, then sandstone bluffs rising to a hundred feet or so in places.

"I'm going to drive around a bit," Ella said. "We need to come up with a good way of approaching the house, since the area is very open in front. I don't know what kind of security she has, and I'd rather not get any last-minute surprises."

The target house, with a small orchard behind it on the west, was actually about a quarter mile down a narrow lane.

That gravel road continued north another half mile until it intersected a dirt road that paralleled the river. Most of the other homes they passed were closer to the river, however, and shaded by one or more cottonwoods or other large trees. The closest house to Dr. Lee's was more than a half mile away, barely visible due to a small apple orchard.

They soon turned around and headed back toward Dr. Lee's house. As they neared the turnoff they saw several churro sheep grazing along the fence line that bordered the lane. They saw no dogs along the highway or near the sheep.

Ella turned down the lane, intending to pass the house at close range. As they cruised by slowly, she studied the grounds, which were enclosed by a white rail fence, searching for possible problems. "All I can see are a few ducks wandering around out back, but it's possible that Dr. Lee has a dog inside the house."

"If she does, I'm very good with animals," Ford said.

"All right then. Let's go farther down this lane, stop by that tree halfway to the river, then circle around. We'll go through the orchard where we'll have cover, and try to get in through the rear entrance. She's renting the house, so it's unlikely she'd equip the outside with anything too fancy, like motion sensors or cameras. The last thing she'd want to do is call attention to herself."

"But she'll still have taken precautions . . . that's all part of this type of business."

Ella parked another quarter mile down the road, beneath the shade tree. They'd be barely visible from the road, and, in a jam, could escape down the lane to the bosque and go either direction along the river road.

After a quick call to Marianna Talk, who assured her that the professor was still lecturing, they headed into the field, discovering an empty irrigation ditch that ran parallel to the lane. Stooping low, they were able to get close to the orchard without coming out into the open.

Ella led the way toward the house, then stopped when they reached another area of concealment within the orchard. A search with binoculars revealed no motion cameras or special wiring that might indicate a burglar alarm.

"We're okay. Let's go," Ella said.

They'd just left the safety of the trees and slipped through a gate into the backyard when they were greeted by loud honking. "Geese! From a distance I thought they were *ducks*!" Ella shooed the aggressive animals away and got pecked in the bargain.

Ford threw several handfuls of feed he found on a potting bench beside the building, and within seconds the geese settled down.

Not wasting any more time, they hurried past an old pickup and made it to the back porch.

Ella handed him a pair of latex gloves and slipped a pair on herself. The cylinder lock was sturdy, but vulnerable to bumping, and Ella had come prepared. Within twenty seconds, they were both inside.

She stood in the kitchen for a moment, but nothing happened. "That was too easy. I don't like this," she said, reassembling the lock to hide her method of access.

"I dislike black-bag work myself. Let's find the computer and get this done," he answered in a whisper.

The kitchen was simply furnished, with a large wooden table and matching chairs, and older-model, white appliances. The living room was bigger and had an overstuffed cloth sofa and coordinating chairs. A large book cabinet lined with textbooks and nonfiction works stood against the wall.

Down the hall, opposite the master bedroom, they found a small office. Atop the desk was an ancient Epson computer with diskette drives and a massive CRT monitor. Ford sat behind the desk, powered up the machine, then waited as the operating system slowly loaded.

"This machine is a relic and doesn't even have a phone connection for dial-up. Look at the directory." Checking the list of recently accessed files, he added, "She hasn't used this computer in months."

"She might have a laptop computer around here somewhere. Let's look around. This one may be what she thinks of as a loss leader. If someone breaks in, this is what they'd see and take—if they can carry it, and if they're totally naive about computers."

They searched through the house, working quickly and efficiently, even looking in places like the heater closet, but found nothing. Pausing, Ella studied the rooms, trying to determine where Dr. Lee spent most of her time when she was at home. As she looked around for the professor's favorite room, she saw the small, expensive, single-unit sound system in the master bedroom. There was a desk in there, too, but no computer.

Crouching down at a low angle, she spotted four evenly spaced spots on the waxed surface. "This is where she places a laptop. I can see where the rubber 'legs' sit."

Ford stepped into the room, looked around, then pointed to the flash drive inside an empty coffee mug beside the phone. "If those aren't marks left by her office laptop, maybe there's a second portable machine hidden somewhere in this room. Keeping it out of sight when she's gone is a good precaution."

Ella felt the phone at her belt vibrate and picked up the call. It was Officer Talk.

"Dr. Lee got a call on her cell, then left Mona Tso in charge of the class. The minute she called over her TA and handed her the lecture notes, I knew she was getting ready to leave. So while she was talking to Mona, I hurried out to her car. She now has two flat tires, so that's going to slow her down. A student's helping her, but the guy will need to find a valve for the second flat, because I've got the two missing ones in my pocket. I figure you've got fifteen minutes plus however long it takes to get another valve and access to a compressor. Of course, that's assuming she's planning to go straight home."

"There's a gas station right across from the college, so we can't count on much more than ten-minutes leeway. Call me back the second she's on the road." Ella hung up and told Ford what she'd learned. "She may be here in a half hour, so we've got to find that second computer quickly."

"Any hunches?"

Ella studied the room, searching for concealed hiding places. They'd checked all the usual spots, such as between the mattress and box spring, in drawers, and even under the bottom drawer. Seeing a large heating vent peering out at her from behind a trash can beneath the window, Ella went to take a closer look. "People don't generally put stuff in front of heating or air vents, and this wall's too thin to accommodate any ducting. Hand me your screwdriver," she asked Ford.

Taking the small battery-powered screwdriver they'd borrowed from Teeny, she attached a small Phillips head, then quickly removed the screen with two quick whirs of the machine. Inside, beneath a black cloth, was a small laptop. It appeared to be the same brand and model as the one Dr. Lee carried with her.

"You practiced on this brand at Teeny's, so it should be pretty straightforward," Ella said, turning it over to him and checking her watch.

Ford placed the computer on the desk, opened it, then turned it on. After it booted up, he brought out a high-capacity flash drive and quickly made a copy of everything on the hard drive. Once that was done, he shut down the computer, closed the top, and turned it upside down. In a minute, using the electric screwdriver, he got the back cover off and placed the monitoring device into it.

"She might have a shadow drive on this computer, hidden within a third partition of the C drive," he said. "Once we're out of here I'll back up her entire drive, then see what we've got. But if I'm right about her, access will require a password, and the data will be encrypted as well. Experience tells me this'll take some serious time to decode, even using a password-cracking program."

After the false battery was in place, Ford reassembled the unit and powered it up again. Quickly, he examined her most recently accessed files, and found nothing obvious. Then he took a quick look at the directory where her temporary Internet files were located.

"Here's something. Jane repeated several ordinary words in the course of several paragraphs. That, in and of itself, doesn't mean much. But it may eventually help me figure out the code."

"If it's not just sloppy grammar, or a first draft," Ella said, then felt her phone vibrating.

She answered and heard Marianna on the other end. "The student wasn't giving her a ride to the gas station as I initially thought," Marianna said quickly. "They're now going west on Highway 64—in your direction. That's after going fifty miles per hour through town. I had to back off to avoid attracting her attention."

"That'll put them here inside fifteen minutes or less," Ella said.

"I've already called in, hoping that there was a patrol officer in the area who could pull them over for speeding. Unfortunately, there's no one except me, and if I stop them they'll know something's wrong. I'm only supposed to be one of her students," Marianna said.

"Okay. Break off and return to the station." Hanging up, Ella looked at Ford and added, "We have to leave. Judging from Dr. Lee's actions, she suspects we're here. My guess is that phone call she got was from her neighbor."

"I'm done," he said, handing her the closed laptop computer.

Ella placed it in its hiding place, screwed the vent back on, then made sure the trash can was precisely where she'd found it.

She and Ford were stepping out the back door when they heard the sound of a car pulling up the driveway. A heartbeat later a car door slammed. Ella looked for the geese, but fortunately they'd moved on, maybe around the side of the house.

"Thanks for the ride," they heard Dr. Lee said. "I've really got a crushing headache."

"Not a problem, Dr. Lee," a young man's voice answered. "I'll get your tire aired up and put it back on for you."

The geese started honking, perhaps after seeing the stranger out front. "Thanks," Dr. Lee answered, her voice barely discernible over the din.

Seeing Ford frozen in place, his anxious gaze on the corner of the house, Ella gave him a hard push toward the orchard. Ten seconds later they were over the fence and among the trees.

NINE

—— ✖ ✖ ✖ ——

After a quick run through the dry ditch and across the field, they reached Ella's vehicle. "Of all the rotten luck," Ford muttered as they climbed in.

"The geese tipped her neighbor off that somebody was near the house. I should have taken a closer look at those birds before we approached," Ella said, taking out her binoculars and looking back.

"Guard geese?" he asked. "Out here? I know they use them on overseas military bases, but there were only, what, five of them?"

"All it takes is one, and when they get upset, the honking is bound to get somebody's attention. These are higher-end houses on the Rez so people probably keep an eye on each other's places."

"We may not have had the opportunity to look around much, but at least we got away clean," Ford said.

"No, I wouldn't quite call it a clean getaway. If I'm right and she was warned, you can bet she'll double-check everything. Hopefully, she'll assume no one got in," Ella said.

He shook his head. "I don't think she'll assume anything. Keep in mind that she didn't call the police. She came herself. That tends to reinforce the fact that she's got something to hide."

"I agree," Ella said after a beat. "Let's drive down to the river road, park among the trees there, and keep a watch on the house. I'm curious to see what she does next."

"How long do you want to stick around?"

"Why? Are you in a rush?"

He smiled. "No, I'm just eager to get started on the decryption. Would you mind if I turned on my computer and took a look at what I copied on the flash drive?"

"No, go right ahead."

Ella parked east of the intersection where the lane joined the river road. If Dr. Lee drove in their direction, they'd still be able to keep their distance all the way back to the main highway. While Ford focused on his work, Ella kept her binoculars trained on the house they'd just left in such a hurry.

For the next hour nothing happened, then Dr. Lee came out and got into the old truck they'd seen parked at the rear of the house.

"She's on the move," Ella said, watching as Dr. Lee came down the lane in their general direction.

Ella started the engine, knowing they'd have to move away if Dr. Lee turned east. "She's going west, farther down the valley. We're going to follow."

Ford didn't react until she'd placed the SUV in gear. Feeling the rocking motion, he looked up at her with a trace of annoyance. "I thought we were going to be here for a while. What are you doing?"

"Following Dr. Lee," Ella said. "I told you."

"Sorry, guess my mind was elsewhere," he said, shutting down his laptop. "Do you think she knows someone was in her house?"

"If she suspects, it's possible she's on her way to report

the news to a coconspirator," Ella said, hoping that they'd get a break on the case. "She's headed even farther away from town, so maybe they plan to meet in a remote location. Then again, she may only be going for a ride to clear her thoughts."

Ella kept her distance, moving slowly to avoid leaving a trail of dust as they proceeded along the old dirt road that ran above and sometimes along the margins of the bosque. The shade from tall cottonwoods helped hide their passage, but Ella was careful not to get into a location where the pickup could double back on them. After a while the road converged with the paved road they'd originally come in on, and Dr. Lee headed east back to the main highway, then toward Shiprock. Back in traffic, Ella was able to blend in more easily.

"What was that drive down the bosque all about? She didn't meet anyone. Come to think of it, maybe the person didn't show up," Ford said.

"I think she was going out of her way to make sure she wasn't being followed," Ella said slowly. "If she's really on her way to meet someone, I'm guessing that'll happen at the college, where we'll never be sure if it's one of her students or not. If I were her, that's the strategy I'd take."

"Looks like you and she are well matched," he said softly. "You're able to put yourself in her shoes and think like she does. For example, it didn't take you long to figure out where she'd hidden her computer."

"Pray the reverse isn't also true," she answered. Her focus remained on the old truck ahead of them, now turning north at the junction of Highway 64 and 491—the road formerly known as Highway 666.

Ten minutes later Dr. Lee entered the college campus grounds. Yet instead of parking in her usual spot, she went behind the student union building and parked in a visitor's parking slot.

"That's in case the person who disabled her car is still around," Ella said, thinking out loud as she drove down another row in the lot to avoid being seen.

Ella parked as soon as she could, then glanced at Ford. "Have you ever done any surveillance work?"

"Electronic, yes, but out in the field, no."

"Stay in the car, but be ready to drive and meet me wherever I tell you. We'll use cell phones to stay in touch. If anyone suspicious sees you and tries to approach, keep your distance, even if it means that you have to drive away. In a case like that, head straight for the police station."

"Got it."

Ella reached into the glove compartment and grabbed a small hand telescope the size and shape of a pen. Leaving Ford, Ella followed Dr. Lee on foot, using the presence of students to screen herself and making no attempt to narrow the gap between them. Before long, the professor was greeted by a small group of students. As she moved through the group, speaking first to one, then another, a man in a tan suede jacket and black cap appeared from around the building and bumped into her. He paused for a brief second, no longer than it might have taken to issue an apology, and then moved away quickly.

Ella went on instinct. *That* was the contact. An exchange had been made. Shifting her target, she stayed on the man in the cap, trying to get a look at his face so she could ID him later.

As he hurried to the north parking area, Ella pulled out her cell phone and contacted Ford, arranging for him to meet her near the bicycle rack in front of the science building. Using her simple telescope, she remained in the shadow of a Navajo willow and kept watch on the man. Almost as if he'd been warned by a sixth sense, he put on a pair of sunglasses.

Ford pulled up a minute later and Ella climbed behind the wheel as he slid over. Her mark had jumped into a large black Ford pickup. The only distinctive thing about the older model vehicle was that the license plate was obscured, despite the relative absence of mud elsewhere on the vehicle. It was a cheap trick, but an effective one.

The truck slowly approached one of the exits. The driver suddenly made a left turn onto the highway without signaling, raced down a block, then made a right onto the next side street. The road was virtually deserted, so had she followed him, they would have been spotted for sure.

Her only advantage now was her knowledge of the area. Ella took a right at the highway, then cut left into a side street, knowing it paralleled the road the suspect had taken. Soon she saw the black truck passing through the intersection to her left.

Turning, she sped forward, made a left, then came up to the stop sign just as he passed through the intersection. Ella purposely allowed two other vehicles to pass, then turned and followed, staying well back.

"He's had some pursuit and evasion training," she muttered, thinking out loud. "I'm going to need help. I'm getting Justine in on this."

When their mark headed north on the road leading out of Shiprock, Ella made arrangements for Justine to get ahead of him on the Cortez highway. They couldn't pull the man over now without blowing their chances of identifying the others working with Dr. Lee. Yet they had to know who he was, or at least get a good look at him.

"Set up a quick roadblock just past the last stoplight and start stopping cars for a driver's license and registration check," Ella said. "I'll come up from behind in case he decides to veer off."

Ella continued following the truck up the hill onto the mesa, staying three cars behind. Eventually, their mark stopped at a light behind another car. Then, without any warning, he whipped around the car in front of him, and made a hard left, running the light and nearly getting struck by an oncoming car. Ella pulled out to follow, but had to slam on the brakes to avoid a car turning toward them from the right. They slid forward, barely avoiding clipping the sedan on the driver's side. Another car behind that first one slammed on the brakes, nearly rear-ending the vehicle she'd almost hit broadside. Both drivers started honking their horns, and the one she'd almost hit flipped her off.

Ella waved both cars on, then made the left turn and pulled over to the side of the road.

"He made you. But how?" Ford said, running an unsteady hand through his hair.

His voice was a pitch higher than normal, yet, considering that they'd barely avoided a major accident, he was handling things remarkably well.

"I had a feeling I was dealing with a pro, but I never saw that move coming," she answered. Ella turned back out into the street and entered a residential area that had once included a large boarding school and faculty housing. "Help me check the roads north and west for that truck. It couldn't have gone far, and we can now bring the driver in for traffic violations without blowing everything."

Ella called in extra patrol units, and, dividing the area into sectors, mounted an intense search. Staying off the main highway, which was covered by other units, she headed along the north side of the river into a farming area less developed than the one where Dr. Lee lived.

"Why did you choose this particular route?" Ford asked.

"In his shoes, I would stay off the main roads, knowing most will be watched, and go someplace where I could find other transportation—something innocent looking."

After several minutes of searching, they found the man's truck abandoned about a quarter mile from a farm building, hidden from view until they got up close. The driver had gone down into a dip in the road where the path crossed an arroyo. The door of the pickup was open, and the engine was still running. Ella called it in, then studied the tracks where the driver had exited the cab. Ford stood back, not wanting to erase any of the marks, and remained silent, allowing her to concentrate.

"He's about five foot eight or nine and wears a size ten shoe, but that doesn't tell us much we didn't know already."

"Maybe you'll be able to lift some prints from the truck," Ford answered.

"Judging from the way he drives, he's a professional, maybe at stealing cars. My guess is that this truck's stolen, too, and the only prints we'll find will belong to the owner and his or her family. But at least for now, our suspect's on foot." She walked a little farther past Ford, toward the road, then stopped and cursed.

"What now?" Ford asked, not bothering to pass judgement on her language.

"Someone picked him up. There was another vehicle here, and they took off cross-country to the highway." She pointed toward the road in the distance, where they could make out several vehicles heading north and south.

"What about a roadblock?" Ford asked.

"The man's probably ditched the cap and jacket, so we have no idea who to look for. All we could get is a long list of names, and there's no sense tying up our officers like that."

Ella called Justine and updated her. "Process the truck, and then the tire imprints of the second vehicle. Then we'll see what we've got."

Ford's gaze remained on Ella. "Don't worry. There are other possibilities. I may have something for you once I go through the materials I downloaded."

She nodded, lost in thought. "I'll drop you off at Teeny's as soon as I finish here."

"While you're working, I'll power up my laptop," he said.

Justine arrived ten minutes later, and although they managed to find and lift several prints from the truck, Ella wasn't optimistic.

"Maybe we'll get lucky, partner," Justine said. "If not from the prints, the way the truck theft went down might give us a lead."

"I hope so." Ella grabbed her cell phone, and ordered Marianna Talk, who'd returned to the station, back to the college so she could keep a discreet eye on Dr. Lee again.

After plaster casts and photos were taken of the footprints and the second vehicle's tire imprints, Ella glanced around and realized that Ford was not in her SUV. After a quick search, she found him sitting in the shade of the overhang from the arroyo, working on his laptop. The hard, angry look on his face surprised her. Those weren't emotions she'd ever associated with Ford.

"Ford?" she called out, but he didn't respond. "Ford!"

He looked up. "I'm sorry. Did you say something?"

"What's up?" she asked, crouching beside him.

"When I tried to access one of these files, it erased itself. I have rescue software that can retrieve almost anything, but I haven't been able to call it back."

"Maybe Teeny can help you with that."

He rubbed the back of his neck. "It's my fault. I should have searched harder for hidden triggers like those, but I got impatient. Maybe I've been out of the game for too long."

Her heart went out to him. He wasn't used to failure—no more than she was. "We all make mistakes. I nearly got someone hurt back at that red light."

"You're good at what you do, Ella. But I got sloppy. I'm doing too many things and none of them well."

She could relate to his frustration, she'd been there herself. "These days no one does just one thing, Ford. I'm a mom and an investigator and both are full-time jobs. When I make a mistake, I dig in, fix it, and keep going. That's the only thing we can do."

"You don't understand. I love being a preacher, but I also needed . . . more," Ford admitted in a barely audible whisper. "Nothing could have stopped me from taking this job for the Bureau. The fact that they came to me was one heckuva rush. I've missed the challenges of pitting my mind against a terrorist's or a criminal's."

"You're benefitting others with your work. Isn't that what you've told me your God expects of you?"

He looked at her in surprise, then smiled. "You might have something there, Slim," he drawled.

Ella laughed.

Forcing her focus back on the case, she gestured to the tribal SUV. "We're almost done here, so get ready to leave. We'll be heading back to Teeny's in another few minutes."

Once they were on the road, Ella tried to push back her frustration. So far, she'd been outplayed, but she was determined to change that.

"If that file you tried to open is irretrievably lost, then she's got some fancy equipment. That tends to support our contention that she's got something to hide," Ella said, for his benefit as well as her own.

"If there's *any* way to bring that file back, I'll find it. I intend to ask Bruce for his help, too."

That was another thing she liked about Ford. Most men would have rather cut out their tongues than ask for help. Ford didn't share that affliction. "Teeny's the perfect person to go to with a problem like that. He loves a puzzle and dinking around with computer problems. He'd give up sleeping and sit at a keyboard twenty-four/seven if he could."

"There's an incredible feeling of satisfaction connected to this type of work when things go right. But it has another side, too. When you work hour after hour and get nowhere, it feels like you're drowning one inch at a time."

"My work's like that, too," she answered. "Take this case, for example. I want answers, but each time I get close, they slip right through my fingers."

"You expect too much from yourself—more so than anyone else does," Ford said. "We're barely out the starting gate."

They arrived at Teeny's fifteen minutes later. Once in front of the computer, both men became completely engrossed in what Ford had downloaded from Dr. Lee's laptop.

Ella watched them for several minutes, then realized that neither of them would have a quick answer for her and there was little she could add to their conversation. Moving away so as to not distract them, she contacted Justine.

"Were you ever able to follow up on the rat poison or the capsules?" she asked her.

"The poison was stolen from Garner Feeds, as Bruce discovered. The capsules are tougher to track. They're sold over the counter at almost every pharmacy in the area, not just health food stores. It's like trying to find a needle in a haystack."

"Nothing about this case is easy. Marianna's keeping Dr. Lee under surveillance, but I've realized that we need to double-team the professor and combine short- and long-distance surveillance."

"If you need my help, I'll squeeze in some extra hours."

"Good. Let's work up a schedule. I'll see you at the station."

Ella and Justine met twenty minutes later in the station's parking lot. They'd just entered through the side door when Big Ed motioned them into his office and asked for an update.

Ella told him about her plan to double-team Dr. Lee, but as she finished speaking, Big Ed shook his head. "Use Joe Neskahi. Justine fits in easier with the student population, but a lot of people know Justine's your partner. I doubt Dr. Lee has ever seen Joe unless he's pulled her over in traffic."

"Good point."

As they left his office, Justine glanced at her. "Guess he's right. Joe's a better choice."

Ella was about to answer when her cell phone rang. One look at the caller ID told her it was Ford. Ella started to say hello, but he broke in immediately with news.

"First we backed up everything I'd downloaded so we'd have a duplicate copy. Then we retrieved part of an e-mail exchange she'd deleted last week. It was an automatic delete, but it was still there because it hadn't been overwritten," Ford said.

Ella could hear Teeny in the background giving Ford information in that clipped voice of his that told her they'd found something important.

"We've learned that Dr. Lee bought a revolver from Jake Rowley—actually Rowley's Pawn Shop in Farmington. What we still don't know is if she's picked it up already," Ford added. "One more thing. She had Jake work on the pistol so she'd have a smoother trigger pull."

"Like a hair trigger?" she asked, thinking out loud.

"Could be," Ford answered. "But why a professor would need something like that . . . well, that's the real question isn't it? All of a sudden she's thinking self-defense?"

"A background check should have been made, but come to think of it, I doubt that her misdemeanor arrests in past demonstrations would be enough to deny her the purchase. I'll check with Blalock and see if the Feds have the application on file," Ella said.

Teeny's booming voice came over the phone a moment later. "Don't count on it being a legitimate purchase, Ella. Rowley does a lot of business under the table. When you go talk to him, watch your back, too. The Farmington PD has arrested him several times, but the charges never stick. He's half-weasel and half-cutthroat, and word has it that he's greased a lot of pockets to keep his firearms dealer permit."

"Good to know. Thanks. Rowley's outside our jurisdiction, so Blalock will ride along with me," she said. "Anything else you can tell me?"

"The stuff that's in the pawn shop is run-of-the-mill. Rowley generates the bulk of his income by offering special services. It's said that he can get any weapon a customer requests, then modify it to suit. I understand that he knows how to convert a variety of weapons to full automatic, and that he makes quality silencers."

"Thanks for the intel," Ella said. She then called Special Agent Blalock and gave him the details. "See if you can find any record of a background check."

Ella drove to Blalock's office on the mesa as they spoke. Ten minutes later she sat across his desk in a building that held mostly tribal offices.

"Give me another minute, Clah," he said, hitting the print button on his computer, then collecting the pages as they came out.

Blalock stacked the pages neatly and added them to what was already inside a file folder on his desk. "I've been working on this since you called, and here's everything I managed to get on Rowley. He's a real gem. From the sounds of it, I think he's got a judge or two in his pocket."

"What about Dr. Lee's gun purchase. Is it legal?" she asked.

"No background check was ever made. So *if* Jane Lee bought the handgun from Rowley's Pawn Shop, it was done illegally," Blalock replied. "But she could have purchased the gun from a private owner, or even at a gun show with Rowley as the middleman. No background check would have been done under those circumstances."

"If that pistol's crossed Rowley's workbench he might

at least be able to confirm its existence. What we need now is his cooperation," Ella said.

"We won't get it without leverage," Blalock said, placing a photo of Dr. Lee in the file as well.

Ella skimmed the contents of the file. "There may be another way," she said slowly. "Let's go. I've got an idea," she added, hurrying back to the SUV.

TEN

—— ✖ ✖ ✖ ——

Ella drove in silence as she firmed up an idea in her mind. Blalock knew her well enough not to interrupt, but she could feel his curiosity working overtime.

"Here's what I was thinking," she said at last. "I read in the file that Rowley's dating a Navajo woman by the name of Wilma Pete. I know who she is, and maybe that's a way for us to get what we want without a major confrontation." She drew in a quick breath, then continued. "When Wilma's mother got sick, my mother and the other Plant Watchers took care of her. Wilma knows my family and, more importantly, she trusts us."

"I almost forgot that everyone knows everyone else here on the Rez—they're either part of the same outfit or clan, or friends of friends."

"Not always, but it does work that way a lot of the time," Ella conceded.

"So we'll be playing on your connection to his girlfriend when you talk to Rowley?"

Ella shook her head. "No, we're going to pay Wilma a visit first and ask her to come with us. I know where she lives.

I dropped off my mother at her place several times. But the Petes are Traditionalists, so this may entail a wait."

Blalock nodded, used to the way things worked on the Rez, despite his occasional grumble of impatience.

Within fifteen minutes they arrived at the wood-frame house just west of Hogback, the local name for the enormous geological formation that ran north and south near the eastern edge of the Rez. *Tsétaak'á* Generating Station, named after that spine-like ridge, lay barely visible farther south and across the river.

Ella saw smoke coming out of the ceremonial hogan in the back, and her brother's pickup parked nearby, along with two others. "There's a ceremony going on, but it's probably not one of the Sings that take several days, or I would have heard something about it. I'm guessing it's a blessing of some sort."

"How long do you think we'll have to wait?" Blalock asked, leaning back.

"No telling," Ella answered, rolling down the window and making herself comfortable. She could hear her brother's monotone chant. The sameness of it was soothing.

Fifteen minutes later her brother came out of the hogan followed by Wilma Pete, who was holding the arm of an elderly Navajo woman.

"If the senior citizen is your brother's patient, whatever he did must have worked. Did you see that huge smile on her face?"

"Even simple *hozonjis*, songs of blessing, can accomplish remarkable things," she said, speaking from experience.

Wilma Pete stopped and, shielding her eyes from the sun, looked at the SUV, trying to make out who was inside. When Ella and Blalock stepped out so they could be seen, Wilma relaxed. Waving, she took her mother into the main house, then came back outside a few minutes later and gestured an invitation to them.

Noting that her brother had returned to the hogan to gather his things, Ella walked inside the house to meet Wilma.

"It's good to see you. Why don't you visit for a spell, or do you need to see your brother?" Wilma asked, waving them to the couch.

"Actually, we came to talk to you," Ella said.

Wilma looked at them curiously, and waited.

"We understand that you're seeing a man from Farmington, the one who owns the pawn shop," Ella said, avoiding names.

She nodded. "You've probably heard some bad things about him, but he's been good to me and my family," she answered, avoiding looking directly at Ella out of respect. "It's thanks to him that my mother was able to hire your brother to do a blessing."

Ella waited, but Wilma didn't elaborate. Silence stretched out. Ella caught a glimpse of Blalock's expression and knew that he was getting impatient. Anglos, even ones who had lived on the Rez as long as he had, usually found it hard to deal with the long stretches of silence which often marked conversations with Navajos.

"The police in Farmington are out to get him," she added at last. "But the judges aren't fooled. They always let him go."

Ella allowed another lengthy silence to pass before she finally spoke. "Have you heard about the tribal police officer who was badly hurt while disarming a bomb at the college?"

Wilma nodded somberly. "Everyone has."

"We believe your friend has information that can help us find the person responsible, but I've heard he doesn't like talking to police officers."

"It's because he doesn't trust them. They're always trying to blame him for something."

"This time it's not about him. It's about our friend, an officer here on the *Dinétah*."

"Then I'll speak to him for you," she said after a pause. "If I do that maybe he'll help you."

"Will you come with us now?" Ella asked.

"Let me make sure my mother's okay, then I need to pay your brother for the Sing. After that, I can go."

"Thank you," Ella said.

Less than five minutes later, with Wilma riding in the backseat, they set out for Farmington—the largest city close to the eastern border of the Navajo Nation. The only thing that disturbed the silence inside the SUV were radio transmissions that would occasionally come over the speaker.

"Jake's a good man. You'll see," Wilma said softly. "People just don't understand him."

Ella and Blalock exchanged a look, but neither said anything.

When they arrived at the pawn shop, which was a few streets south of Main, the paved lot beside the establishment was nearly empty. Only two cars were parked near the back door.

"He's alone right now, except for his clerk," Wilma said. "Let me go inside first and talk to him. I'll call you when he's ready to see you."

Ella and Blalock watched her go inside, but remained in the SUV. Blalock checked his watch. "This is Anglo territory. If she doesn't come out in five minutes, I'm going in."

"Agreed," Ella replied, sorting through the file.

Wilma came out a short while later and waved at Ella. As Blalock approached, Wilma moved to block him from going inside. "He'll see her, but not you, FB-Eyes," she told Blalock.

"That's too bad," Blalock said, refusing to step back. Seeing Ella shake her head, he smirked, and moved away from the threshold. "You sure, Investigator Clah?"

"Yeah, I've got this covered."

Wilma nodded in approval. "I'll wait out here, too," she

said, looking in Blalock's direction. "This has to be between them."

When Ella stepped inside, she recognized Jake Rowley immediately, from his mug shot. If anything, the man looked even less appealing in person. He had a narrow face and frame, with weasel-looking eyes that were too close together. His blue chambray Western shirt, bolo tie, and jeans were a cut above, but weren't enough to salvage his appeal. Love was definitely blind, Ella concluded.

"Ella Clah," he said, giving her the once-over as she stepped up to the counter. "You're well known even in this 'burg. I understand you need information—and maybe a favor," Jake added. "I'll be happy to help you—but there's something I want in return."

"Let's hear it." Ella braced herself and hoped that he knew she had no jurisdiction in Farmington. If what he wanted was to cut a deal with the police here, there wouldn't be much she could do to help him.

"Wilma's brother, Joe Pete, was busted for DWI over by Window Rock. He's awaiting a court date, but he's been busted twice before for drinking and driving and he's going down hard this time. If you intercede for him and ask the court for leniency, I'll guarantee that he goes into the top substance abuse program on the Rez. I'll even cover all the costs."

She blinked in surprise. Knowing Jake's reputation, she'd expected something entirely different.

"He's family," he added by way of an explanation. "Or will be after Wilma and I tie the knot."

Ella nodded slowly. "That's out of my district, you know. But I'll do everything I can for you."

"Good. Now what do you need?"

Ella brought out the photo of Dr. Lee, which Blalock had placed in the file. "Do you know this woman, and have you had any dealings with her?"

Taking a quick look, Jake nodded. "She's a professor at the community college who's having problems with a stalker," he answered. "I sold her a rifle and a .38 revolver I owned personally. It was a private transaction away from my business and didn't require all that background crap. The .38's trigger was stiff, really hard to pull, so I offered to do some custom work for her at the shop if she wanted to bring it in. She did and went away happy with the results."

Ella knew the sale was dubious and she could probably create problems for him, but right now she needed information. "It would be kind of hard to fire a rifle *and* a pistol at the same time unless you're Rambo. Just how dangerous is this stalker?"

He shrugged. "I advised her to get a shotgun instead, but she said that the rifle wasn't for her, that she was planning to give it to a friend. I got the impression that the rifle was more of a bribe—a gift to one of the professors or maybe a neighbor in exchange for backup if it became necessary."

"She should have reported this stalker to a tribal officer. If she returns, will you give me a call?" Ella said, handing him her card. "And keep this conversation between the two of us."

"What conversation? Just remember our deal."

"You've got it," Ella answered.

As she walked back outside, she found herself envying Wilma. She'd found a man who loved her enough to put her and her family first. Not a bad deal, even if he looked like a weasel.

Ella thought of her own life. No one except God would ever occupy the number one slot in Ford's life, but she was happy being number two. In an odd way, considering her own life, it made for a more balanced relationship between them. Whoever needed her most—Rose, Dawn, or Ford— usually got top priority for however long was necessary.

Ella joined Blalock, who was leaning against the tribal SUV. "If you hadn't come out when you did, I would have gone in after you," he said flatly.

Wilma gave him an exasperated look, then glanced at Ella. "Were you able to help each other?"

Ella suddenly realized that their quid-pro-quo arrangement had probably been Wilma's idea and she'd persuaded Jake to play along.

"I'll be asking the tribal court for leniency for your brother," Ella replied, studying her expression.

Wilma nodded, satisfied. "I thought it was a good idea. Without balance, nothing really works. I'm going to stay here, so I won't need a ride. You can get back to your work."

Wilma went back inside the shop, and Ella brought Blalock back up to date as they climbed into her vehicle. "Let's go over to Teeny's and see what they've got," she suggested, turning on the engine.

Blalock nodded. "Sounds good to me."

"I don't know if they've made any progress breaking the code, but maybe they can tell us who else is working for, or with, Dr. Lee. I'd also like to find out what she's done with the weapons she bought. I didn't spot them earlier, during the sneak-and-peek."

"One step at a time," Blalock said.

As they got underway, Ella glanced over at Blalock. "I sure miss the days when crimes were crimes, and terrorism was something that happened only in the Middle East."

"Amen to that," Blalock said. "Speaking of terrorism, Ella, how much has the Saytak—uh, forgive my pronunciation—Hogback Generating Station's security been told about the situation regarding Dr. Lee?"

"They have her photo on file, and were asked to keep her under surveillance if she tried to approach again. Security's on high alert because of all the publicity leading up to the reactor's installation."

"I haven't been there since the combined briefing the week before their staff training began," Blalock said. "Wanna stop by and see how they've implemented all their security plans?"

Ella looked at her watch. "Good idea."

Ten minutes later, they were seated in a small guard house, inside the second line of razor wire fencing, with Captain Henderson, the on-duty head of security. Henderson was ex-military and Navajo, like most of the protection detail, and armed with a handgun, Taser, and a submachine gun slung over his shoulder. Ella doubted that even military bases around the country had such a high level of security personnel and training.

Ella looked at the plastic strap on the man's wrist, a tracking device and heart monitor everyone inside the second fence wore. If they went in any further, Blalock and she would each be wearing one as well.

"As you noticed while coming into the parking lot, officers, we've now completed the concrete barrier. Without authorization from the inside, no vehicles can penetrate beyond the staff and visitor lots. No trucks filled with explosives could get anywhere near these buildings," Henderson said. "And the EDS—explosive detection system—keeps anything like that pipe bomb you described from ever getting inside the gates. We're much tighter here than any airport security. Notice how far you were from the sensor when it picked up the backup pistol in your boot, Investigator Clah?"

"Yeah, that was impressive," Ella said.

"Your remote sensors are effective," Blalock said with a nod. "I'm surprised you felt a need to add human and canine patrols, too."

"We didn't want to rely on technology alone, even though we've got battery backups on all our observation gear," Henderson said. "We want to be ready for anything that could come at us. All of our people have completed their DOD training, just like the crews that'll be transporting the reactor bottle and pebbles."

Ella looked at the low, thick-concrete buildings, sort of a cross between bank and fortress. "How many attackers would it take to fight their way inside to something important?"

"More than fifty, based on our training experiences so far. We've had worst-case-scenario mock attacks as part of our training, with Special Forces teams playing the aggressors. We've sometimes lost twenty percent of our security force, but none of the attackers ever made it inside," Henderson said, smiling. "We even have surface-to-air capability, though I'm not allowed to elaborate."

"How does your anticipated security level compare to other current US nuclear utilities?" Ella asked.

"Mock attacks on other facilities have succeeded in penetrating defenses fifty percent of the time. We feel a lot better about our protection, though we'll continue to hold drills and revise our tactics. The key here, I think, is that our people aren't glorified rent-a-cops. They're highly trained professionals." Henderson stood. "Anything else?"

"No, that's it for now. Once we get more information on the potential threat, especially regarding suspects and specific target areas, we'll pass it along immediately," Ella said.

"Good luck tracking these bad guys down, and give my regards to Officer Tache's family." Henderson led them to the door, punched in a code, then escorted them to the outer fence. Four minutes later they were underway.

"Looks like Dr. Lee is going to have some trouble penetrating their defenses. Compared to the coal-fired plants around here, that place is Fort Knox," Blalock commented, looking back in the side mirror.

"I agree, though that doesn't mean innocent people couldn't die in an attempt against it. Terrorists might try to hijack the reactor en route, too, or gain entry to the parking lot. That's where the big ceremony is going to be held, what, next week?" Ella said. "We need to know what Dr. Lee has planned."

"Let's see how close our code breaker is to reading Dr. Lee's mail," Blalock said as they slowed, nearing the turn-off to Bruce Little's street.

A short time later, after getting past Teeny's cameras and security, they entered his main work room. Ford was at one of Teeny's computers, and with the exception of a quick nod, barely looked at Ella when he started speaking.

"We've studied Jane Lee's blogs, her e-mails, and the rest of her files without incident," Ford said. "Everything looks painfully ordinary, but, considering who we're dealing with, that just means she's using a code we haven't broken. We're still working on recovering that file that deleted itself, but that's going to take considerably longer."

"And here's a heads-up, Ella. My guess is that she'll know we accessed her computer," Teeny said, walking into the room with a can of soda in his hand. "I would."

"You're assuming she's as computer savvy as you are, but I don't think she is," Ella said. "Judging from her initial mistake—trying to communicate in plain language via a supposedly anonymous service—it's clear her focus isn't computers. What drives her is more likely to be her desire to make her mark on the world. For example, she teaches because that's one way to touch a new generation. She knows that a few of her students will always remember her, and she finds continuity in that. Many women find that same deep-seated need fulfilled when they have children. Kids become their legacy to the world."

Blalock looked at her for a long time. "That's certainly an interesting viewpoint. But her motivation isn't our concern—her potential actions are. And the way she bought her handgun and a hunting rifle are borderline illegal. The real question is: Just how far is she willing to go to make an impact on the world?"

"I'll have more for you when I break her code," Ford said, looking up from his keyboard. "And before you ask, I haven't got much so far. It's just a guess, but I think it may be the type of code that requires certain words be said in a certain order—a trigger word or expression, followed by the message. It could be hidden within her blogs or e-mails. If that trigger word or key isn't there, the message isn't valid, it's just words."

"Like baseball signals," Blalock suggested.

"Exactly. If the third base coach wants the batter to bunt, the signal may be him crossing his arms. But the key might be him touching the bill of his cap first. The coach can send all kinds of phony signals, touching his ear, clapping his hands together, or even crossing his arms. But until he touches his cap, *then* crosses his arms, it doesn't mean a thing," Ford explained.

"That's a very simple key. There are other, more complicated ones that are changed daily," Teeny said. "Those are more secure, and if that's the type they're using, the code key may be hidden in something she carries on her person, like her purse. You might want to take a look there. This lady's no novice, so I doubt she'd keep the codes in her computer—the same place as her messages."

"Using the same argument, it's also possible she'd keep the key on a piece of paper in her shoe, but I'll admit, her purse is more likely," Ella said. "In my college days, the women professors always kept their purses locked in their desks. If that's still the case, we have a set of skeleton keys that'll give us access to it."

"Checking inside her purse and putting it back without her knowledge is going to be real tough," Blalock said.

"We'll give it a shot. That's all we can do," Ella replied.

Ford glanced at Blalock. "I'm going to need some extra

security clearance. There's this program I've only heard about . . ."

Leaving Blalock to work with Teeny and Ford, Ella walked back out to her department vehicle. From there, she called Officer Talk and learned Dr. Lee's whereabouts.

"The subject's been in her office for the past hour or so. Students have been dropping by almost continuously," Marianna said. "She also has a class coming up soon, then a thirty-minute break, followed by another class. After that, she has another hour of office time scheduled."

"Stay with her until you're replaced; probably by Sergeant Neskahi. I'll let you know when you can pull back," Ella said. Then she called Justine. "I'll pick you up in twenty. We're heading to the college. I need your help for a little black-bag work," she added.

As she drove, Ella considered her options. What they needed was a diversion, maybe just a touch of confusion . . . like setting off a fire alarm. People would be jumpy enough after the recent bomb blast, and it was possible that in her rush to get out of the building, Dr. Lee might leave her purse behind. Then, in the ensuing chaos, either she or Justine could slip into Dr. Lee's office and get a quick look inside her purse. But setting off a phony fire alarm would require a lot of interdepartmental cooperation. That promised to be trickier than the operation itself.

Ella entered the station a few minutes later, still deep in thought. She was halfway down the hall when she heard a familiar voice.

"Shorty," Big Ed called, waving her to his office.

As Ella went inside, she saw another plainclothes officer, judging by the badge on her belt, sitting across Big Ed's desk. She stood up as Ella came in, but didn't smile.

"This is Officer Anna Bekis. She's your new bomb squad tech."

Considering they were all Navajos here, Ella never made a move to shake hands. "Good to meet you," she said.

"I've been briefed about your situation and know what happened to your EOD tech. I want you to know that as soon as he can get back to the job, I'll be happy to accept reassignment," Bekis said, her voice crisp and professional.

"Thank you for the thought, but that's not going to happen anytime soon. Our officer is still in intensive care, and we have no idea how long his recovery will take."

Just then, Big Ed's phone rang. He answered the call, listened for a second, then looked up. "We're glad to have you on board, Officer Bekis. Now I'll let you two get back to work."

Ella led Bekis to her office. Halfway down the hall, Justine joined them.

Ella waved both women to chairs, then quickly updated Anna on the details of their case. After she finished, Ella studied Anna's calm expression. The woman had scarcely moved a muscle. Ella figured she was in her early thirties, but there was a weariness around her eyes that spoke of someone with serious field experience.

"Our team's badly understaffed," Ella said. "That means pitching in whenever you're needed to work with the Crime Scene Team and putting in unspeakably long hours during crunch times. Are you ready for all that?"

Anna nodded once. "This is where I want to be."

"Then we're happy you're here. But I'd like to ask you a question. After all your years on the outside, what made you come back to the Rez?"

"Personal reasons."

Ella took a deep breath, then exhaled slowly. "Our lives are often in each other's hands and I like to know who I'm working with. Will you reconsider your answer?"

Anna said nothing for a long moment, then answered

her. "There's a sameness about crime on the outside. You work on cases—three, four, or maybe five at a time. You solve some and not others, but you never get the feeling that you've accomplished anything. After a while, you end up forgetting why you're doing the job. On the Rez, we restore order because that's the only way to walk in beauty. That makes sense to me, and puts things in the right perspective."

"In one way or another, life between the sacred mountains always calls to a Navajo. It doesn't matter how far away we go," Ella said.

Justine nodded in agreement.

"So where do you need me today?" Anna asked, her tone all business again.

"I have to get our subject, Dr. Lee, out of her office and separate her from her purse," Ella said. "Here's a recent photo." Ella brought out the folder she had on Dr. Lee. "Since she's never met you, Anna, I was thinking you could be our lookout. But I'm getting ahead of myself. First, I need to run an idea past Big Ed. We can't get things rolling unless I can get his permission and his help."

Leaving Justine and Anna, Ella returned to Big Ed's office. With luck, and a lot of fancy footwork, they'd soon know a lot more about Dr. Jane Lee.

ELEVEN

——— ✖ ✖ ✖ ———

Ella entered Big Ed's office at his invitation and took a seat. "I need a diversion so I can take a look inside Dr. Lee's purse for a code key," she said, getting right down to business. "If we could get our fire marshal to give an impromptu safety update to the college faculty members—a few at a time—pulling them from their offices as available, that'll give me the time we need. Best part, no classes will be disrupted, so administration at the college shouldn't object. The fire marshal could cite the bomb incident and the need for heightened security as a reason, and repeat the presentation he normally gives to school staffs and tribal agencies. If he's quick to assure Dr. Lee that it won't take long, there's a good chance she'll leave her purse behind, knowing her office is locked and supposedly secure."

Big Ed thought a moment, then nodded. "I can do that, but it seems like a big effort just to get a look at her purse. If she doesn't leave it behind, then what?"

"It won't be a total loss. There's still a chance that she keeps the code hidden elsewhere in her office and only takes it with her when she leaves for the day. Once we get her out, we'll be able to search her office from top to bottom, as well as her car."

"Okay. I'll call our fire marshal, Mike Martinez. He's my cousin, and I'm sure I can get him to cooperate."

"That's great. Thanks."

"What do you think of Anna Bekis so far?" Big Ed asked.

Ella considered her answer. "I like the way she thinks," she answered at last.

"She's in my wife's clan. Her family doesn't approve of her work, but I think she's well-suited for the job. I've been told that she has nerves of steel."

"EOD is as dangerous as it gets. Any idea why she chose that?"

"Her dad. He worked EOD for the Albuquerque Police Department. She idolized him. She always wanted to be just like him."

"Idolized? Past tense?"

"He died several years ago of a particularly nasty form of cancer. It was a long, hard process and it changed her. She saw firsthand that you can't run from death, and the 'natural' way isn't always the best road out. According to her supervisors, she's not reckless or suicidal, but she doesn't hesitate to do whatever has to be done. On her application she wrote that the danger and the uncertainty of her work makes her appreciate life more."

"That, I get." The reason Ella never took the time she spent with Dawn for granted was because of the nature of her job. In some ways, she breathed more into one afternoon with her daughter than some parents shared in a lifetime.

Big Ed looked up a telephone number, then glanced at Ella. "I'm going to call the fire marshal now. Could you be ready to roll if I get things set up right away? I'll have better luck if I don't give him too much time to think about it."

"The sooner, the better," she said.

"Good." Big Ed picked up the phone and dialed.

Ella waited as he spoke on the phone. After the usual greetings, Big Ed got down to business. "I need a favor," he said, providing details of what he needed and the urgent timeline. "Can you do this for me? I wouldn't ask if it wasn't important."

There was a brief silence, then Big Ed gave Ella a thumbs-up and slid over a piece of paper with Mike's telephone number. "Thanks, Mike. I appreciate it. Around noon is perfect," he said. "Come for dinner tonight. I'll have Claire fix her special green chile stew."

Ella returned to her office moments later. As she gave Justine and Anna the details, Justine sorted the skeleton keys they'd need to gain access to Dr. Lee's office and desk drawers.

"It's going down within the hour, so let's roll," Ella said. As an afterthought, she looked at Anna and added, "Follow us there in your own vehicle. I don't want to take a chance that Dr. Lee will see all of us together."

After getting an update on Dr. Lee's whereabouts from Marianna, Ella gave Anna additional information, including directions to Dr. Lee's classroom. "She's supposed to be teaching a woman's studies class this morning, then making herself available to students for a half hour in her office. Once she's back in her office, the fire marshal, with administrative backing, will drop by and pull her out for a quick security review. When she leaves, keep her in your sight. Justine and I will search her office and car. Once Dr. Lee's done with the fire marshal, send us the text message 'go.' "

"Piece of cake."

"And Anna? Make sure you keep your service weapon and badge out of sight," Ella said, gesturing to her waist.

"Not a problem. I'll also loosen my hair. When it's not braided like it is now, it's down to my waist. People tend to see the hair, not me or my face."

Ella nodded in approval. "Good thinking."

With a plan ready, Ella and Justine drove together to campus. "What would you rather do, search Dr. Lee's office or car?" Ella asked.

"I'll take her car," Justine said. "I brought a GPS tracker that I'd like to place somewhere on her vehicle. It may help us along the way."

"Go ahead, but hide it well. Jane's sharp. Remember that she found the device Ford dropped into her purse."

They were heading toward the building when Ella's phone vibrated, and Officer Talk's voice came through clearly.

"We have a hitch. Instead of going to her office, the subject dismissed her class, then took off across campus. Her TA, Mona Tso, is still in the room—the same place where Dr. Lee's next class will be held. Looks like Mona is sharing lunch or whatever with an ex-military looking guy in his forties. Guy was waiting around, bucket of chicken under his arm, and Mona sneaked him in right after her boss left. I followed Dr. Lee, but she might have made me."

"Where's she at now?" Ella asked.

"Near the student union building, the north end. It's lunch time, and the commons is really crowded right now. Maybe she's just picking up a salad or sandwich. She has her purse with her."

"You'd think she'd send her teaching assistant to pick up snacks. Or maybe Jane knows about Mona's boyfriend and wanted to give them some privacy. Stay back, but keep her under surveillance. I'll be there and take over for you in another four or five minutes."

Hanging up, she briefed Justine. "We'll have to put the fire marshal on hold," Ella added, then called Mike's number and gave him a quick update.

Soon Justine, who'd been driving, pulled over, and Ella got out. As she hurried across the campus toward the student union building, she saw that it was just as crowded as Marianna had said. After checking in with the younger officer, Ella spotted Dr. Lee in the lobby outside the dining hall.

"I've got her," Ella said, then maintaining visual contact, followed her without narrowing the distance between them. Twice she saw Dr. Lee get jostled by the crowd, and another time, the professor bumped into a young man leaving the building. But as the crowd thickened even more, Ella lost sight of Dr. Lee altogether.

Common sense told her to watch the food line, but she still couldn't locate Dr. Lee. Five minutes later, when Ella spotted her again, Dr. Lee was looking in her purse as she exited the building.

Ella followed, checking her watch. They were running out of time to carry out the plan before Dr. Lee began her next class. Soon Dr. Lee entered the women's studies building and headed back to her classroom. Mona greeted her at the open door. The boyfriend was nowhere in sight, so he must have taken off already.

Ella remained at the opposite end of the hall. She knew in her gut that she'd missed something important, but before she could give it more thought, her phone rang. It was Anna Bekis.

"What now, Investigator Clah?" Anna asked. "Do we still have time to do this?"

"Doesn't look like it. Hang tight, and we'll give it another shot at the end of her next class. If she doesn't return to her office then, we may have to give up on the purse and settle on an office search instead," Ella said. "Stay in touch and keep your eyes open."

"Okay," Anna said, then ended the call.

Ella called the fire marshal and then Justine, informing them of the change in plans. Then she headed for the campus security office. There were security cameras at the student union, so maybe Dr. Lee's activities in the dining hall had been recorded.

The woman in the blue-and-white uniform behind the desk, Vera Hunt, had been a classmate of Ella's back at Shiprock High. Vera had served on the tribal PD for ten years, too, before coming to work on campus.

Hearing Ella's knock on her open door, Vera looked up from her paperwork and smiled brightly. "Hey, Ella, I'm glad to see you. I'm just sorry that it had to take a campus bomb attack to bring us together again. That's why you're here, right?"

"Yeah, I'm following up on a few details," she replied, unable to provide any other information.

"How about a cup of cocoa while we conduct business?" Vera reached for a big thermos.

Ella sat and accepted the cup of hot chocolate Vera offered her. "Hey, this is *seriously good*!" Ella said after taking a sip.

"I've been experimenting with the mix for years. It gets cold in this office, but I can't push the temp up because of the computer equipment. Since I can't stand coffee. . . ." She sat on the corner of her desk and faced Ella. "So how can I help you?"

"I'd like to take a look at the student union building's security video."

"I gave a copy of that to Justine the night of the big blast," Vera replied.

"I need the video for today. It's just follow-up," Ella responded, deliberately being vague.

"You've got it, but I should warn you that our cameras are completely inadequate and the VCRs are ancient. I've told administration that we need better equipment, but they're always more worried about their budget. Maybe they'll come up with the money now that we've had a bomb attack."

She walked around her desk. "What part of the student union building do you want to focus on—the entrance and foyer, or the interior?"

"The interior."

Vera went to the machines in the next room and came back out with two videotapes. Placing the first in the VCR in her office, she turned on the monitor and ran the footage.

The cameras weren't that bad, but the videotape itself had obviously been recorded over many times and was grainy. This particular camera focused on the lunch line from the east side. The images recorded were for the span of time Ella had lost sight of Jane. Ella caught a glimpse of Jane bumping into two different people—or maybe they'd bumped into her. It was impossible to tell.

"Can you zoom in on this person?" Ella pointed to the professor, who was in profile.

"That's Dr. Jane Lee, women's studies. She's your mark?"

Ella nodded. "But keep that to yourself, okay? It's important."

"I understand."

"Let me see the other tape," Ella said. "That should show the reverse angle, right?"

"It does." Vera loaded the second video, then forwarded it to the same time period.

"There, regular speed please," Ella said.

A man wearing a baseball cap and sunglasses approached Dr. Lee, but he kept his face down, making it impossible to identify him. Vera worked with the machine, trying to lighten the image, but nothing helped. The only thing Ella managed to see clearly was the distinctive name brand on the ammunition box Dr. Lee took from the man and quickly slipped into her purse. From its size and shape, it looked like rifle rather than pistol rounds, though it could have been a mix.

Legal ammunition sales were always recorded, and Jake Rowley hadn't mentioned selling any ammo to Jane, just the pistol and rifle. Whether purposely or not, Dr. Lee had managed to prevent both transactions from being documented, at least on paper.

"Sorry we can't get a better look at the man who handed the box of bullets to Dr. Lee," Vera said finally. "He tucked his chin down at the wrong moment."

Or the right one, Ella mused. "Any idea who he is?"

"None."

"He obviously knew about the cameras. . . . Could he be part of your security team? Except for the position of his head, he walked like a cop—or ex-military."

Vera's eyebrows shot up, but she recovered quickly and focused on the screen. "I've got two security guards who might fit the general description of the man on the video, but one's not here today. His wife's having a baby and he's at the hospital with her, which should be easy enough to verify."

"And the other?"

"He's on campus, but our people are always in uniform, Ella, like I am—white shirt and badge, blue pants, and black shoes," she added, pointing to each.

"Can you verify his activities?"

"Let me find out where he was about that time," Vera answered, then checked her log books. "He was answering a call at the administration building. One of the secretaries reported money missing from a cash box. She'd left the drawer unlocked and when she came back from lunch, the cash was gone."

Ella sighed. Another dead end. But at least they had an image. Maybe someone else could ID him.

"Have your security people view these tapes and see if anyone can ID this guy. But don't let *anyone* outside your office know what you're doing. Secrecy's our only advantage."

"You've got it."

Ella stood up. "You're a good cop, Vera. If you should ever want to come back to the department, give me a call."

"Thanks, but no thanks. I'm where I belong," Vera said. "After I was nearly killed by that *glonnie* I pulled over," she said, using a common Navajo expression for drunk, "I didn't have it in me anymore. On campus I deal with people who are looking forward to life, not trying to escape from it. As a cop, I saw too much despair. Here I see hope, and futures in the making."

Ella understood. There'd been times when she'd thought that law enforcement would eat her up from the inside out. The difference between them was that she could no more leave the department than she could will herself not to take her next breath. Police work was too much a part of who she was.

Ella checked her watch. It was almost time for the fire marshal to make his move. She'd have to get in place quickly. "Thanks for your help."

On her way to the lobby of the administration building, Ella asked Marianna for an update on Dr. Lee's whereabouts.

"She's heading to her office—finally. I've called Mike and Officer Bekis. Both are ready."

"Stay with her until she's inside her office, then leave the area. I'll be close enough by then to see when Mike Martinez pulls her out into the lobby," Ella said. "But if you see that she's not going to make it to her office for whatever reason, call me immediately."

Five minutes later, Ella watched from an adjacent corridor as the fire marshal led Dr. Lee and two other professors into the lobby. Unfortunately, Dr. Lee, who hadn't seemed at all happy about the interruption, had decided to take her purse with her.

Ella nodded to Anna, who was reading a newspaper across the lobby, then proceeded down the hall in the direction of the offices that had just been vacated.

Standing in front of Dr. Lee's office, Ella looked down at the lock, noted the manufacturer, and brought out two master keys. The second one opened the door and she slipped inside, locking it behind her.

There were papers and mail in two stacking baskets on Dr. Lee's desk, and Ella took a quick look through it all. Finding nothing of interest, she moved behind the professor's desk and looked at the brand name on the locked, central drawer. This time, it took three attempts to find the right key.

Just as she opened the drawer, there was a knock at the door. "Dr. Lee?"

Ella didn't recognize the voice—a young woman's—probably a student. Ella froze, happy that the walls were solid and there were no windows.

The knock came again, louder. About ten seconds later, she heard a single word—"crap"—and then silence. Not knowing if the student was still out there, Ella worked quickly and silently. She looked at the contents of the open drawer without touching anything, and saw packs of chewing gum, erasers, staples and a stapler, and a folder with a tag that read "class rosters." Other office supplies were in there, too, along with a nail file and a set of keys. From their shapes, the keys probably fit the file cabinets along the side wall.

As she was about to close and lock the drawer, Ella heard a faint sound by the door. A piece of folded paper had been slipped underneath—maybe a note from the student who'd come knocking. She'd check it later.

Quickly going through the other desk drawers, Ella found only lecture notes, reference books on women's issues, and what looked like student assignments and grade sheets from a computer spreadsheet program.

Finally, she got down on her knees and looked up at the bottom of the center drawer. A piece of tape had "9002eele-naj" written on it.

It was a password obviously—Jane Lee written backwards, plus the year 2009. That probably gave access to the files on her office computer, or maybe her grade program.

All in all, Ella thought it was too simple and obvious to hide any big secrets, but sometimes the biggest minds made simple mistakes.

Not wanting to waste time checking out the password now, Ella worked her way around the room. She checked the unlocked file cabinets quickly and found they contained only reference materials and old student papers.

Turning a quick circle, she noted only Southwest landscape watercolors and Indian poster art on the walls. Taking them down to examine the backs wouldn't make much sense. Ella knew the information had to be immediately available to Jane.

Ella took a quick glance at the paper that had been slipped beneath the door. It was a note on a physician's letterhead explaining the absence of Betty Largo from a recent class.

Ella was looking under the office chair for other taped passwords or lists of code words when her cell phone started to vibrate. Seeing the "go" text message, she put the chair back in place, then checked to make sure everything was as it had been before.

Moving quickly she exited the office, walked briskly down the hall, and out a side door.

As Ella headed to the visitor's parking lot, she dialed Anna's number. Notifying the bomb tech that she was clear, Ella instructed her to meet and assist Marianna. Lastly, Ella checked in with Justine.

"I placed the GPS and searched the car, top to bottom, but there was nothing of interest to us there," Justine answered. "How did it go with you?"

"Not good. Jane kept her purse with her. All I found after searching her office was the likely password to her office computer, or maybe her grade program." Ella then gave her partner the code.

"Let me guess—it was written on a scrap of paper and slipped underneath her desk pad."

"Close, it was on a strip of masking tape stuck beneath her desk drawer."

Ella and Justine met at the parking lot a short time later. "Big Ed may not agree, but I'm sending Marianna and Anna back to help Neskahi. When Dr. Lee leaves the campus, you and I are going to stick to her like sand to the desert floor."

It was another twenty minutes before Marianna finally reported that Dr. Lee was heading to her car. Relieved that the wait was over, Ella asked her and Anna to return to the station.

"Where did you place the tracking unit on Dr. Lee's car?" Ella asked Justine.

"I used quick-set epoxy and stuck it behind her license plate." She brought out the small GPS screen and showed Ella the color display. "The red dot is Jane's car."

They set out heading west, Justine behind the wheel and Ella monitoring the GPS. After a while, the route seemed clear. "Looks to me like she's going home," Ella said. "The software doesn't show every unpaved road in the area, but the blip and the direction indicate she's now on that gravel lane."

"Too bad. I was hoping we'd get lucky," Justine said.

"Wait a sec," Ella added suddenly. "She's come to a full stop, and although the scale isn't precise, I don't think she's home yet." Ella paused, then continued after a beat. "She's moving again."

"There might have been something in the road, like those geese. Or maybe she met someone," Justine said.

"No, no way. If she was going to make contact, it wouldn't have been out in the open like that, where she could be seen for a mile in every direction. Something else is going on. Stay sharp." Ella got out a pair of binoculars and studied the area ahead of them. "Nobody's passed us, and I can't see any sign of another car or truck in the distance."

As they reached the lane that led to where Dr. Lee lived, Ella sat up. "Take it slow," she said. "That fence . . ."

Justine glanced at it, then back at Ella. "What? It was there last time."

"Look at the Coke can. See it balanced on that post up ahead?"

"If it's a code or a signal it's definitely low tech, and that doesn't fit with all the electronic gizmos she's been using," Justine said. "For all we know, kids could have done that."

"What a better way to throw people off the trail than to mix a variety of methods. Leaving a marker like that as a sign to pick up a message at a drop, or make a contact, is right out of an old Cold War spy manual."

"We could dust the can for prints. If someone else put it there as a signal . . ."

Ella considered. "Drive down to the end of the lane first and let's make sure we're not being watched, or that Jane isn't out in her yard looking this way. If it's clear, we'll stop and I'll keep watch while you dust the can. Then we'll wipe it clean and put it back exactly where it is."

As they were circling the area, they found a place beside the river road where somebody had been dumping garbage, a common problem in an area where public sanitation services were scarce. "Stop a second, Justine," Ella said, pointing toward the debris pile.

"Yeah, I see the Coke can. We can use it as a substitute while we work on the other one. Good idea, partner." Justine stopped the unit, and Ella walked over to the mess. A few seconds later, they were on their way, empty can in hand.

Not spotting another moving vehicle, Ella, wearing latex gloves, walked over, switched cans, and, after looking inside the one from the post and finding it empty, put it into a paper bag she used to transport evidence.

Five minutes later, down by the river and out of sight, Ella stood outside the vehicle and watched while Justine dusted the can.

"I've got a lot of smears and a partial or two, but no complete prints," Justine said, placing the can back into the paper bag.

"When we get back to the office, process what you've got. See if you can get anything by matching comparison points."

"I'd like to have this fence staked out for the next day or so. Let's see if the can gets removed, or placed elsewhere—anything that might constitute a signal. Joe and Anna can take turns keeping watch."

"We have no guarantees that this is for real, or if it is, that the message hasn't already been delivered. Will it be worth the manpower?" Justine asked.

"It is, when you consider our only known suspect lives a half mile from here." Ella remembered the ammo Dr. Lee had been passed. "Something's brewing, cuz, and it might involve a long-range weapon and some up-close firepower. The problem is, we can't stop what we don't see coming."

Ella called Ford and gave him the password she'd found in Jane's office, then continued surveillance on the two targets—Dr. Lee's home and the fence line. With the open terrain, a pair of binoculars were all that was needed.

"This is making me nuts. She's not going anywhere," Ella said.

"Let Joe take over for us here," Justine said. "Our time's better spent elsewhere."

Ella nodded. She still had a feeling she was missing something, but before she could say anything, her phone rang. It was Big Ed.

"We just got a call from the Bureau lab. They've completed processing the bomb fragments and have a sketch of the likely design and components. The electric timer was a cheap version that's readily available, but we got a hit on the blasting cap. It came from Valley Construction. The charge used in the bomb was black powder, and that's something Valley doesn't carry or use. But they recently reported the theft of several bags of ammonium nitrate and sticks of dynamite, along with a few electrical blasting caps."

"When was the report filed?" Ella asked.

"Late yesterday. They keep their supplies in a steel storage unit, and didn't discover anything was missing until one of their foremen came to pick up supplies and noticed the break-in. The moment it showed up on the federal hot sheet, FB-Eyes called me."

"We'll get on that right away," Ella said, hanging up and giving Justine the highlights.

"Black powder is mild compared to what they could do with dynamite, or that much ammonium nitrate," Justine said. "If the bomb in the backpack had been dynamite instead of black powder . . ."

Ella nodded. "I wouldn't be here right now."

"Want me to follow up on the theft and get a complete list of what's missing, and how much?" Justine asked.

"Yeah. I'll check in with Ford and Teeny and see if they have anything new for me."

Less than an hour later, they were back at the station. Ella, after getting herself some coffee, went directly to her office and called Ford's cell phone number. From the tone of his voice when he answered, she knew instantly that they hadn't made significant progress.

"This code's so random, it's nearly impossible to break," he said, frustration evident in his tone. "Whoever made it up is extremely intelligent or very lucky."

"Don't let it drive you crazy. Experience tells me that to

make progress you sometimes have to get away from it for a while." People usually had things in their lives that gave them a sense of purpose and made them feel good about themselves. With Ford it was God, and then ciphers. Right now the first didn't seem to be listening, and the second wasn't cooperating.

"You're right. I need a break. Why don't you meet me for an early dinner at the Totah?" he asked at last. "A little while ago Bruce took me back to my place to pick up my stuff and get Abednego. My car's here now so after I stop for gas, I'll join you there."

Ella checked her watch. It was a bit past four. "Okay. You're on."

About fifteen minutes later, Ella was on her way to the Totah Café in downtown Shiprock. As she passed Tsosie's Gas and Goods, all her muscles suddenly tightened and a chill ran up her spine. Maybe she'd seen something only her subconscious had registered, or maybe it was that special instinct all cops developed, but something was wrong.

The badger fetish around her neck grew uncomfortably warm as she pulled into the station. The last time she'd felt on edge like this, the bomb blast had followed. Ford, who was at the pumps, recognized her SUV and waved, obviously unaware of any possible danger.

Ella parked in a slot beside the building, then hurried to join Ford, who was putting the gas cap back on his car.

"Is something wrong, Ella?" he asked, watching her carefully as he walked toward her.

She barely heard, turning in a slow circle, looking for the source of her uneasiness. Catching a flash of light at eye level from a figure standing beside a tree atop the mesa, Ella suddenly tackled Ford to the ground. Something thumped into the wall of the store just beyond them as the echo of a gunshot reached their ears.

"Get down!" Ella yelled to the other people nearby, simultaneously drawing her handgun. Crouching low, she placed Ford's vehicle between her and the tree in the distance.

"Stay behind the engine block," she called out to Ford, feeling the heat flowing from her badger fetish. "This isn't over yet."

TWELVE

× × ×

As Ella brought out her cell phone and hit speed dial, another bullet struck the car with a thud. A third whistled by so close she could almost feel it. The sniper had a high-powered rifle with a scope, and judging from the way he was shooting, he was an expert marksman.

Ella reached the dispatcher and asked for backup. As soon as she ended the call, Ford crept closer to her, staying low.

"Who's doing this?" he asked, his voice shaky.

"An expert who's got us zeroed in. Stay down." Yet even as she spoke, she could feel the badger around her neck cooling. Unwilling to trust that completely, she waited another few minutes.

At long last, Ella moved to the rear of Ford's car and risked a quick look. The shape she'd seen by the tree was gone. By the time she rose to her feet, the fetish was cool to the touch, as all turquoise should be.

After backup arrived, Ella turned the job of interviewing witnesses over to the officer. As he worked, she processed the scene, searching for the places where the three rounds had struck.

The first bullet fired had ended up striking the foundation of the store, just below the wood. The copper-jacketed round that had mushroomed upon impact appeared to be a hunting round from a .308. Ella knew those bullets were designed to do maximum damage. Unfortunately, that caliber wasn't difficult to acquire and was available for many weapons.

Ford came over while she was inspecting the second bullet hole from the round that had struck the engine block instead of them. His pallor said more about his state of mind than words could have.

"How . . . ," he managed, but his voice broke. With his hand clenched around the cross he wore around his neck, he tried again. "*How* did you know? You reacted *before* he fired."

"The badger fetish my brother gave me . . . it warns me. The stone gets hot whenever there's danger." Seeing his reaction, she wished she hadn't said anything. His hand was now wrapped so tightly around the cross, his knuckles had turned white.

Justine and Marianna, the only available members of her crime scene team, arrived next. As they processed the scene, Ella phoned Joe Neskahi.

"Where's Dr. Lee?" she asked.

"At home. She hasn't moved."

"Are you absolutely certain that she never left the house? Is it possible she went for a walk without you being aware of it, and someone else picked her up?"

"No way. I've got a clear view of the fence line as well as her house. Since her curtains are open, I can see inside her living room with my binoculars, too. Right now she's reading a book."

Anger wound through her. While her prime suspect was relaxing at home, Ford and she had been dodging bullets.

Ella hung up, looked around for Ford, and found him inside Tsosie's store, drinking a cup of hot cocoa. "That looks good," she said.

"Comfort food." He held it out to her, but she declined. "When I was a kid, my mom would always make hot chocolate whenever we had a big problem. Her cocoa was nothing special, but the whipped cream made the difference," he added with a shaky smile.

"Are you okay?" she asked softly.

He nodded. "God was keeping watch over us today. It was His hand that brought us through this."

Ella noticed that he was staring at her badger fetish. "Does it matter whose side kept us alive? Maybe one of your God's people makes the fetish change temperature."

"This isn't a matter of my side or yours," he said quickly.

"That's not what I'm hearing," Ella countered. "But what difference could it possible make who or what's responsible? We're alive. Take it as a win."

"It matters to me," he said quietly. "But there's something neither of us can refute: You've saved my life twice now," he added in a gentler tone.

"It's all part of my job. You save souls—I save lives," she said with a smile. "And speaking of jobs . . . I'm going to need you to answer some questions for me."

"Go ahead."

"Do you always gas up at this place?"

"Yeah, they've got the best prices. I usually come here once a week—about this time, come to think of it."

"You're being targeted. You can't afford to follow any of your regular routines or schedules."

"I should have thought of that, but today I was more focused on other things," he admitted. "But why would someone want me dead so badly?" He looked around, making sure no one but Ella was close enough to hear. Even so, he lowered his voice. "I'm nowhere close to breaking that code. And killing me wouldn't solve anything. There are others who could do the job if I couldn't. I'm certainly not irreplaceable."

Teeny drove up before Ella could answer. "Wait here, okay?" she asked Ford, then went to join her old friend. "I'm glad you're here."

Teeny nodded. "I heard the police calls on my scanner and thought I might be able to help. What do you need me to do?"

"Take Ford with you and keep him out of sight. He was the sniper's target."

Within the minute, Teeny and Ford drove away. Ford's car was still parked by the pumps. After the bullet strike on the engine block, she had no idea if it would even start. She'd have it towed to the impound yard to be checked out. Ford would be without transportation for a while, but it didn't matter. He'd have to stay in protective custody anyway. Experience told her the person after Ford wouldn't stop until he was dead.

Ella met Teeny two hours later at his secure compound just east of Shiprock. Ford was sitting outside in the enclosed courtyard, a Bible on his lap and Abednego at his feet.

"That episode with the sniper really threw him, Ella," Teeny said quietly. "I don't think he ever really believed that the bomb had been meant for him—not until now. He told me that the sniper would have taken him out if you hadn't knocked him out of the way when you did." Teeny paused for several moments. "Something about that is eating at him, too. I can't put my finger on it, but I don't think it's male pride."

"It's not," Ella answered grudgingly. "He needs to believe that it was his God, not my badger fetish, that gave me advance warning. But the badger, for whatever the reason, turns hot when danger's close by. Whether or not he can accept it, it's the truth."

Teeny shook his head. "No, that's not it. I suspect that what's bothering him is that you can't—won't—share his beliefs."

Seeing Ella, Abednego yipped and Ford looked up from his reading. Ella smiled and waved, asking him wordlessly to come back inside and join them.

"Have you made any progress finding the sniper?" Ford asked quickly as he came up.

"We've learned a few more things about him," Ella said, following Teeny to the conference table. "We know he's a confident shooter who can fire accurately at what must have been four hundred yards. He's also cool enough to police his brass afterwards. All we found were some scuffed-out bootprints. He parked on the asphalt road that runs along the rim of the mesa so he wouldn't leave tire tracks. The area is now being canvassed to see if anyone saw the sniper or his vehicle. Most important of all, I believe the shooter is afraid of you."

"Afraid of *me*? Why?" Ford looked at her as if she'd lost her mind.

"Look at the facts. In each attack he's kept his distance. That leads me to believe that you know your assailant and he—or she—is afraid of coming too close in case the attempt to kill you fails and you end up recognizing him."

"She?" Ford stared at her.

"It might be a woman," Ella said. "What I need you to do now is think hard. You deal with a lot of people, some of them deeply troubled, I'd guess. Who hates you enough to want you dead?"

"What about Dr. Lee? She's the one I've been investigating. She might have figured out that I was the one who placed the device in her purse. If she's really planning an attack against the power plant, she might see me as a serious threat."

"She was at home when it went down. But there's another alternative I think we need to consider. Maybe we're dealing with two separate, unrelated crimes. Number one, Dr. Lee's involved in some kind of covert ops, and number two, someone's got a grudge against you."

"No one has a serious grudge against me, Ella. I'd know about it. Dr. Lee is the best bet," Ford said. "Although we've yet to establish who her associates are, we know she has them. Their interest in the *Tsétaak'á* Generating Station makes me their common enemy."

She nodded, lost in thought. "Our sniper might be the man who slipped her the ammo," Ella said, then filled him in on what she and Vera saw. "We didn't see a rifle at her house, so I'm guessing she gave it to the sniper before we started watching her every move. Thing is, the shape of the box looked wrong. The bullets that were passed could have been for her .38, which she might have easily stashed almost anywhere."

"Maybe some of the interesting bits we've turned up will help you," Ford said.

"Wait—you've made progress?" Ella asked quickly.

"I was going to tell you when we got together at the To-tah," Ford said.

Ella gave Teeny a hard look saying without words that they shouldn't have waited.

He shrugged. "I was hoping for a little more time to run some new decryption programs. That way we could have given you something more definitive," Teeny said.

"What we've discovered was that her blog, dated the day before the bomb incident on campus, mentioned the words 'Red Rock' and 'dawn.' Those were the *only* references to time of day and location. The rest read like a travel brochure and were totally different from her other blogs, which dealt with women's issues. Also, the *only* times she ever mentions locations is when she's using it to make a point about poverty, or the need for medical care in remote areas on the Rez," Ford said.

"Any idea who visits her site?" Ella asked.

"We can identify servers, and have picked up some screen names that we were able to track back to some of her students. But there are others we can't identify for various reasons," Teeny said.

"Does she get a lot of hits per day on her Web page?" Ella asked.

"We counted ten to twelve on average," Teeny said. "Most have URLs that can be tracked back to the college. The others came from well-known, popular servers, and those are harder to isolate to individuals."

"I checked her e-mails and she's also been getting messages from individuals who have obvious, phony addresses," Ford said. "Like spammers who want to avoid being nailed, those URLs are used only once and are virtually untraceable. I was trying to find something that would give us a lead when I saw that one of the letters mentioned plaid shirts sold at the trading post near Hogback. But I've been there and know they only carry a few of those tourist T-shirts. So I'm sure that was code, but I haven't been able to correlate it to any other incident that happened around that time."

"Anything based on a system or mathematical analysis of speech or word patterns and letter placement, like the code generated by the famous Enigma machines of World War II, can be broken," Teeny said. "But something this random is practically unbreakable. The message only becomes clear after the fact. Without the key, we can't break the code unless we can link each portion to an action, date, time, individual, or location."

"We need to stick to what we know, then," Ella said firmly. "Besides Dr. Lee and her associates, who else is your enemy, Ford? Give me some names."

"That's just it, Ella. I have no enemies," he said flatly. "My mission is to counsel people spiritually and to love them no matter what they do or say. As I said, no enemies."

"Not admitting a person's your enemy doesn't change the hard facts."

"You're wrong about that," Ford said softly. "The way you perceive someone can ultimately change how they think about you . . . and themselves. Love can turn an enemy into a friend."

She exhaled softly. Her father would have said pretty close to the same thing. Yet the police officer in her just wanted to pick Ford up and shake him until his brains rattled.

"All right. Let me rephrase this. Who might have a reason to resent you? Think of anyone you might have counseled, telling them things they didn't want to hear. Or maybe someone who has made it clear they don't like you, either personally or because of something connected to the church. And, Ford, think hard. Your life's on the line."

"My life is in God's hands," he said flatly.

Ella exhaled loudly. "I'm just asking you to tell me the truth, Ford. How could that offend your God?"

"If you love, you can't see your brother as your enemy."

"Do you believe in evil?" Ella countered.

Ford paused.

"If you do, Ford, and if you believe that evil presents a danger to everyone, then you owe it to the rest of us to help restore the balance."

"That's exactly what I do, though our methods are different."

Ella glanced at Teeny, looking for help, but he shook his head and shrugged. Ella focused on Ford once more. "Don't think of it in terms of enemies then. Who in your congregation is capable of violence against you or anyone else?"

"At any given time we all lose our tempers. I don't judge my brothers and sisters in Christ."

Ella felt her frustration turning into anger and knew it was time to stop going in circles. If he couldn't admit that a parishioner might be gunning for him, that avenue of discussion was closed, at least for the moment. "All right, Ford. Focus on the code, and see if you can find some answers we can use," she said, standing up.

As Ford turned back to the computer, Teeny walked her to the door.

"The Way is closed to him now, so you can't expect him to react to threats and aggression as if he was a Navajo *hataalii*," Teeny said in a whisper-soft voice. "He's rejected a lot of what it means to be Navajo, maybe because he associates it with a past he wants or needs to suppress. As a minister in his new life, he's cut from a different mold—maybe more so than most, in order to refute his take-no-prisoners background. That's part of the reason you're drawn to him."

"There's a lot I admire about him, but our beliefs . . . they're poles apart," she said at last. "Sometimes, around him, I feel pressured to reject my own background and culture, and my family."

"Nobody can make you do that. You believe too much in yourself. At least your ultimate goals are the same. Navajos try to restore the balance one way, while Christians work from a different perspective."

"One that can turn them into victims."

"Sometimes, but in the long run they tip the scales on the side of good. That, in itself, helps restore balance."

Ella smiled at him. "You're a smart man."

On her way minutes later, Ella decided to follow a hunch and head directly to Ford's church. For a brief moment, she considered calling Reverend Campbell and letting him know she was on the way, but then decided against it. She didn't want him to prepare. She'd have a better chance to get the kind of answers she needed if she caught him off guard.

When Ella arrived at Good Shepherd Church, she was relieved to see Reverend Paul Campbell's old blue sedan parked by the open side door. Ella went inside, and as she walked down the hall, heard the reverend practicing his sermon inside his office.

A second later, Reverend Campbell stepped out into the hall. "I thought I heard footsteps. Welcome, Investigator Clah," the tall, balding Anglo man said, greeting her with a smile.

"Do you have a minute, Reverend? I'd like to talk to you," she said.

"Of course. Come in, and have a seat. Tea?" he asked, gesturing to the kettle atop a hot plate. "It's decaffeinated green tea, which is supposed to be good for you. I'm trying to lay off the caffeine, particularly these days."

Ella didn't ask the obvious question, but looked at him and waited. In her many years as a police officer, she'd learned that if you just waited, and appeared interested, people would tell you just about anything. Reverend Campbell didn't disappoint.

"I'm glad to fill in for Reverend Tome, but the workload's been staggering," he said, sitting behind his desk. "And, of course, the fact that someone actually tried to kill a minister keeps me looking over my own shoulder."

"I think it's target specific—they want Reverend Tome, for whatever the reason. Mind you, it's good for you to stay alert, but I don't believe you're in danger."

"I just don't understand what's happening. Our job's to help people, to love them as Christ loved. To us, combating violence means loving more. It's not an easy road, believe me, but it's the one we were called to follow."

Ella stared at a spot on the wall just beyond the reverend. His words sounded so much simpler and easier to accept than if they'd come from Ford. Maybe it was because Reverend Campbell was more flexible. Or maybe it was because she wasn't in love with Campbell. Either way, she had to get answers, and to do that, she'd have to approach him in just the right way. Remembering her father's views, and

trying to put herself in Reverend Campbell's place, she finally spoke.

"An officer of mine is in the hospital and may never
completely recover. You can't allow this disturbed person to
harm another one of God's children. Loving your enemy
means protecting him from himself, too. By placing him in a
position where he can receive help, you save two souls—his
and the potential victim's."

"That's very true. Well said."

"Which brings me to the reason I'm here. I need your
help, Reverend Campbell. Ford's too close to this situation
and I need someone who can be objective. There's a good
chance that the person trying to kill Ford knows him personally. Does anyone here at the church have a problem with
him?"

"Minor skirmishes break out between different committees when it comes to the ministry and budgetary matters,
but all-out violence?" He shook his head.

"Think hard, Reverend Campbell. Has Ford had a dis-
agreement with anyone who might be prone to violence?"

"You should be asking him this," Campbell said.

"Ford's in a bad place mentally right now. In his eyes,
admitting that the person after him might be a parishioner
will also mean admitting that he and this church failed that
person. I don't think he can deal with that at the moment.
Will you help me?"

Reverend Campbell fell into a thoughtful silence.

As Ella waited, she wondered what Ford would say
when he found out she'd spoken to Reverend Campbell. By
his own rules, he'd have to forgive her. . . .

"I can recall two instances of trouble in the past few
months. When the wife of one of our parishioners, Edna Billey, left for Albuquerque on business, she asked Ford to make
some routine stops at her home to check on her husband, who
was bedridden. Ford agreed, but one afternoon when Ford

went to the house, he found that the man had passed away. When Edna returned, she blamed Ford, convinced that he hadn't checked on her husband closely enough. She was very upset, but Edna's a gentle person. She wouldn't harm anyone."

"What about their children? What was their reaction?"

"They only have one son, who's in the Marines. He was granted leave to attend the funeral, but I understand he's scheduled to be shipped back to the Middle East soon."

"I'll need his name," Ella said.

"Louis Billey. They're both currently staying at a rented single-wide trailer over in Waterflow. Edna moved in there right after her husband's death. There's nothing wrong with the house, but no one will go near it now that a death's occurred there. You know how that works."

Ella knew about fear of the *chindi*. It was said that when a man died, the evil in him wouldn't be able to merge with universal harmony, so it stayed behind to create problems for the living. It was a powerful belief on the Rez, even among churchgoers.

"You mentioned two instances of trouble. What's the second?" Ella pressed.

"Kim Mike. . . ."

The name sounded familiar, but she couldn't place it.

"It was a very sad situation. Her husband Henry used to beat her up. She'd come to church a total mess—busted nose, black eyes, split lip, the works. We both tried to work with Henry and Kim because, believe it or not, Kim didn't want to leave him, despite the abuse." He shook his head, then took a deep breath before continuing.

"The beatings grew so severe that Ford and I were both worried that he'd end up killing her. Then last month, Henry put her in the hospital and got arrested. While he was in jail, Kim finally took our advice. She left the Navajo Reservation, telling no one where she was going. When Henry got out on bail he came over here drunk, threatened Ford, and started pushing him around. Things got really bad fast, so I called the police. They took him back to jail and put him in a detox program. After that I was told that he'd moved over the mountains to Many Farms."

"I appreciate your help, Reverend Campbell," Ella said, standing. "Thanks very much."

He nodded. "Tell Ford that I'll be praying for him and everyone else involved in this case."

"I will, and thanks. We need all the help we can get."

THIRTEEN
✖ ✖ ✖

As Ella headed back to the station, she telephoned her team for a meeting. It was time to get more minds on the problem. Maybe together they'd be able to come up with new strategies.

It was already dark by the time Ella walked into the station. Time seemed to be slipping through her fingers, just like the answers she was trying so hard to find.

As she entered her office, Ella glanced at the group already gathered there. Blalock was sitting in her chair, sipping coffee from one of the machines down the hall, Justine was leaning against the wall, and Anna seemed restless, fidgeting in her chair. Marianna was typing on a laptop.

"Phillip Cloud has taken over surveillance from Joe, who's en route back. Dr. Lee didn't leave her home again today," Justine said.

"Maybe she knows we're keeping tabs on her," Blalock said, standing and motioning Ella to her chair.

"I suppose she could have made us," Ella said. "Except for Anna, we've all been part of this community for years, so she may know who to look for." Ella sat down and glanced at them. "Okay, moving on. Anyone have anything new to report?"

"I spoke to the construction company foreman, Don Zahnes, who reported the theft," Justine said. "He says this is the first time they've had an explosives locker broken into, and they've been in business for twenty-five years."

"When Justine mentioned that it was Valley Construction, I volunteered to go talk to the owner, Gary Ute," Anna said. "He and I were . . . friends . . . once."

"What did you get?" Ella asked her.

"The explosives are stored in a ventilated steel shed out in the back of the yard. The shed—actually a concrete locker with a steel door—is kept locked and they've never had a problem. Gary said that he went out to take inventory yesterday and that's when he realized that someone had cut off the locks and helped himself. Missing were five blasting caps, and three electrical and two non-electrical detonators with fuses. Also fifty pounds of ammonium nitrate and ten sticks of dynamite."

"The lot number of one of the missing electrical detonators matches the one used to set off the pipe bomb on campus," Justine added.

"What did you get from the prints, anything interesting?" Ella asked Justine.

"Lots of partials, most belonging to the crew who deals with demolition over at Valley Construction. None of the men have criminal records beyond minor traffic violations."

When no one else spoke, Ella glanced around the room. "I have a theory. Despite my hesitancy to believe in coincidences, it's possible we may be working two cases with separate motives," she said, then told them about Ford's problems at church. "Right now I'd like to go over all the hard facts we have and see what we can make of them."

She paused for a moment, and, assured she had everyone's attention, continued. "At least one of our suspects is an expert shot. We're also dealing with someone who knows how to make a bomb. This person may or may not be the leader, but he's well-read, or trained in setting up and running a covert operation."

"And someone who's familiar with codes," Blalock added.

"If you lump it all together, then it looks like we're looking for people from law enforcement and/or the military," Anna said.

"A non-Navajo would stick out on the Navajo Nation, and have trouble enlisting other Navajos. We're probably talking about one of our own people," Marianna said.

"Let me do a little digging and take a closer look at Navajo officers who serve in departments adjacent to the Rez," Justine said.

"Look inside our own department, too," Ella said in a heavy voice. "And, Justine, don't go through channels. We can't afford to tip anyone off, and we don't know how highly placed the individual or individuals might be."

"That'll take some finessing then," Justine said.

Anna regarded Ella thoughtfully but said nothing.

"Got something on your mind?" Ella pressed.

"Just a thought," Anna answered. "You can learn just about anything you want about bombs in a library, more via the Internet. The Patriot Act gives us the right to monitor the reading and search patterns of people of interest. Since we don't have any names, maybe we can get a lead from the librarians at the Media Center. It's possible they can point us to someone who has visited suspicious sites or has been reading books on explosives."

"I suggest that you forego the fishing expedition, Officer Bekis," Blalock said. "Get a name first. Then, providing you're able to demonstrate probable cause, get a warrant before you monitor a specific person. It keeps things clean. I'm getting close to retirement and I'd rather spend my future wading in a trout stream, not slogging through court proceedings."

Ella looked at Justine. "Try to locate Henry Mike for me. He's supposed to be living on the Arizona side of the Rez at Many Farms. Just don't make the trip unless the locals can verify his location. No sense in wasting half a day on the road. Recruit extra personnel if you need to, but only with the intention of interviewing Henry on domestic charges."

As Anna and Justine left, Ella glanced at Blalock. "Let's go talk to Louis Billey. We know he's got the weapons skills, at least."

Following the directions Reverend Campbell gave Ella, they soon arrived at an area of single-wide trailers on the mesa north of the highway, about ten miles east of Shiprock. In the headlights they could see that most of the homes had torn or missing window screens. Roofs were held down by old, junked tires, to keep them from shaking loose. Running water came via garden-type hoses running inside windows from a common faucet, and each mobile home had an out-house at the back.

Ella found the right trailer, judging from the number on the white sign facing the hard-packed dirt road.

"At least they have electricity, but I've never figured out why people stay in places like this," Blalock said. "If they'd leave the Rez, they could get decent jobs and better housing."

"Jobs here are few and far between, that's true enough, but leaving the Rez is equally hard for some of the *Diné*. Here, we have the sacred mountains and other Navajos who understand and value the same things we do. We have clans, and that means family nearby no matter where we go on the *Dinétah*. That's worth something, isn't it?"

He shrugged. "I've always made my own rules and I was never close to my family. They went their way, I went mine."

Ella had heard this before, but she didn't understand it. She couldn't even count the many ways her family enriched her life.

"Don't look at me like that, Clah, I like the way I live. There's freedom in it," Blalock said.

"Freedom to be lonely," she answered. She'd seen too many people on the outside wandering through each day of their lives, lost and searching for meaning and purpose. What a Navajo family gained by staying on the *Dinétah* couldn't be measured easily, but the rewards were there. Her own life with Dawn and Rose kept her connected to the past, the present, and the future.

Ella turned off the headlights and the engine and sat back. "We want cooperation, so we're going to afford them the courtesy of waiting for an invitation to approach."

Time passed. Ella saw the curtains of the old trailer move as a figure she couldn't see clearly peered out, but no one came to the door.

"No cars are parked here, Clah. We're wasting our time."

"She's there, and there's a light on. She's just testing us."

At long last, a middle-aged Navajo woman wearing a long skirt and a velvet blouse tied at the waist with a concha belt came to the front door, turned on an outdoor light, and waved.

"Good. The fact that she invited us inside will make things easier," Ella said.

The woman ushered them into the narrow living/dining room. Shelves and cabinets were loaded down with an overflow of canned goods and dishes from the kitchen. On top of the portable television, which rested on a window seat, was a photograph of a stern-looking young Navajo man in his Marine dress uniform.

"Are you here because of what that Navajo preacher did to my husband?" she asked immediately.

"We'd like to hear your side of the story," Ella said.

"Reverend Tome *promised* that he'd check on my husband. I wouldn't have left him otherwise." Her voice broke and she turned away, handkerchief in hand. "Everyone says that it wasn't the preacher's fault, but he didn't take care of my husband and neither did his God." She took a deep unsteady breath. "I should have taken my husband to a *hataalii*. My grandparents relied on them and they lived into their nineties."

A daddy longlegs spider crawled onto her chair and she captured it between her two hands and set it outside. After a moment she returned to her chair. "So you gonna arrest him?"

Ella blinked, but managed to keep all expression from her face. "We're here because we wanted to talk to you about him. It appears that someone wants the reverend to die. They've tried to kill him twice in the last three days."

"I didn't know that someone went after him a second time, but like everyone else, I heard about that bomb in Shiprock. And just in case you're asking, I had nothing to do with that. I've seen enough of death, believe me," she added in a whisper-thin voice.

"I know it's been difficult for you," Ella said, then focused her gaze on the photo of the Marine. "We understand your son came home for the funeral."

"He's here on leave, but he spends most of his time at some bar over in Bloomfield." She pointed to a matchbook on the tiny kitchen table.

Ella picked it up and read the name: Bottoms Up. "Is that his photo?" she asked a moment later, walking to the picture on the TV.

Seeing her nod, Ella took a closer look at the young man's face, memorizing it. She then handed the photo to Blalock, who'd come up behind her.

"How does he feel about what's happened to his father?" Blalock asked.

"I don't know. He won't talk about death . . . or much of anything else, either. He wasn't always like that, but the war . . . it changed him."

"Thanks for inviting us into your home," Ella said, heading back to the door.

Inside the tribal SUV, Blalock fastened his seatbelt, then glanced over at Ella. "It's still Sunday, Ella, but we're heading for the Bottoms Up, right?"

"Yeah, so keep your weapon tucked in and hard to reach. I've been in there once or twice and it's a rough joint," she said.

"Yeah, I know. It's a gas and oil field-worker hang-out, with enough overflow of local cowboys to stir things up. More often than not, there's a fight brewing."

"I think the guys go there to test themselves, you know?"

"Some men enjoy that type of thing," Blalock answered. "And that includes a few cops I've worked with. The theory is that it's a good way to keep their skills sharp."

"Or get knifed. I still hate that place," Ella muttered.

"Some women enjoy it. They go there 'cause they like rough men."

"I prefer wusses," she answered and Blalock laughed. Growing serious again, she continued. "I'm going to keep my badge pinned to my belt. Not in plain view, but I want to be able to move my jacket back if I have to, and flash it."

"They'll know you're out of tribal jurisdiction."

"Probably, but it may slow them down, and sometimes that's all that's needed. It'll be seven by the time we get there and by then, those who got off work at five will be working on their fourth or fifth beer."

"I've got your back, but I'm getting too old for bar fights, Clah."

"Don't give me that. I've seen you in a fight," she said with a grin. "You cheat and win." She still vividly remembered one time when Blalock had feigned a punch, then delivered a crushing kick to his opponent's groin, sending him to the floor in a moaning heap. The man couldn't even stand at the booking desk.

Blalock laughed. "At my age you take whatever advantage you can get."

Forty minutes later they arrived at the Bottoms Up, just south of the main highway junction in Bloomfield. The vast parking lot was filled with rows of big trucks and trailers, oversized company pickups, and a half dozen older models with construction gear and ladders in the beds. Ella took two ASP collapsible batons from the cup holder where she kept them for emergencies and tossed Blalock one.

"Would you believe a crowd like this on a Sunday? I can't imagine what it must be like on Friday night. Let's just find the Marine and get on with it," Blalock said as they strode toward the steel door of the sprawling one-story cinder block building.

To their surprise, the interior of the bar was nearly empty. Blalock looked at Ella and shrugged.

Seeing the bartender opening beer bottles and placing them on a serving tray, Ella went up to him. She pulled back her jacket, showing him her badge, and Blalock did the same before wandering off.

The Anglo bartender looked bored. "What can I do for you, detectives?"

"Where *is* everyone?" Ella asked, glancing at the few patrons watching an East Coast baseball game. "The parking lot's filled."

The bartender pointed to the big-screen TV on the wall. "The owner got tired of replacing the TV every time a fight broke out, so he built an outdoor patio with wooden benches and a big kerosene heater. If there's a problem, the boys have to settle it out back. The bouncers make sure everyone plays by the new rules and, best of all, the plasma TV stays intact."

"So most of your customers are outside right now?" Ella asked.

"Yeah. No big games are on tonight, so the guys got restless. When tempers started flaring, our people showed them the back door. They can have their drinks served out there, too. We have a small bar outside and kegs on tap."

Ella turned around to look for Blalock and saw him waiting for her by the back door. Joining him, she brought him up to date.

"I've already taken a quick look outside. There are a couple of drunks going at it. Everyone else is standing around watching, just like back in junior high. Can this day get any better?" he grumbled. "You want to split up while we look for our guy?"

"Yeah. The plus is that everyone's attention will be focused on the fight, so we shouldn't get any interference."

They made their way to the crowd that was gathered under the open-sided loafing shed and illuminated by lights on poles. Ella could see two men fistfighting in the center of a circle of about twenty men. Both fighters were Anglo, so she didn't give them more than a passing glance. Blalock worked his way around to the left. Ella took the opposite direction, passing a matter-of-fact waitress gathering up empty beer glasses left unattended at the wooden picnic tables. Two burly men in red muscle T-shirts, no doubt the bouncers, were on opposite sides of the circle watching the fight closely but making no effort to break it up.

Ella was about halfway around the tight circle of cheering onlookers when someone placed a hand on her hip. "You've got a nice ass, honey!" she heard in a whiskey-laced growl.

Ella spun around, brushing the redheaded man's hand away in one fluid motion.

The man, wearing the local gas company's uniform, laughed and moved toward her again. Just then a Navajo man in blue jeans stepped between them. Ella got no more than a quick glance at his face, but she recognized Louis Billey. Whose side was he taking, she wondered.

Before she could speak, two other Anglo men wearing gas company uniforms grabbed both of Billey's arms, answering her question. An enemy of her enemies might turn out to be an ally, but right now, they were both in trouble.

Ella stepped up and kicked one of the men, but her aim was off and she only managed to get his thigh with the toe of her boot. The man stumbled back, then lunged, throwing an off-balance jab.

Ella slipped under it and landed a fist to his right kidney. As he folded to the brick floor, another drunk reached out to grab her.

Blalock, his flexible nightstick extended, whipped the guy across the forearm and the man yelped, jumping back. He collided with another patron, who grabbed him in a headlock. Both stumbled into a wooden table, then fell to the floor.

"Cop!" Somebody yelled, and that only galvanized the attack against Blalock.

As Blalock moved to Ella's side, two more patrons rushed in, throwing blows. Ella blocked one attack with a jab to the man's substantial belly, but the big man quickly grabbed her by the hair.

Blalock slapped the man across the forehead with the nightstick, but then another grabbed him around the neck, trying to wrestle the FBI agent to the ground.

"Get the cop!" people started chanting in unison.

Billey moved in, watching Ella's back as she stomped on the instep of Blalock's attacker. The man let go and jumped back, barely avoiding Ella's kick. Ella, Blalock, and the Marine stood back to back, ready to take on all comers, but that only seemed to incite the crowd. There was no sign of the bouncers, and Ella couldn't really blame them for ducking out.

At least four more men came at them, the first ducking in low with a tackle. Ella grabbed the man's jacket and threw him into another man standing beside a table holding two beer bottles. Beer flew everywhere, and the men who'd collided started punching wildly at each other.

Ella called out to Billey, but he couldn't hear her above the din. When she grabbed the back of his shirt to get his attention, he spun around, swinging, and she had to duck fast to avoid the punch.

"Parking lot," she managed quickly, pointing toward the courtyard's wooden gate.

Blalock, at her side, also heard and nodded, then began moving in that direction.

Ella felt a thrown beer bottle brush her head as she hurried through the gate into the parking lot. Blalock was half a step behind. Once among the cars, she heard a third set of steps, and spun around, fists up.

"Whoa, it's me. You okay?" Billey said, his eyes bright with excitement. "You're good in a fight, lady. You a Marine?" he asked, a dribble of blood slipping out between his lips.

"I'm another cop. Special Investigator Ella Clah of the Navajo Tribal Police," she said, catching her breath. "Thanks for watching our backs."

"No prob. I've heard of you," he said nodding. "You out on a date, looking for a little action? Maybe I shouldn't have stepped in."

"No, I'm glad you did," she said, laughing. "Actually, we came here looking for you."

His expression darkened. "My mother . . . she called you?"

"No, but she told us where you'd be," Ella said, then introduced him to Blalock. "We're trying to make some sense out of a few things that have been happening on the Rez and were hoping you could help us," Ella said, telling him about the attempts on Ford's life.

"The attempts on Reverend Tome's life have nothing to do with either my mom or me," he answered before she could ask. "He's nothing to us now. My mom's going back to Traditionalist ways, and I'll be shipping out in another week." He paused, started to say something else, then changed his mind.

"Go on," Ella encouraged.

"I was just going to say that even though he's Navajo, that preacher sure has a way of making enemies among the *Diné.*"

"What makes you say that?" Ella asked, puzzled. She hadn't heard this before.

"I haven't been back for long, but I've already met an ex-GI who hates his guts."

"Who are you talking about?"

"Henry Mike. He blames the preacher for the split between him and his wife. Says it wouldn't have happened if the reverend had minded his own business," he said, and shrugged. "The guy's got an explosive temper, and the way he's been drinking, all you have to do is look at him wrong to set him off. He's dangerous as hell."

"So where can I find him?"

Louis shrugged again. "All I can tell you is that he was here two nights ago. I saw him take on three guys when one of them spilled Mike's beer. The bartender had to Taser him twice to bring him down. The guy's the size of a truck, so he can do a lot of damage."

Ella handed him her card. "If you find out where he's at, or if you run into him, give me a call. It'll stay between us."

"I don't think he'll be coming back here anytime soon," Billey said, frowning. "His head's not screwed on right. Just before that last fight, he told me he needed to hole up someplace. He said something about making a last stand that no one would ever forget. I have no idea what that was all about."

"Did he say where he was going?" Ella asked.

"According to him, a relative's place up in the mountains. Said it was empty now and he needed to get back in tune with Mother Earth, or something like that."

"Thanks for your help," Ella said.

They were back in the SUV a few minutes later, driving west toward the city of Farmington. Ella called Justine, and after relaying what she'd learned, added, "Find Mike's relatives and ask them where Mike would go if he wanted to hide out in the mountains. Our intel suggested Many Farms, so maybe we're looking for a place east of there in the Chuskas."

"Got it. I'll get back to you."

Ella glanced at Blalock. "Wanna pick up some dinner?"

"Let me guess. You're trying to get a bead on this guy so you can see him *tonight*?" Blalock asked, with a martyred sigh.

"Yeah, if it turns out he's still in-state, I'd like to find him," Ella said.

Blalock gestured to a fast-food restaurant just ahead. "Go through the drive up."

"You don't want to eat inside?" she asked.

"Not tonight. Just park where we can see anyone who tries to come up to us. You and I made some enemies in that dive, so the only way I'm going to be able to eat in peace is if we can watch our backs."

Ella and Blalock were just about finished with their jumbo burgers and fries when Justine called. "I've got a few interesting things for you. First, Henry Mike. According to a source in town, a distant relative of his, he did move to Many Farms after his wife ducked out. But since then, his aunt back on the New Mexico side of the Rez walked down into the desert to die. Now her home west of Sanostee is empty, so he may have decided to use it instead. A neighbor of the Mikes said Henry's always had his eye on the place, though he has to haul water, and the only heat comes from an old wood stove."

Getting directions, Ella ended the call and glanced at Blalock. "We won't get there for at least two hours. The last ten or fifteen miles will be on crappy mountain roads— more like jeep trails than anything else. But the middle of the night is still a good time. We'll catch him off guard."

"Dawn's even better on that score," Blalock said, "and we'll have the rising sun at our backs."

Ella nodded slowly. He was right. The only reason she'd suggested tonight was because she really hadn't wanted to go home.

"All right Dwayne," she agreed. "We'll wait and set out at three a.m. I've got the four-wheel drive vehicle, so I'll pick you up. Where you going to be, your apartment in Farmington?"

"No, let's meet at my office. Drop me there now instead of at home so I can pick up my car. I'll return to Shiprock in the wee hours and we'll be able to shave a half hour off tomorrow's travel time. Okay?"

After Ella dropped Blalock off at his office, she headed to the tribal police station. Still wanting an excuse not to go home, she finished some overdue paperwork that had been on her desk for days.

An hour later, Ella stood and stretched. There were two more reports she still needed to read, but she was dead tired now and might miss something important. It was time to go.

By the time she arrived home it was close to midnight, and the only greeting she'd expected was from the dog. But to her surprise, Rose was sitting in the living room, waiting.

"Mom? What are you still doing up?" Ella asked, knowing Rose was an early riser and usually in bed by nine-thirty.

"I wanted to speak to you, daughter."

It was her tone that signaled trouble. Ella sat down and scratched Two behind the ears, not interrupting her mother's silence.

"I spoke to your daughter tonight," Rose said at long last. "She sounds happy in the city and that disturbs me."

"She loves being with her father, Mom, and she's eager to experience new things. That's all there is to that," Ella said, trying to put a positive slant for her mother's benefit.

"She told me that her father took her to see a girls' school outside the capital, in Maryland. It was a beautiful country campus with a summer program, and she met some students her own age. She was the first Navajo the girls there had ever met. She said it was really cool. Those were her exact words, daughter."

Ella swallowed back a flash of anger and forced her voice to remain even for her mother's benefit. "I know that her father would like to see her go to private school back East, but he shouldn't have done this. He knows—or should know—that she's much too young to be away from home full time."

"Her father asked that you call him when you got home."

"Did he give you a cut-off time? It's late."

"I asked him the same question, but he said for you to call no matter what time it was."

Ella nodded, then went to her room, still feeling the chill of Rose's disappointment. This was one call she didn't want to make in front of her mother.

Ella shut the bedroom door, then called. Kevin answered on the first ring. "I just got in," she said, her tone guarded. "What's going on?"

"Relax. It's not bad news."

She waited.

"Dawn called for you earlier and left a message. Then she tried again and managed to speak to your mom," he said pleasantly. "Have you checked your messages yet?"

"No. As I said, I just got home." Ella looked at the answering machine on her desk and saw that the red light was blinking. "But I've already heard about her outing at that private school. You shouldn't have done that."

"She had a lot of fun, Ella, and the school is top-notch. There's no harm in letting her see the options open to her."

"It's *not* an option. A girl her age needs to be with her mother."

"Which brings me to the reason I wanted you to call me tonight. There's a private corporation here in D.C. that's looking to hire someone with your background and training. It's a terrific opportunity, Ella, and you'd more than double your salary. You'd be investigating white-collar crime and doing background checks on potential employees for businesses in the area. You'd have the challenges you need to be happy, but you wouldn't have to be in the line of fire every day. That means our daughter wouldn't have to worry every time you were late for dinner. The biggest plus of all is that Dawn would be able to attend one of the finest schools in the nation."

Stunned by the news, Ella didn't say anything.

"Did you hear me?" he asked, laughing.

"I—" She swallowed hard. She wasn't sure whether she should thank or shoot him. "What kind of a job did you say it was?" As the words left her mouth, she cringed. She'd worked hard to make a place for herself here at home. Why had she even asked such a question? The answer echoed in her mind—providing for her child, a better salary, better schools. . . .

"The company was formed by three retired FBI agents and handles everything from industrial espionage to government security projects. Your work would be varied and interesting, and you'd be making a difference, Ella. The biggest difference, of course, is that you'd be earning a top-notch salary for a change."

She started to argue that her present salary was more than adequate, but then stopped. Kevin knew better. New Mexico's salaries were among the lowest in the nation. But there were other considerations. "We have beautiful landscapes, abundant sunshine, clear blue skies, and a home that's paid for," she argued. "Not to mention tribal health care."

"You'd have even better health care here, and with the salary you'd be making, you could afford to live very comfortably," he said, and quoted her a figure.

Ella heard the number and although her thoughts were racing, she remained silent, too stunned to comment.

"And Dawn loves it here in D.C., too," Kevin continued. "She wouldn't miss the reservation all that much."

"She'd miss her grandparents."

"They could fly over. It would be a new experience for them, too. Or you could go home to visit. Weekend flights aren't all that expensive with the corporate discount."

Exhausted, Ella could barely process everything he'd thrown at her, but a sudden, disturbing thought renewed her energy. "You didn't tell Dawn any of this, did you?"

There was a pause before he answered. "I haven't spoken to her about this, but she may have put it together on her own. When I spoke to the former agent who planned to offer you the job, I thought Dawn was in her room. But as it turned out, she was in the living room right next to my office."

"You're not that careless, Kevin. You're a good lawyer, used to playing people. So save the excuses. Is that what her phone call was about?"

"No. She'd already spoken to Rose, but she'd wanted you to know all about her day, too. She really loved that school."

Before Ella could argue further, Kevin continued. "This job offer could open all kinds of doors for you, Ella. And it would give Dawn the kind of opportunities neither one of us ever had. Don't decide now. Give yourself a few days and think about it."

"I'll be in touch," she said and slammed the phone down hard.

She'd wanted to think about things a little more before going to sleep, but after a hot shower, exhaustion took its toll. She took a few moments to hear Dawn's excited voice on the answering machine—twice—but then knew she had to call it a day. The second her head hit the pillow, the warm comfort of her bed led her into a welcoming void.

FOURTEEN

— ✘ ✘ ✘ —

The alarm on Ella's wrist-watch went off at two-thirty a.m. She got out of bed and dressed quickly, grateful now for having taken her shower last night. Though still groggy, she moved noiselessly through the house and stopped by the kitchen to make herself some strong coffee. She downed the first cup quickly after cooling it with cream, then poured the rest into a thermos, black.

Ella met Blalock at his office twenty minutes later. As she pulled up, he was standing beside his vehicle, waiting. It was three twenty-five, and the sky was bright with stars and a full moon.

"If my calculations are right, we'll be there at around five," Ella said. "What a way to start a Monday."

"With luck, he'll still be passed out, or nearly so," Blalock said.

"Don't count on anything being easy. Think the worst and it won't take you by surprise," she muttered.

"What's eating you?" he said. "Something I should know about?"

She shook her head. "Nothing to do with the case."

"If you need to talk, I'll listen," he said. "I know from our conversation yesterday that *you* still have a life outside the job."

Ella considered it. She did need a sounding board, and some information. . . . "Have you heard anything about a new investigative firm in D.C. headed by former FBI agents?"

"Yeah," he said, looking at her in surprise. "PPS—Personnel Profile Security. In fact, I've been offered a job with them once I retire. One of the men running it is John Blakely, my former SAC in Denver," he said, meaning the Special Agent in Charge. "The work would put me behind a desk, overseeing operations, but the pay . . ."

"Is fantastic." Ella finished for him.

"Yeah, and I'd be getting my Bureau retirement check on top of that, too. The firm's got so much business they're thinking of expanding and setting up regional offices in Denver and L.A." He paused. "But how did you find out about them?"

"I heard that I'm going to be offered a job."

He stared at her. "I didn't realize your reputation had grown so much. Or did you know one of the agents from your days in the Bureau?"

"I know Blakely, but I have a feeling this was Kevin Tolino's doing," she said.

"Don't sell yourself short," he said. "I have a feeling it wouldn't have been a hard sell at all. Ethnic diversification makes them look good in D.C., and would be a plus if they set up shop in other major cities. Plus, it adds credibility to what they're pitching—that there's no case they can't crack."

"So you think I'd be the token Indian?"

"No, Blakely hires on talent and skills, not skin color," he said flatly. "So, you gonna take it?"

"The salary they're offering would tempt just about anyone with a pulse. And my kid seems to like D.C. and the advantages big-city living brings," she said. "But *I* have to be sure it's the right step, and I'm not there yet."

"You could really go places in a job like that, Clah," he said.

"Is that about me—or you?" she asked, accurately reading the undertone in his voice.

He expelled his breath in a hiss. "It applies to both of us. For me, the real question is do I want to keep working after I retire? If I took this job, I could build up a really impressive nest egg. Then, after a few years, I'd be free to do a lot of things I would have never been able to do on my pension alone."

"Face it, Dwayne. You're not the kind to retire anyway," Ella said.

"Not completely, no," he admitted after a brief pause. "The biggest draw for me is the type of work I was offered. I'm getting too old to be out in the field, chasing suspects down dark alleys or into bars, you know? Sitting behind a desk, earning that kind of salary, might just the ticket for an old war horse like me."

"If you want to continue to do investigative work, this is the perfect solution for you. But for me . . ."

"You actually like it here," he said flatly.

"Yeah, I do. I've got a good life, and my daughter is well taken care of. She's learning about our ways firsthand, which is important to me—and will be important to her, too, someday. I'm afraid that outside our borders she'll lose more than she gains."

"Why don't you talk to Dawn and tell her that? See what she says, then make up your mind. An offer like this one from PPS might only come once in a lifetime."

"True, and I *will* be talking to her. But, ultimately, it's got to be my decision. The thing is, I don't want to make a mistake I'll end up regretting."

"Then talk to Blakely or whoever makes the offer, and get all the details you can. Visit D.C. if it sounds promising, but do nothing until you're really sure. That's the best advice I can give you."

Ella had to concentrate on her driving as they left the main road, a narrow, gravel path that only gained the distinction when compared to the two ruts they were on now. It was darker than black in the narrow canyon, and the pine trees at times brushed the sides of the car with a soft whisper.

"I've worked on the Rez for nearly fifteen years, Ella, and I still can't wrap my head around some things. Living out here, for one. I've backpacked into some pretty isolated places on fishing trips, but living full time in the middle of nowhere? Not on your life."

As they turned a switchback in the trail, they got their first glimpse of the house—a low, corrugated-metal roofed structure with wood siding and a big stovepipe. The windows were small, and the door very solid looking. There was no vehicle visible, but that didn't mean Mike wasn't home. A wooden shed, big enough to contain a pickup, stood fifty feet beyond the house, and recent vehicle tracks led up to it.

Ella turned off the headlights, and used the parking lights to guide her a little farther before coming to a stop near the side of the house. They exited the SUV quietly, not closing the doors.

Ella pointed to the back of the house, then to herself, and Blalock nodded.

They moved forward with turned-off flashlights in hand and guns drawn. Blalock reached the front door as Ella moved into place near the back. He knocked hard, identifying himself, but nothing happened.

Ella tried the handle next and the door opened easily. She stepped inside, switching on the flashlight and aiming it low, and to her side. A quick sweep around the one-bedroom house revealed several boxes of rifle ammo and a bag of ammonium nitrate, but the suspect wasn't anywhere to be seen.

Blalock came in through the front door, having found it

unlocked, too, and glanced around. "Looks like Henry Mike's getting ready for a serious firefight. The question now is, where is he?"

"He's got to be around someplace," Ella said. "I doubt he'd leave this stuff just sitting here."

"Let's try the outhouse."

They slipped out the back door and went about twenty yards into the woods, along a narrow path, when they heard loud snoring. Ella glanced at Blalock and pointed ahead. A man was lying face down on the trail, next to an empty bottle of whiskey.

"This is how they freeze to death during the winter," Blalock whispered, shaking his head.

As they moved in, Ella saw that the suspect had a semi-automatic rifle next to him. Henry was also as large as she'd been led to believe. She motioned for Blalock to cover her, put her flashlight away, and crept toward the prone suspect, intending to grab the weapon.

The second she got close enough to do that, Henry reached out and tugged hard at her ankle.

Ella lost her balance and fell on her back, struggling to hold on to Henry's rifle with one hand and her own pistol in the other.

"FBI! Don't move!" Blalock ordered.

In a lightning-fast move, Henry rolled to his feet and dove down the slope into the trees.

"I've got him," Ella called to Blalock, tossing the rifle over. It would only slow her down.

"I'll cover the house in case he doubles back," Blalock called out.

Ella scrambled down after Henry. She moved as quickly as she dared through the pines, trying to avoid tripping over logs or rocks that were sticking up on the path.

Failing to find him as quickly as she'd expected, she considered the possibility of an ambush. Ella took several quiet steps, then stopped and listened for movement. At first, she was sure she'd heard the sound of footsteps, but then it grew quiet.

It was still dark, so Ella brought out her flashlight, checking the forest floor cautiously, but found no footprints. Henry might have feet the size of an elephant, but he knew the terrain and how to avoid leaving a trail.

After a few minutes, she finally stopped looking. It was dangerous to continue peering at the ground this intensely, knowing he was capable of a sudden rush when her back was turned. Her handgun was her only comfort now, though she wished it were a .45 instead of a 9 mm. Henry Mike was a moose, and a little extra stopping power would have been reassuring.

It wasn't long before she was forced to admit she'd lost him. Henry knew the area. If he didn't want her to find him, it would be nearly impossible for her to do so now.

Ella headed back and met up with Blalock, who was standing behind cover at a spot where he could watch both the house and the SUV.

"No luck, I see," he said, expelling his breath in a hiss. "Maybe I should have gone after him, too, but guarding his stash here at the house seemed like a better idea at the time."

"Even if both of us had given chase, we wouldn't have been able to corner him. He knows the area better than either one of us, and is incredibly fast." Ella looked at the shed. "Is his truck in there?"

"No, I already checked. According to the DMV he has an old Chevy pickup, but maybe he stashed it somewhere down the mountain. It's a long walk from here to the trading post otherwise," Blalock said.

"True enough," Ella said. "Too bad we didn't have a Taser handy."

"Yeah. I chose not to fire when he bolted because we

needed answers, not a body. I just never expected we'd come out empty-handed," Blalock said.

"At least we've neutered him for a while." She pointed to the rifle in Blalock's hand, a Remington autoloader. "What caliber, Dwayne?"

"It's a .308, and fully loaded. Let's see what else our boy stashed in there," Blalock added, gesturing to the house.

"Rifles are common out here," Ella said, falling into step beside him, "but I've never seen anyone outside an arms dealer with so much ammo on hand. Then there's the ammonium nitrate."

"Maybe he was involved in that burglary over at Valley Construction," Blalock said.

"Could be. If we also find some of the dynamite and detonators inside, we'll know for sure. As for the ammo, it looked like military issue to me, at least at first glance," Ella said. "Some of these guys have been known to smuggle back whatever they can."

"Yeah, but the bullets you recovered outside the gas station were civilian, not military issue," Blalock said as they entered the cabin.

"This guy's definitely not playing with a full deck—and his profile says loner. Look at this," she said, opening the closet door and showing Blalock a row of rifles, some of them military and dating back to World War II.

"That British SMLE and the Springfield are still top-notch sniper rifles," Blalock said, helping her search. "There's plenty of ammo here for those weapons, but I don't see any detonators. Look, a can of black powder. We should check this against what was used in the pipe bomb."

Ella took out her cell phone, verified that she could still get a signal, then called in the rest of her team, requesting an arrest-and-hold on Henry Mike. She then went back to studying the rifles, beginning with the two weapons they found in .308 caliber. The one in the closet was a hunting rifle with a scope. "Neither of these weapons have been fired recently."

"Here's a cleaning kit and it looks well used. He seems to take good care of his firearms. So what have we really got here, Ella? Someone who collects weapons because they make him feel secure, or something else altogether?" Blalock asked in a faraway, thoughtful voice. "These weapons are better suited for forties-era guerilla warfare, not present-day terrorism. Not an automatic weapon or handgun in sight."

"Maybe it's his way of maintaining an arsenal without really breaking any laws," she answered. "Or he could be selling them to collectors, or to hunters for cash."

"He doesn't have a criminal record except for the spousal abuse, but he's armed himself like one of the old-fashioned survivalists. What are we missing?" Blalock asked.

"Let's keep looking," Ella said. "It's getting light to the east and maybe we'll find something else."

Ninety minutes later Justine showed up with Neskahi and Anna Bekis. "Did you see anyone on your way here?" Ella asked the moment she saw them.

Justine shook her head. "No, and we were looking just as you asked us."

"This is quite a stash," Anna commented, looking around.

"Process everything here and let me know what, if anything, is on the stolen-weapons hotlist. Also, see if you can turn up any detonators or dynamite," Ella said, then looked at Anna. "We need to find Henry Mike's wife. She's going to know more about him than anyone else. I'd like you to focus on that as soon as you get back to the station."

"I'll find her," Anna said. "Count on it."

Something about Anna's tone of voice and the determination in her eyes told Ella that the job was as good as done.

As her team got back to work, Ella glanced at Blalock. "The sun's up so let's expand our search around the cabin.

He must have had a vehicle someplace. Maybe now we can find some tracks."

They hiked around carefully and eventually found a forest trail and tire tracks among a grove of ponderosa pines. Continuing down the narrow path, they came across an old abandoned pickup with its hood up. Though the keys weren't in it, it was unlocked, and the DMV papers in the glove compartment revealed that the truck was registered to Henry Mike.

A quick look under the hood revealed that a battery cable had worn out and corroded completely through. "He fiddled with the battery cables for a while and still couldn't get it to start up again, so he hoofed it from here," Blalock said. "But where to? The highway must be twenty miles away on these winding roads."

"Yeah, but the Sanostee Chapter House is only about five miles northeast of here," Ella replied, pointing down the mountainside. "He could have run down the mountain and helped himself to someone else's ride. Let's check out that possibility first. If not, then Mike's still in the area, and we'll need to go after him. We have some excellent trackers and it wouldn't take long for them to trailer in their horses."

As they hurried back up the forest trail, Ella used her cell phone to caution her team in case Henry doubled back to hijack one of their vehicles.

After Ella listened to Justine's preliminary report, she hung up and glanced over at Blalock. "They found some diesel fuel at the cabin. There was a small barrel with about twenty-five gallons just beyond the shed. Henry's pickup had a gas engine, so you know what I'm thinking?"

He nodded slowly. "Ammonium nitrate, diesel fuel, and a detonator are the basics for a really nice bomb, like the one used in the Oklahoma City attack. Fortunately, this bomb would have been way smaller than the one McVeigh constructed."

"How big does it have to be to kill one man?" Ella mumbled, picking up the pace.

About forty minutes later, they spotted a home they hadn't seen during their night approach. They parked and went in on foot, but soon it became clear that no one had lived there for years. The windows had been smashed and the doors were missing most of their hardware. Tumbleweeds were almost as thick inside the house as around the outside. "There's no hole punched in the side, so no one died here," Ella commented.

"Cheery thought," Blalock muttered.

"Abandoned places like these aren't uncommon. Squatters could have been kicked out, or maybe it's a matter of people walking away from a place that's falling apart because they can't afford to fix it," she said.

"When we first got out of the vehicle, I noticed the roof of another home just over the hill. Let's go check it out."

They arrived two minutes later at a stucco home. Its windows and doors were intact and smoke was curling out of the stovepipe poking through the tar-paper roof. There was no hogan visible, nor any sheep or other livestock, but the occupants had what looked like a pump house and a well.

"So, are they Traditionalists, or can we go up to the door and knock?" Blalock asked.

"When in doubt, wait," Ella said.

Just then, the front door opened and a young woman wearing a traditional long Navajo skirt and cotton-print blouse came out and waved.

"Are you here about our pickup?" she asked as they approached.

"Excuse me?" Ella asked.

"You're the police, right? My husband told me he'd use the phone at the trading post on his way to work to report the theft. We don't have a phone of our own. We figure the thief must have taken our pickup either late last night or early this morning. When I got up to fix breakfast, I looked out the window and it wasn't there anymore."

"I'm Investigator Clah of the Navajo Tribal Police. Can you describe the truck for us?"

"It's a faded blue, '66 Ford. It's no prize, but you've got to get it back for us. It'll take months and months for us to save up enough money to get another one."

"We'll do our best," Ella replied, then called in the description of the stolen truck. Manpower was thin on this part of the reservation, but a description of what Henry Mike was driving would help.

Continuing the investigation, they followed the tracks to the chapter house where the paved road began. From there it was about ten miles to the main highway.

"So what now?" Blalock muttered. "He could have gone south, then turned off in a dozen different places. Or maybe he went north?"

"To Shiprock, you mean. We better find him fast, then. He's a disaster waiting to happen. Henry's probably armed, has a problem with alcohol, and a reason to resent Ford. And he could have more bomb supplies stashed somewhere."

Ella updated her team, then she and Blalock headed back toward Shiprock. They'd been driving for about ten minutes when her cell phone rang.

"Got a problem, and thought you'd want to know," Teeny said in a clipped tone. "Someone's outside the fence line watching my place, so I called the PD. Unfortunately, the closest officer can't get here for another half hour. I've got things covered for now, so you don't have to worry. I just wanted to keep you informed."

"Be careful," she said, giving him an update on Henry Mike. "He may have another weapons stash, and bomb making supplies."

"Good to know," he said. "I'll keep you updated."

"For what it's worth, I doubt you're dealing with Henry Mike," Ella added. "There's no way he could have known Ford was at your place."

"Don't be so sure," Teeny answered slowly. "Ford took the dog and went over to the church by himself yesterday while I was out purchasing supplies. He never mentioned the trip to me, but I found out later when I reviewed the surveillance tape. When I asked him about it, he said that he'd gone to help Reverend Campbell. There was an emergency with one of the parishioners Ford had been counseling. She'd gone to the church looking for him and Reverend Campbell couldn't calm her, so he asked Ford for help."

"Let me talk to him," Ella managed through clenched teeth.

"Hang on."

A moment later Ford answered. "Before you say anything, I made sure I wasn't followed. I wouldn't have risked endangering anyone, but I had to answer that call. What you need to remember is that I'm a minister—first, last, and always."

"Your actions may have ended up endangering both Teeny and you," she said.

"Bruce has told me that the person out there can't come into the compound without frying himself. We're safe inside. He won't even be able to get a clear shot at either of us as long as we stay away from the windows."

"*Listen* to him, Ford, and do whatever he says. He'll keep you alive."

Ella hung up and briefed Blalock. "Looks like we'll be the first ones on the scene, so let's go in quiet and fast. If it's not Henry Mike, and I suspect it isn't, we're up against another unknown. That makes it even more urgent that we catch whoever's there."

"I hear you," Blalock said.

Ella contacted the station, advised the officer en route of her plans, then ended the transmission.

Once they were through Shiprock and within a mile of Teeny's place, Ella pulled over to the side of the highway. "Wanna grab the shotgun? It's time to armor up with some serious firepower," she said, opening the storage compartment and bringing out a ballistic vest. "You wearing, right?"

"You didn't think this manly chest was entirely mine, did you?" Blalock said, thumping his vest. "I noticed you'd stopped wearing yours—not that I've been staring at your . . . torso, Clah."

"It's been too hot lately," she said, taking off her jacket.

"I'd rather sweat than not be able to anymore."

"Good point." After strapping on the heavy tactical vest, she struggled back into her jacket, then brought out the case holding her long-range rifle and ammunition. "How good a sniper are you?"

"Truthfully? I suck. Wish we had time to go by my gun safe and pick up the two HKs. A submachine gun could swing any firepower problems back to our side."

Ella had used one of the Bureau-supplied Heckler and Koch MP5 weapons favored by many SWAT and other teams, and found them very accurate in urban situations and for clearing buildings. But the terrain around Teeny's place was more open, and she preferred the precise, longer range of the Remington .308 with the variable scope.

"How about the shotgun then?" Ella held up a bandolier with extra twelve-gauge shells. "I've got slugs and number-four buckshot loads."

"Your rifle will give us the range, so I'll take the buckshot and increase my chances of a hit, Ella. What's the plan?"

"The suspect will probably be positioned so he can keep an eye on the west, the direction he'd undoubtedly reason help from the tribal police is likely to come. Once we get an indication of his likely, or last, location from Teeny, we'll approach him from the opposite side of the building, using it as a screen."

"Sounds good. You can keep him pinned down with the rifle, while I advance from around the other end of the building."

Ella placed her rifle on the backseat beside Blalock, who'd taken that position so he could hold the shotgun for a quick exit. "I'll try to get a fix on our suspect," she said, climbing in behind the wheel and phoning Teeny.

"Last time the cameras caught a glimpse of him, he was on the north side of the compound, hiding around the cottonwoods at the base of the hillside," Teeny said. "From what I can tell, he's armed with either a rifle or a shotgun."

"My vehicle's unmarked, so we won't be sending out any alarms when we drive past your building. We'll park out of sight, then approach from the south. Hang tight and stand by on the phone. We're coming in."

Ella turned around in the seat. "Dwayne, you're going have to duck down so he can't see you as I drive past the compound. Once we get around the corner and out of his view, I'll pull over. Hopefully he won't have shifted positions much, but be ready to move once we stop. Teeny says our man is armed with either a rifle or shotgun," Ella said, adding, "This is sure turning out to be one heckuva morning."

FIFTEEN

— ✖ ✖ ✖ —

As they drove past the compound, Ella tried to locate the suspect without turning her head. That would have been a dead giveaway if he was checking every passer-by. She called Teeny to verify. "You sure he's there, Teeny?"

"Absolutely. My cameras don't lie."

Suddenly there was a loud gunshot. Ella felt a jerk on the steering wheel and the front end of the vehicle veered hard to the right. "Tire's gone and we're taking fire! Hang on!"

Ella did her best to control the SUV as it dropped into the shallow drainage ditch, but she could barely hang on, much less steer. She thumped her head hard on the roof of the car, then slammed her shoulder against the driver's side window as the front end came up the far bank.

The soft earth dragged the crippled car to an abrupt stop in a cloud of dust. Ella dropped down hard, bumping her stomach against the steering wheel. The impact knocked the wind out of her for a second, but then another bullet hit the rear of the vehicle, and that jarred her into action.

"Out—my side!" she yelled, pushing open her door and diving to the ground. Seeing the butt of her rifle beneath the door, she reached over and grabbed it.

The back door on her side opened slowly, then she heard a groan and a thump on the ground. "Dwayne? You okay?"

There was a one word curse, then another groan. "I'll live," Blalock said. "Your damn rifle came down on my foot, and the shotgun bounced over the back of the seat. Give me a sec. . . ."

Another bullet struck the side of the car, motivating Blalock. He dove away from the car, then turned and shoved the door shut with his left hand. Rising to his knees, he pulled out his pistol, crawled to the rear of the car, then looked around the rear bumper. "He's got us pinned. I vote for a new plan."

Ella checked her rifle and realized the scope had been damaged. She'd have to aim down the barrel, but it would still fire, and the barrel hadn't been dropped into the dirt, so blockage wouldn't be a problem. She flattened on the ground and fired beneath the car, hitting one of the cottonwood trees. The entire car reverberated from the blast.

"Damn, that's loud!" Blalock grumbled, but he dropped to prone, rolled back to the rear tire, and fired two quick shots with his pistol.

"Ella, Ella? Can you hear me?"

Ella recognized Teeny's voice coming from the telephone that was still inside the car, but she couldn't answer now. Her gaze remained on the cottonwood tree ahead until she saw movement. Both she and Blalock fired, and once again the car shook from the blasts.

"Ella, you've got him on the run!" Teeny yelled.

They heard two blasts from another weapon farther ahead, then silence.

"That's a shotgun," Blalock said, sneaking a quick look.

Ella scrambled up to her knees, set down the rifle, then found her cell phone on the floor of the front seat. "Teeny, I'm here. Was that you firing?"

"Yeah. The guy ducked down just as I fired some buckshot in his direction. I think he's taken off now. Move on in, and I'll provide cover fire."

Blalock stood, then opened the back door and retrieved the shotgun. "Glad to have an armed ex-cop around. Shall we?"

They advanced carefully, using the shallow ditch as cover, but once they reached the cottonwood trees it was clear that whoever had been there was gone. They found one brass .308 shell casing half buried in the dirt, apparently missed by the shooter, who'd again tried to police his brass.

A thorough search followed, revealing boot prints running down the gully to a side road that led from the highway to a trucking company's yard. Blalock volunteered to ask workers there if they'd seen anyone as Ella called to have her vehicle towed to the department's repair shop.

Leaving Blalock to his work, Ella went to the compound gates where Teeny, at the door and holding a Remington pump shotgun, let her in. Ella followed Teeny inside and joined Ford at the monitors. They replayed what the cameras had recorded, but all they could see was a hooded figure wearing a baseball cap and sunglasses. The distance was too great to show any distinguishing features.

"He stayed far enough from your cameras so the image would be marginal at best. That was no accident," Ella said.

"Then maybe it was Henry Mike. He's been around similar equipment in the military," Teeny said.

"So have most people who ever worked security. And if it's not Mike?" Ford asked. "Any ideas who it might have been?"

"I think this shooter was smaller than Henry," Ella said. "That guy's a moose. I'll have to check on Dr. Lee's whereabouts, but this doesn't strike me as her thing either, and the shoe size is wrong, too. To me, this had the earmarks of a law-enforcement professional, or maybe military. The way this person moved also makes me think we're dealing with a man."

"I tend to agree—but only to a point," Ford said. "Oversized boots can create a false impression."

Ella studied his expression carefully. He had that faraway look she'd learned to recognize. "What's going through your mind, Ford?"

"I think the time's come for me and Abednego to leave. You almost got killed today, and by staying here I'm endangering Bruce as well."

"That's the worst idea you've had so far," Teeny said firmly. "*You're* the target. It's the suspect we need to neutralize. By staying here, you're insuring that he'll have to come for you in a place we control. We drove him away, remember?"

"Yes, but he shot your vehicle—what, three times?" Ford noted, looking at Ella. "You and Agent Blalock could have both been killed."

Ella noticed that Ford's fists were clenched around Abednego's collar and the vein at his temple was throbbing. Anger . . . it was an emotion he rarely let escape.

"I've been shot at before, and chances are it'll happen again. Risks are part of my job. This is what I'm trained for, Ford."

"I want to stop the violence, not escalate it," he argued.

"To stop it, you need to take a stand and fight. The road to a greater good often demands payment in blood."

"Even that of the gentlest man who ever walked the Earth," he said, nodding and reaching for his cross.

"What's next?" Teeny asked, eager to get back to the business at hand.

"I'm going to bring in my team and scour the area for evidence and possible witnesses. Then we'll have to talk to Henry Mike's neighbors and locate his wife," Ella said.

"I advised her to leave the Rez, but not to tell anyone where she was going," Ford said. "Look for relatives and friends of hers who live outside our borders. She knew that the more distance she put between Henry and her, the safer she'd be."

"We'll handle it, Ford, but you've got to stay here."

"All right," he said, looking back at his computer.

Ella felt him sliding away mentally, going back to something he understood. But she knew he'd stay, and that would keep him alive. She'd ask him for nothing else.

Ella joined Blalock and her team and helped them sweep the area, searching for anything the sniper might have left behind, but he'd been pretty thorough. The only thing they managed to retrieve was the bullet lodged in their car. Like the other slugs recovered at the site of the previous attempt on Ford's life, it was a .308 hunting round in a caliber common to many military, sporting, and police-issue rifles. Unfortunately, the bullet was too damaged for them to be able to make a positive forensic link to a particular weapon.

Hours later, Ella met with her team back at the office. All but Marianna Talk, who was watching Jane Lee, were present. Blalock was there, too, as well as Teeny and Ford, via telephone speaker.

"I spoke to Marianna. Dr. Lee called in sick today and hasn't left her home," Justine began.

"She's also received no phone calls," Teeny said over the speaker from the compound. "Ford's found several more e-mails mentioning Red Rock. All of them were written an hour or so after the assault on Ella and Agent Blalock."

"So we have reason to suspect that she knows what happened. The question is, does she know who ordered the attack," Ella asked, "and how much advance notice was she given?"

"That's the key," Blalock agreed. "The media reported the story almost immediately, so even if she knew about it shortly after it went down, it proves nothing."

"It was on local radio stations ten minutes after it happened," Anna said. "Someone in one of the cars that passed the shot-up vehicle must have called it in. It didn't take long for officers with drawn weapons to respond."

"That sniper has serious skills. Hitting the front tire of a car going twenty-five—at that angle and distance—was an incredible shot," Ella said.

"Maybe he was unbelievably lucky," Justine said, then seeing the expression of disbelief on Ella's face, shrugged and added, "It happens."

Anna Bekis opened the notebook on her lap, then glanced up at Ella. "You asked us to research the background of people here in our department and in adjacent agencies who might fit the profile. I've been taking care of that and have come up with something interesting. . . . It's not exactly a perfect fit, but it was close enough to get my attention."

She cleared her throat. "About eight months ago an Anglo ex-Army sergeant named Frank Atwood bought some land in The Meadows area, south of the Hutch Canyon Road."

Noticing the confused looks, she clarified. "In the county, several miles north of Kirtland and that old gas flare tower."

Several individuals nodded, so she continued. "Atwood started his own survivalist group—The Freemen. Their compound is called Camp Freedom. According to the county sheriff, they stay to themselves and haven't posed a problem."

"Possibly because no one lives out there except rabbits," Ella said. "I read a story about them in the Farmington paper."

"Have you ever noticed that what they choose to call themselves is usually the opposite of what they really are?" Blalock commented. "In this case 'freedom' is probably the last thing they have."

Anna chuckled. "I also found out that they have their own Web site and it's filled with their cult propaganda. Near as I can tell, Atwood and his followers distrust everyone who doesn't think exactly like they do. He blames the absence of God from people's lives for everything bad that's ever happened," Anna added.

"So he's their spiritual leader, too. I suppose that means he could have a grudge against Ford for, say, theological reasons?" Ella asked no one in particular.

"The Freemen also have quite a bit to say on their Web site about the upcoming nuclear power plant. The Freemen think that something with that potential for disaster shouldn't be on the reservation. They're convinced that Navajo Nation leaders can't be trusted with something that has such a 'capacity for misuse,'" Anna said, reading from her notebook. "Those are their words, by the way, not mine."

"Maybe we should go pay them a visit," Ella said, looking at Blalock.

"We won't be able to get into their compound without a warrant, and we don't have enough to get one," he said.

"They've made significant purchases of weapons, reloading equipment, and supplies—including several types of gunpowder—but it's all legal," Anna said.

"What about their leader's background?" Ella asked. "Who's Frank Atwood and how did he end up here?"

"He served overseas in the Army and was wounded in Afghanistan bad enough to be sent home to Denver," Anna answered, holding up a photo of the man. "According to my background check, Atwood's held a number of jobs after his discharge, but has had difficulties adjusting. He writes weekly letters to area newspapers blaming the system, big business, and the failure of established religion for every problem facing the nation. He's an advocate of smaller, self-sufficient and independent states, and the elimination of income taxes, which he considers illegal. He's swayed others with his party line and that's how the Freemen got started. Those who become Freemen have to sell all their assets and put their money into Camp Freedom's nonprofit account, which also has tax-free status as a church. The official line is that it all goes to support the members, but I'd be willing to bet that good ol' Frank, the minister, gets a generous salary," Anna said.

"Sounds like a cult with a strong leader whose sheep follow him without question," Blalock said. "And the way he's got things set up, he doesn't have to deal with anyone he doesn't approve of—like the rest of the world outside his compound."

"Agreed, so why is he taking issue with events outside his walls? Those guys are usually isolationists," Ella said.

"Normally that's true," Anna said, "but about six months ago, he began trying to spread his influence and recruit new followers." She looked down at her notes. "He went up against the coal generating plant several miles west of Camp Freedom, and the older tribal facility farther south. The emissions from the smokestacks, according to him, were poisoning the land. The operators of the big drag line they use to scoop out the coal started finding bullet holes in their cabs. On two occasions the bullets caused damage to the machinery. That forced them to shut down and make expensive repairs. The companies have since posted more perimeter security."

"I can't say I know Atwood, but I've met him," Teeny said, his voice coming over the speaker. "He wanted to hire me to get something on John Buck, the man who owns the ranch just north of his compound. Buck wouldn't sell, so Atwood wanted something he could use against the guy to force his hand. He thought I was the man for the job because I'm Navajo and so's Buck. When I said no, it took him by surprise. He insisted on a meeting, hoping to change my mind."

Teeny paused, then continued. "When I met with him, he had two of his bodyguards with him—ex-Navy SEALs, judging from their tattoos. The plan was to lean on me if I refused." There was a pause. "Turned out he didn't have enough SEALs."

Ella smiled, but said nothing. Blalock burst out laughing.

"Here's the thing though," Teeny added. "These guys have learned from the Waco episode several years ago. They're very careful not to break any laws, or flash any weapons, and no one gets near Atwood unless he grants them an audience."

"We can't force him to talk to us," Ella said, trying to figure out a way around that.

"I know of a way to persuade Mr. Atwood to let you inside his compound," Ford said, his voice coming over the speaker. "I could go over officially—as a minister—and say that we're soliciting donations for our youth programs. I'll even issue an invitation for their children to attend our Bible classes. You could come along as my assistant, Ella."

"I don't think it's a good idea for you to go anywhere near that compound, Ford," Ella said slowly.

"From what I've heard, it's your only shot at getting inside," Ford answered.

Blalock nodded. "He's right."

"But if Atwood's behind the attempts on Ford's life . . . ," Ella said, letting the sentence hang.

"Neither Atwood nor his people would dare try anything there, not with you and the rest of his followers as witnesses," Ford answered. "I'm sure he's learned from the Waco disaster."

"Ford's right about that," Blalock said. "I've studied the tactics of these religious fringe and cult leaders, and their control over their followers hinges on their ability to present themselves as larger-than-life role models. Atwood wouldn't dare risk an open confrontation with a man of the cloth."

Ella thought about it, studying the faces of those around her. Most seemed to agree with Blalock and Ford. "All right," she said finally. "We'll say that we're part of a group that's canvassing the area. That way he'll know we're not alone."

"I like that," Justine said with a nod. "It adds another layer of safety to the operation and still gets the job done."

"Looks like your plan's the way to go, Ford," Ella said.

As everyone began leaving the office, Blalock lagged behind. "Stay sharp the moment you enter that compound," he cautioned, "And you might see if you can borrow some extra gadgets from Bruce Little. Hearing and seeing whatever you're doing would be very useful to those of us providing backup outside."

"But any evidence we'd get from an unauthorized transmission like that wouldn't be admissible in court," Ella answered.

"That's not the point. I was only thinking of it as added protection. That's why I suggested Bruce Little," Blalock said.

Ella toyed with a pencil on her desk, lost in thought. "I still don't like the idea of taking Ford out of Teeny's secure compound. If our sniper today had spotted Ford, he'd have become the target, not you or me."

"Ella, there's something you need to remember," Blalock said. "Reverend Tome's past wasn't all peace, serenity, and turning the other cheek. And from what I've seen, a part of him misses the challenges of those days. Preacher or not, he won't become a liability. He's got serious training and he'll be able to handle himself."

She didn't answer. She didn't have to. They both knew that truer words had never been spoken.

SIXTEEN

✖ ✖ ✖

Ella arrived at Teeny's the following morning wearing a conservative blue suit and sensible shoes. As Teeny ushered her into the main room, Ella saw Ford at the computer, Abednego at his feet.

"Ella," Ford said, standing. "I've never seen you in a suit and skirt. You look nice."

"Don't get used to it, buddy. When I left the Bureau, I thought I'd seen the end of city clothes," she replied, grinning. "So how are you three getting along?" she added, anxious to change the subject.

"The reverend's good company," Teeny said, his lips stretching back to reveal a healthy set of teeth.

Ella knew that was Teeny's version of a smile, but even his grins had a deadly edge.

"As far as I'm concerned, it's good to be able to talk to someone who understands codes, and the latest software— particularly the kind that's not even available yet," Ford said.

Ella chuckled. "My two favorite guys are nothing more than computer geeks." Taking the seat Teeny offered her, she explained what she needed.

Teeny went to one of the desks at the back of the room and came back holding a pair of devices the size of shirt buttons.

"These will relay whatever you see and hear. The reason I suggest that each of you carry one is because if one's compromised, we'll still have the other. You're going straight into the lion's den, Ella."

"I know," she answered softly.

"Since they're not exactly legal, I offered to wear both of them, but his way's safer," Ford said.

"By the way, Ella, here's an important heads-up," Teeny said. "Atwood's got a thing for Navajo women."

"He'll never place a hand on you," Ford said quietly.

The expression on his face took her off guard. It was more than determination—it was the cold confidence of a man who'd tested himself and knew exactly what he was capable of.

"If anything goes wrong, you'll have backup immediately. I've arranged things with a few . . . friends," Teeny said as he placed the bug on Ella's jacket.

"Don't say another word," Ella answered. "I'd rather not know."

Ella stopped by her car long enough to pick up a few things. Afterwards, she and Ford set out in his old sedan, which had been fixed then kept out of sight in Teeny's two-car garage.

"I know Bruce's place is basically a warehouse," Ford said, "but it's sure a comfortable one. I like having access to the wide range of computers he has in there, too. The only thing I hate is that, under the present circumstances, I can't leave whenever when I choose. I miss my freedom."

Ella nodded. "I couldn't stand being cooped up either."

"The most frustrating thing about it is that I know I can take care of myself. I would never take a life to save my own, but I'd never hesitate to kill an attacker to protect the life of an innocent." His gaze was direct as it settled on her.

"If you mean me, let me assure you, I'm no innocent.

And I'm quite capable of taking care of myself—and you, too—if need be," Ella said.

"And I, you."

There was no particular emphasis to his words but she hadn't expected the undertone of strength . . . and power . . . behind them. "You've never told me much about yourself— your past, that is," Ella said.

"I'm a minister now. That's all that matters."

"I've been deluding myself all these months, haven't I?" Ella said, her eyes narrowing as a sure realization swept over. "I barely know you at all."

Ford didn't answer right away. "The past isn't nearly as important as the present. You know how I feel about you. What happens next—that's up to us. But let's not discuss this right now," he said, pointing to the listening device.

Ella smiled and nodded, knowing Teeny was as close as if he'd been sitting between them.

"Once we get to the Freemen's compound, I'll take the lead," Ford said. "I'm more of a draw there," he said giving her a smile. "And I'm glad to see you came properly armed." He pointed to what she held on her lap.

"It was my father's Bible. Under the circumstances, it seemed more appropriate than my service weapon." She didn't bother to add that she *did* have a backup pistol nestled between her breasts. "Just remember that we need to see At- wood," she added. "He's the only one that matters."

"I know, and I've got a plan. I'll tell them that in exchange for a one-hundred-dollar donation, their children can attend fall Bible camp at Waterflow, tuition free. The way I figure it, only Atwood will have the clout to approve that."

She nodded. "Good plan. Also, if by some odd chance I get recognized, I'll point out that I'm the daughter of a well- known former Christian minister on the Rez, and I'm a vol- unteer. They can look it up on the Internet and verify who my father was. He was a fixture in the Four Corners until his death."

"I could also say that you're my bride-to-be." He smiled at her. "I can be *very* convincing."

"You don't have to tell me that, Reverend," she said, laughing.

They arrived twenty-five minutes later at Camp Freedom, a collection of metal-roofed buildings constructed on a rise in the rolling desert east of the Navajo Nation. The entire property was surrounded by tall, chain-link fencing topped by three strands of barbed wire. Further in was another even taller stretch of coyote fencing that added privacy and formed a wind break. The front gate, a solid metal structure that rolled sideways to open, was closed. At first glance, parked in their car fifteen feet from the barrier, there seemed to be no way for Ella and Ford to announce themselves.

"There's no one at the gate," Ford said, "and if we can't see them, they can't see us."

Ella drove a little closer. "Look at the left-hand gatepost. There's a video camera inside the shadow. They can see us, so let's do this Navajo style. We'll just park out here and wait until they get tired of staring and come out to check."

"That could take a long time," Ford said slowly.

"Fortunately, if there's one thing a cop and a preacher have in common, it's patience," she said, leaning back against the seat.

It took over forty minutes, but finally the green-painted gate slid open. A muscular man wearing a communications earpiece, olive green T-shirt, and camouflage jacket stepped out and came over to the driver's side. A leather strap on his chest and the bulge beneath his arm indicated he was armed.

"You're trespassing," he said. "Move on."

Ford smiled up at the man. "I'm Reverend Tome. The

Good Shepherd Church in Shiprock is conducting the sacraments of evangelism and community service, and we're soliciting donations for our youth program. We've come to Camp Freedom with fellowship in mind, and have something to offer you, and your children," he said, mentioning the Bible camp scheduled for fall.

"Sorry, Reverend, we're just not interested," the man said, shaking his head. "There's nothing for you here."

"At least let us introduce ourselves to those inside and invite them to The Good Shepherd services," Ella said, leaning forward.

The man took a step back, touching his earpiece and turning his head as he spoke into the microphone. After about a minute, he stepped up to Ford's open window. "You're welcome to come inside. Park in the center, next to the barrier."

As the gate slid to the right and they were waved inside, Ford glanced at Ella. "That was an unexpected reversal. Stay on your guard," he said quietly.

The compound, only visible from higher elevation and a considerable distance, was larger than she'd expected. There were six metal portable buildings of various sizes surrounding a central, larger two-story cinder block structure. Three large vans were parked at the barriers. A simple playground lay beyond the last row of buildings, flanked by two flourishing vegetable gardens. A line of concrete barriers, like those in business parking lots, kept vehicles from getting close to any of the structures.

They came to a stop before a barrier in the center. A man wearing a sidearm and headset exited the central building and walked over to join them as they climbed out of their car. He was older than the one who'd greeted them at the gate, but similarly attired.

"Excuse me sir, ma'am. I'm required to screen for weapons before you go any farther."

Playing their roles, they both managed a look of surprise. "You're kidding," Ford responded after a beat.

Ella sighed loudly. "Here. Start with my purse," she said, handing it to the man.

He looked inside, handed it back, then expertly patted Ford down. When he turned toward Ella she stiffened and raised her eyebrows.

The ruse worked, and he smiled, stepping back with raised palms. "That's good enough. Please follow me, sir, ma'am."

He led them to the rear of the compound toward one of the largest portable buildings. Ella saw two boys about eight years old playing catch beside a swing set, and a woman, armed with a pistol at her waist, walking from one building toward the other carrying a basket of laundry.

They finally stepped inside. The room they entered, judging from the portable chalkboard, textbook-filled shelves, and student desks, served as a school, though at the moment it was unoccupied. Across the room, through an open doorway, Ella saw two men in desert-camo fatigues with pistols at their thighs, military style. The guards were standing in a narrow hall, watching them.

"These men will take you from here," their escort said.

When the men motioned them forward, Ella's body stiffened.

"We're here to do the Lord's work, sister," Ford said, placing a hand on her shoulder as they circled around the rows of desks. "Don't let their appearance concern you. Our Lord protects His own."

The guards exchanged a quick look, but neither commented. The man who'd escorted them to this location didn't follow. After saying something into his headset, he turned and exited the building without further comment.

Ella was acutely aware of the .22 Derringer nestled in a custom holster between her breasts, and felt a certain degree of comfort from the weight. Despite years of undercover work, back in the days when she'd been Special Agent Clah of the FBI, the passive demeanor she was being forced to maintain was now starting to wear on her. She was itching for some action, and distracted herself by formulating a strategy for their defense, if it became necessary.

"Down the hall and into the office at the end, on your right," one of the men in fatigues said, pointing.

Ella walked ahead, though Ford tried to step past her. There was nothing noteworthy in the hall except for a half dozen children's watercolor paintings on construction paper taped to the walls. Each depicted a smiling, tall, muscular, short-haired man standing in front of the chalkboard, and was titled "Father Frank." For some reason the presence of this particular art gallery made the hair on the back of her neck stand on end. Perhaps it was the pistol on the hip of every Father Frank painting—or maybe it was his exaggerated smile.

Before they reached the door at the end, a tall, powerfully built man with closely cropped brown hair stepped out. The leader matched his photo perfectly—and, to varying degrees the watercolors of Father Frank. He was clean shaven and was, as accurately depicted in the juvenile art, carrying a .45 Colt auto at his hip.

"I'm Frank Atwood," he said, smiling and waving them inside. He nodded, but didn't offer to shake hands, apparently familiar with traditional Navajo customs.

"I understand you're here to ask for a donation for your youth program," he said as they took a seat in simple wooden chairs across from his heavy metal desk. "The Freemen aren't wealthy, Reverend, but we're God-fearing people who value the religious education of our children. I'll make the check out to the Good Shepherd Church, if that's correct."

Ford nodded. "On behalf of our youth program, we thank you."

Atwood wrote out the check and handed it to Ford.

Ford stared at it in surprise, then glanced at Ella.

She could see enough to note that it was for five hundred dollars. Her eyes widened, but she said nothing. She wasn't sure how Atwood defined wealthy, but in her book, and by reservation standards, someone who could casually give away that much money was certainly prosperous.

Ford was placing the check in his jacket pocket when one of the men in fatigues appeared at the door. He was holding a printout of some sort, and promptly handed it to Atwood.

Atwood read it over quickly, then looked back at his man. "Alert the gate to watch for intruders," he said, clipping his words.

Then Atwood trained his gaze on Ford. "I know that there are people in this area who have recently made you a target, Reverend Tome. Yet I was willing to invite you into our compound, and I was going to offer you our help. But I feel nothing but contempt for people who try to trick me," he added, his tone and gaze as cold as ice.

"There's a problem? I assure you that I am who I've said," Ford answered calmly—a direct counter to the anger in Atwood's voice.

Atwood's gaze was as cold as ice. "What kind of church business requires you to bring along a cop?"

SEVENTEEN

—— ✖ ✖ ✖ ——

From the second the guard had stepped into the room, Ella had known they were in trouble. The guard's body language—his stare, his stance, the way he rested his hand on the butt of his pistol—had signaled her in advance. Hopefully their backup outside the compound was well hidden from Atwood's lookouts, otherwise she and Ford could become hostages in an instant.

Knowing that diplomacy and training, not firepower, would be their best chance now, Ella smiled at Atwood. To keep the situation from escalating she had to convince Father Frank that no Waco-type raid was forthcoming. "I *am* a police officer, but we also have lives *away* from our jobs. I'm here on church business, and my defense at the moment is the Good Book."

Atwood stood, then took a step back, positioning his right hand within a foot of his holstered pistol. He nodded to the guard, who whistled. The second man in fatigues appeared, carrying a riot gun at quarter arms. "Convince me," Atwood said.

"My father was the pastor of The Divine Word Church until he died several years ago. This is his Bible. His name, Raymond Destea, is engraved on the front," she added, showing it to Atwood. "There's a lot more to my background you might want to read before you . . . overreact."

She wanted to demonstrate anxiety and uncertainty—not that difficult really, at the moment—but it had to be subtle and believable. Playing a role that didn't fit her background would simply make him more suspicious.

Atwood gave the man who'd brought in the printout a nod, and the underling left. The guard with the shotgun remained, not taking his eyes off of Ella and Ford.

"I greeted you as a friend, Reverend, and I'd sure hate to be proven wrong about you," Atwood said, his gaze flat and hooded.

"You won't be," Ford said easily. He turned to Ella and nodded, placing his right hand over her left.

Atwood took a step forward, his own hands resting atop the desk now. "You're a very attractive woman, Officer Clah."

"One of many reasons why I'm courting the lady, Brother Atwood," Ford answered while her jaw was still dropping.

Recovering quickly, Ella managed a composed nod and smile, though she would have much rather punched Atwood in the nose. Playing the lamb while among wolves went against her nature.

The man who'd left moments ago returned and gave Atwood another printout.

Atwood read the text, motioned with a simple gesture for the two guards to leave, then relaxed and eased back in his chair. "You have quite an interesting past, Investigator Clah. You even brought your father's killer to justice. I'm glad to see that you share The Freemen's concept of loyalty to family," he added, his annoying smile back again.

Ella met his gesture with a nod, but said nothing. She could almost hear Teeny breathing again, back in his compound. Atwood had no idea how close he'd come to a face-to-face meeting with the gate crasher from Hell.

"You mentioned something about Reverend Tome's enemies before, Mr. Atwood," Ella said, working to produce a pleasant conversational tone despite the tension in her gut. "What did you mean by that?"

"Like everyone else, I've heard the news about the attempts on Reverend Tome's life," he said, focusing on Ella. "We may have chosen to remain separate from the largely Godless, secular world, but we still have our sources. It's a matter of survival—our own."

"So what I've heard about Freedom Camp is true. You have very few dealings with the community outside these grounds?" Ford asked casually.

"It's better for us to keep to ourselves," he said. "That's why we have to decline your invitation to bring our children to your youth camp. But I would like for you to come to our compound and give our young people Bible lessons."

"I would be happy to do that," Ford answered without hesitation.

Ella wanted to take advantage of Atwood's apparent shift in attitude. There were questions that needed to be asked, but she had to go about it indirectly. "I'm curious. You mentioned that to survive, you have to be aware of everything that happens on the outside. But why not join the rest of society and help define what happens? You and your people could influence your neighbors more through direct contact, couldn't you?"

"Not as much as we need, unfortunately. There are things we're already forced to accept that may end up causing great damage to us."

"Like what?" she asked.

"Your new Hogback power plant, for one," he answered. "Your tribe claims it's doing a good thing, something that'll benefit everyone. It's supposed to be safe from catastrophic accidents, and non-polluting. All we hear are promises."

"You think tribal employees lack the competence to operate the generating station safely?" she asked.

"In matters like these there are things that are always kept secret. That's the nature of the beast, you see," he added. "I'd be willing to bet that it's nowhere near as safe a design as they've been claiming. Think of Three Mile Island or, much worse, Chernobyl. Nuclear power can be dirty and extremely dangerous."

"So you'd like to see it shut down?"

He shook his head. "No, not shut down, just closely monitored by local residents who have a vested interest in keeping their community safe. But there *are* people who want to see the plant shut down for good."

"Like who?"

"If the rumors are right, your enemies are in your own backyard, not out here. Haven't you noticed that all the protests have suddenly stopped? I'm reminded of a mountain lion—quiet but closing in, waiting for the right moment to strike. I hope your security is up to the task."

He paused and looked at Ford. "But as far as the attempts on your life, Reverend, that's an entirely different matter. You serve God, and you're not involved in political causes. The whole thing makes no sense to me."

"If the Freemen avoid contact with the outside, how do you stay so current on what's happening locally?" Ella asked.

"We don't watch TV or read the newspapers, but we *do* have some communication with members of the community," he said.

"How about sharing your sources?" she asked. "Lives could be at stake."

Atwood shook his head. "That's the cop talking now, and we're not compromising ourselves by becoming informants."

Atwood stood, indicating the meeting was over. An instant later one of the armed men reappeared. Ella suspected that their entire meeting had been monitored and recorded.

"My Freeman brother will escort you out." Atwood

looked at Ford and added, "You'll always be welcome here, but leave your woman behind from now on. An off-duty cop is still a cop."

When they were in the car, clear of the gate and driving away, Ella finally breathed easy. "We managed to avoid a real confrontation. That's a win—and maybe a miracle," she said with a tiny grin.

Before Ford could answer, Teeny called Ella's cell. "I've been monitoring everything and I wanted to let you know that the tone of Atwood's voice changed slightly when he told you to look in your own backyard."

"The man knows more than he's admitting," Ella said. "I could feel it in my gut."

"I'll ask one of my people to follow anyone who leaves that compound, and keep tabs on whoever they meet. Maybe we can track the information Atwood gave you back to its source," Teeny added.

"Excellent idea."

Ella hung up and glanced at Ford. "You've been very quiet."

He gestured to the bug Teeny had placed on his jacket and shook his head.

Knowing Ford was uncomfortable with it, Ella called Teeny and asked him to turn off the device. Once both had been deactivated, she focused on Ford once again. "What's bothering you?"

"This visit. . . . I went there undercover, propagating a lie, or at the very least, shading the truth and misleading people. That's in direct opposition to what God expects from me. I've betrayed a trust."

"You risked your life to serve the community and our country, Ford," Ella said. "That's brotherly love—the greatest of all the commandments."

He looked at her in surprise.

Ella smiled. "I *am* a minister's daughter."

His eyebrows shot up. "Until now, I never realized that any of what he'd taught you had actually sunk in."

"Most didn't," Ella answered. "Well, let me clarify that. It's not that it didn't sink in, it's that I didn't agree with a lot of the doctrine he was pushing. What I saw as just one of many ways to live a good life was the *only* way to him. I was caught in the middle, forced to choose between his religion and my mother's traditional Navajo beliefs. So I walked away, choosing not to choose," Ella said. After a long pause, she added, "Rather than disappoint either one of my parents, I ended up disappointing them both."

He nodded, understanding. "Could you still live with a servant of God even if you disagreed with the doctrine?"

"Excuse me?"

"Let me put this another way," he said, struggling to find the right words. "What I said in front of Atwood wasn't all talk. I'd like for our relationship to eventually progress . . . you know, to the traditional conclusion." He paused and cleared his throat. "I'd also hope that you'd say yes when the time comes."

Taken by complete surprise, she stared at him, dumbfounded. In her occasional daydreams, she'd envisioned a romantic proposal at sunset, or maybe at daybreak—but not in the car, on the job, and sounding so odd.

"I'm sorry. I'm bungling this big time. I can only imagine what you're thinking right now. Please don't feel pressured, this isn't an official proposal," he added with a shaky smile. "I just want to know how you feel about the whole thing. If it's something you can't see happening between us—ever—I need to know."

Ella smiled. "I wouldn't say never—not to anything."

"That's not a yes."

"Yours wasn't a question. We were talking possibilities," she teased. "Nothing official, remember?"

He took a deep breath, then let it out slowly. "I love you,

Ella. I have from nearly the moment we met. But our beliefs are very different. I know that hasn't been a problem between us, but if we ever had kids—"

"Whoa! Kids? Aren't we jumping the gun?" She gave him a gentle smile. "We're both happy the way things are. Let's not change anything for now."

"There are things we need to settle before we can ever look to the future, Ella. You're an open book with few secrets. Could you accept the fact that there are some things you'll never know about me?"

"Like what really drove you to become a pastor?" she asked, and his reaction told her she'd struck a nerve. "It wasn't just God's call, was it? You were trying to leave something behind. . . ."

He nodded slowly. "But you never can, you know. Certain things follow you."

"Could something from back there be the reason you're a target now?" she asked instantly.

"The Bureau people I worked for have looked into my past assignments and they've assured me that's not the case."

"And that's all you can tell me?"

"I trust you, Ella, but these aren't my secrets to tell."

Ella's curiosity fueled her imagination. More than ever she wanted to find out about Ford's past, but the last time she'd tried to pursue information, doors had shut firmly— and irrevocably—everywhere she turned.

"Now you're wondering who I really am . . . and if you want any part of the baggage I'm sure to bring," Ford said softly.

"No, that's not it. I'm just very curious about you, that's all. You were a little too cool and calm back there, even when that guy was waving around a shotgun."

Ford shrugged. "You already know that I used to do special work for the Bureau, Ella. Don't try to dig any farther into my past. You'll bring down a ton of grief on yourself. Believe me."

She did.

Less than an hour later, Ella was in Big Ed's office, along with Justine, Blalock, and Anna. Joe Neskahi was on surveillance detail now that Dr. Lee was back on campus, and Marianna was getting some much needed sleep.

"I want an update," Big Ed said.

"We don't have much," Ella said, giving him a report.

"The reverend's past, and the possibility that his former bosses are missing something . . . How much clearance do we need to open those files?" Big Ed asked Blalock.

"I've handled special ops in the past and have TS clearance," he said, referring to top-secret clearance. "When I tried to read his file I found critical information redacted—blacked out. To access everything, I would have needed even more clearance than I have. The Washington Bureau agent who studied the file told me that there's nothing in it that can help us. I insisted on taking a look for myself, but was told we had no need-to-know, so the file would remain closed."

"Need to know . . . ," Big Ed said slowly. "How are *they* determining what *we* need to know? They're not part of this investigation, *we* are. If anyone has the need to know, it's us."

"They told me that they've studied the matter in depth and have reached the conclusion that what's happening now is not related to the past. But I can tell you this much," Blalock said. "Bilford Tome is still considered an important asset."

"Because of his skill in cryptography, right?" Ella asked.

Blalock shook his head. "From what I've been able to put together, that's only *part* of his area of expertise."

"Unofficially, what else can you tell us?" Big Ed asked.

"Officially or unofficially, you now know what I do," Blalock answered.

Big Ed, visibly annoyed, nodded once, then looked at Ella. "What else have you got for me, Shorty?"

"My team has compiled a list of possible suspects who may or may not be working in conjunction with Jane Lee," she said, then gave Anna a nod.

"Only a few officers fit our suspect profile—expert marksman and proficient with explosives," Anna said. "Here they are, in no particular order. There's John Butler, an Anglo sergeant in the County Sheriff's Department. He served with the Los Angeles Police Department for ten years and has all kinds of specialized training, including SWAT."

"Where was he when the last attempt on Ford's life was made?" Ella asked.

"Backpacking into the Gila Wilderness," Anna replied. "So it's unverifiable."

"Does he have any connection to Dr. Lee?" Ella asked.

"None that I found."

"You checked his background without tipping anyone of your search, right?" Ella asked.

"My information didn't come from their personnel files. I couldn't access those without pointing a finger back to myself and this department."

"Then how—," Ella asked, then quickly held up a hand, and shook her head. "Never mind."

Anna continued. "Officer Danny Martinez is with the Farmington PD. He's taken a lot of special classes, most notably he underwent SWAT training with the Albuquerque Police Department. He's half-Navajo and his sniper skills are really extraordinary. His kill scores at six hundred yards are 100%, and 90% at a thousand."

"That's impressive," Big Ed commented, voicing what they were all thinking.

"Lastly, there's San Juan County Deputy Henderson

Whitefeather," Anna continued. "I think I've seen him somewhere before, I just can't recall where. He's Navajo and lives somewhere on the Rez. He was a sniper in the military, which puts him on a par with Martinez, maybe better. He has some explosive-ordinance training, too, but I'm not sure how extensive," she said, closing her small notebook. "I wasn't able to verify the whereabouts of these last two men during the times in question."

"It's still an impressive bit of investigative work," Ella said. "Good job."

"One last thing. I also managed to get photos," Anna said. "I thought Reverend Tome could take a look and see if he recognizes any of these men."

"Good thinking," Ella said, taking the photos from her and glancing down at the faces. "I know Reverend Tome met Whitefeather recently, though we were outside in the dark at the time. He was the deputy who visited Ford's home after the attempted break-in. That happened the same night as the bomb attack."

"Coincidence? Or something more?" Big Ed asked.

"Whitefeather took the call, and responded pretty fast for a non-emergency stop," Ella said, thinking back. "It might not hurt to find out if he's usually in the vicinity around that time. Also we should check and see if Dispatch sent him or if he volunteered."

"I'll handle that," Justine said. "And one more thing comes to mind, now that I think of it. The county lab never could find that lost .22 bullet Whitefeather said he turned in. What if he never did?"

"If it came from one of his personal weapons, he certainly wouldn't have wanted it booked in as evidence," Ella responded. "And I remember something about him using air freshener. That could have been used to cover the scent of recent gunshots originating from his vehicle."

"So we keep him on the suspect list. But what about

Henry Mike? What's going on with that part of the investigation?" Big Ed asked.

Ella brought him up to date. "He's still on the run. At the moment, we're trying to track down his wife."

"I've got a lead I'm following on that, Big Ed. I'll know later today if it pans out," Justine said.

Big Ed nodded to the group. "All right. It looks like there's plenty of work to go around. Get to it."

As everyone began filing out, Big Ed signaled to Ella to remain behind. "I'm thinking that you may be too close to this case, Shorty. Perspective is everything, and if what I hear is right, you and Reverend Tome are pretty close nowadays."

"Yes, we are. That's no secret. But if anything, that's an asset to this case. He'll trust my judgement far more than he would a stranger's, and that'll help me keep him safe."

"I'll take your word on that for now, Shorty. You've got good instincts, but be careful," he said. "This case is running your team in circles, and we still have no idea what Dr. Lee and her people have up their sleeves concerning the power plant."

Ella paused for a long moment, then spoke. "I think we're being played, chief. My gut tells me everything's connected somehow, but we'll need a lot more to go on before we have any definitive answers."

"Watch your back," he said somberly. "I have a real bad feeling about this one."

Absently, Ella reached up and touched her badger fetish. It felt cool to the touch, but she knew he was right. There was too much beneath the surface that had yet to be uncovered.

Ella drove to Teeny's shortly thereafter. As she took a seat in the main room with the wall-to-wall electronics, Ford swung his chair around and faced her. "I don't have anything new for you, Ella. I'm still working on the codes."

"I won't interrupt you for long. I just wanted to show

you some photos. I need to know if you recognize any of these men," Ella said, handing him the file folder.

Ford set each out on his desk, studying the faces. "I know this man," Ford said. "He's the deputy who came to the house the night someone tried to shoot Abednego. His last name was Whitefeather." He paused for several seconds. "But I also recall having met him somewhere else in the past. His hair was longer back then . . . I think."

Teeny, standing behind him, shook his head. "I've never seen Whitefeather before, Ella." He then glanced at Ford. "Maybe you remember his face from one of those traffic blitzes—the roadblocks checking for DWI. Or maybe it was at the scene of an auto accident?"

"He apparently lives on the Rez. Could he be one of your parishioners, Ford?" Ella pressed.

Ford's gaze remained on the photo. "No. I know the people at my church. Whitefeather. . . . I definitely recognize the man's face, but the name doesn't seem to fit. What's his first name?"

"Henderson," Ella answered. "Disregarding the fact that he's now a deputy, does his face strike you as someone you met in pleasant or unpleasant circumstances?"

Ford continued to study the photo, his eyebrows knitting together. "I can't tell you. There's just something about his face . . ."

"Then keep thinking about him, okay? You might be interested to know that the bullet from your front porch, which I gave Whitefeather to have processed, has disappeared. The county lab said they have no record of it ever being turned in," she added.

"Those people are top-notch, so my guess is that Whitefeather dropped the ball. He's either bent or incompetent. So what now?" Teeny asked. "Would you like my help digging up something on Deputy Henderson Whitefeather?"

Ella considered. Teeny had no equal when it came to getting information discreetly, but one slip could blow things sky high. Other departments were understandably protective of their people, and she knew Sheriff Taylor, Whitefeather's boss. If he thought the tribe was investigating one of his men without his knowledge, an irreparable breach would result between their departments. "Hold that thought. I've got some things I want to try first."

"Good enough."

Ella petted Abednego when he came over. "Anything more on Dr. Lee's blogs or e-mails?" she asked.

"We've been looking for the appearance of the words 'Red Rock' but so far there's been nothing," Ford said.

"The second you see them, let me know," Ella said.

"Of course," Ford answered. "And Ella?"

She stopped halfway to the door and glanced back at him.

"Watch yourself. It's the ones you think you can trust, like a fellow police officer—or a deputy—that'll pose the greatest risk."

"Have you remembered something else about White-feather?" Ella asked immediately.

"No," he answered, leaning back in his chair, his gaze focused on her. "It's just an observation."

She respected his instincts. Staying alert for whatever lay beneath the surface of things was what good investigators—and cryptographers—did best.

A short time later, Ella was driving west again on her way back to Shiprock and the station. She was lost in thought when her cell phone rang.

"It's Justine." Her partner's voice came through clearly. "Can you meet me at home? I've got an idea."

"Sure. See you in ten."

When Ella arrived, she saw Sergeant County Sheriff Emily

Marquez's unit parked outside. She realized then what her partner had in mind. Emily, Justine's roommate, was in the ideal position to provide them with additional information about Whitefeather. Most importantly, Emily trusted them, and would keep their interest to herself.

EIGHTEEN

✖ ✖ ✖

Ella walked up Justine's driveway. Although from the front it looked like a perfectly ordinary middle-class suburban tract house, Justine's home was large by reservation standards. The five-bedroom home, built by a wealthy Navajo businessman who now lived out of state, also had all the modern amenities.

Justine rented it for an extremely reasonable price because of the deal she'd struck with the owner. He'd wanted someone he could trust completely to take care of his horse, a surly stallion no one could ride. The horse was also known to bite and kick without provocation.

Justine came out from around the back of the house as Ella reached the front door. From the wet, gooey spot on her jacket, Ella surmised that Leggar, the horse, had tried to take another chunk out of her partner.

Justine followed her gaze and nodded. "I went to give him an apple, but my cell phone rang and he freaked."

Ella laughed. "I hope you smacked him on the nose."

"I threw the apple at him."

Ella sighed. "You two really do need to establish a better working relationship."

"It's hopeless."

Justine led the way inside. "By the way, I finally got a lead on Kim Mike. It turns out my sister Jayne's a friend of hers. The problem is, Jayne refuses to tell me where Kim's living now. She's afraid Henry will follow us, track Kim down, and hurt her again. I was thinking that if you talk to Jayne yourself, she might listen to you."

"All right. But first let's talk to Emily. That's why you wanted to meet here, right?"

"Yeah," Justine said with a grin. "Together, I'm sure we can talk her into giving us some unofficial help."

Ella nodded. She'd been the one who'd introduced Justine to the blond San Juan County sheriff's deputy a couple of years ago. Emily Marquez, divorced, had needed to split housing costs, and Justine had also needed a roommate, though for different reasons. After living at home, and being part of a huge family, the silence had gotten to Ella's second cousin.

"She's in the greenhouse right now. She loves those orchids of hers," Justine said.

Ella smiled. Orchids and the desert didn't exactly mix, but they were Emily's way of relaxing and staying sane, and somehow she managed to manipulate the humidity and other growing conditions.

"But Jayne's here, too," Justine continued, "and has to leave for work pretty soon. Maybe you should talk to her first."

"What's she doing these days?" Ella asked as Justine motioned her toward the long, black-leather sofa.

"She finally gave up the desk job at the motel and began working the evening shift at the Stargazer Café on campus. She says a lot of people who come in to buy coffee are really just looking for someone to talk to, and Jayne loves dispensing advice. She's never been happier."

"That's great," Ella said.

"Hi, Ella. You two talking about me again?" Jayne flashed

them a playful grin as she came in from the kitchen holding two large mugs filled with coffee and whipped cream. "This is Stargazer Café special mocha mix. It's terrific and not heavy on the caffeine, so you don't have to worry about staying up all night."

Ella tasted the chocolate and coffee mix through the thick mound of whipped cream. "This is really good," she agreed. "You've given me a new vice."

"Glad to share one of mine," Jayne responded.

Justine nodded. "This *is* terrific."

"Didn't I tell you?"

Jayne was a year older than Justine but nearly as petite. They looked so much alike that they were often confused with each other, a source of embarrassment for Justine sometimes when strange men came up and started flirting. Jayne was the wild one of the family, and had only recently shown signs of settling down with one man.

She sat down on the couch, then waited for Ella and Justine to follow suit.

"I need a favor, Jayne," Ella said after a moment, and started explaining.

Jayne shook her head. "I know what you're going to ask, and I'd love to help you, but I gave Kim my word of honor that I'd never tell *anyone* where she was. That idiot husband of hers is dangerous. She's lucky she's still alive, the way he used to beat her."

"What we're really trying to do is find Henry. Kim might be able to tell us where he's likely to hide out."

"And after you catch him, will you be putting him away for good?"

"We don't have enough to hold him. We just need to question him at this point," Ella admitted.

"Then I can't help you," Jayne said flatly. "You don't realize how crazy Henry is. Did you even know that he's been following you? He's been leaving messages on Kim's cell phone telling her all about it. He's determined to use you to lead him to Reverend Tome."

"No way he's been following me. That's just a bluff. I'd know if I'd picked up a tail—particularly recently. We've been extra careful about that."

"When I heard about the shooting that took place over at Bruce's place, I figured Henry had gone there hunting for Ford. If *I* know Ford's there, maybe Henry figured it out too," Jayne said.

"Back up a bit. What makes you think Ford's there?" Ella asked. Jayne and Teeny had been hooking up over the past few years, but she seriously doubted Teeny would have told her anything about this. Jayne was one of the biggest gossips in the Four Corners.

"He didn't tell me, if that's what you're worried about. You know that Bruce and I see each other, so when he broke our last date, I started wondering if he was seeing someone else. I decided to drive by his place and take a look. That's when I saw Ford in that old sedan of his, pulling into Bruce's garage. No visitors ever park there so I realized he was hiding out. After the bomb that hurt Ralph Tache, and the shooting over at Ford's place, it was obvious he needed someplace safe. What a better place than Bruce's? The last piece of that puzzle fell into place for me once I spoke to Kim. That's when I realized that Henry Mike's after Ford."

Ella had been afraid all along that Ford's little excursion to help Reverend Campbell had been tracked. Now that she knew she'd been right, she had to minimize the damage, if she could. "You're reading way too much into things. We don't know who was responsible for that incident at Teeny's. But if you are right and it was Henry Mike, all the more reason for us to find him—fast."

"If Henry's on a rampage, nobody's safe, especially his wife. Kim's not like you or Justine. She's not a fighter. She took his beatings for years. She loves the a-hole."

Ella grimaced. She'd never been able to understand why any woman would remain loyal to a man who abused and terrorized her. That was one of the main reasons officers hated responding to domestic calls. All too often, the woman would turn on the officer and defend the man who'd just hurt her, rather than see him get arrested.

"I'll do my best to ensure I'm not followed. But we have to talk to Kim," Ella insisted. "Other lives are at stake here, too."

Jayne considered it, then at last, nodded. "How about a compromise? Even if you can't see anyone, and all you have is a *feeling* that someone's tailing you, will you back off?"

"Yes, and I'll do you one better. I'll have Justine come with me. Between the two of us there's no way we'd miss a tail."

Jayne took a deep breath then nodded. "All right," she said, then recited an address in Farmington. "She planted a trail west into Arizona but doubled back and is now living with her second cousin, Alyce, who's a nurse practitioner. She found Kim a job working afternoons with her at Dr. Sanchez's office."

"Everything will be fine. Don't worry. We know what we're doing," Ella said.

"Henry Mike is really bad news, Ella. Kim says he has all kinds of rifles and ammunition, too. If he even hears that you know where Kim is, you and Justine will be in a world of trouble."

"Actually, I hope he does come after me for whatever the reason," Ella said with a lethal smile. "He'll find out the hard way that I'm not as easy a target as his wife."

Jayne looked at her watch. "I better get going. You know where to find me if you need me."

"Thanks for the coffee, Jayne," Ella said.

As Jayne left, Justine glanced over at Ella. "Shall I go get Emily?" she asked, finishing the last of her mocha.

"Get me for what?" Emily asked, coming into the living

room and sniffing the air. "That's Stargazer's coffee, isn't it?" Seeing their empty mugs, she sighed. "Next time pick one up for me, too, okay? I'm addicted to the stuff."

Emily sat down and stretched out her jeans-covered legs. "It feels so good to finally have time off! I'm not due at the station until the day after tomorrow, and I'm going to enjoy every single second of it. I've been working double shifts and I'm beat."

"Personnel problems?" Ella asked.

"Other law enforcement agencies pay a lot more for their services, so after four or five years, our deputies grab their résumés and move to greener pastures."

"The county and the tribe are going to have to wake up. Without enough officers out on the streets, everything will fall apart," Ella said.

"So what do you need from me?" Emily's gaze narrowed and she gave Ella a hard look. "I hope you're not going to try and recruit me for a special assignment. Unless County's working with you and will cover my shifts, the answer's no."

"All I need from you is some information, and your discretion," Ella said.

"What kind of information?" Emily asked cautiously.

"I can't tell you why I'm asking—not now at least—but I want to know everything you can tell me about a Navajo County Deputy named Henderson Whitefeather. I need to get a feel for who he is, what he believes, and so on."

"That's a tough call, Ella," Emily answered. "W—that's what he prefers to be called—doesn't socialize with the rest of the officers, not even for an off-duty beer or a pick-up game of basketball behind the station. I don't think he's ever said more than a few words to me, and that was in passing."

Ella gave her a surprised look. Emily was a tall, beautiful blonde and men gravitated to her. "Are you sure about that? Think hard."

"I'm positive. As far as I know, he's never hit on any of the other female officers, either. Come to think of it, I remember him saying that he had a girlfriend at the college."

"What else can you tell me about him?"

Emily considered it for several long moments. "Nothing, except that he stays to himself generally and isn't much for small talk. Do you want me to nose around some more? Maybe see if anyone knows his girlfriend's name?"

"Yeah, that would be great, but only if you can do it unofficially, and discreetly," Ella said. "Under no circumstances do I want Whitefeather to find out we're interested in him."

"I'll see what I can do," Emily replied. "And when you can, tell me what's up."

"I will."

As Emily left the room, Ella stood and Justine followed her out the door. "Are we going to talk to Kim now?"

"I'd like to stop by my brother's first. Then, afterwards, we'll go," Ella answered, leading the way. "Let's take my unit and you drive. That way I can use the time to try and figure out some of the things that are bothering me about this case. You can pick up your wheels later."

It was shortly after four when they set out. Clifford, like Rose, still refused to carry a cell phone so Ella couldn't call ahead. Clifford had told her more than once that he didn't want to be tied down to an electronic gadget, even if it was the Anglo world's lifeline. Rose, on the other hand, hated the cell phone on principle. She didn't want to be available *all* the time.

Ella's mother and brother were cut from the same mold. They were two fiercely independent people who were determined to fight the intrusion of what most considered a modern-day necessity.

"What do you think is at the root of the threat against Ford—a terrorist cell or an angry husband?" Justine asked her.

"I honestly don't know, partner. So far on this case, I

don't have even one clear answer. We'll just have to work the leads as we get them. If the terrorists are worried that Ford will manage to expose them, then it's also possible they'd come at him through surrogates."

"If that's what's happening, then Whitefeather's expertise and position as an officer might be worth a great deal to them," Justine said.

"We've been told that Whitefeather lives on the Rez, so there's bound to be someone who knows him. That's why I'm going to get my brother's and mother's help on this. They'll be able to find out more about him in a way that won't point back to us."

As they drove up the road leading to Clifford's hogan, Ella spotted her brother chopping wood behind the house. "Good. He's not with a patient. Do you want to come in with me?"

"Naw, I think I'll call the hospital and see how Ralph's doing," Justine answered, taking out her cell phone.

"Good idea. I'll be back in a few minutes, hopefully."

Clifford, who'd seen the SUV coming, smiled as Ella stepped out of the vehicle and approached. "It's good to see you! I've heard what's been happening—the shooting at the gas station, then the problem you and FB-Eyes had over at your friend's place. Are you okay?"

"Me? Sure. I'm fine. It's all part of my job, brother."

"Is there any way I can help you? I see your partner's in the car, so I suspect you're here on business."

"You're right," Ella answered with a smile, and quickly told him what she needed.

"I've never met this deputy, but I'll ask around. I should be able to get something for you fairly soon. Maybe even something about his woman."

"Thanks. I appreciate it." As she looked at her brother, she realized that there was something else on his mind. Rather than returning to her unit, she waited.

Long minutes passed before he spoke. "I'm very worried about our mother's husband," he said at last, following tradition and avoiding the use of names.

"Why? What's going on?" she asked instantly.

"My wife saw him visiting the heart specialist at the hospital."

Ella's blood ran cold. "Could he have been there with someone else?"

"It's possible, but when I tried asking him about it, he told me I was mistaken, that he'd never been there. He made it clear, too, that he didn't want to talk about it."

"Could your wife have made a mistake?" Ella asked.

"No. My wife was at the hospital visiting a friend when she saw him coming out of the doctor's office. They were less than ten feet apart, though our mother's husband didn't see her."

Ella felt a shiver run up her spine. Rose had buried one husband, and Ella wasn't sure that she was strong enough to go through that a second time. Herman was not only her husband, he was her best friend. Rose depended on Herman more than most people realized.

"I'll see what I can find out," Ella said. "But it's going to be difficult. Doctor/patient confidentiality trumps my badge."

"This doesn't necessarily have to mean that it's bad news, but I know he doesn't like going to a doctor, so I thought it was worth checking into," Clifford said.

Ella nodded in agreement. "Do you think Mom knows about this?"

"I have no idea."

"All right. I'll take it slow and see what I can find out."

Worried about her old friend and stepfather, Ella returned to the car. Herman had created a place for himself in all their hearts.

"Hey, partner," Ella said, climbing back into the car. "Help me brainstorm. Besides the obvious, why would a man who hates doctors go see a heart specialist?"

"To get information for someone else?"

The answer didn't make her feel any better. It only made her worry about her mother as well.

"Is something wrong?" Justine asked.

"I don't know," she said, confiding her worries to Justine. "But don't tell anyone. I need to find out more in my own way."

"If there's a problem, let me know, okay?"

Ella nodded, then changed the subject. "What did you find out about Tache?" she asked, hoping for good news.

"He's out of intensive care, and apparently lung function has been completely restored because he's off the ventilator. They're giving him antibiotics to stave off infection and he's improving steadily, but they still won't allow any visitors except family."

"I'm glad to hear he's on the mend," Ella said with heartfelt relief.

"Should we go see Kim Mike now?"

"No, not yet. Stop by my house first. I won't be long."

They pulled up at Ella's house less than five minutes later. "I need to talk to Mom for a bit. While I'm in there, find out if Emily knows anything about Whitefeather's schedule. It's about time for a shift change, so if he's just getting off, I'd like to risk trying to follow him home."

"Sounds good to me."

Ella went inside and found Rose in the kitchen, fixing a casserole for dinner.

"Tamale pie—your favorite," Rose said. "I hope you can make it home at a decent hour and share a meal with us."

"I can't promise, but even if I come in late, I'll be nuking myself a serving in the microwave."

Rose sighed loudly. "What brings you home this early? It's still afternoon."

Mentioning Henderson Whitefeather by name, Ella told her what she needed. Although the use of names was generally avoided, certain situations made it a necessity. "The man's supposed to live on the Rez somewhere."

"I've never heard of him, but I'll ask my friends and see if anyone knows him or his clan."

"Where's your husband?" Ella asked, looking around.

"He's been wanting more time to himself lately," Rose said, giving her a worried look. "Something's bothering him, but he won't talk about it. Men are strange that way. A woman will talk about whatever's troubling her, but men . . . well, they're different, aren't they?"

Ella thought of Ford. "Men are always difficult to figure out, Mom," she said with a thin smile. "It's all part of the package."

"But life's sure a lot better with them," Rose said, gazing out the window at Herman, who was outside grooming one of the horses.

"Then be happy you're together and don't worry about the details, Mom," Ella said, placing a gentle hand on Rose's shoulder.

Rose patted Ella's hand. "I have a Plant Watchers meeting later this afternoon, daughter. I'll ask around and see if anyone knows the man you spoke of."

"Thanks, Mom."

Ella was back at the car moments later. As she slid into the passenger seat, Justine closed her cell phone. "Emily said that she'll get us Whitefeather's schedule if she can do it without raising questions. But she also said that she's seen him at the Save More Grocery a few times, with a grocery bag in hand. She thinks that he probably stops there on his way home."

Before Justine could say anything more, Ella's phone rang. It was Agent Blalock.

"I've got some interesting news," he said. "We need to go back to Valley Construction. Can you meet me at my office?"

"I'm with Justine right now, but she can drop me off."

"Good. I'll see you then," he said.

"What's going on?" Justine asked.

"Blalock's found something of interest over at Valley Construction."

"Guess that puts another hold on finding Kim Mike." Seeing Ella nod, Justine continued. "I thought Anna checked them out. What's the deal?"

"I don't know." She wouldn't voice her suspicions— words had power and could bring things into being—but she couldn't stop wondering if Anna's friendship with Gary Ute had compromised her perspective. The problem was, she didn't know Anna that well.

When they arrived at Blalock's, Justine glanced at Ella. "Unless you have an objection I'd like to be in on this. I've trusted Anna to follow up on everything—from the original list of suspects, to processing evidence. If she's dropping the ball, I need to know."

Ella nodded. It was important for all of them to find out how much they could rely on the newest member of their team.

Blalock greeted them both amicably, offering them a seat when they stepped into his office. "I figured we needed to start exploring tangents and seeing where they led. With that in mind, I focused on the *amount* of explosives being purchased by appropriately licensed companies in the area. I started with Valley Construction, and discovered the volume of explosives they've purchased doesn't mesh with the inventory figures they gave Anna."

"Some *were* stolen," Ella said. "We've established that."

"That's not it. They've been buying a lot more than can be accounted for with the jobs they do—a lot more. We need to pay Gary Ute another visit," Blalock said. "He and his crew are working late up in the Glade, north of Farmington, on a road under construction between La Plata and Flora Vista."

Justine looked at Ella. "While you go with Blalock, why don't I go pay Betsy Dan a visit? She's the owner of the Save More. I can ask her to give me a heads-up next time she sees Whitefeather."

"Excellent idea," Ella said. "Also, keep what we're doing at Valley Construction confidential for now. I don't want Anna to know we're retracing her steps."

They arrived at the site about forty-five minutes later. The gravel road they came in on was blocked off by orange barrels and sawhorses with flashing yellow and orange lights. A white Valley Construction pickup and several pieces of construction equipment, including a big bulldozer, were clustered just beyond the barrier. A man in a yellow vest and hard hat stepped forward, waving a red flag, and another worker with a handheld radio to his ear motioned for them to stop and park to one side. Blalock steered into the indicated spot and parked. A second later, a loud explosion went off, shaking the ground, and dust rose from a location about a quarter mile farther up a long hill.

Ella ducked instinctively and so did Blalock. "I *hate* that sound," she said, remembering Tache and what had happened at the community college.

"I'm not big on explosions myself," Blalock said. "Every instinct I have tells me to duck and draw my weapon."

As they approached the road crew, Blalock flashed his badge, and Ella did the same, despite knowing she was out of her jurisdiction. "We need to talk to Gary Ute," she said.

The man picked up the two-way radio that he'd reattached to his belt and spoke quickly. "He's on his way here," he said, moments later.

Gary Ute soon appeared, walking briskly out of the juniper forest bordering a dirt trail lined with red flagged wooden stakes that mapped out the future roadbed. He stepped between two sawhorses and joined them. "We've got a lot going on here," he said brusquely, "and will be running out of light soon. What can I do for the FBI and the Navajo tribe?"

"It seems that there are certain things you forgot to mention when our investigator met with you," Ella said. "First of all, there's a considerable discrepancy between the amount of explosives your company orders and the number of charges you've actually set off."

"What are you implying? That I'm stockpiling explosives, or juggling the books?" he challenged. "Either way, you're way off base. I have a business reputation to maintain, and I can't afford mistakes like that."

"Then explain the discrepancy," Blalock pressed.

"I can't, not without looking at the books and checking out the explosives locker," he answered. "Give me some time."

"So you don't actually purchase the explosives?" Ella asked, playing a hunch.

"No, not me. My foreman handles that."

"Then that's who we want to speak to. Where is he right now?" Ella said.

"Up the trail about a quarter mile. We're loosening some stubborn bedrock from the right-of-way. Regulations require hard hats if you want to go beyond this barrier, so hang on while I go get some for you." Gary went over to the truck, then returned with two blue hard hats. "Here you go," he said, handing one to each of them. "Let's go."

As they approached the work area, Ella could see a second, larger bulldozer clearing away big chunks of rock that had been blasted loose from a large formation in the middle of the apparent new roadbed.

Ella glanced at Gary. "What's your foreman's name?"

"Ernest Haske. He's over there, next to the guy with the clipboard. Haske's the one with the metal box and the blue hard hat." Gary let out a shrill whistle, then pointed his thumb at Blalock and Ella.

Haske turned his head, set down the metal box, and took a step back.

"Crap, he's gonna bolt," Blalock said just as Haske spun around and raced off, heading toward a steep ridge.

They both took off after him, but a chase uphill on rocky ground was tough. Ella paced herself, making sure her breathing stayed even. She'd lived in this country most of her life and still ran several miles a week when she wasn't on a big case.

Blalock fell behind almost immediately, and she could hear his wheezy, labored breathing. "Clah, where's he going, to the top of the hill so he can—what, fly off?"

"Go back to the four-wheel drive," she called between breaths. "Make sure he can't get to the highway." For a man close to sixty, Blalock was in good shape, but this was no weekend run. The terrain was uphill and uneven. "I can outdistance him," Ella added. "Keep him moving up while I circle around and cut him off."

As she raced around the hill in an intercept course, she saw the suspect slowing down, looking around in a panic for a place to hide. The rocky hill was naked of vegetation higher than grass, however, and there were only a few rock formations big enough to provide any cover at all. She stopped and watched as he circled a big rock, then slipped down into a gap where the shade quickly hid him from view.

She waved to Blalock, who'd driven up, and pointed to the hiding place as she approached from above and behind.

For a minute she was reminded of a rattler seeking cover under a rock. If you reached in, or got too close, it would strike. Ella moved in cautiously, gun drawn, then peered down into the dark, narrow crevice. The split in the rocks extended to the far side of the hill, but it was clear there was no safe exit at that end. The only way out was to jump—more than a hundred feet straight down—onto a rock-covered slope.

Ella climbed around to the place where he'd dropped down, then stood there, blocking the exit, her pistol drawn. "Ernest Haske, I'm Special Investigator Clah of the Navajo Tribal Police. Give up and climb out," she said. "Unless you can sprout wings, you're not going anywhere."

The man didn't answer, looking back at the drop-off, desperately trying to find another option.

"You don't have any way out of this, guy, except past me. Be reasonable and climb back up. Keep in mind that I can sit here and wait you out. There are others who would come up and spell me when I got tired or hungry, but you don't have that choice."

"Okay, I'm coming," he said after a long pause. He was halfway up the crevice when he muttered a curse, grunted, and stopped.

"Don't play games, Ernest. I'm not in the mood for this crap," Ella said.

"I'm not playing with you, I'm stuck," he said. "I had the two-way on my belt, and now I'm jammed tight."

"So take your belt off," Ella said.

"Yeah, yeah, okay."

Two minutes later, Haske emerged. He held one hand up in the air, but his jeans had slid down around his hips and he was using his other hand to hold them up. "Let me go back for my belt. I've lost weight and these pants won't stay up."

"Stay where you are," she ordered.

Blalock appeared just then, breathing hard, and slipped far enough into the crevice to grab the belt. Seconds later the man was handcuffed.

"Why did you run?" Blalock demanded.

"I didn't know you were cops. I owe money to the pueblo casinos and I thought you guys were here to collect."

"Try the truth," Ella said.

"I want a lawyer," he answered.

"Okay, play it your way," Blalock said. "Makes my life easier, turning you over to Homeland Security. The bombing of a school . . . well, that goes under the category of terrorism." Blalock shrugged.

"No, wait a minute," he said quickly. "Terrorist? No way, man. I'm a good American."

"Thing is, Ernest, you've got access to explosives. In fact, you're the one who buys them for Valley Construction, and we know there's a big discrepancy between what was ordered and what Gary Ute has on hand. Since he doesn't order the explosives—you do—that makes you a person of interest," Blalock said. "Hey, don't worry. I hear Guantanamo isn't all that hot this time of year."

"No, listen, you can't turn me over to the military. I've got nothing to do with that bombing. I just do a little business on the side, that's all."

"What kind of business?" Ella snapped, urging him back down the mountain.

"A lot of small construction companies on the Rez are subcontractors on bigger jobs. Problem is, they don't have the permits they need to get explosives that'll cut away a hillside or break loose stubborn rocks. That's when they come to me. I provide them with small amounts of both explosives and detonators—just enough to do the job," he said, then added, "We make a small profit, that's all."

"Meaning you and Gary Ute?" Ella pressed.

"Well, um, Gary's doing real well for himself, and subcontractors get paid, too, so actually I'm picking up the extra money. That way Gary doesn't have to give me a raise."

"How noble of you," Ella said. "Then Gary approves of this little side operation—which, of course, is illegal?"

"I never told him about it. I work long, hard hours, and I never complain. I figure it all balances out in the long run."

"You're a treasure," Blalock spat out.

As Ella loaded him into the back of the tribal SUV, Gary

Ute came over. Once the prisoner was secure, Ella told Gary what they'd learned.

"That piece of slime," he said, his fists clenched. "I trusted him, and now he's going to rain down all kinds of crap on my company."

"We'll need to track down the people he sold the explosives to, but you'll probably be cleared of any charges. He's already admitted that you were in the dark about this. Unless we discover otherwise, you'll undoubtedly keep your license," Ella said.

"Will I need an attorney?" he asked.

"It wouldn't hurt to provide initial representation for him and yourself in order to protect your company, but from what we've heard so far, it's likely he'll be the only one going down. You'll be called to testify against him, though," she responded.

"No problem," he said, understandably relieved.

On the way back to the station, Ella noted that Blalock's color and breathing were normal now.

"I'm going to have to start working out again," he muttered.

"If you want a jogging partner, I'd be glad to come along."

"Great. You're bound to have enough breath left over to call the paramedics," Blalock said, laughing.

NINETEEN
———— ✖ ✖ ✖ ————

Ella and Blalock split a can of soda while taking a break in Ella's office. They'd wanted to let Haske wait—and worry—before questioning him.

After thirty minutes they went into the interrogation room, and found Haske eager to cooperate.

Ella slid a notepad and pen across the desk. "You can start by giving me a list of your customers."

"They're all legitimate businesses." He wrote down four names and the companies they worked for, then pushed the notepad back to Ella. "I was making their lives a little easier, that's all. Permits cost money. This way, they saved some, I made some, and nobody got hurt."

Ella studied the list. She recognized all but one of the names. "Anyone else? And keep in mind that if I find out that this is incomplete, I'll fry your butt. You get me?"

"That's it, I swear."

Ella reached into the file she'd brought in and pulled out Whitefeather's photo. It had been cropped so that only his face showed. "Do you recognize this man?"

He studied the photo, then leaned back in his chair and shook his head. "Don't know him."

"Take another look," Blalock said.

Haske did as he asked, and then shook his head once again.

"I recognize three of the names and the companies on your list, but not this last one," Ella said. "I've never heard of Jim Nafus or Roadrunner Construction."

"Guy's an Anglo. He works off the Rez."

"So how did you two hook up?" Ella asked.

"He used to work for Valley Construction as a day laborer. We sometimes need extra help, so we hire temporary workers."

"How often did you sell explosives to Nafus?"

He considered the question for several moments. "I think I've sold to him twice. He's the new foreman at Roadrunner Construction. They've got a small operating budget and low credit, so he was looking for ways to save the company money up front."

"We'll be back in a few minutes." Ella stood and signaled Blalock. "See if you can remember anything else. If you do, write it down."

Blalock met her out in the hall. "What's up?"

Seeing Justine farther down the hall, Ella called her over. "Forget about seeing Kim Mike at all today. I want you to check out Jim Nafus and Roadrunner Construction," Ella said, then motioned Blalock back to her office. "I'm trying to figure out the best way to proceed with Haske," she said, still standing, but offering him a seat.

"What have you got in mind?" Blalock responded, sitting and putting his feet up on her desk.

"With his access to explosives, Haske might be an asset we can turn. . . ." Before she could continue, Justine came to the door.

"I couldn't find Nafus or Roadrunner in the phone book. I'll need a little more time."

"Okay. Think in terms of a small company—and new. Check with the phone company and county records."

As Justine walked away, Blalock spoke. "Haske would be a great asset, but let's give him a few more minutes to worry before we offer him a deal."

A moment later Justine ducked her head into Ella's office. "I just got a call from Betsy at the Save More. Whitefeather's there. He's driving an oversized white truck, but she can't see what make it is from where she's standing. She did notice that it has a PAL, Police Athletic League, sticker on the rear bumper. If we hurry, we might be able to get there before he leaves."

"Let's go," Ella said. "Blalock and I will ride together. You take another unmarked and we'll work in tandem so he can't make us."

Seeing Anna coming out of the lab, Ella went over to meet her. "We've got Ernest Haske in room B. If we're gone for more than thirty minutes, offer him a cup of coffee and a bathroom break, then put him back in the interrogation room. Tell him we're checking out his story."

"No problem."

Ella and Blalock were back in his sedan five minutes later. "Tailing a suspect at night is going to be tricky," he said.

"That's why I'm getting Justine's help. We'll have to stick close."

"What part do you think Whitefeather plays in all this?" Blalock asked. "You think he could have planted the bomb and been the shooter in both incidents?"

"He certainly has the skill levels necessary, and his position of trust would give him some latitude and access. The night of the attempted break-in at Ford's house, Deputy Whitefeather showed up almost immediately, then admitted being one of the officers who helped at the bomb scene earlier. No better way than that to get a close look at the results. The county lab also insists he never signed over the bullet I recovered from Ford's porch. Being Navajo, he might have a serious problem with the power plant, nuclear or not," she answered. "But what's really bugging me is that Ford can't remember where he first met him. My instincts tell me we're missing an important connection."

"Trust your instincts. If it happened during Tome's previous occupation, that could be a motive for the attacks—not Ford's code-breaking efforts. Whitefeather may have had no problem remembering Ford. Have you been able to find any connection between Whitefeather and Dr. Lee, romantic or otherwise?"

"Not so far, but your speculation about Ford and Whitefeather intrigues me. We'll have to follow up on that. Without a motive, we can't be sure, but at this point we've got more reason to suspect Whitefeather than we do anyone else who fits the profile."

"Which makes it even more important that we find out where Whitefeather lives," Blalock observed.

"Yeah. I'm also trying to find out what clan he belongs to, or anything else that'll give us some personal information about him. Unfortunately, we can't get access to his personnel files without turning too many heads."

"I'm guessing you asked your family to ask around? The Navajo network?"

She nodded. "It was the best way of making off-the-cuff sounding inquiries that wouldn't necessarily get back to him."

He nodded slowly.

"In fact, let me call my mother right now and see if she's got something for me." Ella tried her mother at home and Rose picked up on the third ring.

"You sound kind of winded, Mom, are you all right?" Ella asked quickly.

"Yes, daughter, I'm fine. I ran to the phone, that's all. I just got back from my Plant Watchers meeting."

"Anything on the person I asked you about?" she asked, avoiding the name this time.

"Your brother and I know just about everyone on this part of the reservation—if not individually, we can usually link them to their clan. It's part of being Navajo and knowing that we're all connected. But this man is a complete stranger to us."

Ella heard Clifford's voice in the background. "What about my brother? Did he have better luck?"

Her mother asked, and Ella heard Clifford's negative reply. "We'll keep trying, daughter," Rose said.

"Thanks, Mom. Thank my brother, too."

"Are you coming for dinner?"

"Probably not. Just leave a piece of tamale pie in the fridge and I'll get it when I come home."

Ella hung up and glanced at Blalock. "A Navajo without family or a clan is almost an impossibility. Clans include second and third cousins and so on. I can't even imagine not being able to track him down through his relatives."

They crossed the river on the old steel trestle bridge, heading west. As they rounded the curve in the highway, now running north and south, Ella could see the Save More on the right, just ahead. Blalock slowed as a big white Ford pickup pulled out onto the highway, headed south.

Ella's cell phone rang with Justine on the line. "He's on the move," she said. "Betsy just called."

"We've got him. We'll follow, then let you pick him up if he makes a turn. At least we've got some go-home traffic to blend in with."

Blalock stayed well behind the truck, focused on the taillights ahead. When the truck turned west on Highway 64, Blalock was forced to brake hard for a car pulling out in front of him.

"Damn. The headlights blinded me for a sec. Where'd he go? He didn't know he had a tail. I'd stake my life on it," Blalock said, making the turn and peering ahead.

Ella looked off to the left. The parking lot by the high

school was nearly full, and two cars ahead of them had stopped in traffic, waiting for a chance to turn onto campus. "There's a summer league playoff game tonight. Maybe he slipped in while we were occupied. I don't see him farther down the highway."

"It's either that or we lost him," Blalock muttered, then in a more hopeful voice, added, "Unless those taillights down the road are his. . . ."

Ella contacted Justine again on the cell phone. White-feather was a police officer and if he had the right equipment in his car he could listen in on police frequencies and monitor their communications. "How close are you? We lost visual on the subject."

"I'm passing the Save More. You want me to go south, or turn west on '64? I can race ahead and maybe catch up to him."

"Forget south. He either went west or ducked onto the high school grounds," Ella said. "We'll pull off at the gas station just past the campus and keep watch. You drive on and see if he managed to get way ahead. We'll keep an eye out for anyone coming out of the school parking lot. No one leaves playoff games early. If he turned in there, he'll have to come back out this way."

Ella closed up the phone and glanced at Blalock. "If he didn't spot us, and we're right about that—"

"We are," Blalock said interrupting her.

"Then he's one cool, careful customer."

"Yeah, one with something to hide," Blalock said. "He's working real hard to make sure he's not followed, that's for sure."

As they waited, Ella reached up and touched her badger fetish. It felt cool to the touch. Seeing Blalock looking at her, she placed her hand back on her lap. There was no way she was going to try and explain to him how that worked. She couldn't even explain it to herself.

They'd only been waiting about five minutes when Justine called. "White Ford pickup, coming your way. It just passed me, moving east on '64."

"Got him," Ella said, seeing the truck in the glare of the streetlights as it stopped at the red light. When the light changed, it turned left, heading back into Shiprock. Blalock was quick enough getting back on the highway to also make the light, taking a yellow, and keeping Whitefeather in sight.

They followed him back through Shiprock, allowing a vehicle to pass them and provide a screen, yet going slow enough for Justine to close the distance from behind. When Whitefeather turned north onto the Cortez Highway, they followed at a distance, allowing the streetlights to help keep the pickup visible.

Twenty minutes later, north of Shiprock on the open highway, Whitefeather turned left opposite the Black Bear Trading Post. He then drove west up a dirt road that led to several small residences.

"I can't follow. He'll see our headlights for sure. We'll turn into the trading post parking lot and keep watch," Blalock said.

"You make the turn and see where he went," Ella told Justine. "Stay on line."

They waited, watching the fading taillights. Then Justine arrived, making the turn.

A few minutes passed before Justine spoke again. "He made a U-turn at the end of the road and is coming back to the highway. I'll have to turn into one of the driveways."

A few seconds later, Justine spoke again. "He just passed by, but he slowed down to take a look at my unit. I think he made me."

"Okay, in case he's still watching, get out of your vehicle and walk toward the residence, like you're visiting. We'll pick him up once he reaches the highway again," Ella said, ending the call.

Blalock and she were soon heading back down the highway, south toward Shiprock. They stayed well back, giving Whitefeather lots of room. It was easy keeping him in sight. The desert in that stretch of road was particularly barren, punctuated only by a few tall, isolated columns of rock, east of the highway, remnants of an ancient mesa.

About halfway back to Shiprock, Whitefeather turned east, driving quickly up a dirt track that led to a small dwelling in the middle of the plain.

Blalock who'd maintained his speed to protect their surveillance, glanced at his instrument panel, then set the trip meter as they passed the turn-off. "My guess is that's his final destination. I say we back off for now, then come take a closer look tomorrow, when he's at work. Just make sure that on her return trip, Justine verifies Whitefeather really settled in for the night and isn't waiting us out."

"Good plan. With the terrain and a rising moon, it'll be almost impossible not to give ourselves away if we try getting any closer."

"I'm sure that's why he chose that place," Blalock answered.

Ella informed Justine of the situation and their plans, then ended the call. "When we get back to the station, I'll find out if he rents or owns this house," Ella told Blalock.

"I thought no one could own a house on the Rez," Blalock said.

"You can own a house, but the land belongs to the tribe."

"Once we're back at the station, we need to start working on Haske again. He's been cooling his heels for over an hour," Blalock said, his eyes on the road. "And remind me to check the trip meter to see exactly how many miles it is to where Whitefeather turned off the last time. Otherwise, you might have trouble checking on the right house."

Ten minutes later, Blalock and Ella entered the station and headed down the hall.

As they passed Anna's office she came out to meet them. "Justine asked me to track down Jim Nafus and Roadrunner Construction. I searched for new permits issued off the Rez and here, and did a full search. A lot of businesses have the word roadrunner in their name, but there's no Roadrunner Construction listed. Same thing with Jim Nafus. The man has no driver's license and no Social Security number. I searched several databases and got zip."

"Thanks," Ella said. The news didn't come as a total surprise, but she had no intention of giving up on that lead yet.

By the time they entered the interrogation room, Haske was pacing nervously. "What took you guys so long?"

"Is there a problem?" Ella asked cooly. "We had to verify some of the names you gave us." She glanced down at the cup on the table. "I see you got some coffee."

"Yeah, one of your officers came in, but that was a long time ago," he said, showing her his empty cup. "I was going to start banging on the door next. I thought you'd forgotten I was here and went home."

"Have you remembered anything else about Jim Nafus, like where he lives?" Blalock asked.

"I have no idea. Like the others, he came to me. Word got around that I did business on the side," he answered with a shrug.

"What did he look like?" Ella asked him.

"Anglo guy with a buzz cut and an armload of tattoos. The one that sticks in my mind was a bulldog with USMC below it," he said. "The guy had a thing for black, too. Every time I saw him he was wearing a black cap and a black T-shirt." He paused, gathering his thoughts, then continued. "Something else I remember about him—no matter what the temperature, he always looked like he was hot. I think that had something to do with his weight. He's carrying an extra fifty or sixty pounds, most of it on his gut. He also wore a tiny hearing aid behind his right ear."

"What kind of wheels did the guy drive?" Blalock asked.

"Blue Dodge pickup. Plenty of chrome on it. Double tool-box in the bed."

"License plate?" Blalock pressed.

"All I can tell you is that it was a New Mexico license plate," he said. "Otherwise, I would have noticed that."

"How much did he buy at a time?" Blalock asked.

Before Haske could answer, there was a sharp knock at the door.

Ella opened it and found a tribal attorney she recognized, wearing his usual thousand-dollar suit.

"I'm an attorney, Mr. Haske," he said, breezing past her. "Mr. Ute hired me to represent you today. Don't answer any more questions until I've had the chance to speak with you privately."

Martin Tallman was one of Ella's least favorite attorneys. He was young, slippery, and out to make a name for himself by taking on the most notorious cases and winning—no matter what the cost. His high, flat forehead resulted in his nickname around the department—Hammerhead, like the shark.

Ella gave him a curt nod.

"I need time to confer with my client."

Ella nodded to Blalock and then stepped out into the hallway with him.

"I was hoping to get Haske to work with one of your sketch artists," he grumbled, as the door closed behind them.

"Tallman will want to deal. Let's see what he has to say," Ella answered.

Before they could give it much thought, Tallman appeared in the hall.

"That didn't take long," Ella commented.

"Feeding frenzy," Blalock mumbled.

If Tallman heard, he ignored the crack. "You read my client his rights and he's cooperated with you. How about a quid pro quo?"

"What did you have in mind?" Ella asked coldly.

"Give him full immunity and he'll testify, and also work with you to help get whomever you're really after."

"How do you know we're not after Haske?" Blalock countered.

"Judging from the questions he said you've asked him, you need my client to nail whomever set off that bomb at the college. He's willing to work with a sketch artist and whatever else you need. Also keep in mind that if you release Haske under his own recognizance, and he gets contacted by the bomb suspect, you'll have a chance to take down a genuine bad guy."

"Full immunity, you say?" Ella said, shaking her head.

"It's either that or his cooperation comes to an abrupt end. I may even be able to argue that he didn't understand his right to legal counsel."

Ella knew Tallman had effectively used that argument before, in the trial of a convenience store robber. Since the man's first language was Navajo, Tallman had convinced the court that his client had been confused by questioning conducted in English. The defendant had walked.

"Let me talk to my people," Ella said.

"I'll be inside with my client," Tallman said with a nod.

As Tallman left, Ella glanced at Blalock. "Looks like we're going to have to play this their way."

"You could dump everything into the lap of Homeland Security and threaten to have Haske locked up as a terrorist," Blalock suggested.

"Throwing in agents from yet another agency will only slow things down and we need answers now. Haske will be of more use to us if *we* cut him a deal."

"I agree, but I'm curious. *Who* were you going to talk to about this?"

"Just you, but I wanted Hammerhead to sweat a little," Ella said with a grin.

After another ten minutes had passed, Ella and Blalock went back inside the interrogation room. "You've got your deal, counselor."

"Does that mean I'm free to go?" Haske asked, his voice rising with relief and excitement.

"Not quite. I'd like you to work with one of our sketch artists," Ella said.

Haske looked at Tallman, who nodded.

"Yeah, okay," Haske said, looking back at Ella.

They brought in their department's top forensic composite artist—a local painter, actually, who worked at a tribal tourist stop sketching caricatures. As the woman worked on her laptop using high quality drawing software, an image based on Haske's description slowly took shape. It took over an hour to get the details right, but Ella and Blalock hung back and watched with interest.

Once the work was completed and several copies of the image were printed, Haske left with his attorney. Ella then met with Anna, Justine, and Blalock in her office. "We're looking for a former Marine. He likes tattoos, so visiting the various parlors is a good idea, in case he's had local work done." Ella paused, then continued. "This Marine may have served around artillery, aircraft, or maybe explosives."

"Because of his hearing problem," Blalock observed, with an approving nod.

"But the name's a fake?" Anna asked.

"Yeah, we're pretty sure of that," Ella said, handing them copies of the composite sketch and giving them the suspect's physical description. "Get on this right away."

Anna walked out, but before Justine followed, Ella stopped her. "Tomorrow morning first thing, you and I are finally going to pay Kim Mike a visit. Pick me up at the house."

"You've got it."

As Justine left, Blalock leaned back in his chair, and

stretched. "As much as I'd like to call it a night, I've got a feeling you've got something else on the agenda for us."

"I want to hack into Whitefeather's computer and set up a tap on his phone conversations, but I don't have a warrant."

"Not a problem," Blalock said. "We've had a terrorist-style attack on a federal employee who's investigating a potential terrorist cell. We'll have all the clearance we need. We can get a judge to sign off on this pronto. The Bureau can also get us a national-security letter which will require Whitefeather's ISP provider to turn over records and data pertaining to his e-mails and other communications. That requires no probable cause or judicial oversight. Plus, a gag order prevents the ISP from telling Whitefeather what we've done."

"Things have sure changed in the past few years," Ella said in a thoughtful voice.

"Progress."

"Sure, and I heard that it was safer to walk the streets in Moscow when the Communists were in charge. How much are we willing to give up? Maybe balance will be restored again someday," Ella answered.

"It's a different world. That requires new tactics," Blalock said with a shrug.

Ella sighed softly. "Have the monitors routed through Teeny's network once you've got things in place," she said at last. "Ford can tap into it from there."

The Bureau's clout, and the cooperation of Whitefeather's Internet provider, smoothed out what might have been a difficult process. It took less than forty minutes to get things set up.

Ella was at Teeny's an hour later, when he and Ford received Whitefeather's backlog of e-mail. "Even with the both of us, we're going to need time to go through all of this, and it's one a.m.," Ford said. "We might be able to do some tonight, but the bulk of this should wait until tomorrow, when we've got clear heads."

"I agree. And there's something else you might start thinking about," Teeny told Ella. "What we need most is to keep current. Waiting for the provider to send the e-mails to us isn't a good idea. A delay of even a few hours could be disastrous."

"What's our alternative? Can you think of a way to hack into his system?" Ella asked.

"Wireless connections can do the job, but I need to be close enough to set up the router. I won't need actual physical contact with his computer because I'll be picking up his WiFi, his radio signal, then relaying it here."

"It's pretty open around his place," Ella said.

"It's nighttime now and late—optimum time to do what I have in mind. Let's drive up there. I can set up what I need from a quarter mile away."

"Let's go." Ella looked over at Ford, then back at Teeny. "Will Ford be safer with us than here alone?" she asked, thinking out loud.

"I can be of more use here," Ford answered before Teeny could comment. "I could start going through this backlog of e-mails from the ISP."

"And Ford won't be here alone," Teeny added. "I'll call one of my men who specializes in bodyguard services. He lives in Kirtland and can be here in less than fifteen."

Good as his word, by the time Teeny got all his equipment loaded into the SUV, someone was coming through the gates. Ella immediately recognized the man—a short, stocky Navajo with a buzz cut and prominent ears. "Gerald Kelewood . . . I didn't realize he was back from overseas deployment."

"Yeah, for about six months now. He came to me when he needed a job and I hired him on the spot. He's not good with electronics but he's sharp in the field. He can handle himself and protect a target."

"I don't need a babysitter," Ford said irately.

"You need an extra pair of eyes to monitor things *outside*. Yours will be on the screen," Ella said.

After making sure Gerald was in place, Ella and Teeny left. Studying road maps that Teeny called up on his laptop, they soon agreed that the best access into the area was using one of the gas-well service roads east of Shiprock. This would give them the opportunity to approach the isolated home from a direction other than the main highway.

The terrain contained numerous arroyos that extended out like veins on a leaf. Choosing one of the low washes, they drove within several hundred yards of the small home without silhouetting the vehicle against the eastern horizon.

Once there, they walked as close as they dared, then Teeny got to work. He would access Whitefeather's computer first, then activate the relay as quickly as possible. Afterwards, they'd hide the remote transmitter in a waterproof bag within a trash bag and hold it to the ground with a big rock. At a distance, it would look like windblown litter, not uncommon within a mile of most New Mexico highways.

Teeny typed in commands on his computer then, after a while, shook his head. "I can't get past his firewall, even with this proprietary software. The only explanation I can think of is that he's got a really sophisticated system—one that's not generally recommended, or available, to the public. To hack in, I'm going to have to identify his software, and that means I'll need direct access to his computer."

"We can't risk breaking in to his house," Ella said, shaking her head. "Not yet, anyway."

"I can tell you this much—the kind of system he's got isn't something an ordinary computer user would even know about. That alone speaks volumes," Teeny said.

"It does," she answered nodding. "Thanks for trying."

They returned to Ella's unit and began the drive back toward Shiprock. "I'll drop you off and then head home, Teeny. I'm beat, and need to get some sleep," she said, stifling a yawn.

They'd been on the road for several minutes when Teeny broke the silence between them. "If anyone can find and break the codes this group's using, Ella, it's Ford. He's good, and he's like a pit bull once he gets going."

Ella thought about the sweet minister she'd thought she knew. He had more sides to him than she'd ever dreamed. Yet instead of pushing her away, this drew her to him. It was the curse of curiosity—and an overactive imagination.

TWENTY

——— ✖ ✖ ✖ ———

Ella's first phone call of the day came shortly after seven the next morning, Wednesday. She was at the table eating one of her mother's fabulous breakfast burritos when she heard her daughter's excited voice.

Ella felt love's pleasant rush of warmth course through her as she listened to Dawn speak at her usual, rapid-fire pace. "Mom, will you be coming to work here in the city? There's so much to do, and it's so—big!"

Ella heard Kevin's voice in the background telling her to calm down. She was glad that he was doing that much, at least. It was clear that Kevin wanted his daughter back East full time because he was convinced that was the right step for Dawn. Yet Ella wasn't so sure about that.

"Oh—Dad wants to talk to you," Dawn finally said. Before Ella had a chance to protest, he was on the phone.

"Will you be accepting the job offer, or do you know yet?" he asked without preamble.

"I'm in the middle of a case. I haven't had time to breathe, let alone think."

"Okay, but heads up: A former agent by the name of John Blakely will be calling you soon. He's one of the men

who started PPS—Personnel Profile Security—here in D.C.
I believe you've worked with him in the past."

"Back up. Blakely's going to be calling me? You gave
him my number?"

"Not yet, no, but I will when I get together for lunch
with him later today."

"No, hold off on that. I need time to think things through
before I speak with him."

"You really do need to talk to this guy. It's the opportunity of a lifetime, Ella. Wait until you hear about the benefits
package this company gives their people."

Ella thought about her daughter. Never having to worry
about finances again would change their lives forever. It was
all so tempting. "If he's that big on offering me a job, he can
wait a few more days. Tell him I'm in the middle of a very
complicated case—"

"The campus bombing? He already knows. He's the one
who told *me*."

"He *knows* what I'm doing?"

"Not specifics, no, but he mentioned that it's a sticky
situation—interagency—and that you're leading the investigation. Even with all his connections and his security clearance, he couldn't get anything more than that."

Ella breathed a sigh of relief. "Have him contact my
office and leave a message. Or send me an e-mail. I'll call
him back as soon as I can."

Ella closed up the cell phone and saw that Rose's unwa-
vering gaze was focused on her. "What's this about a job?"

Ella told her, expecting Rose to be angry but instead, her
mother nodded thoughtfully. "If what you've heard is true,
then you're facing a great career opportunity. What will you
do now, daughter?"

"I have no idea," she answered honestly.

"Remember that everything has two sides. Consider all
the aspects before you give them an answer."

"I wish my daughter's father hadn't opened this particular door right now. I have more than enough on my mind."

Before Ella could reply, Herman came in and Rose's attention quickly shifted to her husband. "I've made an extra breakfast burrito for you," she said.

"They're second to none, but I'm just not very hungry this morning."

"You should eat something anyway," Rose insisted. "I could fix you some oatmeal, just the way you like it."

"Yes, oatmeal, that sounds good," he said in a more spirited voice. "And whole wheat toast."

Rose glanced at Ella and, in that brief moment, she saw the fear in her mother's eyes.

"Are you feeling okay?" Ella asked Herman.

"Sure. Just watching my figure," he answered with a quick half-smile.

Ella was about to gently press him for more of an answer when Justine walked in. Seeing the uneaten breakfast burrito still on the stove, she looked at Rose hopefully.

Rose laughed and nodded. "Help yourself, youngster."

Justine didn't have to be asked twice. While Ella went to retrieve her gun and grab her jacket, her second cousin ate breakfast. They were on their way moments later.

"Your mother is still the best cook around. You're lucky to have her," Justine said, licking her lips.

Ella thought about the job offer in D.C. and all the changes that would bring into her life if she accepted. For one, Rose wouldn't make the move with her.

Ella considered talking to Justine about the offer, but then decided to wait until she had more information. Leaving would also break up their team, and that wasn't something she wanted to mention as a possibility until all the details were on the table and it became a serious consideration.

"Kim's staying on Farmington's south side, across the Animas River. It's an area of modest housing off of Hydro

Plant Road. I have a friend who lives several blocks east from there, along the Bloomfield highway."

Ella kept her eyes on the passenger-side mirror while Justine concentrated on the road. Morning traffic was heavy today and fast moving, but she was sure that they weren't being followed.

Once they reached Farmington, she had Justine circle several blocks in the downtown area off Main and Broadway, to shake any potential tail. Satisfied at last, they crossed the Animas River, where Broadway became Bloomfield Boulevard, and headed back west to Kim's.

"There's no guarantee she'll be home when we get there," Ella said, thinking out loud. "But I didn't want to call and let her know we were coming. She's supposed to work afternoons, so this looked to be our best shot."

"If she's not there, do you want to wait?"

Ella nodded. "At least for a bit."

They arrived at the address, an old stucco house with a sagging roof. An '80s-model Ford sedan was parked in the driveway. "It looks like someone's here," Justine said.

Ella went up to the door, Justine beside her, and knocked. Moments later, a young Navajo woman wearing jeans and a sweatshirt answered the door. Ella immediately noticed that she stayed well back, in shadow.

Though Ella had her badge in plain view, it was Justine who first caught Kim's attention. "You're Jayne's sister," Kim said, not making it a question. "You look a lot like her." Glancing back at Ella, she added, "Jayne told me you two would be by. You're *sure* you weren't followed?"

"Absolutely certain," Ella answered.

Kim invited them into the tiny living room and waved them to the sofa. "Make yourselves comfortable," she said, taking a quick look out the window.

Declining coffee, Ella got down to business. "We have to

find your husband because we believe he has information about a crime we're investigating."

"Have you tried his aunt's house in the mountains? He's happier there than anywhere else."

"We looked. He's not there," Ella said, not wanting to give any details of their previous encounter with Henry.

Kim thought about it for a few minutes. "There's one other place I know he likes to go. His father built a hogan close to the river, north of the Hogback oil field. His dad's gone now, but Henry goes there when he wants to be alone, which is most of the time these days. Thank goodness for that."

"Thanks. We'll check there," Ella said, standing up.

"Be careful," Kim said softly, seeing them to the door. "Henry was really poor growing up and it's made him really bitter. That's what led to his awful temper."

Ella had to bite her tongue, but managed not to reply. By the time they were back in the car, she noticed that Justine was grinding her teeth.

"Lots of Navajos were poor growing up," Ella said, shaking her head. "That's no excuse for cruelty and abuse."

"The guy's walking garbage. I'm surprised anyone would have stayed with him as long as she did."

Ella took a steadying breath and forced the thought out of her head for now. "Let's drive over to the hogan, but take Highway 64 and cross the river at Fruitland instead of at Hogback. If he's in the area, he might be watching bridge traffic."

"Should we get backup?"

Ella considered it, then nodded. "See if Joe can meet us there, but have him hang back and be ready to block the Hogback escape route with his vehicle. Call Phillip Cloud, too. That's part of the area he patrols, I think, and he can come in behind us and cover the road east with his unit."

Justine made the calls and as soon as she was done, Ella continued.

"We'll park a ways off from the hogan itself, and check it out for signs that'll confirm he's there. We should also go on the assumption he's heavily armed."

"Yeah. He could have another stash," Justine agreed.

The road from Fruitland ran along the bluff south of the river and they stopped beside the road, at a point just east of the hogan, putting the morning sun at their backs. Walking away from the vehicle, they approached the edge of the bluff and looked down. They could see a pickup not far from the hogan.

"A true New Mexico son, he's got the standard-issue gun rack in the cab and I see a rifle or shotgun there, along with a fishing rod," Ella said. She focused her binoculars on the hogan next. It was constructed close enough to the base of the cliff to be protected from a westerly wind, but far enough away not to be caught in runoff from the high ground. A metal chimney poking through the roof indicated the owner had a wood stove.

"Should we look for a way down there?" Justine asked.

"No, not yet. He just came out of the hogan and he's walking around, weaving slightly, so I'm guessing he's been drinking," she said. "Yup, I was right. He just dropped a bottle onto a pile of empties on the ground. He has a pistol on his hip, too—an autoloader. Let's sit tight and wait for Joe and Phillip. Once they have our backs, we can move in."

"If he's drunk, that'll make him meaner," Justine said in a taut voice. "And even without binoculars, I can see he's as big as a sumo wrestler. I bet he'd give even Tee—Bruce—a good fight."

"I wouldn't want to be in the same room if that ever went down," Ella said somberly. "The good news is that his drinking should slow his reaction time and destroy his aim."

"Why do you think he's wearing a pistol? Do you think he's expecting trouble?" Justine asked.

"He knows he's a fugitive and my guess is that he's hoping for some action. There's not much out here to keep him occupied besides a bottle—and maybe a little fishing," Ella added. "He's going back into the hogan now."

"What strategy do we use to get him out of the hogan once we're ready to move in?" Justine asked.

"We'll approach on foot from his blind side and pretend we're breaking into his truck."

"As long as he doesn't see us coming through a gap in the logs, that should get him out," Justine agreed.

Ella examined the log structure with her binoculars. "The gaps between the logs look completely filled with mud. It's also got a wooden door instead of a blanket, so my guess is this place is used year 'round. From what I can see, it has been well maintained."

"Let's hope this is over quickly," Justine said.

"Just be careful, and we'll have him under arrest before he knows what hit him," Ella continued, reaching for her cell phone. "Now, let's find the best way down and get our backup on scene."

Joe and Phillip arrived on foot, having met and joined forces. Ella gave them a quick rundown before they all moved into position. The men came off the bluff farther west, blocking any escape routes north into the river, and points west. Ella and Justine walked down the access road, using Henry's pickup to screen them from view from the hogan entrance.

As they got closer, Ella could hear country music coming from inside the hogan, which meant their approach had been masked. She looked over at Neskahi and Cloud, who were nearly at the rear of the hogan. The hogan had no windows so their arrival, too, had apparently gone unseen.

"We're going to have to step up the noise a little, part-ner," she said, kicking the door of the pickup with her steel-toed boot.

Justine picked up a rock and used it as a hammer, pound-ing the back bumper, then ducking down. Using the truck for cover, she brought out her pistol.

"What the—?" Henry Mike yelled, slurring his words as he rushed out, pistol in hand. As he cleared the door, he wove for a moment, almost falling down.

"Tribal Police. Put your weapon down," Joe called out firmly, coming around the hogan from the south side.

"Do it," Phillip added, moving in from the river side, shotgun aimed at Henry's chest.

Henry Mike swayed but never let go of his pistol. "I'm not going in—not while I've got breath in my body. If you want me, you're going to have to shoot me."

Ella glanced over the hood at Justine, who'd moved up on the opposite side of the truck and was now standing by the passenger door. "Suicide by cop. That's what he's after," Ella said, recalling a similar situation years ago. She still had nightmares, but maybe today would be different and she could do and say just the right thing.

"No matter how much training we've had, real life al-ways throws you a curve ball. I doubt a Taser would work on somebody that big—if we had one. So now what?" Justine muttered.

"Drop your weapon, Henry," Ella called out, hoping to get a dialogue started. "It doesn't have to go down this way. You'll spend some time in jail, but, hey, this is New Mexico. You'll probably be out for good behavior in six months."

"Serve time for what? I know what you're thinking, that I had something to do with that bomb. Right? It wasn't me. Hell, I'd have taken a .45 to that weasel preacher if I wanted him dead—up close and personal, right between the eyes."

"Then you have nothing to worry about." Instinct told

Ella to keep her eyes on Henry. His expression would reveal what she needed to know to stay alive.

"You're lying. You need a fall guy to keep the tribe happy. But I had nothing to do with that bombing and I can prove it. I was at the Nakai's wedding in Fruitland the day the bomb went off. There's a photo inside that shows me there with my buddies."

"Then it's settled. Now lay down your weapon so we can talk," Ella said, feeling the badger fetish at her throat grow hot. "Don't throw your life away."

"There's nothing for me back in Shiprock. This is the end of the road."

"It doesn't have to be. Let's talk about this once you have a chance to calm down," Ella said, keeping her voice steady.

"You're not hearing me. The only way I'm going back is in a body bag." He took a step back, inching toward the hogan entrance.

The fetish at her throat felt like it was on fire now. There had to be a way to stop this. "We're *not* going to kill you. We'll wait until you're ready to come with us peacefully. Just stay where you are."

There was no answer for several very long minutes. Finally, he called out to them. "Okay, I'm putting my weapon down. Tell Kim I love her."

Henry crouched and set the pistol on the ground, but as he stood, he made a sudden grab for something underneath his jacket.

"Gun!" Phillip shouted.

Henry whipped out a second pistol, bringing the barrel up as he went into a crouch. Four simultaneous blasts shook the river canyon. Henry's body shuddered and he collapsed, face down.

None of the officers could move. "Good eyes, Phillip," Ella finally said. "Thanks."

"Don't mention it," Officer Cloud muttered, visibly shaken.

Ella stepped over to where Henry Mike lay, automatically kicked the pistol away, then confirmed he was dead. "I should have seen this coming from his last words," she said quietly.

"There's one good thing—he'll never threaten her again," Justine answered in a whisper-thin voice.

Ella turned away, staring with unfocused eyes toward Shiprock Peak to the west. Henry Mike had taken four hits to his torso, one of them from a shotgun at close range. Though it had been a righteous shooting, she wasn't the only one who looked ready to vomit. Things like this never got easier. Like a highly corrosive acid, police work ate away at your humanity. But if you ever stopped feeling the pain, you'd know it was time to turn in your badge.

Ella remembered the D.C. offer Kevin had mentioned. Maybe it *was* time to turn in her badge. Yet even as the thought formed, her stomach tightened. Leaving would be the toughest decision in her life right now. The tribe needed her, and her career—her mission in life—wasn't about pocketing the biggest paycheck.

"Officers," she said to the others, "bring your vehicles down and park them over there." She gestured to a spot against the cliff side. "I'll begin a preliminary search of the hogan. Justine will take over Tache's normal duties. I'll call the ME and also get the Crime Scene vehicle delivered to us as soon as possible. We'll split up the rest of the duties when you return."

The three officers moved up the dirt road, preferring the longer route rather than a climb up the bluff.

Pulling on a pair of latex gloves, Ella went inside the hogan. On a small wooden table were five twenty-round clips of ammo and a HK semi-auto assault rifle in .308 Winchester caliber. It was a deadly weapon with plenty of power, capable of penetrating most police-issue vests. There were also several boxes of ammo, probably for the second rifle in the truck, and two pistol magazines. Dangling from a nail was a military-surplus gas mask, and on a shelf were flares and smoke grenades.

Ella checked a large cooler next and, not surprisingly, found several beer bottles floating in a mix of ice and water. As she continued her search, checking around the other hogan contents and the bedding, Ella heard a vehicle pull up. It was Justine, who'd had the shortest distance to go.

Ella motioned for her partner, who had a camera, to join her. "He's got an armory in here but I still haven't found any explosives or detonators. Looks like he planned all along to make his last stand here. Suicide by cop—and we obliged."

"We didn't have a choice," Justine said, stepping into the small hexagonal space. "If we'd have held off just another second, you or I might be lying on the ground instead of him. That hidden weapon came as a surprise to all of us, and if he'd managed to get back inside . . ."

While Justine took photos of the interior, Ella continued to look around. That's when she noticed a collection of photos taped to a wooden cabinet. One showed Henry Mike at a wedding with the groom.

She was looking at the images when Phillip Cloud came up behind her carrying an electric lantern, which provided much-needed light to the interior.

"That's John Nakai next to the deceased," Phillip Cloud said. "I was invited, too, but had to work that day. The wedding was the same day the bomb went off at the college."

"He could have made a quick trip to the college to drop off the package," Ella said. "We need to find out if the deceased spent the entire day there or not."

"I'll check into that," Justine said, "but with his obvious taste for alcohol, I can't see him skipping the reception."

"Let me know as soon as possible what you find out," Ella said, looking through the photos.

Dr. Carolyn Roanhorse, the medical examiner, arrived a few minutes later, and Ella gave her friend a nod as she exited the van. With no need to discuss the cause of death, Ella kept to her own tasks, and got busy checking out the pickup.

Dr. Roanhorse went to work, immediately enlisting Sergeant Neskahi as her helper.

Despite an exhaustive search, Ella found no trace of explosives, anything resembling codes, or correspondence with a terrorist cell or anyone else. She was walking back to the SUV when Blalock contacted her on the radio.

"I couldn't reach you on your cell phone, so I'm using the tribal tactical channel. Your hunch paid off," he said quickly. "Nafus didn't know Haske was in custody and left a message asking Haske to call him back. The number belongs to one of those throwaway cells, so we can't trace it. Haske set up a meeting. Nafus wants to buy more explosives."

"Where's the meet?" Ella asked quickly.

"A place they've used in the past, off Highway 64 just south of the Nenahnezad Chapter House."

"On the Rez. I'm surprised that a big Anglo would think he wouldn't be noticed here," Ella said. "Where's Haske now?"

"At home," he said, giving her directions to the house, which lay not far from the river, in the bosque a few miles northwest of Shiprock. "He'll have to leave in another twenty minutes."

"Tell him to stay put until I arrive. My ETA should be inside that time frame if I leave right now. I'll follow him from his home to the meet. Meanwhile, call for tribal backup and set up surveillance at the site of the meet."

"Copy that."

Ella signaled Justine and gave her a quick update.

"I should go with you," Justine said. "You'll need backup."

"Not until Haske meets with Nafus. Contact Blalock and coordinate with him on the takedown. He'll fill you in on tactics. But stay in touch with me."

Ella was on the road less than a minute later, heading west toward Shiprock, about ten miles away. Lights flashing, she made her way in record time. Haske actually lived out of town, where houses were surrounded by cultivated fields or barren desert rather than developments.

As she reached the general area, she followed Blalock's directions past the farmhouse. Ella stopped just beyond the dirt lane which led from the main gravel road to Haske's house. The residence, about two hundred yards downhill, was almost hidden by the tall brush along the bosque.

Ella called Haske on his cell. "I'm uphill from you. I can see your front door from here but don't look for me," she instructed. "Just go about your business. I'll follow at a discreet distance."

"I'll leave now, then," he said.

Ella saw Haske come out the front door, then turn to lock up. Suddenly there was a burst of gunfire. Haske fell to the ground.

As the shots continued Ella pressed down on the accelerator. She spun and fishtailed all the way to the house, hoping to raise the biggest cloud of dust possible. Driving up as close as she could, she slammed on the brakes, sliding sideways to a stop and shielding Haske's body as much as possible.

Diving out the passenger's side, she crouched behind her tribal unit and called for backup on her hand-held radio. The shooter continued firing, bullets passing just over the hood of the car and slamming into Haske's home. One struck the top of the car, then the wall. That gave her a general fix on his position. Rolling to the right, she fired two quick rounds into the bosque.

A shot came in reply, striking the front bumper with a thud, not a foot from her head. Instinctively, she hugged the ground behind the front tire. He wasn't backing off—and now she was a target, too.

Knowing the shooter had fired at least five rounds and might need to reload, she rolled in the opposite direction and squeezed off three rounds at the best hiding place she could pick.

"Crawl closer to the car," she called out to Haske as she reached into her left pocket, feeling for the reassurance only a spare magazine could give her.

Haske didn't respond.

Turning her head, she risked a look at the victim, who was face down, half on and half off the concrete pad that comprised the porch. There were two holes in his back: one in the spine, and the other on the left, where his heart was located. The third round had struck the left side of his neck.

Any of those hits were potentially fatal, but having sustained all three of them, Haske was either dead or beyond help, Ella knew. Faced with another senseless death, anger filled her.

She took a deep breath, trying to focus solely on the shooter now. Firing back twice, she rolled to her right again. The sniper's bullet struck where she'd been just two seconds earlier, its impact stinging the side of her face with sand. But now she had a better lock on his location.

Ella fired three more times, then rolled back, ejecting her spent magazine and inserting the fresh clip in a well-practiced motion. She waited, her sights on the spot beside the thick clump of willows, looking for movement or shadow.

The silence was disturbed only by the metallic tick of the car engine above and to her left as it cooled. Knowing the sniper's advantage of patience, she watched, not moving, her gun hand steady. After five minutes, she slowly snaked down her left hand, flipped her cell phone open, and punched Blalock's number on speed dial, looking away from the target area for only a second.

"I'm still here," she whispered.

"We're on our way, Ella. Our ETA is less than ten minutes. We were halfway to Hogback when your call for backup came through. Hang in there," Blalock said.

Several more minutes passed, but the sniper hadn't fired again and there was no movement. Ella wondered if she'd scored a hit or if she was being set up. She waited behind cover, noting that no birds had settled on the branches above what she'd determined to be the shooter's mostly likely location.

After two minutes, she rolled to her right, sneaking a quick look out from behind the front tire, then rolling back. The front bumper clanked loudly, and a bullet struck Haske's door, just six inches above porch level.

She looked at the bumper, less than a foot to her right. A shiny two-inch-long groove had just been scratched into the chromed steel. If she hadn't rolled back immediately, the bullet would have blown away the right side of her head.

Shaken, she took a deep breath. The badger fetish around her neck felt scalding hot against her skin. Death surrounded her now, she could feel it calling. Shutting out her fear, she focused on survival.

Hugging the ground, Ella rolled below the open passenger door, planning to reach up behind the seat and grab her rifle. Two more shots rang out in rapid succession. As she looked back, she saw new holes in the side of the house, low and close to the foundation. Had the bullets actually passed beneath the car this time? If so, there were only two places to hide.

Ella rolled to the right, using the front tire to physically conceal herself. Though it was a relatively cool day, her body was bathed in sweat. She swallowed, trying unsuccessfully to moisten her throat.

She called Blalock on the cell phone again. "He's south-west of the house, at the edge of the bosque. He's got me pinned," she said.

"We're on foot now, a few hundred yards from the house. We're going to come in behind him from the south, along the river, and send a car down the road as a diversion. Be ready when he's forced to break cover."

Seconds ticked away, each its own version of Hell. The car's cooling metal had stopped ticking but the stillness didn't reassure her. She was alive, but two men had died in her presence today. She felt poisoned by evil. Her brother and mother would insist on her having an Enemy Way sing done, but the nightmares would still follow her for a long time—that is, if she lived through the next half hour.

As she waited, Ella held tightly to her pistol, sighting toward the willows and wondering if she had five rounds left in the clip or four. Others would be arriving soon, but did the sniper know? She moved again, rolling to the left then rising to a crouch as she reached the rear tire.

This time, there was no answering fire. Deciding to push it, Ella moved forward again, reached into the SUV, and brought out her rifle. Nothing.

The busted scope had been removed, but she had the iron sights and five rounds in the weapon. Rifle in hand and safety off, she moved to the front again and waited.

She heard the vehicle before she saw it. A police cruiser pulled up, sliding to a stop beside hers and placing another layer of protection between her and the river.

Ella touched the badger, felt the coolness of the stone, then stood, placing her rifle across the hood. Instinct told her the sniper was gone. And Haske . . . The poor man had only wanted his freedom, and they'd played on that. His blood was also on her hands now.

Blalock came into view among the willows, then waved his shotgun in the air. "It's clear. I think he waded across the river to a vehicle. We heard an engine starting up a few minutes ago."

Ella stepped out into the open, watching the river beyond as she lowered her weapon. "I had a feeling he'd left," she answered in a low and heavy tone.

"You're not blaming yourself for this, are you?" Blalock asked, as he glanced over at Haske's body.

"That sniper . . . he wasn't content with just taking Haske out," she said, not answering his question. "He wanted me, too."

"But you won, Clah. You're alive."

He was right. She'd lived to walk in beauty again . . . someday.

TWENTY-ONE

——— ✖ ✖ ✖ ———

After filing all the necessary reports, Ella sat alone in her office, lost in thought. The attempts on Ford's life, the probable existence of a terrorist cell, four shootings with two dead and an unknown shooter on the loose—these were just the job highlights of a very long week.

On top of everything else, she was going to have to make a major career decision soon. An e-mail from Blakely at PPS had been in her in-box when she sat down to the paperwork. Though she'd put it off for over two hours, she'd finally broken down and read the message.

Kevin had been very accurate in his earlier description of the offer. Though John Blakely hadn't mentioned an exact dollar figure in his e-mail, he'd promised more than quadruple what she was making now. The job description and benefits were tempting enough even without a raise. John had suggested she visit their D.C. operation at her earliest convenience, at company expense, of course. He left her his office, cell, and even his home phone number, requesting Ella call him to discuss the job offer in detail.

Ella had e-mailed back, agreeing to a phone call but asking for a few more days because of work responsibilities.

Life was definitely brimming over at the moment. On top of her current case, she had serious home problems as well. Herman appeared to be ill, her mom was upset for a variety of reasons, and Dawn was away from home and sorely missed. Too much was coming at Ella at once.

Experience told her to deal with one thing at a time or she'd get nowhere. Ella forced herself to take a very deep breath, then let it out slowly. Before she'd finished exhaling, her cell phone rang. It was Ford.

"Are you all right?" he asked quickly.

"You heard?" she asked, surprised. As far as she knew the shooting hadn't been on the news—at least not yet.

"Yeah. Bruce has a receiver that picks up all emergency radio communications."

Ella suddenly had one of the answers that had eluded her till now. The shooter had accessed the Navajo Tactical frequency. That's how he'd known where she and Haske would be.

"Are you there?" Ford asked.

"Yes, I'm sorry. You were saying . . . ?"

"We've intercepted some of Dr. Lee's e-mails and a very interesting picture is starting to emerge. Can you stop by?"

"I'll be there shortly," she said, then hung up.

Justine came in just then. "We're processing the scene at Haske's, but the shooter was careful. The rounds he used weren't particularly distinctive, but we found some brass. From the caliber and brand, it looks to be the same weapon that was used both times before. It's the same guy, Ella, I'd bet anything on that."

"I agree. And it's now clear to me that he was listening to our radio communications, too. That's how he got to Haske's ahead of me. Make sure the others know about that."

"Since he failed to take you out, he's likely to try again. He did with Ford," Justine warned.

Ella stood up. "Speaking of Ford, he's intercepted more

of Dr. Lee's e-mails, so I'm on my way over there now. Let me know if you turn up anything new."

When Ella arrived at Teeny's, Abednego came up to her holding his favorite stuffed monkey. His tail was wagging and he looked a lot happier than either Ford or Teeny.

"Well guys, what's up?" she asked.

Ford waved her to his chair. "Going through her previous e-mails and blogs, we've been able to narrow down certain elements of their code. I've already told you about the words 'red rock' being a trigger for events, but what we've also been able to determine is that it only holds true if they're preceded by the word *aqalani*."

" 'Greetings' in Navajo," Ella said. "Interesting."

"The words they use when referring to the attempt to kill me are *aqalani*, red rock, and Wednesday. I believe 'Wednesday' is their code name for me," Ford added.

"They're going to an awful lot of trouble to neutralize you," she said slowly. "Any idea why yet?"

"No, I just can't figure it out. I wouldn't have given myself away. I'm too well trained for that."

"Yet Dr. Lee found the tracking device you planted," she said. "They must have made you, Ford, and know that you're trying to compromise their operation. That's the only answer."

He nodded slowly. "But they also want *you* out of the way. I've been studying this carefully and an e-mail sent less than twenty-four hours ago mentions problems with *ha'asídí*, 'watchman' in Navajo. That correlates to the attempt on you today." He showed her the e-mail and the time it had been sent. The name of the sender had been blocked out, but the addresses of the three recipients showed clearly. "The addresses you see were originally blind copies, but we got past that. What we haven't been able to do is identify the sender."

"Do you think the sender is their leader?" Ella asked Teeny, who now stood behind her.

"There's a real good chance of that. We never figured Jane Lee as the brains behind this operation."

"Whoever it is, that person sure knows how to run a tight ship," Ella said quietly.

"I'd like to run a program that'll check out the other recipients of the e-mail, but I wanted to make sure you were okay with that first," Ford said. "I can't guarantee it won't tip them off."

Ella considered it briefly, then nodded. It was time to start taking more chances.

"Then I'll get started on that right now," Ford said. "All I have to do is designate the key words and phrases we know about. The fact that some of the words are in Navajo should get us more reliable hits."

The vast, data-mining program originated in a major computer network that Ford wouldn't identify, but Ella got the idea it was either the NSA or the CIA. The program searched millions of recent messages on the Internet, looking for anything that contained the search words. After several minutes, it produced an e-mail address. The recipient was an ex-Marine named John Baker, according to his profile on one of the Internet sites.

Ella sat up quickly. "Get a photo on screen."

As Ford pulled one up and moved aside, Ella studied the picture. "There's a strong resemblance between this man and the composite sketch we got from Haske. Chances are this is the guy he knew as Nafus."

Ford smiled. "That's an anagram for SNAFU: Situation Normal—All Fouled Up," he said.

"I've heard that phrased a bit differently," Teeny said, chuckling.

Not commenting, Ford switched to a DOD database, checking service records. "Baker served in the Marines fifteen years ago, in artillery. Now he's a truck driver. According to this, he receives regular benefits."

"Get me his address," Ella said.

A moment later Ford read an address off the screen while Ella wrote it down. She'd need Blalock on this, since it was off the reservation. "One more thing," she added. "See what you can get me on Henderson Whitefeather."

Although Ford tried several searches, there was little on Whitefeather online, other than a few newspaper articles where he'd been mentioned as a deputy at an accident or arrest.

"I can hack into the county's files," Teeny suggested, "but it'll take time. The sheriff's department has a really good firewall."

"And you would know because . . . ? Never mind, go for it. But be careful. If Whitefeather hears about it and spooks, I have a feeling we'll lose him for good," Ella said.

"If he's *not* involved and hears about it, there'll be all hell to pay with the county," Teeny added. "But I'll take precautions."

"There's another way to go about this if all you want is his background," Ford said. "I have a facial recognition program the Bureau gave me. That could uncover a great deal of information based on his photo alone. I might be able to remember where I met him, too, by the time I'm through."

"Go for it," Ella said.

Ella waited as Ford accessed Ella's terminal at work, using her password, then retrieved the photo she'd stored there.

"How long does it take?" Ella asked Ford as he brought up the file and began to run the program.

"Have a cup of coffee with us," Ford suggested. "If by the time we're finished, this hasn't come up with something, then it's going to take some serious time."

"I'll keep watch. You guys go ahead," Teeny said, his attention riveted to the screen.

Ford led her to the coffee machine Teeny had set up. "You

place a coffee packet in the center and you get a perfect cup every time," he explained. "There are tea and cocoa packets available, too, and even decaf for sissies. It's really a wonderful gadget, but I don't think our church can afford it."

Ella accepted the coffee he made for her with a "Thanks."

He put in a new packet and made himself a quick cup. "Am I losing you?" he asked, glancing over.

Ella blinked. "No, I get the packet idea. It's like the vendor at the station, but more hands-on."

"No, I'm talking about man to woman," he said.

Ella reached out and placed her hand on his cheek. "I want *more*, not less," she murmured.

"So do I," he admitted. "But we've been through this."

Ella sighed. "I won't marry you just because I want to make love to you," she said, moving away from him.

Ford started to say something, but Teeny came in just then.

"Guys, come see this."

Ella hurried back into the main room, Ford a step behind her. The program had found a match. Ella looked at Henderson Whitefeather's photo, but the name listed below was Ernest Blackwater. The biographical information showed Blackwater, a Navajo, had worked at a tribal casino in California.

"His father died of acute radiation poisoning contracted while working in the uranium mines here on the Rez," Teeny said, skimming faster than Ella.

"I think we just found our motive," Ella said. "All things considered, he's got a really good reason for wanting to keep anything nuclear off the Rez."

"*Now* I remember where I met him before," Ford said, studying one of the images on the screen. "He was Ernest Blackwater to me. I was working undercover at the time with the FBI as a tribal gaming consultant—looking for corruption."

"Blackwater must have seen you or your photo and realized that the second you remembered *him*, his new identity would be compromised—along with whatever else he was planning. As a sheriff's deputy working the reservation borders, it wouldn't have been hard for him to find out you did consulting work for the Navajo Tribal Police. He had two reasons to be gunning for you."

"But even if we assume he's working with Dr. Lee and John Baker, what exactly are they hoping to accomplish?" Teeny asked. "Do they want to prevent the power plant from ever becoming operable, or will they wait until test operations begin, then try to cause a major accident that'll force it to shut down?"

"I don't see how they could assault the place, not without a dozen more just like them and a lot more firepower. Even then, their chances are slim. I'm sure they have a different point of attack," Ella said. "And we need to find out what that is."

"We'll keep digging through the e-mails, and see what we can come up with," Ford said.

"I'll concentrate on Baker," Ella said. "I think he killed Haske and, with luck, he'll lead me to the others."

"That'll take too much time," Teeny pointed out. "The reactor vessel is scheduled to be delivered and installed in just a few days. That will be their last opportunity to act before everything's sealed up tight inside their grounds."

"The design of the power plant and the use of helium coolant would eliminate the chances of a catastrophic accident like Chernobyl," Ford said. "There's a dome to seal off any accidental radiation leaks, too, and a fire suppression system that cuts off all the oxygen. Yet the facility's opening could be indefinitely delayed if they were able to damage the reactor bottle before it's put into place."

"The question is, other than step up security on the bottle and pellet delivery convoy, how do we stop something we haven't quite nailed down yet? All we have are guesses," Ella mused.

"The time for playing it safe is long past," Ford said. "We know at least three members of the cell. If they want me so bad, I need to set myself up as a target and force them to take action," he said, then mapped out his plan.

Ella listened, liking what he was saying less and less. When Ford finished, she remained silent.

"It's our only viable option," Ford added.

"All right," she said at last. "I'll talk to Big Ed and, providing he okays this, we'll get things rolling tomorrow. But no matter how well we plan, Ford, they might make their move *before* we can react," she said, meeting his gaze.

"Then that's the way it is. By keeping innocent people from being injured by these terrorists, I'm honoring my Lord's commandment to love my neighbor as myself. Your job is to restore harmony, Ella, but *this* is the essence of what I do."

"I wish I could do or say something to change your mind," she said.

"I've often felt the same way about your police work," he answered gently. "But we each have to follow our own path."

Ella nodded, then bracing herself, added, "Teeny, we need to borrow some of your equipment. It's better than what we have in the department."

TWENTY-TWO

—— ✖ ✖ ✖ ——

Ella arrived home late, and, though exhausted, she doubted she'd get much sleep tonight. As she sat at the dining table alone, sipping a hot cup of her mother's special herbal tea, she could just make out Rose's voice speaking softly with Herman in the next room.

Although it was close to midnight and well past her mother's usual bedtime, Rose joined Ella moments later. "Your daughter called earlier. She wants to stay with her father a few extra days. I told her you'd be home late, but that I'd ask."

The fact that Dawn didn't seem to be at all homesick niggled at Ella. Sensing that, Rose smiled.

"You were the same way. You loved whatever was new and different. Something in you needed adventure."

Ella smiled, remembering their many arguments. As far as Ella could remember, she'd always welcomed any excuse to leave the Rez. Where she went hadn't been nearly as important to her as the chance to explore unfamiliar ground.

"Your daughter needs you to make the right decision for her, even if she doesn't like what you decide," Rose said softly. "That's all part of being her mom."

"I'm not sure what's right anymore—for her, or me," Ella said, running a hand through her hair.

"Many Navajos grow up away from our Sacred Mountains. There are more opportunities on the outside. But a lot of our young people end up getting lost outside our borders. They learn Anglo ways, and soon start thinking of themselves as Anglo," Rose said. "Eventually, they find out the hard way that no matter how well they speak, or how they dress, they'll never quite belong. Only then do they try to reconnect with the tribe. But by that time, they often find they don't feel at home here either. The end result is that they belong nowhere, and they spend their lives trying to understand why."

"Jobs are few and far between here. My daughter will need all the advantages she can get to find her own way in the world. This will always be her home, but her future may lie outside our borders."

"Our tribe makes us rich in ways that the outside world can't even begin to understand. What else do you want for her? A big bank account? At the end of the day, what comfort is there in that?"

"I want her to have it all, Mom—a future where she'll never have to worry about money, and the strength that comes from family. I just don't know how to make sure she gets that. I received an e-mail from a representative of the security firm and they want to fly me to Washington and see their operation for myself. I told him I'd be giving him a call in a few days to at least discuss the job offer."

She'd expected her mother to argue, or maybe even get mad, but instead, Rose leaned back in her chair and regarded her thoughtfully. "You're worried about how this would change all of our lives. Am I right?"

When Ella didn't answer, Rose stood up. "We're both tired. Let's get some sleep. There's always tomorrow."

"Before you go, how's your husband?" Ella asked her.

Rose's expression became guarded. "He hasn't said anything to me yet. If he doesn't soon, I'll have to convince him that I need to know what's going on. I can deal with whatever it is, but not knowing . . ."

"Is the worst," Ella agreed, then hugged her mother tightly. "I love you, Mom."

"I love you, too, daughter."

Ella watched her mother go down the hall, then stood and rinsed out her cup in the sink. Leaving her pistol and gear in its usual place, she went to her room. Ella checked for e-mails from Dawn and finding none, checked her phone messages. There was one call. Listening to her daughter's excited voice telling her all about her day, Ella smiled. Life was a lot less complicated when you were ten years old.

Too tired to undress, Ella lay back on the bed, closed her eyes and soon drifted off to a restless sleep.

Ella woke up before sunrise, bathed in sweat. She'd dreamed of a barren canyon covered with blood. Death had been everywhere, consuming the land, dogging her footsteps.

She got up slowly. An Earthway Sing was said to counteract bad dreams involving the land, but her nightmares were the price of spilt blood. She'd need to have an Enemy Way done first, and an Earthway later.

Sometime during the past several years she'd moved closer to her mother's Traditionalist beliefs. Though she was still a skeptic, Ella couldn't argue with results. Over time, she'd stopped trying to explain why certain things attributed to The Way actually worked. Knowing that they did was enough.

Ella made herself a quick breakfast, scrambling some fresh eggs and pouring some of her mother's perfectly seasoned chile sauce over them. It was fast, but indescribably delicious. After filling a thermos with coffee, she set out.

By the time she walked inside the station shortly after seven, Blalock was already there, and to her surprise, so were Teeny and Ford.

"Why did you guys leave the compound before we had things in place?" Ella demanded, glaring at Teeny, then looking at Ford.

"We took precautions, but I wanted to send the message that the tide has turned," Ford responded. "They should be afraid of *me*, not vice-versa."

"You should have waited," Ella argued. "But it's too late now. Let's go see Big Ed."

Ella gathered Neskahi, Justine, and Anna, and they all went to the chief's office. Marianna was on surveillance duty.

Once inside Big Ed's office, Ella gave him the highlights of their plan, which included Ford paying Dr. Lee a visit and goading her into action. "I admit it's extremely dangerous. Too many things can go wrong, like Reverend Tome getting killed before we can intervene. But things are coming to a head. We can't interfere with tribal plans to install the reactor bottle, and if we arrest the players we know about, others could slip through our fingers with whatever explosives and resources they've gathered. Ford's plan is our best option," she concluded.

"But you'll be keeping Reverend Tome under tight surveillance?" Big Ed asked.

"Absolutely," Ella answered. "What we need to decide now is where he'll go *after* his meeting. That's when he'll be the most vulnerable. We have to find a secure place, a location that'll seem natural for him to go to but won't endanger anyone else. It can't be his church, or the campus, for example."

"I've been giving that some thought," Teeny said quietly. "Your home is the perfect place. Your daughter's visiting her father, right?"

"Yes, but my mom and Herman are there," Ella answered.

"How about getting them out of the house for the day?" Blalock said. "Officers could pass themselves off as your mother and stepfather, and guard Ford from inside as well as out. It'll look perfectly natural to anyone watching and give him maximum protection."

Ella considered it, then nodded. "That sounds good, but I'll have to talk to my mom. It's her house."

"Do it now, Shorty. We'll wait for you," Big Ed said.

Ella stepped out of the office, and walked down the hall. After deciding how best to broach the subject, she called Rose. "Mom, what are you plans for today?"

"Why? What's on your mind?"

Ella sighed. Had she honestly believed that Rose wouldn't know something was going on? "Mom, I need your help," she said at last. "Is there someplace you and your husband can go to spend the day?"

"We've already decided to do just that. It's such a beautiful day, my husband and I are going to drive to Navajo Mountain. On the southern slope, near the top, are some black rocks that form a circle. That's where Monster Slayer was born. Offerings can be made at the sacred spring by there. Afterwards, I was thinking we could spend the night in Page, then return tomorrow afternoon."

"The car ride will give you hours to talk. That's a good idea, Mom," Ella said.

"And the offering will give my husband strength to face whatever's disturbing him," Rose said. "We'll be leaving in about a half hour."

After getting her mother's permission, Ella returned to Big Ed's office. "It's set. We can use my mother's home. Joe, you have Herman's general build so you'll take on his identity. He's been spending a lot of time outside lately, messing with the cars and doing chores. That'll give you the opportunity to watch the property. Justine, you're closest to

Mom's size, and you're most familiar with her habits and mannerisms. Go outside once in a while, but not beyond the garden. Your job will be to stick close to Ford once he arrives."

"You've got it," Justine said. "Where will you be?"

"I'll be positioned on the mesa behind the house. I can keep watch on the arroyo from there. That's the best way of sneaking up on the house. But heads-up, people. If they strike, it'll be fast, and if they use a sniper, he'll be likely to make another long-range attempt. Never stand still in a place where you present a sight picture. That includes you, Ford."

"I'll direct the watch on the suspects—those we can locate," Blalock added.

"Okay, then down to another detail," Ford said. "Shall I make the initial call from here using my cell phone? I know you'll all want to hear firsthand, and I could put it on the speaker, but I'd recommend against that. People can always tell."

"No need," Teeny said. "I can place a small recording device on your phone. We'll have the conversation on record then, and there'll be no telltale sounds."

After Teeny had the recorder in place, Ford called Dr. Lee's office on campus. The professor picked up on the first ring.

"This is Reverend Tome, Dr. Lee. I'd like to meet with you this morning to discuss a matter of interest to both of us."

While Ford listened, Ella bit her bottom lip, wishing they'd used the speaker anyway.

"All right, the faculty break room in an hour it is, though I would have preferred someplace more private, considering what I have to say." He listened again. "It's entirely your choice. I'll see you soon."

He hung up, then looked at the others. "She doesn't trust me, that much was clear. That's why she insisted on a public place. I could have argued, but I think that would have been a mistake."

"Once you start telling her why you're there, she may regret her decision and opt to take you elsewhere, like maybe her office," Ella said. "But stay on campus, whatever you do."

The remaining details were worked out quickly, and Ford left to meet with Dr. Lee. Teeny and Ella followed him at a distance. They'd be monitoring the microphone Ford was carrying. Despite their careful planning, Ella felt her stomach tying itself into knots.

"We've got him covered, Ella. Stop worrying," Teeny said.

"This group has had us running in circles for a while. I don't trust them to act in the way we would expect. They're unpredictable—and that's what makes them so dangerous."

"*We're* even more dangerous," Teeny answered.

"True," Ella said and smiled.

Finally on campus after thirty minutes, they parked and waited. Soon Ford's voice came over the monitor's speaker.

"Dr. Lee, I'm glad we were able to get together."

"I was surprised to hear from you, but I am intrigued, Reverend Tome. What's on your mind?" Dr. Lee asked casually.

"Everyone in the community knows that there've been at least two attempts on my life. Although I should have probably left the investigating to the police, I got involved because I needed to understand why I'd become a target."

"I would have done the same thing," she admitted.

"Before I became a minister, I worked for the government, creating psychological profiles for persons of interest— frankly, political and environmental activists with extremist views. Using avenues that were still open to me, I looked into the backgrounds of people I've had contact with lately. You got my attention almost immediately."

"Me? Why?"

"I've learned about your opposition to nuclear power in its many forms—including our new tribal facility. I also noticed that now when the plant's about to become operational, you've abruptly stopped protesting. To me, that sends up a huge red flag. If it meant so much to you, why stop now? Taking that a step further, I've wondered if you've become involved in something far bigger than you bargained for— one that you must now keep secret at all costs."

"That's quite an imagination you have, but there are flaws in your logic. If, as you suggested, I'm against the power plant, why would I have wasted my energy attacking you and not the plant?" Dr. Lee asked in a pleasant voice.

"Because it's an ideal way to keep the cops distracted. It'll also draw manpower while something of greater importance is taking place—maybe a move directly against the Hogback facility."

Ford waited, but Dr. Lee said nothing.

"I'm not out to condemn you, Professor, nor do I doubt the sincerity of your concerns against nuclear power. I'm here as a minister, hoping you'll see the danger you present to yourself and others by choosing a path of violence. Ask God to forgive you, and choose peace. I assure you it's not too late."

Dr. Lee cleared her throat. "Your suppositions are way off base, Reverend. As I've said before, I've given up fighting the power plant because it's a lost cause. I'm now focused on a mission that'll bring about real change—women's rights."

"My theory's on the mark, Professor. We both know it. Others charged with protecting our nation's utilities will soon come up with the same idea, too, if they haven't already done so. If you know anything about any threats against *Tsétaak'á* Generating Plant, you have to go to the police now. That's your only way out. The government has a lot of latitude these days regarding the ways they investigate acts of terrorism. You don't want to go down that road."

"This has been fascinating, but I have to go back to work," Dr. Lee said firmly. "Good-bye, Reverend Tome."

Ella and Teeny heard a door open and close, then the sound of footsteps. A few minutes later, Ford spoke. "Okay, I'm outside. I've done my part. I'm going back to my car and over to your place, Ella. I'll drive slowly to make sure I can be tailed."

Ella then called Justine and verified that everything was in place. "Ford's on his way."

"Good. We're ready. Officer Michael Cloud's keeping an eye on Dr. Lee as we speak."

"Make sure Ford wears a vest even inside the house. He may not like it, but it's necessary."

The morning turned into afternoon, but nothing happened. No one made a move on Ford. They had officers on every major player, including Baker and Whitefeather, but since both those men were outside their jurisdiction, Blalock was in charge of watching them.

Ella routinely checked in with the others via cell phone. It was now time to make a call to Teeny, who'd been monitoring Dr. Lee's calls and her computer.

"I've got nothing so far," he said. "You?"

"All three subjects have been involved in normal-looking activities. Baker has a laptop in his pickup truck. While running around town, mostly to auto supply stores and such, he has gotten it out a couple of times, briefly. Whitefeather, according to the deputy watching him, has been in the Bottoms Up bar in Bloomfield for the past hour. It's possible he may have used his unit's computer to check his e-mail prior to going in. Michael Cloud followed Dr. Lee home—part of her normal routine."

"Jane hasn't logged on," Teeny said. "Wait a sec—here she is now. She's on MySpace, and she's edited the content of her profile. She's also changed the music on her page. It used to be something classical, but now it's a Paul Simon song, 'Slip Sliding Away.' "

Before Teeny could finish, her call waiting beeped. Ella switched to the other caller. Emily Marquez, the county deputy Blalock had chosen to keep tabs on Whitefeather, was on the line.

"I lost him, Ella. I got worried when he failed to return to his car, so I went inside to check on him. I ran into some goons and got held up for about five minutes. He'd apparently told the bozos that I was stalking him, and they kept me there just long enough for him to slip out the back. His unit's gone."

"Head west, then. Maybe he's on his way back to Shiprock," Ella said. "We can't have county dispatch asking other deputies to call in if they spot him because that would alert him as well. He's probably listening to the calls."

After ending the conversation, she switched back. "Teeny, I need your best guess. Could Jane have sent a signal via computer to one of the others without your knowledge that Ford's out of hiding and ripe for a hit?" Ella asked.

"No way. If you're worried about the changes in her page, those are more likely to be a panic button signal. Check on the truck driver and see how he's reacting," he suggested.

Ella called Phillip Cloud next, the man assigned to Baker. "Whitewater has managed to ditch us," Ella told him. "How about your subject?"

"He almost lost me for a while, but I've still got him."

"What happened?"

"He pulled into the parking lot of a coffee shop, fiddled with his laptop for a few minutes, then went inside. After he failed to come out, I went in for a look, keeping an eye on his pickup through the store window. The clerk said he'd gone out through the back. I tracked him down an alley, and am currently following him at a distance along the street. We're both on foot, and he doesn't seem to be in a hurry."

"Stay with him, and keep a vehicle handy in case Baker catches a ride."

"Baker's not ditching me, I guarantee it."

With Whitefeather gone, Baker and Jane Lee were now of prime importance. Making a fast decision, Ella called Justine. "Change of plans. I want you and Joe to take Ford back to Teeny's. Just make sure you aren't spotted. Then pick up Anna, go to Dr. Lee's place, and take the professor into custody. Work quickly so she can't raise another alarm, and then leave Anna behind in her stead. From a distance, they look alike and, with luck, the others won't know we've made a switch. I'll meet you and Joe back at the station."

TWENTY-THREE

──── ✖ ✖ ✖ ────

A short time later, Ella met Justine in the station's hallway. "Is Dr. Lee in custody?"

"You bet. But she's steaming mad and screaming for a lawyer," Justine said.

"Stall. Don't let her have contact with anyone. Is Anna back at Dr. Lee's place?"

"Yes, and Michael Cloud's covering her. A few calls came in for Dr. Lee from her teaching assistant, Mona Tso, but that's about it. Anna didn't answer the calls."

"Okay. We've got the first part of my plan down. Now we move to the second part, and this'll have to play out in a very public way. The only hitch is that I'm going to need the college administration's cooperation."

Before she could continue, Blalock came in. "Not necessary. I have the authority to force the issue. Whaddaya need?"

"I wanted to get someone in administration to call Mona Tso, Dr. Lee's teaching assistant, and tell her that Dr. Lee will be unavailable for class because she's helping the police on an important matter."

"You want the other members of Dr. Lee's group to

believe she's turned traitor and is a threat to their operation," Blalock observed, putting things together quickly. "But do you really think they'll make a move on her here at the station?"

"No. That's why I also wanted the TA told that Dr. Lee can be reached at home in the evenings, and if any of the students have a problem they can contact her there. Word will get around fast. If I'm right, the group will go after Jane at the house—only we'll be waiting, one guard showing, the rest under cover," Ella said.

"They'll need a *very* good reason to believe Dr. Lee is there," Blalock said slowly.

"That's where Anna comes in. She's about the same height and weight as Dr. Lee. We'll make sure she's seen from a distance, briefly, maybe walking around the house tonight—along with someone known to be in law enforcement. The rest of us will be in hiding, ready to seal off the area and close in. When they make their move, we'll make ours."

Blalock nodded slowly. "You're thinking that they'll have to neutralize her quickly because they have no way of knowing what she's telling us. You're probably right about that, but the problem is that they might also decide to scatter. Depending on what she knows about the rest of the cell, it could go either way."

"They've shown dedication to their cause so far. Their actions are well planned and coordinated. Even if she hasn't been told enough to unravel *all* their plans, she still constitutes a risk by knowing their codes. I think they'll strike, the sooner the better," Ella said.

Blalock considered this, then nodded. "Let me call the college president and bring some pressure to bear."

"Actually, Ella, if you want to word to spread fast, there's a better way," Justine interrupted. "You and Blalock should go talk to the president in person. Mention that Dr. Lee is helping the FBI catch the bomber. If the *right person* is in a position to overhear and spread the tale, everyone in the entire county will know within the hour," Justine said.

"And the right person happens to be?" Ella asked, thinking she already knew.

"Jayne, my sister, who works on campus. Who else? And the fact that she's been seeing Bruce Little will add credibility to her story because people will see her as someone who's on the inside track."

"The woman is a blabbermouth," Blalock replied, nodding. "No offense, Justine," he added quickly. "But it can't look like a setup, so she'd have to be in the right place at the right time to be convincing."

"I can call her and arrange for her to be in the president's office when you're there," Justine said bringing out her cell phone. "Shall I call her now?"

Ella smiled. "Do it, partner."

The plan was put in motion quickly. Jayne had been happy to cooperate. She'd always liked having others see her as someone "in the know."

Sticking to their plan, Ella and Blalock went to the college and within forty minutes had completed the first phase of the operation. Jayne, who'd delivered coffee to the president's office, waved at them and headed to the college cafeteria to spread the news.

It was now time for phase two of the operation. Ella and Blalock drove to Dr. Lee's home, where the rest of the team was waiting.

Inside, Ella met with Anna. "You'll be wearing a vest, but it's still risky. Any second thoughts?" Ella asked her.

"None. It's all part of the job," she said in a firm voice.

Ella saw the flash of excitement in her eyes, and knew precisely what Anna was feeling. That adrenaline rush was one she'd felt many times before, and it was addictive. There was nothing like coming face to face with death to make you appreciate life even more.

"Joe, you came out first in our last rifle competition," Ella said. "I want you out of sight with the sniper gear, up in one of those cottonwood trees across the road. Use the infrared scope to monitor the perimeter." Ella focused on her partner next. "Justine, you're with me. We'll be in the orchard watching the road and that ditch in the back—a potential access point. Marianna, I want you in uniform and visible through the windows *but only briefly and intermittently*. Blalock will be inside the house, but away from outside view. Stay on the floor if you have to, Dwayne."

"Crawling from room to room? Sure, why not? Impersonating a rug rat will add a new dimension to my personnel file," he said straight-faced.

"I've been reading the reports that Joe and other officers filed detailing Dr. Lee's habits around the house. I'll be sure to sit on the back step for a little bit like she's known to do," Anna said. "But I'll keep my face down."

Ella realized how carefully Anna had prepared. That thoroughness might help keep her alive tonight.

"What'll happen to Dr. Lee while we're working?" Justine asked.

"She'll stay in holding. No one questions, or even approaches her," Ella said. Then as an afterthought, she added, "We need to make note of what she's wearing so Anna can match her outfit."

"She's wearing jeans and a red sweatshirt with the community college's logo on it," Justine answered.

"I've got the jeans part covered, but I don't own any red sweatshirts," Anna said, looking at the two other women in the room.

Justine went down the hall to Dr. Lee's closet and returned with a sweatshirt. "Here you go."

"Then we're all set," Ella said, standing up. "Double-check the video cameras, Justine, and make sure they're positioned to record everything as it goes down."

"I would have gotten top-notch electronics from the Bureau if we'd had more time, but come to think of it, Bruce probably has better hardware," Blalock said.

"I agree," Ella answered with a chuckle. "One last thing, people. Communicate via cell phones, unless you have no other choice. At least one of the suspects has access to our tactical radio frequencies." Ella looked at each person. "All right. Let's roll."

Long after the sun had settled over the Carrizo Mountains to the west, Ella and Justine, in camouflage clothing, sat in the orchard at the rear of Dr. Lee's house. From their position, they could see the rear of the house, the road leading in both directions, and the rim of the ditch running through the field behind them. Minutes ticked by slowly.

Ella checked with Phillip Cloud. "You're still watching Baker?"

"For a while it looked like he was going to return to his vehicle, but then he hoofed over to Broadway and hitched a ride to Shiprock with a Navajo family. Now he's at the Dog House, eating dinner. I can see him through the window from my vehicle, across the street. He doesn't look like he's going anywhere for a while at least."

"Stay with him," Ella said.

Lapsing into a long silence, Ella checked her weapon, a department-issue AR-15 assault rifle, identical to the one Justine was holding.

"What's been eating at you lately, partner?" Justine asked her quietly. "You've been tense about something these past few days, and it's not just the job. We've worked tough cases before."

"Actually it is the job. I have an important decision to make and I haven't had time to think things through," Ella answered, her eyes on the ditch. "It's something I'd like to discuss with you in a few days. But now is not the time."

Before Justine could comment, Ella's cell phone vibrated. She flipped it open with one hand and answered.

"It's Joe," Neskahi said, his voice coming through clearly. "We've got a brown delivery truck turning down the lane. It's headed toward the house."

"Keep an eye out for passengers. I'll alert everyone inside," Ella replied.

Ella called Blalock and put him and Anna on alert. Not knowing if the delivery was legitimate, they'd have to be careful not to overreact. Ella then glanced at Justine. "Check out the driver, partner."

Justine focused the infrared binoculars on the approaching truck. "Looks like the parcel delivery company's regular step van. The driver's wearing the uniform and matching baseball cap. But he's delivering awfully late for this time of year. By now they're usually done and back in Farmington."

Ella smiled. "It's hard to make a delivery on the Rez with so few street signs. But let's play it safe. Since the truck could screen out Joe, I'm going to approach from the right and cover the front. I want you to move in to the other corner, but keep checking our six in case this is a diversion that allows someone else to come in from behind the orchard. And stay out of sight as much as you can."

Ella walked around to the right end of the house and waited, watching from around the corner, her weapon lowered. The deliveryman got out, package in hand, walked up to the door, and knocked. His stride and stature didn't match that of Whitefeather as she recalled, so Ella relaxed slightly. Everything looked perfectly normal.

As the door opened, the deliveryman stepped aside and reached into his pocket, dropping the package. Flashes came from the cab of the van as two shots rang out. Almost simultaneously, the deliveryman dropped something on the front step, then ran. Ella heard a pop, then white smoke quickly billowed from the ground.

"Justine, get a shot from your side," Ella shouted, now unable to see the van clearly.

Ella ran into the cloud of smoke, then stopped, blind, remembering the fence. She heard the van's metal door opening, then there was a loud thud on the road, like something being dropped, and a gunshot went off.

Something bright red appeared to her right, low, on the ground, and she recognized the scent of a road flare. Inching forward, Ella saw the four-foot-high fence just as she bumped into it. Feeling her way, she vaulted it with one hand.

Hearing the sound of a motorcycle starting up, Ella ran toward the sound. She came out of the smoke just as the cycle raced down a ramp at the rear of the van. From the light of the red flare on the road, she could see the bike was carrying two people in brown clothes.

A spurt of dust kicked up beside the bike as a gun roared from the left and above. It was Neskahi, with the rifle. Ella stopped, raised her own weapon to her shoulder, then lost her sight picture as a flare and then another smoke bomb went off on the road behind the bike.

Grabbing her cell phone, she dialed Blalock's number. Almost simultaneously, she saw his vehicle racing by, Justine on the passenger side.

"Already in pursuit," Blalock answered crisply. "I'll call for backup. Check Officer Bekis."

Ella hurried through the drifting smoke, which had dispersed enough now for her to orient herself. She located Anna sitting on the porch.

"Are you okay?" Ella asked as Anna looked up, her back against a post.

Anna nodded, fingering a hole in her sweatshirt. "Glad

he didn't take a head shot, but it still feels like I've been kicked by a horse."

Seeing her struggle to stand, Ella helped Anna up. "Are you sure you don't want to stay down a while longer?"

"I'm okay," Anna said, shaking her head. "I didn't get a good look at the delivery guy. The cap was over his eyes. But he was Navajo."

Hearing a clank, they both turned and saw Neskahi coming through the front gate. "You hit, Bekis?" he asked.

"The vest held," Anna answered, her voice strained.

"Damn flare blinded my optics. I had to fire at the sound. Sorry, boss," Joe added.

"These guys knew what to expect and came prepared. We needed more protection, I see that now," Ella said, muttering a curse. "Let's start processing the truck. Maybe we'll get lucky and find something useful."

Remembering Blalock was in pursuit, Ella called Justine and asked for a situation report.

"The cycle went down an arroyo and into the bosque to the north," Justine answered quickly. "We're trying to find a route down there, but the sand's making it tough to keep going without bogging down."

"Get back along high ground, then listen for the bike and try to stay parallel to him," Ella said. Then realizing she was trying to micro-manage the pursuit, she corrected herself. "Forget what I said. Just use your own judgment. You're in the best position to make the right tactical choices."

"We've got backup on the way. They'll block the main routes," Justine added. "I need to hang up now so we can park and listen for the bike."

Ella called Phillip Cloud next, and learned that Baker had checked into a Shiprock motel using a phony ID.

They turned their attention back to the van then, and soon learned it had been stolen a few hours earlier, when the real deliveryman had been inside a business. The "package" delivered to Dr. Lee's door had been one apparently pulled from a shelf within the van to serve as a prop. Again, the perps had planned carefully.

Twenty-five minutes later, Blalock pulled up with Justine, a sour look on his face. "We found the cycle abandoned right beside the river," he said. "It looks like they used the same plan that Haske's killer did—wading across the river at a shallow point, then taking a vehicle parked on the opposite bank."

"There was still water on the rocks where they came out on the far side, and we could see tire tracks in the sand over there with the binoculars," Justine said.

"We've got the Colorado police manning a roadblock on 491 northbound. There's another unit checking southbound out of Shiprock for Whitefeather—if he was the shooter—and the other perp. But they could have already slipped by on a side road. Without a vehicle description, we're operating blind. Whitefeather, or whoever's calling the shots, has played it smart all the way, Clah," Blalock said.

"Neither of these guys was Baker. That much we know for sure. He's at a Shiprock motel. Let's check what the cameras picked up," Ella said, pointing to Teeny's video console.

A moment later, they were playing back the recordings on a split-screen laptop. The cameras had been placed at two locations to cover the house from the outside, and were low-light devices that recorded in black and white, not color. The first camera caught the deliveryman from behind, and only for a second as he turned and ran after dropping the smoke grenade. After that point, the images were indistinct, obscured by the choking cloud that had engulfed everything.

The second camera covered another angle, but from the distance, the image of the shooter inside the truck was too vague for them to make a positive ID.

Ella called Teeny, and he gave them quick instructions on how to transmit the recordings to his home, where he'd try to clean and filter them for clarity. He called back just five minutes later.

"What do you have for us?" she asked.

"I've got a partial image of the deliveryman, but he kept his head down, and the bill of his cap hides his eyes. I've got less on the shooter—just enough for a general description, nothing facial. These guys did everything they could to obscure the scene once the shots were fired, and it was effective."

Ella said nothing for several long moments. "Teeny, put your enhanced images onto a DVD and bring it to me at the station. I've got an idea."

After leaving her people to process the evidence, Ella left with Blalock.

"Update me," Blalock said, taking his eyes off the road long enough to glance at her. "You've got something running through your head, and I don't like being kept in the dark."

Ella grunted, busy squirming out of her camouflage pants and jacket, which she'd worn over slacks and a blouse.

"Okay, *after* you lose the duck-hunter suit," he added.

Ella tossed the pants and the camo jacket into the back seat, then snapped her seat belt. "I'll have to get Big Ed's okay first, but here's what I want to do. I'd like to release the camera images that show Anna taking the hits and going down and let the press assume that Dr. Lee died in the attack. We'll then move Dr. Lee into a safe house. Once she sees what went down tonight, I think we can turn her."

"You may be underestimating the woman," Blalock said. "A lot of zealots will take a bullet for the cause."

"From their own people?" She shook her head. "I don't think so. We'll show her Anna's vest and let her verify what she sees. She's smart enough to understand that once her associates find out she's still alive, she'll be nothing more than a walking target. One thing's for sure, if Whitefeather *was* her boyfriend, Jane'll discover right away how much he *really* cares. . . ."

Once at the station, Ella and Blalock went directly to the chief's office.

Ella gave Big Ed a full report, then added, "I'd like permission to put my plan in motion. I called Bruce on the way in, and he's going to make sure we have exactly what we need."

Big Ed leaned back in his chair and rubbed his chin absently. "I hate to purposely mislead the press. In the past, that's always come back to haunt us."

"This may be the last shot we've got to grab these people. Once the reactor vessel is put in place, it'll take the equivalent of a Ranger or SEAL team with air support to be any real threat to the facility, and they know it," Ella said.

"All right," Big Ed said. "You've got my approval. Let's make it work."

Teeny knocked on Big Ed's open door and came in. "I've got the video," he said, holding up a DVD.

"You made sure no one can tell the victim wasn't Dr. Lee?" Ella asked.

"You saw the original. This is nearly identical, except I played with the depth of field and filters to make sure you could read the number and name on the mailbox beside the gate. It was easy enough because that camera angle was set to capture the entire front of the house. Blalock's in the background, and you come into view from the margins with that assault rifle. That'll add credibility to the whole package. The segment ends with a freeze frame on the delivery guy—cleaned up as much as possible."

"All right. We're going to send the whole thing, digitally, to the *Diné Times*, the Farmington newspaper, the cable channel, and the Albuquerque TV stations and newspaper," Ella said. "We'll also send a request for the public to help us ID the suspect."

"Maybe you'll get lucky," Teeny said.

"We'll be making our own luck," Ella said. "What we really want people to see is Dr. Lee going down, and that's exactly what's going to happen."

TWENTY-FOUR

——— ✖ ✖ ✖ ———

It was close to midnight by the time they moved Dr. Lee out of the cell and into the Crime Scene van via their loading dock. Ella sat on a folding chair beside her.

"I know my rights. I *demand* to see an attorney. You can't do this. You have to charge me or let me go."

"Calm down, Dr. Lee. We're trying to save your life," Ella said quietly.

Dr. Lee's eyebrows shot up. "What on earth are you talking about?"

"We'll explain as soon as we reach the safe house," Blalock said from the front, where he sat at the wheel.

Jane Lee's eyes grew even wider. "Safe house? Why do you think I need that? What's going on?"

"Let us concentrate on getting you there safely. We'll explain what you need to know then," Ella said, keeping her eyes out the rear window, searching for any possible tail.

Dr. Lee slumped back in the seat and stared at the crime scene gear attached to the sides of the interior.

An hour later they arrived at a cabin in the eastern foothills of the Chuska Mountains, near Owl Spring. The compact log structure among the tall junipers and piñons belonged to Big Ed. The nearest communities, about equal distance to the east and west, were Sheep Springs and Crystal, neither of them bustling cities this time of night—or any other time for that matter. Window Rock was the closest big town, if any Rez community could be said to qualify, but that was only as the crow flies—over the mountains and south.

Ella led Dr. Lee inside. "Sit down, please, Professor," she said, gesturing to the couch.

"I don't want to sit down. You're violating my civil rights. Where are we, and what's going on?"

"We're on Navajo Nation land. We could let you go, but if we did, you'd be dead by Saturday," Ella replied calmly. "We know about your coded e-mails—the use of certain trigger and message words like red rock and *aqalani*—and the other signals you've used, like the Coke can on the fence."

Jane said nothing, her expression still one of defiance, but it was now mingled with a trace of fear. She was a professional activist, but as a terrorist, Dr. Lee was clearly an amateur.

"We have no intention of allowing an act of terrorism to delay or prevent the operation of the *Tsétaak'á* Generating Station," Ella said. "What you and your friends are trying to do isn't going to happen."

Jane sat perfectly still and said nothing.

"Many things have changed in the past few days, particularly for you," Ella continued. "We're now the only hope you have of staying alive," she added, recounting what had happened.

Jane stared at her blankly for a moment. "They shot the woman they *thought* was me?"

Ella nodded. "I allowed word to spread that you were cooperating with us. Part of the reason I did that was to show you exactly what kind of people you're dealing with. You're an activist, but they're terrorists out to further their own agenda at any cost. Right now they see you as a traitor, so you're of more value to them dead than alive."

Jane seemed to crumple before their eyes. "What have you done to my life . . . my future?" she muttered in a barely audible voice.

"We've bought you some time by bringing you here, but the second they realize you're still alive, they'll be lining up crosshairs with your head again," Blalock said.

Jane shook her head. "No, you're just playing me. None of what you've said is true."

Ella retrieved the DVD from her jacket and placed it inside the laptop Blalock had carried into the cabin.

Jane stared wide-eyed at the screen. "I don't understand. Our plan *never* included taking lives."

"You're kidding yourself," Ella said. "You discovered the bug Reverend Tome put in your purse, that pen, and told the others about it, didn't you? You knew he suspected your involvement in the attempts to disrupt the nuke plant. Soon after that he became their first target."

Jane broke eye contact and stared across the room. Her eyes were moist.

"Still can't face the truth? Well, the bomb at the college was intended to *kill*—a bomb placed in a class full of young people. And now, one of my officers is in the hospital because of it, fighting for his life," Ella said.

"At least no innocents died," she said in a whisper-thin voice.

Rage suddenly filled Ella. She picked up the laptop, and called up the photos of Ralph Tache taken for evidence purposes shortly after his arrival at the hospital. They were the stuff of nightmares.

"This is one of the results of that bomb," Ella said, shifting the screen toward Dr. Lee.

Jane Lee stared at the photos, stumbled to her feet, ran to the kitchen sink, and vomited.

Ella handed her a glass of water moments later. "Are you okay?" Despite the horrific photos, Ralph was expected to live and most of the scars left behind would respond to plastic surgery.

She nodded. "I swear to you, I didn't know about the bomb. Minutes before Reverend Ford's presentation, I got a phone call telling me to go outside. I didn't know what was going on until much later."

"Who gives the orders?" Blalock demanded. "Your boyfriend?"

"What boyfriend? I never even met the guy. I just supplied most of the money and stayed quiet, like I was told."

"Does the name Henderson Whitefeather mean anything to you?" Ella watched her carefully, reading her body language, but Dr. Lee showed no signs of recognition when she heard the name.

"Sounds Navajo, but I've never heard of him. Who is he?"

"How did you get recruited and by whom?" Blalock pressed, not stopping to answer her question.

"A letter was slipped under my office door at school. It praised my work against nuclear power, and was well written. It spoke of the Church Rock disaster, where a hundred million gallons of radioactive liquids leaked into tribal waterways. People live in those contaminated areas and are subject to its effects. In the letter, I was told that we all needed to do our part to make sure that never happened to our people again. I was asked to join the fight, and told to go to the library on campus that night. It was signed 'ak'is.'"

"Friend," Ella translated for Blalock. "Do you still have the letter?" she asked.

"No. He advised me to burn it, and I did."

"So you saw the man? What did he look like?" Blalock pressed.

"I can't tell you. I only saw what he wanted me to see," Jane said, then explained. "We were in a public place, right outside the library, but it was dark, and he was wearing what was clearly a disguise. He had a thick beard and mustache."

"I've never seen a Navajo who could grow a thick beard or mustache. Maybe you're wrong about him being Navajo," Blalock said.

"No, I'm right. Although the beard and mustache looked real enough, he spoke to me in our language, and his accent was too perfect for him to have been anything but a Navajo," she said.

"Did you meet any of the other members of your cell?" Ella asked.

"I know one man, but he doesn't give the orders. I know that for a fact."

"What's his name?" Blalock asked.

She hesitated.

"You have no friends out there now," Ella reminded her.

"Thanks to you."

"I've read your profile," Ella said. "You're an activist because you want to save lives. You don't take them. Or has that changed?"

"No, it hasn't," Dr. Lee said quietly. "I got into this fight because nuclear power always leads to loss of life—one way or another. Despite all the claims, it's not clean fuel. Think of all the miners who've died digging up that yellow earth. There'll be even more deaths when the stored waste gets out into the environment again—into the air and groundwater. Rocky Flats, WIPP, Los Alamos, Yucca Mountain, Three Mile Island, all dangerous places for our children, and their children. Somebody has to do something."

"The causes we champion say a great deal about us. Yet it's what we're willing to do—and not do—that define us." Sensing that Jane's mind was still not made up, Ella continued.

"You can't convince anyone you're trying to save lives if you're willing to kill the ones you're trying to protect. Help us stop these people. Give us a name."

"John Baker," Dr. Lee answered at last in a thin whisper. "He's committed to our cause, but he's no killer. Go easy on him."

Ella and Blalock exchanged a quick look, then Ella focused back on Dr. Lee. "You're wrong about him," Ella told her. "He's been busy illegally buying explosives—probably with your money—from a construction foreman here on the Rez. When he realized that we were on to him, he killed Haske—the man working with us—and tried to take me out, too. I have photos of Mr. Haske, who died, literally, on his own doorstep, if you want to see them. They aren't pretty."

Jane stared at Ella in shock. "I don't understand any of this. How could I have been so wrong?"

"Because you agreed with the cause and *wanted* to believe the people you saw as your allies. That clouded your eyes and thinking," Ella said. "To put it simply, Professor, you were used."

"Why do you know Baker but not the others in the cell?" Blalock asked Jane.

"Security. He and I were supposed to work together. Just before the reactor vessel was scheduled to be delivered, we were to dig up some dead bodies and dump them around the facility to alarm the Navajo workers. But John didn't show up when he was supposed to, so I waited. I expected to hear from him fairly quickly but, as of today, not a word."

"Would you recognize 'ak'is' voice?" Ella pressed.

Jane took a deep breath, considering it. "I think so."

Ella stepped away with Blalock. "We need to get a recording of Whitefeather's voice. I could ask his department for one—their dispatch system records all their calls—but that'll tip our hand and could compromise everything."

"If I ask for it, it'd be even worse," Blalock answered.

Ella weighed her options, and, as a new thought occurred to her, smiled. "Emily. She can get one without raising questions. She's in his department."

"It's around four in the morning," Blalock reminded.

"Let me call her cell. It's always on."

Ella called Emily and learned that she'd been called in to work the graveyard shift. "I need a favor," Ella said, and explained. "Even voice mail's fine. Can you help?"

"Yeah, I think so. I'll get back to you shortly."

They fixed strong coffee, knowing that they'd all be pulling an all-nighter. Jane Lee took some, but from what Ella could see, she was wide awake already. Unable to sit still, Jane was pacing around the room when Emily called back.

"I've got something," Emily told Ella. "Should I play it over the phone or bring it to you? It's just the message on his machine at home, and the one on his cell, but it's his voice and it's clear."

"For quality purposes, I'd rather you bring it," Ella said. "Can you get away?"

"I'll have someone finish out my shift. I'll say I'm not feeling well."

Ella gave her directions. "Let me know if there's a problem."

While they waited, Ella and Blalock questioned Jane and got the remaining code words the group had used, along with their security procedures. Jane also confessed to having bought weapons and ammunition which she'd then leave at a specific drop site in the bosque for the others.

Once it was clear that the professor had told them all she knew, Blalock took Ella aside. "We need to anticipate 'ak'is and Baker's next move."

"I've been thinking about that myself. My guess is that Dr. Lee was a patsy—their source of money—and they never told her their real plans. Their next move, if they intend to do more than generate bad publicity, will be to interfere with the delivery of the reactor vessel. That's scheduled to be trucked in two days. Since the public already knows where it's coming from, the likely route is easy to surmise. A sniper attack or assault against the transfer vehicle seems the most likely method of attack."

"You've got a man on Baker so we've got a good chance of stopping them," Blalock said.

Ella checked in with Phillip Cloud next. "You've still got a fix on Baker, right?"

There was a pause. "He hasn't left the motel room for hours. I've been watching the front, but I can take a walk around the building, just in case. The bathroom windows look too small to climb out, so I haven't been checking regularly in the back."

"Go ahead, then call me ASAP." Ella hung up, then waited.

Five minutes later, she got the bad news she'd feared.

"Ella, he's not in his room. I walked by and looked through the front window. The bed was torn apart, so that immediately caught my attention. Then I noticed that there was an open passage door—you know, for families renting adjacent rooms. Baker must have kicked it open and, while I was watching one room, left through another."

"Crap. Any idea how long ago that was?"

"A big, heavy woman left that room about two hours ago, heading toward the Totah Café. That must have been Baker in disguise. From what I can tell, he used sheets, blankets, and stuff in the rooms to fashion a scarf, shawl, and a wraparound dress. I blew it, Ella."

"See if you can track him from the Totah," Ella said. "Maybe he met someone there or stole a vehicle."

Blalock cursed when Ella told him. "We've been outplayed again."

"No, not yet," she answered, seeing Emily Marquez's county vehicle arrive. "I'll be back in a minute," she said.

Ella met Emily at the door, and they stepped out where it was dark to talk. "I'm glad you were able to get away."

"I got lucky. Two deputies were returned to patrol after their stakeout assignment was cancelled, so the manpower problem went away. So here I am," Emily answered.

"If we get a positive ID on the voice, will you stay with our informant? She needs protection right now. We'll send backup, so you won't be alone for long."

"Sure, not a problem."

"You've helped our department considerably, Em. If there's ever anything we can do for you . . ."

"Don't mention it. And I mean that, Ella. *Don't* mention it. I've played fast and loose with the rules, and Sheriff Taylor would nail my hide to the wall if he found out I hadn't gone through channels."

Ella chuckled softly. "You've got it. But we still owe you one."

TWENTY-FIVE

—— ✖ ✖ ✖ ——

As Ella played the recording to Jane Lee, the professor closed her eyes and listened to the voice. After several long moments, she finally nodded. "That's him."

Ella turned the recording off. "All right. We're going to keep you here under guard. The person you've been dealing with is in law enforcement, and we have to make sure you remain out of his reach. Officer Marquez will stay with you, and backup will be arriving soon."

Ella moved to a corner of the room with Blalock. "We need to figure out where and when Whitefeather intends to strike."

"My guess is that Baker had someone, another player we still haven't identified, pick him up somewhere in Shiprock. What we need now is someone with experience tracking a fugitive on Navajo turf. One thing working for us is that Anglos should be easier to find—considering there aren't that many living here," Blalock said.

"Bruce isn't the man for our hunt because we need him elsewhere, but he might know of someone. . . ." Ella called Teeny, then after explaining what she needed, added, "Can you recommend anyone?"

"Melvin Bidtah," he answered. "He used to be a Federal Marshal. Melvin's a real bloodhound when it comes to jobs like this."

"I remember Melvin. He got tired of all the travel and retired."

"He works for me occasionally. Fewer rules, more money."

"I can see how that would tempt him," Ella said, remembering that she, too, now had the option to move on to greener pastures.

The drive back out of the mountains to Ella's home took about forty minutes. The air was clear and bright with stars and an occasional meteor flashed across the sky.

Eventually Blalock came to a stop in Ella's driveway. "Try to get some rest, Ella. Some is better than none, if you intend to think clearly."

Ella nodded, and slowly walked into the house. Undressing quickly, she lay down on her bed and within seconds was fast asleep.

Three hours later, as her watch alarm went off, Ella groaned and opened her eyes. Rose was standing at the door.

"You work too hard, daughter," she said. "It's Saturday. You need a day off."

Ella wasn't about to deny it. Moving slowly, and reluctantly, she got to her feet. "I've got to get back to the station."

Rose nodded. "First there's something I wanted to tell you. Your brother and I have been asking about that man you were trying to find out more about."

Ella knew Rose meant Henderson Whitefeather. "What have you got for me?"

Rose motioned with her head toward the kitchen. "Your brother's here right now. He'll tell you what you need to know. I've put on a pot of coffee for both of you, but I have to get going."

"What's wrong?" she asked, accurately reading her mother's worried frown.

"It's my husband. We had a long talk yesterday and I found out that he went to see a doctor because he was having chest pains. He didn't mention it to me because he didn't want me to worry until he knew more. The doctor has now told him that it wasn't a heart attack, it's something called angina, but his blood pressure and cholesterol are too high. The doctor wants to see him again today so we're both going this time."

"High blood pressure and high cholesterol can be treated, Mom. Try not to worry too much."

Rose nodded absently. "I know. I just wish he'd told me what was going on from the beginning instead of waiting."

The hitch of helplessness in her mother's voice revealed more than her words did. "And now that you know there are things he'll keep from you, you'll always worry."

"Yes," she said softly.

"Talk to him, Mother."

"It won't do any good. That's the way my husband is. When something scares him, he won't voice it, because then it has even more power."

Ella nodded slowly, realizing that was part of the Navajo way, and there were some things that would never change.

"For now, I'll just be happy that we're dealing with something that can be fixed." Hearing Herman calling, Rose hurried out the bedroom door.

Ella walked into the kitchen moments later and found her brother wolfing down a breakfast burrito.

"Mom made one for you, too. And there's plenty of coffee," he said. "Take time to eat, sister."

"Good advice. I'm starving," she said, sitting across from him.

"The deputy you're looking for is engaged." Clifford slipped her a piece of paper. "The top name is his woman's, the bottom belongs to her brother who lives with her. The deputy can usually be found at her house. I've drawn a map to the woman's place on the back."

The brother's name, Chester Tso, sounded familiar to her, but she couldn't place it. The woman's name she recognized immediately. Ella cursed herself for not having discovered the connection sooner. Mona Tso, Dr. Lee's teaching assistant, was Whitefeather's fiancée. She'd been in the ideal position all along to keep a tight watch on Jane for her boyfriend. He'd probably been the man Marianna had seen sneaking into the classroom that day, to be with Mona. He'd been on campus, out of uniform, the day Jane had met a man in the cafeteria. "Thanks very much for this."

Grabbing the burrito off the table, Ella ran out to her pickup and drove east toward the highway. The tribal SUV she'd been assigned after her original had been shot up would be waiting for her at the station.

Once she was on her way, Ella called Justine on her cell phone. "I need everything you can get me on Mona and Chester Tso. I also need you to get an officer to watch their place," she added, giving Justine the address. "There's a chance Whitefeather's there. Mona's his girlfriend."

"Got it."

Justine met her at the side door fifteen minutes later, as Ella walked in. The look on her partner's face told her that Justine had hit paydirt.

"Chester Tso does plumbing and electrical maintenance on tribal buildings—including the community college," she said.

Now Ella remembered where she'd met him. "He was there after the bombing. He said he was checking the electrical connections and light fixtures, but I'll bet he was trying to figure out how much damage the bomb had done."

"He's got a clear motive, too," Justine said. "Turns out Tso's father was a uranium miner who died of radiation poisoning. Their mother died six months later of unrelated causes. Chester raised Mona, and though they've kept away from any public protests, they're very opposed to the Hogback plant. They believe that the tribe's repeating the past, and other families will have to go through what they did."

"Who's your source?" Ella asked.

"One of our officers dated Mona Tso when she was in high school. He's the one who filled me in on her background."

"That's good intel. Now we have to find Whitefeather. Any sightings?"

"None. Whitefeather's not at home, nor is he at work. He called in sick. We'll have officers watching the Tso residence soon. Right now both Mona and Chester are at the community college, working."

Big Ed came out into the hall. "Shorty, my office."

Ella started down the hall, then stopped and turned to her partner. "Justine, get me a list of all upcoming ceremonies related to the installation of the reactor vessel and the opening of the plant."

Ella joined the chief in his office, sat down at his invitation, then proceeded to make her report.

Big Ed listened. "Time's the enemy now, and it looks like they've gone to ground. Do you think you can get a bead on Whitefeather?"

"Either he or Baker will surface soon. They've gone this far, and experience tells me that they won't cut and run until they finish what they set out to do."

Justine came back into the office and gave them each a copy of the schedule she'd printed out.

Big Ed glanced at the sheet, then back at Ella. "I'll send plant security what we have on our suspects, and contact the officials in charge of the reactor vessel delivery. But there's an army of security covering these events—not only private, but state, county, and tribal officers. I can't see them targeting any of these."

"Convoy security should be checking for potential bombs at every bridge and possible bottleneck, and be on guard for a sniper attack."

"Those truckers have DOE training, satellite communications systems, and a couple of carloads of heavily armed security," Big Ed said. "Attacking them is practically suicidal. With the protection that's in place it's going to be nearly impossible for anyone to stop the opening of the plant."

"I know," Ella admitted, "and that's what bothers me about this. Whitefeather would know that, too. To stake months of planning on the hope that they'll penetrate those kinds of defenses . . . and with what? Less than a half-dozen people with dubious training? We're missing something, Chief."

"The plant *must* be the target," Big Ed said. "All the evidence points to that. Let's take a look at the schematics again," he added, calling them up on his computer.

"The only vulnerable area is the parking lot, and that's fifty yards outside the complex," Justine said.

"Even if they had a bomb large enough to take out all the vehicles there, that still wouldn't get them inside," Big Ed noted.

"And taking out the cars wouldn't make any difference anyway, not to plant operations. Wait a minute," Ella said slowly. "That's it. All this time we've been working under the assumption that their target is the facility, or its equipment. But the easiest way to stop the plant from opening is to target the workers themselves."

"Yeah, but they won't be at the plant for several more days, and, more importantly, they'd never all be there at the same time," Justine argued.

"Prior to the installation of the reactor vessel, what's on the agenda for the workers?" Ella asked Justine quickly.

"I have no idea. Let me go back and check," Justine said.

"Good thinking, Shorty," Big Ed said as Justine left.

"This is the first plant of its kind in the country. Without trained personnel, the tribe will be stuck for months with nothing more than a billion-dollar monument."

"That'll make the StarTalk fiasco seem like kid's stuff, and put the tribe in deep financial trouble," Ella said. "If that's Whitefeather's plan, he's been two steps ahead of us all along. He even misdirected his own people."

Justine hurried back inside the office moments later. "The entire staff is meeting today and tomorrow at the community college auditorium. They've been receiving extensive training for the past six months so they can operate our country's first pebble bed reactor. This is their final orientation before taking charge of the facility. The first session begins in . . . fifteen minutes," she said, looking at her watch.

"Without them, the plant won't be able to open. *They're* the target," Ella said.

"If you're right, then it's the perfect inside job. He's got the help of his future brother-in-law—a man with keys and unlimited access to the community college's buildings," Big Ed said. "Get over there, Shorty. I'll make sure you have as much backup as you need."

Ella contacted Vera Hunt, the head of campus security, as she ran out to the tribal cruiser with Justine. Updating Vera as quickly as possible, Ella added, "I'm sending you a copy of Whitefeather's photo ID, but be aware that if he's on campus he may be in his deputy's uniform or wearing a disguise. He's been known to use a mustache and a beard. Since that would call even more attention to him during the day, I'm guessing he'll opt for a hat or cap of some sort, and sunglasses."

"Okay, I'll get my people out looking for him."

"It's likely their plan will make use of an explosion and/or fire," Ella added. "The heating and electrical units are vulnerable, especially to Chester Tso. Working maintenance, he has every key he needs. Where exactly are the heating and cooling units in the auditorium building?"

"The basement," Vera answered in a flash, "in the rear, north end. Should I evacuate the campus, or at least the auditorium?"

"If we start evacuating, we could force them to act right now with whatever they have. Worst-case scenario, they might have an alternate target that we know nothing about. Let's stay low key for now. That's the only way to guarantee we won't start a panic and warn off Whitefeather and the others."

Ella thanked Vera, then glanced at Justine. "You and I need to check out the auditorium. I'll take the basement while you watch the front and ground floor. Make sure the exits remain open. If the plant employees really are the target, one possible strategy would be to block the exits to maximize the body count."

Less than five minutes later, they arrived at the rear of the building and parked in a red-zoned space near the loading dock. After finding the rear door locked, they walked along the side, and stopped at the corner of the building. Glancing ahead, Ella saw a twin-door entrance at the front. Both doors were wide open. Someone was standing there beside a heavy-looking canvas book bag. Ella recognized Mona Tso and saw her slipping a big chain through one of the door handles.

"Mona's chaining the doors," Ella told Justine.

"We need to take her out without tipping off the others," Justine whispered.

"She'd recognize me, but not you," Ella said, thinking fast. "Can you get the drop on her?"

"Sure thing."

Justine brought out her cell phone, held it up to her ear, then turned the corner, looking away, toward the street, instead of at Mona.

Ella watched as Justine approached Mona, phone still at her ear, and smiled. "Hi, need some help with that door?"

Mona stared at Justine in surprise for a moment, then dropped the chain, and reached into her jacket pocket.

Justine lunged forward, punching Mona in the throat.

Mona gagged, throwing her arms up in vain, then sagged to her knees, grasping her throat in agony. Ella was there in a flash, grabbing Mona's hand in a painful pinch-hold and yanking her off the steps.

"You!" Mona gasped, her eyes bulging and wet with pain.

"Check her pockets!" Ella ordered.

Justine reached into Mona's jacket and brought out a Taser.

"Police brutality! I'll have your badge," Mona croaked at Ella.

Ella increased the pressure on Mona's hand, forcing her to her knees again. "Check the lobby, Justine."

Justine looked inside, then stepped back. "She must have Tasered the guard. I can see him on the floor just down the hall to the left. The auditorium doors are shut but not blocked. Nobody else is around, but I smell gas."

"Where are Chester and Henderson?" Ella demanded, still applying the pinch hold.

"I have no idea," Mona said, her face contorted in pain.

"Cuff her," Ella said, maintaining the pinch hold while Justine worked. "Chain *her* to the door, then get everyone out as quietly as you can. Tell them there's a small gas leak and order them to stay off their cell phones until they're well outside. While you're at it, prop open every door you can. Just don't flip any light switches. One spark might set off an explosion. I'm going down the hall, then taking the stairs to the basement."

Mona suddenly jerked free of Justine, kicking out. Justine took a blow to the shin, but shook it off, punching Mona in the gut and doubling her over. Ella helped with the chain, and within ten seconds, Mona was held fast. Justine, thinking quickly, stuck her scarf in Mona's mouth, effectively gagging her.

Not wasting any time, Ella ran down the hall and checked the guard. He was unconscious, but alive. Noting that his handgun was missing, Ella touched the butt of her own pistol, wondering if a gunshot would set off the gas in the basement.

Ella reached for her baton, then, finding the door labeled "basement," opened it slowly and peered inside. The gas smell was much stronger here.

Ella heard footsteps from the bottom landing and stepped back, suspecting they'd placed another lookout below. Continuing quickly down the hall, she reached another door also labeled "basement." She went in slowly and sneaked a look down the stairwell. Nobody was in sight, and the air was fresher here.

Ella went down two flights, then stopped at the bottom step and listened, breathing through a handful of tissues now. The basement itself was a maze of pale green concrete walls, overhead pipes, and utility lines. Directly in front of her was a long hallway with doors on each side.

Ella crept down the corridor, making sure her boots didn't clack against the concrete floor. At the hall junction, she looked to her left and saw an open storage area filled with carts, folding chairs, and tables.

Ella moved to her right, aware that she was circling around toward the rear of the building where the heating and cooling systems lay. Using the intensity of the odor to guide her, she walked quietly toward the source of the gas.

Ahead was another junction in the hall system, and as she approached, she heard a muffled curse and the sound of metal against metal. Moving carefully, Ella homed in on the sound. As she turned the second corner, she saw a man in a gas mask loosening a pipe from a big heating unit. He had his back to her, but from his size and build she knew it was Chester.

Before she could make her move, Ella saw a sudden flash of fabric ahead. Moving a few steps forward, she spotted Whitefeather, in dress slacks, white shirt, and tie, at the bottom of the other stairway. He was the one she'd heard earlier, standing guard.

As Chester struggled with the hissing pipe, using a wrench with plastic jaws to avoid a spark, Ella crept up behind him. He turned just as she brought the baton crashing down on his skull.

As he sagged to the floor, Ella reached out and grabbed the wrench from his unfeeling hands. Moving quickly, she reattached the pipe, then located the shut-off valve. Once she'd turned off the gas, the hissing sound dropped in intensity. That leak was plugged, but more gas was still flowing into the basement from elsewhere.

Ella handcuffed Chester, then dragged his inert body into a utility closet about ten feet away. Working quickly, she removed his gas mask and slipped it over her own head. She was straightening the face mask when a sixth sense warned her of danger.

Ella turned quickly and saw Whitefeather standing less than five feet away, mask over his face, gun pointed straight at her.

"You shoot, and we're both dead. One spark will set off the gas," she warned. As Ella called his attention to another hissing pipe, she spotted a timer, lantern battery, and electrical detonator taped to the wall above it. The detonator would be more than enough to set off the gas.

When Whitefeather hesitated, Ella realized that he wasn't a fanatic after all. The man wanted others to die for his cause, but he hadn't planned on including himself in the body count.

Whitefeather jammed his pistol into his belt and raised his fists, and Ella leaped to one side, reaching for the power switches on the main electrical panel. Whitefeather blocked her path, but Ella caught him in the chin with the tip of her right boot. He fell back, the mask knocked halfway off his face, and blood gushing from his mouth.

Ella dove for the panel and pulled the big-handled switches, turning off all power to the building. Almost instantaneously, pale emergency battery-powered lights came on along the top of the wall. Whitefeather kicked out, keeping her at bay while he struggled to place the gas mask back over his torn lips.

Ella knew she'd have to disable the bomb. The gas was building up quickly. She caught Whitefeather as he lunged at her, kicking his knee. As he fell, she ripped the device from the wall, yanked the wires off the terminals, and threw the battery as far as she could down the hall.

By the time she looked back at Whitefeather, he had a knife in his hand. Ella tossed the detonator and timer into a trash can in the utility closet and turned to face him. He'd have to get past her now to retrieve the detonator.

Limping badly from his damaged knee, he forced her back, swinging the blade in low arcs directed at her belly. He jabbed at her chest next, but Ella grabbed his arm, and using his own momentum, propelled his hand and knife into the concrete wall. She heard a crack, and knew it was either the knife or his wrist.

Ella grabbed Whitefeather's mask and slammed his head forward into the wall. The mask's cartridge filter broke away, and he began coughing.

"You can't set off the gas without killing yourself. Give it up. It's over," she yelled.

Whitefeather didn't waste time. He pulled out his pistol, waving it in her direction and stumbled away, dragging his damaged leg behind him.

Ella wanted to follow, but first she had to cut off the gas. After finding the wrench and closing the last valve, she took out her baton and followed Whitefeather's blood trail. He was heading for the rear basement exit.

He was halfway up the flight of stairs when she came around the corner. As he half-turned, pistol out, she threw the baton at his ankles.

Whitefeather tripped, his weakened knee betraying him now. Grasping in vain for the handrail, he tumbled down the steps and hit the floor head first, coming to rest at her feet. Ella knew from the angle of his neck that he wouldn't be getting back up again. He'd lost the fight.

Ella hurried back to where she'd left Chester, dragged him up the stairs one step at a time, then outside to the parking level.

Justine raced up seconds later, Vera right behind her. "Guess you don't need our help anymore, huh?" Justine asked, panting.

"You might want to prop open the door," Ella said, removing her mask, and gasping from the exertion now that the adrenaline was wearing off.

"The fire department is on its way," Vera said, grabbing Chester.

"Where's Whitefeather?" Justine asked quickly, opening the basement door.

"At the foot of the stairs," Ella said, shaking her head. "Once the building's aired out, we can go back in and recover the body." Ella took several deep breaths of fresh air. Her job, for now, was done.

TWENTY-SIX

—— ✖ ✖ ✖ ——

On Sunday afternoon Ella sat with Blalock and her team in the chief's office. All known members of the cell were now accounted for, or in custody. Phillip Cloud and the other officers working with him had caught John Baker hiding in the brush beside a bridge along the intended route of the reactor vessel convoy. His truck had been loaded with the stolen explosives.

"For the time being, the attempt to eliminate the entire power plant work force will remain under wraps—orders from the Feds," Big Ed said. "The tribal government went along with the gag order because we don't want to create a panic here on the Rez or, more importantly, give anyone else any ideas."

"All the suspects will be facing trial in federal court, and paying for what they did," Blalock said. "Dr. Lee's testimony and their decoded correspondence will add to the evidence we've already gathered."

"Good job everyone," Big Ed said at last, looking around the room. "All of you have been working long hours lately, so take the rest of today off. Of course I'll expect all of my people back here by tomorrow noon to write the mother of all reports."

"Almost an entire day off . . . ," Ella said with a rueful smile. "What the heck. We'll take it."

The room cleared in record time. As Ella reached the door, Big Ed said once again, "Really good job, Shorty. If I could, I'd give you a raise."

Ella nodded, but didn't comment. A raise would have been great, but she had other options now she'd never had before. More money, a new challenge . . . so why wasn't she happier about all the possibilities that D.C. had to offer?

She drove home slowly, thinking things through. No answers came to her—at least none that felt right. After she called John Blakely, if the offer still sounded good, she'd have to discuss the situation with Justine—and Big Ed. Taking a new job back East would have an impact on the department, and if she was seriously going to consider the offer, those working closest with her deserved to know.

She also had to consider her relationship with Ford. Leaving now would change everything with him—if there ever *was* going to be something more, that is. Her life could be about to turn upside down, and she'd need time alone to sort things out.

Ella arrived at the house a half hour later and, as she parked, Rose came out to meet her.

"Daughter, I have wonderful news! Your daughter is coming home."

"I thought she'd planned to stay with her dad for a few more days. What happened?"

"Her father called me late last night. The tribe's sending him to China to study options for adding a second reactor. Our people are already thinking of doubling the new power plant's capacity, and they want him to visit a place where that's already been done."

Ella didn't comment. "So when is she getting here?" she asked, looking forward to seeing Dawn again.

"In about an hour. Her father hired a small plane to fly them from Albuquerque to Farmington. He said he'd have a car waiting for him there, so don't worry about picking them up."

"Good. That'll give me time to get ready."

"Why didn't he just drive from Albuquerque like most people?" Rose asked.

Ella smiled, remembering one of their past conversations. "It bores him, Mom. He just can't see the beauty anymore. He says it's miles and miles of nothing and nothing. In his heart, he's adopted the city."

Ella was finishing lunch when a big black SUV pulled up in the driveway. Rose ran outside just as Dawn climbed out of the vehicle, followed by Kevin.

"*Shimá*," Dawn yelled, using the Navajo word for grandmother and launching herself into Rose's arms.

Seeing Ella a heartbeat later, Dawn ran up and hugged her tightly. "I've got so many things to tell you!"

Ella laughed. "I've missed you, too."

Before Ella could say anything else, Dawn heard her pony whinnying and ran to the corral to greet Wind.

Kevin, dressed in a gray business suit, came up, watching their daughter as she talked to the horse. "Have you thought any more about the job offer, Ella? I know that a part of Dawn will always belong here on the Rez, but the city has a lot to offer her—and you."

Ella nodded slowly. "It's tempting, and I haven't said no, not yet. I'll be calling John Blakely in a few days to check out the details, and I want to talk it over with a few people. But no promises. I've already got everything I need and want right here."

Dawn came running back. "Mom, Wind *missed* me! Did you hear him whinny?"

"I did!" Ella said.

"Did anything exciting happen while I was gone?" Dawn asked, walking with them toward the house.

Ella smiled. "Nothing as exciting as your homecoming."